The Forest of Hours

The Forest
Of Hours

Kerstin Ekman

Translated by Anna Paterson

Chatto & Windus
LONDON

Published by Chatto & Windus, 1998

2 4 6 8 10 9 7 5 3 1

Copyright © Kerstin Ekman, 1988

English translation © Anna Paterson, 1998

This translation is published with the support of the Svenska Institutet and the European Community's Ariane Programme.

Kerstin Ekman has asserted her right under the Copyright, Designs And Patents Act 1988 to be identified as the author of this work.

First published as *Rövarna i Skuleskogen* by Albert Bonniers Förlag AB, Stockholm

First published in Great Britain in 1998 by
Chatto & Windus
Random House, 20 Vauxhall Bridge Road,
London SW1V 2SA

Random House Australia (Pty) Limited
20 Alfred Street, Milsons Point, Sydney,
New South Wales 2061, Australia

Random House New Zealand Limited
18 Poland Road, Glenfield,
Auckland 10, New Zealand

Random House South Afric (Pty) Limited
Endulini, 5A Jubilee Road, Parktown 2193, South Africa

Random House UK Limited Reg. No. 954009

A CIP catalogue record for this book
is available from the British Library

ISBN 0 701 16614 2

Papers used by Random House UK Limited are natural, recyclable products made from wood grown in sustainable forests. The manufacturing processes conform to the environmental regulations of the country of origin.

Typeset by Deltatype Limited, Birkenhead, Merseyside
Printed and bound in Great Britain by
Biddles Ltd, Guildford and King's Lynn.

Translator's Note

The Forest of Hours is a wonderful story, but also a work so full of learned and witty references that I felt many readers would welcome some notes. In this I followed the author, who provided a section of notes for the Swedish edition of the book. Unfailingly helpful in the preparation of this longer version, Kerstin Ekman also pointed out that there are some deliberate errors in the text, for reasons which will become clear to the reader.

Throughout the novel, the language reflects the passage of time with great inventiveness. This includes the use of words and forms of words rooted in northern Swedish dialect. When possible, these have been translated into Scots – or, when appropriate, Old English – and a glossary of Scots words can be found with the notes at the back of the book.

Apart from making technical points, a Note is essential for a translator with as many debts of gratitude as I. Many friends at the University of St Andrews have been generous with their time, intelligence and learning. Greta Arnott has read, discussed, criticised and encouraged. Invaluable help has been given by Tom Duncan, Jill Harries and Lawrence James. Alan Paterson, my patient husband, could not have been more supportive and nor could Joan Tate, an old friend and expert translator.

But most of all, I am indebted to Rebecca Carter, the editor, for her expertise and dedication, and to the author of *The Forest of Hours*, which has taught me more and made me read and think more widely than any other book.

Contents

The Children from Markom

There was once an old crone, who lived in Oringen with her two grown sons. They were called Granarv and Groning, and had never been among people. One day when they were felling trees in the forest, Groning got separated from his brother. The trunk of the fir tree he was felling came down on top of him, and pinned him to the ground. He shouted, but Granarv did not hear him and went home instead, because it was time to eat. Groning was sore, and made an ugly face as he tried to twist himself free. But he was stuck.

A long day passed. Ants crept over his face, and midges crawled into the corners of his eyes and stung and sucked. He was pinned down and helpless. All the tiny vermin of soil and air, all that was crawling and winged, seemed to have noticed the smell of his warm body. He was surrounded by humming and whining. Groning was no longer a man-like giant out felling, and every now and then chasing gnats and clegs from his sweaty neck. No, he had become a large forest larder, a supply of food for those who fed on fresh blood.

Lying there, he could picture in his mind only too easily how other things would soon come crawling and flying and padding along, all the forest creatures which lived off the weak, whose blood and juices were stilled. They would probe with their tubes into fermenting parts, and tear with their teeth at flesh which had started to smell. Hopelessness welled up inside him.

Some time later, he sensed he was being gawked at, and thought that it must be the trolls. He was alerted by an eye-gleam, and noticed something moving among the ferns. A little later he glimpsed a hand. It was thin, with long fingers, and looked like the bare roots of a birch. Well, he was not at all sure, perhaps it was no more than a bundle of roots with their bark worn away by the wind and the snow. Then there was another gleam. It really was an eye. Groning, who by now had been lying there for many a long hour with his legs caught under the fir tree, saw that there was a troll in the undergrowth. Just one, though, and rather a puny one at that. Its body was thin and willowy, and its head covered by a rough mat of hair, full of scurf and lice nests.

'Look you, Scurfhead, come here,' Groning said.

He had a notion he might get some help from a troll like that, small and probably more innocent than most. But it did not answer him.

The Siberian jays were of course just as curious as always. On soft, fluttering wings, piping and whistling confidingly, they flew down to sit near his hands. It was false comfort. They cared nothing for him. But he remembered how they would come for scraps of food from his satchel, if he threw them a bit away. It came to him that the scurfhead over there in the bushes might do the same. Maybe giving scraps to that hiding thing would be a way of befriending it and getting it to help him.

Groning was right. A troll was gawking at him from the undergrowth. It was a scrawny little troll, unknowing and guileless, and not much given to thinking at all. There was little more than fluttering, like the wings of jays, going on under that tussock of hair. It was amusing to watch the big one, heaving and groaning under the trunk of the fir tree. This was something new in the wastelands of the forest, and the rumbling voice made a change from the harsh, piercing whistles of the brambling which were heard day in, day out, throughout the long summer.

The scurfhead had been ambling through the forest, collecting snails and cracking dung-beetles between his fingers, and then chewing them carefully to savour the crunchiness. Nothing more exciting than that all day. This big contraption of skin and cloth and hair and clasps and tied straps, and the shiny blade of the axe, which the troll thought was a beak, and the big boots, which he thought were hooves – this was the strangest thing he had ever seen. The tied bootstraps he found the most wondrous part of all the bits which were stuck fast under the tree trunk. Crooked juniper bushes he had seen, growing in weird twists and hooking into each other. But he had never seen anything make a join as infernally coiled and hard to follow as the two ends of the straps when they came together.

4

There was something like a hoof fungus, but made of hairless skin, lying close to the big contraption, who pulled out a large ear from inside it and tore off bits, which he threw into the thicket. A jay got there quickly and snapped up the first morsel. This happened again and again. After a while the troll became so curious about the small ear-flakes that he pinched one. He fingered it and then decided the flake was meant to be eaten, because it smelled like white clover or grass-of-parnassus, and the inside of it was like the innards of a large caterpillar. The scurfhead ate it and it was good. It was the best food he had ever eaten. It was goodness itself.

He had only one thought, if that is the right word for what was fluttering under his tufty hair: he wanted more. How was he to get it? The big one had put a lid on the hoof fungus, after putting the softear inside. Then the big one said, 'You get more if you fetch my brother.'

Now, Groning did not say this in his mother's language, because the old crone spoke like people, but tried instead the language the birds use for speaking together. Not chaffinch speaking to chaffinch, and siskin to siskin, but the language used between raven and finch, grey siskin and peregrine falcon. It is a language that foxes can understand and mimic, with some difficulty, and it is known by weasels and hares.

The scurfhead, crouching among the ferns in the thicket of alder and birch saplings, saw no point in being contrary. He would bring the brother to Groning. After all, it meant getting more mouthfuls of that yellow goodness in the big one's sack. But because he was a troll, he could not be bothered to move. His eyes swivelled, and caught sight of a crow sitting in the top of a pine. His fluttering thoughts and his will entered her. The crow took off and flew away between the trees, without knowing quite what had got into her head. She just knew that she had to keep flying for a long time, over the blue mountain ridges and small glittering tarns. Finally something in her head said it was time to descend and search among the trees. And then she heard the blows of an axe.

There was Granarv cutting the branches off felled birches, without a thought for his brother and what might have happened to him. But he did notice the odd behaviour of a crow perched on the top of a pine. She was hovering about, and clattering with her beak like a capercaillie. When he stepped closer to the pine, she flew off, but in a peculiar, shambling way, as if she had been waiting for him. He walked across the mountain ridges with long strides and in that way reached his brother. By then Groning was swollen and half crazed by thirst and midge bites.

His brother gave him water from the stream, sawed up the fir tree and heaved the pieces of the trunk off his legs. He pulled Groning up on all fours and spoke to him slowly and sensibly. When Groning could stand upright and had begun to recover what little wits he had had, they set out for home. And so they forgot all about the troll.

Skord – for it might as well be said at this stage, that is who it was – followed them, and never stopped watching the large grey fungus dangling from Groning's shoulder. He called like a cuckoo, rustled like a hoarse aspen and snapped like a beetle, all in order to remind Groning of his promise. But neither of the brothers noticed anything.

So they came back home to the old woman, and she took care of them. The smoke billowed from the hole in the roof of the cabin, and Skord sat behind a fir tree sniffing the smoke, which was fatty and smelled just like the delicious ear. But nobody in the house remembered about him.

That autumn things went badly for the crone and her giant sons far away in Oringen. Smoke from the fireplace filled their hut, because a crow got stuck in the smoke-hole. Carrion turned up in the freshwater well and rose to the surface with bloated belly. And then the axe blade was ruined by cutting into a stone.

Granarv started thinking. Groning could not manage this, but his brother tried his best and came up with a question: 'Did you promise anything when you were lying there under the fir tree and wanted to free yourself?'

'I'll be damned,' said Groning. 'It's just come back to me.' And so he told of the troll and what he had said.

Then Granarv asked their mother, the old crone, to bake a large pancake, and she did as he wanted. He carried it out into the forest, put it down on flat rock and said:

'You take what's yours

and I take what's mine
You walk your way, and I walk mine.'

After that, life in the cabin became peaceful again. The well ran with sweet water, the fire burned well in the grate, and Granarv honed and whetted the edge of the axe so it stayed keen.

Skord stayed in the forest near the hut. Now and then one of the giants would put a piece of pancake on a rock or throw the crust of a loaf in the direction of the forest. Their home was little more than a lean-to, with a rock face forming one side. But Skord had never seen a building before, and marvelled at it. When it was pouring with rain, it gave better cover than the branches of a fir tree. He noticed how they would come out dry after a storm. Inside it was the secret of the smoke, which had something to do with the goodness, and they had things like a wooden pail for carrying water and a pottery dish for the porridge. When the crone scraped out the cold porridge before washing the dish in the well, Skord was lurking among the aspen seedlings. As soon as she had gone, he was there with his long fingers.

Then winter arrived, and things were not the same in there any more. He saw no smoke, other than a sour little twist once in a while, and then it did not carry any good smells. Neither Granarv nor Groning showed their faces for days on end, and when they did come lumbering out to piss by the wall, they looked swollen and daft with sleepiness. They never threw anything into the forest now, not even when Skord played wicked tricks on them.

In the end he went wandering, drifting further and further away. Time passed, and he no longer remembered very much of what he had seen and done at Oringen. Troll brains do not hold many memories. Mostly, their minds flicker and ripple like the glossy water in a forest tarn ruffled by the wind. There are fluttering movements and faint whispering or whirring noises as of wings, and there are thin roots twisting round each other and searching ever downwards, looking for something with their fine, hairy points. But they find so little. So much happens in vain and is drained away, so much drifts down towards a smooth surface, is sucked in and disappears. Pulled down, it sinks into the slime and becomes one with the thick, black darkness.

Besides, it was winter, which is always a hard time for those who live in the forest. They are half starved, their chilly legs are covered in sores caused by the frozen crust of the snow, and there is an evil, whining hollow inside them. Forest creatures would gnaw at practically anything. Early buds on the rowans or cones dropped by the crossbills. Icy leftovers of carrion, in the hope of extracting some small sweet piece of flesh. They would suck their nails. Still, Skord was used to all that. Nothing special about it. Yet there was this small worry, a hurt inside which made him feel almost ill. It was because of something that kept surfacing in his mind. Every time it happened he had to move on. Then he would follow the deep tracks left by the elks, and sometimes wander all through the night, for as long as snow crust held under him.

It was not possible to send anybody else if one wanted some of the goodness from inside that hillside lean-to up there in Oringen. Neither raven nor crow would do. There was no way to get inside the head of a fox and make it run across the ice-bound forest floor. You had to do it all yourself, stumbling and plunging through the snow and keeping at it, with a runny nose and snow-cut legs, until you arrived.

But it was all so silent there.

The cabin was buried under the snow and there were no tracks. So he hid inside an old abandoned fox's lair, curled up and lived on what he could find under his nails and inside his ears. Then he slept like a bear, and later more deeply still. He slept the way the root of a fir tree sleeps in the frozen soil. He did not wake until drops fell on his face. By then the sun had etched holes in the surface of the snow, and water was burbling everywhere. He had no stomach any more, just skin glued to the front of his backbone.

But now it was easier to survive. He collected frozen cranberries under the snow, and rummaged to find ant eggs. Then came the time for picking bird's eggs from their nests, and he ought to have been fine. One day should have slid into the next, through the pale-blue dusk of the long early summer nights. He found such things as he needed, and once in a while got to suck on something sweet-tasting. All the same, he was drawn to the cabin. He stared at it, lingering at the edge of the forest clearing. Nobody came, nobody went and there was no smoke coming through the hole in the roof.

Only later in the summer, when the foam of grasses and cow parsley reached high up the stone at the entrance, did he dare go closer. He noticed then that a thin-stemmed plant with pink flowers had grown tall in front of the doorway. It was obviously on its way in. Lying still in the grass he also noticed that the field mice had made themselves busy inside. They ran to and fro as if they had been living there all their lives. Wasps were building a byke somewhere in the darkness. They buzzed out and in again, with chewed wood from an old slaughtering block by the cold-water well.

Later the wall leaning against the rock face caved in; the long fir trunks covered with mossy peat-blocks collapsed. It happened one morning when the sun had just started rising above the fir-edged crest of the hill. Now he could see straight into the cabin, and that was very strange. He did not know the names of all the things he saw: the table that Granarv had made by splitting tree trunks, and the hearth he had built from stones and mortar. He had made the stones stick together by using a mixture of sand and clay. There was cold soot and blackness where the fire had been, and Skord understood very little of what he saw.

He went closer still because now he realised that many creatures were slipping in and out without a care, or, at least, with only their own troubles in mind. In the end he too stepped inside. It was dangerous but he did it anyway. Coming up to the hearth, he looked into the cold pit where the ashes still smelled of piss. He recognised the porridge bowl and the wooden pail and a big spoon carved from a tree root. The axe and the saw were gone.

In the box-bed was a pile of bones partly covered by dried brown skin. Skord still recognised the head of the old crone. There were a few bits of cloth lying around her and instead of eyes she had empty sockets. He had seen carrion before and was not surprised. He understood that there would be no more having to listen to her girning, but no more porridge cooking or pancake frying either.

Smoke and the flapping of wings. Vapours rising from the marsh during summer nights. Moths in drifting flight over dewy grass. As we have agreed, there is little else inside the heads of trolls. Not much memory, not many thoughts.

But still Skord's thoughts kept clustering round that goodness, because he now knew how goodness tasted and had watched how Granarv and Groning and the little old crone, who was their mother, went about their lives. He had heard the way they spoke together, and seen them stay dry during rainstorms. Clusters of thoughts may be putting it too strongly. More a case of chance encounters of thoughts which were beginning to congeal, to form clumps like butter in the churn separating out from the cream.

In the past, voices had always made him withdraw deeper into the forest. Now he loitered near the paths instead, listening to the passers-by. These were creatures much smaller than the two Oringen brothers. More like the size of the old crone, their mother, as she had been when alive. But there were those who were smaller still. Skord preferred to stay close to that sort, because they did not scare him as much as the bigger ones. He took note of the way these little ones kept company in groups, and were carrying bags. There were edibles in the bags and he wondered where they got them. To find out he began following the small ones. That was how he got closer to inhabited places and came to see many strange things, which would have been utterly unexpected, had he not been watching the hut in Oringen.

Smoke rose from the common huts, and from those which were much bigger and made from tree trunks stripped of bark. The small ones went to these places, held out their bags and were often given things they chewed on afterwards. He wanted to go with them and get things to eat too. But he had neither a bag nor any rags to use for clothing, and did not dare to show himself in case they should understand that he was of a different kind. Then it occurred to him that he could return to the forest hut with the old crone's skeleton and take her clothes, and so he did just that.

He made a bag out of her long skirt and put on the rest. But falling into company with the small ones was not as easy as he had expected. He understood their language. He tried to speak it too and found it could be done, though at first he sounded like a starling mimicking human speech, toneless and whistling. By the by, it improved and he spoke well enough to be understood, even by himself.

He had an extraordinary facility for imitating sounds. This had been the case throughout his life in the forest. But it was still hard to get close to the small ones. The larger ones beat him with sticks and threw stones at him whenever they saw his face in the undergrowth. The smallest ones spat and shouted abuse after him. It did not take him long to realise the group did not want any hangers-on. He also observed that the smallest ones were picked to go along to the farmhouses with their bags. The bigger ones stayed behind in the forest and waited for them to come back. When they did, the crusts of bread and the soup bones were taken from them and eaten by the bigger ones. The smallest ones only got to suck on the bits and pieces the bigger ones left behind as the group walked on. Often, they had to find forest berries to eat. Skord felt that somehow the smallest ones were not too different from himself. Like him, they had nits in their hair and coughed when the weather was cold and did not speak very much.

There were many wanderers following the paths. Some of them, similar in size to the crone, had lost their noses and the end-joints of their fingers. People were scared of them, though Skord thought them less dangerous than the small ones. To him, losing one's nose or a couple of finger joints did not seem worth worrying about. He was used to bits like that growing back soon enough. But then he had learned that humans – this was what they all were, even the small ones – preferred a particular appearance. They wanted to look like one another, and not like rotting tree stumps or twisting branches or foxes or mossy stones. Looking like these things frightened them. Skord tried to tidy himself so that he would be allowed to join one of the groups, but they spat at him and sharp stones flew round his head. He followed anyway at a distance and at times he got to suck on something they had dropped.

One morning he woke to find the sun shining on his face, and as he stretched his cold limbs, still stiff with sleep, he could hear voices. Two small humans were talking to each other. At first he listened as usual to the flow of words, without taking in much of their meaning. He just realised they were speaking nicely and sensibly to each other. This was something he had not heard before. It sounded like the faint twittering of siskins or tits, chatting quietly and trustingly.

He crept forward and caught sight of the two small ones sharing the bread from a bag. They urged each other to please have some more, and each wanted the other to eat plenty. As they finished by shaking the crumbs out of the bag, they saw Skord. He hid quickly, expecting a stone to come flying his way. But it did not.

For a while all was silent, but the piping and twittering began again, low and eager. Then stillness fell once more. When he peeped, he saw they had gathered up all the crumbs and put them on a flat stone. They were sitting there, looking at his hiding place under the bushes. In the end he could not stop himself, and grabbed a handful of crumbs. After getting them into his mouth, he looked at the small ones for a long time, trying to work out what they wanted from him. Was he meant to send a crow to look for their brother?

But they said nothing of the sort. They were busy making a bag from a piece of cloth, which was worn and full of holes. The bigger one stuck it in his belt, which was made of birch bark, and then they started walking again. Skord followed, and kept an eye on what they got up to. He saw how they went to the farms and were given nothing. Angry dogs would snap at their legs. In the evening, they settled down next to a stream and tried to keep the midges at bay by waving birch twigs. They drank a lot of water and searched under the moss for the roots of ferns. But they only found the bitter kinds. The smaller of the two began to cry. There was not much left of the morning chatter and the fine piping noises. In the end they fell asleep close together next to the root of a fir tree, and he could hear them whimpering in their sleep like fox cubs. They were still sleeping the next morning when he looked. Skord, who had noticed that they picked the wrong ones when looking for sweet roots, pottered around on the rock faces pulling up common fern until he had collected a good handful. He shook the soil off the roots, and carefully put them on top of the bag next to the sleeping small ones.

Waking, they saw the roots and looked about in surprise. Maybe they had caught a glimpse of Skord's eyes gleaming in the shadows, because they spoke towards the forest. He could not hear their words over the gurgling noise of the stream.

Then they started walking again, and had a better day. When an old woman gave them a crust of dry bread, they divided it up and put one piece on a stone. Skord did not dare crawl out to get it. Only at dusk, when the two small bundles had fallen asleep, did he come out and grab the crust.

He spent of lot time thinking that night. It was like trying to catch midges in your hands without killing them. He did not get much out of it. But finally he scurried away and began looking for this and that, all the things he used to feed on. He found some really tasty morsels: a couple of black forest snails, a yellow caterpillar with a hard, waxen carapace. He dug out some pine-weevil larvae and wrapped them in a large, soft willow leaf. He put it all on the stone and withdrew into the undergrowth, staying close enough to be able to see what would happen.

They were still asleep. Skord had plenty of time to practise catching his swarming, humming thoughts. He stayed there, pondering why he had done what he had done. There seemed to be no answer.

When they woke and saw the gifts, they looked at each other and then into the forest. But they did not eat any of the things he had put there for them. The same thing happened for several mornings. At last he understood that they only ate fern roots and berries. He thought it peculiar that they preferred starving to good food.

They had started to speak to him from a distance. They wanted to know his name, and who his parents were, and where he lived. Of course, there was nothing he could possibly say. But he learned from listening to them that it would be dangerous to walk the roads and paths without being able to answer such questions. So he told them anything that came to mind. He said that his name was Skord.

'What a strange name,' said the bigger of the two small ones. 'My name is Erker, and this is my little sister, who is called Bodel. Our home is in Markom, and our dear father and mother died there from weakness after the years of famine. Our grandmother looked after us. Now she too is dead. She died from old age and we have to go begging for a living. Is that how it is with you?'

'Yes,' said Skord. He did not quite understand it all but memorised it carefully.

'Then let's keep together,' said Erker, 'because the way you look you'll get nothing from the farms. You could be taken for a tr–'

'Hold your tongue now,' said Bodel. Then she said, 'Come to the stream, Skord.' He hesitated, and then walked up to her.

'Now, I want you to take your clothes off and put them here in the pool.' Skord did not mind this at all, because he did not think much of wearing clothes anyway.

'Put a stone on top, so they don't float away.'

'Look at the nits, they are coming up to the surface,' said Erker, and so they were. Bodel rubbed the clothes against a stone and hung them up to dry in a large elder.

'You have got to get into the stream now,' she said. He did not like the idea, but her voice was quite forceful though she was small. Soon he was lying in the stream with only his head sticking out, and she scrubbed him with a bundle of the long grass which grew there and waved in the clear brown water. The current played round Skord's shoulders and tickled his stomach. He found it pleasant to lie immersed in the stream, once the first chill had passed.

Afterwards he was made to sit on a stone while he dried. Bodel produced a small knife from her bag and cut his hair level with his shoulders except in front, where it only reached to his eyebrows. He felt very naked and strange without his hair. Then she cut his nails back to the tips of his fingers. At the back of his mind was a faint worry about how he would be able to get at weevil larvae. But he said nothing because he did not want her to stop touching his body. He wished she would go on forever.

She started cleaning his feet. He had to sit and soak them in the water for a long while until the dirt softened. Then she trimmed the nails. She did it so neatly with her small knife that nothing bled or hurt. When she had finished she wrapped his feet in a piece of cloth and patted them dry. They emerged looking much lighter than the rest of his skin. While she was carrying on with her tasks, a thought started flitting round in Skord's mind. He got hold of it and turned it into the kind of words they used. He asked why she did all this for him. And little Bodel answered, 'For the sake of Jesus Christ and His mercy.'

He could make nothing of this. But he did not dare ask any more questions. She must have her reasons, he said to himself. He had seen the way the bigger ones used their knives to cut the small ones before they went begging in the farms. When they looked hurt they sometimes got more in their bags. He thought that she might like to cut his foot off. He would let her, and they could send him to the farms afterwards. But when he told her of his idea she just said, 'You're silly. How could you manage with only one foot?'

'It would grow back soon enough,' said Skord.

Bodel and Erker started laughing at that, and they kept laughing until Skord joined them. He had never laughed before, and could not fathom what this barking noise of theirs was about, but it was irresistible, and he had to imitate it. All three of them laughed so hard that tears came to their eyes. At first, Skord was frightened when he noticed that his eyes were filling with water, but then he laughed even harder. In the end little Bodel said that they had to stop laughing and start behaving properly again. They soon did as she told them, and wiped their eyes.

They laughed. They were given food to put in their bags and shared it with Skord. They kept talking together, and this made a pleasant humming noise. But there was something odd about them as well, something cramped which he could not understand. If they had wanted to, they could have moved along like squirrels. He showed them. But no, they had to plod along on the ground and preferably on a path.

When he got fed up with the plodding, he took on the shape of a buzzard and rose high above the forest. He could see other groups of cramped-looking figures, carrying bags and sticks. But he also saw the black forest tarns, and rain drifting over the mountain ridges and the high slopes of the hills, bare and swept by the wind. The children pulled him down with their calling. They said he had been a lazybones, just lying there on his back on the mossy ground. They thought that he too had to stay with his pile of flesh-clad bones.

Long before they realised, he would know when they were approaching a place where people lived. The forest clearing reeked with their scent. Bodel and Erker were afraid at night, when the moonlight outlined the sharp branches of the fir trees and gleamed in the black water of the tarns. They started shaking when they saw the tracks of a bear, even though it wanted nothing from them. But when it came to walking up to farms, they were almost fearless. Bravely they kept furious dogs at bay with their sticks. But what did they know about those who lived inside? The farmer might be like a bear, disturbed in his winter sleep. Maybe his wife would be like an adder, alert on a warm rock. In they walked, between the jaws of stone and the sharp claws, right up to the hard chins and the talking fleshy tongues.

He tried to put one of his commands inside them, to make them come back. But they were not like foxes or crows. They went their own way. Crouching in the undergrowth at the edge of the forest, he watched what they got up to inside the houses. He saw a great many things. Snakejaws was a housewife who kept a log in swaddling clothes and cradled it in her arms in front of the fire, all the while howling like a she-wolf. It looked bad. But Bodel taught Skord that all was not what it seemed. The farmer did not take a scythe to the meadow in order to cut off the heads of the voles. And he did not put the voles away in jars once they had stopped bleeding. And he was even less likely to do any of these things to children.

'But he does it to pigs,' said Skord. And she did not deny it.

Nor could he understand why humans were forever bending double over sticks and sharp iron blades, rooting around in the soil and cutting grass and the branches of trees. Then Bodel told him about how the very first human beings had lived in a forest where only the finest trees grew, without scrubby thickets or piles of dead branches. Linden trees danced in the wind, and the hazel bushes bore golden leaves. The wolves would lick the leverets as they lay next to springs which flowed out of rock faces of silver. There was a tree there with special fruits, which they were not allowed to eat, because He who was the Master had said so. He was called God, our Father in Heaven. But then a snake came wriggling along and told the Wife to pick one of these fruits, which were called apples, and eat it and give the Husband a piece to taste.

When they had done this, they were banished, and outside were the midges and gnats and all the other kinds of misery. Since then, all human beings are enslaved until Judgement Day. Bodel would recite, in a loud voice, these words, which Skord understood just as little as the rest of the story:

> 'You will eat your bread with sweat on your face
> and suffer all the worst ills of this place.
> The soil you'll till because you must live,
> but thistles and thorns is all it will give.'

Again and again he asked her to say these words in the quiet of the evenings, and he smiled when he listened, as if hearing the song of a blackbird.

For a while, Bodel and Erker had belonged to a band of children trailing along the roads with their bags. But things had gone badly for them. Now they were on their own, and would hide in the forest if they met another band. Skord trundled along with them, and it did not take him long to find out how to make himself useful. He frightened the others away. Stones would whistle past his head, but after a while the throwers would give up and leave. The villages were far apart and the forest scared the two children. For Skord, the forest was home. He could make the night-time creatures rustling in the undergrowth go away. On the other hand, the moment they came close to a village he became much less brave.

The only house he had been into was the ruined hut up in Oringen where he had found the dead crone. It was hard for him to understand what a house was for. True, in the rain it was less leaky than the branches of a fir tree. But then, he had seen people protect themselves against the rain by putting sheets of birch bark over their shoulders, so really from that point of view, houses were unnecessary. There was always a very strong odour coming through their front openings. Skord kept away when Erker and

Bodel approached the houses. He feared that the children would be trapped inside them and never come out again. Instead they would turn into dried-up hulks like the old crone, just skin and bones, and lose their shining eyes, their warmth and firm flesh.

But he was curious, and tried to peer into the openings in the houses, especially when the smoke smelled of the good things. This way, he managed to work out what houses might be used for and, ultimately, what they signified.

The fact was, inside the houses, they had imprisoned fire.

They had caught the roaring, raging fire, capable of rushing through a whole forest, turning it into blackened hills and smoking tree stumps and exposing the burrows of the voles. They kept it enclosed in a hole in the wall or, by some magic, on a flat stone base. The fire did not burn them. Instead of leaping at the insides of the house with snapping jaws, it warmed them nicely like the sun shining on a meadow, and beamed prettily on their faces. They in turn honoured it, and fed it with sticks and logs. Thanking them, it heated their pots and pans. They behaved almost arrogantly with the fire, in the same way that an undersized man might behave with a big bull or a stallion. A man like that can lead a bull by a ring through its nostrils, and hold a horse back with a bridle, even though it is furious and the corners of its mouth are filling with green froth. They also kept flickering points of fire inside cages, which they carried around to light their way.

In the end, Skord's curiosity got the better of him, and he made himself go into a house even though fear prickled inside him. Inside it was dark and the fire glowed on the hearth. Smoke rushed towards the hole in the ceiling, carrying sparks of fire with it. He looked at the hole and suddenly it all became clear.

These people had made the hole so that the fire could get out when it wanted to, but stay with them all the same. The stream of sparks flew between them and the sun. He could not work out which way – from the sun? Away from it?

Now he knew what houses were for.

In places like this, pissing on the floor was not allowed. Of course, the animals that knew no better did, like the piglets and puppies. Hens, too, seemed not to understand the meaning of houses. The animals were there to make the house like the forest. Because by now Skord had realised that the house was made in the likeness of the forest. Tree trunks rose towards the sky. The ground was covered with crackling dry grass and pine needles. A stack of stones surrounded the sky-hole which served as their sun. Ignorant, the animals went about their daily lives. Only the people knew what they had done. They liked likenesses. They had created an image of the forest. Inside it, there was no green unruliness, no undergrowth and dead wood and barrenness. Instead there was order. They had put a bridle on the sun and a nose ring on the moon. Water was contained in pails instead of gushing over rock faces. People were sensible and cunning and skilful beyond belief. They had even made themselves burrows in the forest, and crawled in there and stayed after dark. They buried food the way bears and foxes do, and found it again and pulled it out when they needed to eat.

Right at the back of the house, a bent old woman would deal with the fire. Skord reckoned she must be the most powerful being around. She would poke the embers with tongs and rakes. She fed the fire to still its hunger, then stirred it up and seemed to play with it, all the while looking grim and preoccupied.

In return for the food they were given, Erker and Skord had to cut logs with a sharp piece of metal on a handle. They carried the logs inside and gave them to the small crone by the hearth. Skord was filled with wonder, and there were strong stirrings and heavings inside his chest each time he entered the house. He felt very anxious, even frightened, and could not get away fast enough. If the fire-crone screamed at them, he got sweaty with fear and badly wanted to leave. Once he ran off, head over heels, and disappeared into the forest. He wanted to forget fires, houses and people. That night, he took cover under a fir tree, and listened to the hooting of the owls and the water rustling under the stony ground. He thought it sounded like human voices, but disjointed and senseless. It hurt his brain more than the shouting of the fire-crone. He could not escape from his need to hear human speech. In the morning, he longed for a crust of bread. When he looked for food in the forest, everything tasted bitter and bad. He kept hearing voices. It sounded as if Erker and Bodel had got lost among the trees and were talking to each other in a confused and worried way.

That evening, they really did call out for him. When he was quite sure it was not just the murmuring of the stream, he ran towards them. Bodel wept when they found each other.

S he was so small and so wise. The top of her head was protected by a grey and tufty woollen hat, tied on with a piece of cloth; underneath was her plaited blond hair and under that the arched vault of her skull. It was in there that she kept everything she knew.

And she knew everything there was to know about the world.

Knowing things about the world does not occur to the daddy-longlegs or the fox. Nor had it ever occurred to Skord. But people made many images of what the world was like, and to them these images were full of meaning.

At Christmas-time, they would put up woven cloths on the timbered walls of their houses. The crowded pictures on these tapestries showed the order of Earth and of the heavens. This is what it was like under the skull-vault of little Bodel.

In the forest, the stalks of bog rosemary and bilberry and flowering whortleberry, intertwined with shivering sedge grass threaded with raindrops like pearls, would trace embroidery patterns on the mossy ground. But these were meaningless. Some days, it was even impossible to discern a pattern. No, forest life went on in a green wilderness of rustling leafy canopies, in black bog pools, in holes and clefts, and over mossy surfaces that gave way under foot and crumbling piles of dry branches.

In the human world, people lived on a disc that was the Earth and it was like the wooden platter for serving meat. It reached to the edge of the sea. There, at the very edge, wandered a wild creature called Behemoth. It ate mud and had stiff hairs all over its head. And a rough-skulled monster called Leviathan was floating in the sea, human bones protruding from its jaws.

Ships like white swans sailed on these seas and often perished. But those who stayed on land lived in houses. They kept a fire in the hearth and smoke coming through the hole in the roof, slept in beds, used the cesspit behind their houses, pulled milk out of cows and goats, made cheese. They ploughed the soil, turning it into deep black furrows, sowed seeds, waved ropes across the plots to keep the frost away, put up leafy branches shaped into crosses to protect against evil flying through the air, cut the corn when it had grown tall, crushed the seeds between millstones, baked loaves of bread and ate them.

It was a complicated and demanding way to live, always planning ahead, cautious and full of care. For the winter, they cured meat in barrels, saved up bread with holes in the middle hanging on rods close to the roof, and dug down the turnips into sandy trenches.

Just fancy remembering all these things, and where they were put away and dug in!

But at that point Bodel would tell him to shush. Of course you remembered where the food was put.

Skord knew that martens and stoats went on running around on the snow cover in the winter. But he also knew of many creatures that slept in nests and burrows. He himself had always thought it best to go to sleep before his stomach started aching with emptiness, and while there was still some fat left on his ribs. Besides, there was no point in getting cut on the sharp crust of the snow.

But Bodel explained that this could be avoided by putting on snowshoes. First ordinary shoes, of course. Then snowshoes, made from plaited willow branches and leather straps shaped into a grid. These supported you and stopped you from sinking through the snow right down to the vole burrows.

But why leave the warm house?

To collect from the traps.

Skord's gorge rose. He remembered drops of blood staining the snow, glazed eyes and broken limbs.

I shall never go and live in a house, he thought. I shall never put a woolly hat on my head.

But he never tired of hearing little Bodel tell of the world.

Everything in the end reached for the sky. Just look at the well handle and see where it is pointing, she said.

The lowest people on Earth's crust, crawling like the worms, were those who for ever busied themselves with the soil. They dug to lighten it and then spread cow muck all over it.

The foreman was above them. He wore a coat with short tails and used the whip if he wasn't obeyed at once.

The best horses for riding were above him. These were the ones the Master himself would ride. Or, at least, that was how Skord saw it. Bodel insisted that no animal could be higher than a human being, not even those animals, with their decorated, silver-trimmed bridles, small, delicate hooves and their eagerness which made greenish froth drip from their mouths. Could it be that creatures with mud clinging to their boots, who crept about dragging hoes and wooden ploughs through the earth, were still meant to be above the slender-limbed horses with their finely embroidered saddle blankets?

Well, yes, because they had souls.

What was that – souls?

Souls were like moths over the marsh pools during a summer's night. If a soul found a body to bide in, it would light up from inside the way a wick lights the inside of a horn lamp. Souls set free from dead bodies would drift at night over the marshes and the clearings blackened by fire.

He had seen souls trying to push their way in through the skin of elks, tough as it was, Skord said.

But Bodel said that was a silly notion. Nothing Skord had seen in the forest counted as knowledge.

He wanted to know who was above the boss man, the next one along the well handle pointing towards the sky.

Her Ladyship was, she of the white face and the hat covering all her hair; she who had no eyebrows.

Above her was the Master. He could run a horse to death if he liked. He wore tall boots made from soft deerskin.

Above him was the Bishop, who lived in a house made of the clearest glass and took his boiled eggs from a cup of gold. Above the Bishop was the Pope in Rome, who somehow was the father of everyone and wore a ring on his forefinger with a red stone in it. If you got to kiss the stone, you would be cured of the plague.

And above the Pope in Rome?

God, Our Father in Heaven, said Bodel, and then she would start speaking of something else. This was the end of her knowledge of the World Order reaching towards Heaven. But she knew a lot more about what went on in the hidden corners of the World, and that way, she had come to find out many more things about Heaven too.

In Heaven, at the side of Our Father, sat the Saviour and He was the Sweet One, whose wounds dripped with blood and honey.

Even further away lived the Mother of God, the Virgin, the Pink Rose, who was called Mary. When She wept, dewdrops fell on the grass. Her bed straw was sweet-smelling flowers. She would sit on the stile, showing Her round white knees. If bees stung you, it helped to call out to Her.

She was like her Ladyship, though Her skin was whiter still. Anyone who knocked on Her door would get bread. A man who had owned a farm, but left his home for the road, had told Bodel that the Virgin had given birth to the Earth, which She had carried inside Her round white belly. But if you said so because you believed it, they would take you and put you on top of a pile of branches and burn you. That was because God the Father did not like it, and it was He who had created Heaven and Earth.

But He liked it well enough if you prayed to the Mother of God for help against famine and wasps and evildoers and snakebites and the ague and the hay rotting, the water turning bad and the meat becoming tainted, and also against earache and summer draughts and flaws in the weave, and the time the tithe was due and also when your skin cracked between thumb and forefinger and the bed linen crawled with lice, and the plague.

Mary, who was the Rose in Heaven, was also all that was most lovely in life. She was warm milk and soft bread straight from the oven. She was the clumps of cheese forming in the whey of the world. She was downy and warm like the flank of a cow, and dry and glossy like fresh straw. She was as pure as a spring deep in the forest and as soft as the breast of a goose and as clear as a dewdrop on a leaf. She was the life in living things and true happiness. So, Skord asked, was she like pancakes?

When it rained, and if they asked nicely, the children might be allowed to sleep in one of the outbuildings. They wanted Skord to come with them, but he did not dare. He lay down outside, and listened to the faint murmur of their voices through the rushing of water pouring from the roof-covering of birch bark. There was also a rustling sound from thin, dry stalks of grass, and a powerful smell of flowers and herbs, mixed with the odour of wool. Sheep were kept in there. He could hear their stomachs rumbling. The children's voices stopped. Now, the only sounds were of ruminating sheep jaws and rats' feet pattering on the floorboards. He would have liked to sleep with the children if only the walls had not closed them in so tightly.

One night he found a shed without walls. It was just a roof supported by poles at the corners. He went in and sat down on the earthen floor, just next to one of the corner posts. Stiff skins were piled underneath the roof. He curled up and listened to the rain being sifted through the gills of the fir trees. The world had turned to water. It seeped through the grass and the layer of red soil, down into the cold gravel. It was dry under the roof, but the air was heavy to breathe.

As he lay there, curled up and surrounded by the stench of skins ready for tanning, his soul freed itself from the mustiness inside his ribcage. It slid outside into the grey light, and it had paws. It put the cold tip of its nose into the wind, which blew strongly and sadly. Like a stoat, Skord's soul slipped between the rocks. It came across a house in the forest. There was just enough room to hold a fox, and sure enough, a fox-body was inside and it stank of fox piss and fox fear. Skord's soul asked the fox-body what it was doing in there.

'Let me out and then I'll tell you,' said the fox-body.

'I don't have the strength,' the soul answered. 'But if you tell me, I'll be back here tomorrow, with my hands. Then I can pull back the bar across the door and let you out.'

The fox was reasonably satisfied with this.

'I came in here to get a bird,' he said. 'But it was a bitter bird. Never get stuck in a house.'

Skord's soul slipped away through the night. It saw the long-eared owl strike and heard the squeak of the vole. It heard the water of the lake lapping against the stones, licking them with many soft tongues. When the soul returned to the shed with the skins, it settled next to Skord's resting body and hesitated about joining it again. Then the soul realised that the skins stacked on the earthen floor had once been bodies. The bodies had not been struck down by beak, claw or paw. The skins could not answer any questions and their eyes were empty slits.

In the morning Skord woke, back inside himself. He remembered his promise to the fox, and decided to go at once into the forest and let it out. Knowing someone like the fox could be very useful. But when he reached the clearing he saw the body of the fox hanging on the wall of an outhouse. It had been killed by a blow which had crushed its skull and forced its eyes out of their sockets. It was strung up by its hind legs, blood seeping from its nose and its thick tail drooping.

So Skord sleeps during the day under fir trees. He does not want to enter a shed again. His body stays warm as he sleeps in the smell of sun-dried resin. He hears voices far away. The aspens swing their stiff bunches of leaves, the well handle creaks. He sleeps the way the guard dog sleeps in the farmyard, eyes peering through slits, ears wide open, hurting in advance from the sounds of iron hitting wood and whips hitting wounds. Little birds fuss about, minding their own business somewhere above his head, taking no more notice than if he were a mossy stone.

When night falls and the moths are dancing, white in the grey light, he goes forth, taking hands and feet with him. Mist rises like smoke from the tarn. It whirls above the pools in the marsh, where a brew is always boiling. He picks snails from their slime, pupae from their shells and caterpillars from their rolled-up leaves. The long-eared owl strikes and the vole squeaks. The water of the lake softly licks the stones, as is its habit. The night is always the same. The marsh brew boils and the steam drifts from sour-pit and cold-hole.

In the morning he is back sheltering under the fir tree, sleeping in the dripping rain. From far away comes the sound of voices and the stench of blood and shit, of frying, of fatty meat, sooty smoke and rancid straw. A fox ambles past under the fir trees, carefully protecting his fur from the rain, pulling back the corners of his mouth. His yellow eyes gleam. He says, without moving his tongue inside rows of white teeth, 'Never enter a house.'

Skord and little Bodel often spoke together. Of course, they would shout if one of them saw a clearwater spring or tracks of wolf paws on the ground. But this was something else: sitting talking together. Bees flew out and in, making honey in waxy combs. Words created trust between them.

Skord had always found it easy to imitate talking. In the very beginning, his voice sometimes became toneless at the end of a long phrase, the way a starling's would. But by now the words were ready inside his head. They were lying in wait for the evening, when Bodel's words would come flying along. Then his words would start shrieking and twittering and hooting.

It was high summer. The sun was warm, even late into the night. The people were more generous than in the spring, when their stores had emptied. Skord and Bodel could talk together in the evenings because by then their stomachs no longer ached with hunger.

Bodel would often sit there picking over things she had found. There were sticks and cones and pebbles, and she made patterns with them and looked at what she had done. Sometimes she smiled at him, as if she meant him to understand why things were arranged a particular way. Sticks forming crosses or squares, pebbles piled up into little cairns. He thought it strange and pretended he did not notice what she was up to. But he understood her words.

For a long time, they had been staying near a village where the people gave them bread and porridge in return for Erker chopping wood and sweeping up the muck from the cattle path and putting it in a midden. There was hardly anything the people took such care of as the muck, from the cows and from themselves. They even tried to collect the goat droppings. Bodel said the soil grew richer from the muck, and in the winter, they would pile it into sledges and spread it on the fields. It worked especially well when the strong spring sunshine made it soak through the snow. No one would think of leaving what came out of the body just anywhere. It had to be kept in the dung pits or one of the many privies.

This was a village with plenty of houses. It had a twisting cattle path called a coo-run, well handles pointing upwards, and outhouses, byres and stone-lined cellars. The farm where Erker chopped and swept was at the edge of the village. Skord did not dare to go there with him. He had seen the farmer beat a horse across the back. The farmer had a loud voice, and people did what he told them to do. When he was watching them, they would shuffle away quickly with bowed backs.

Bodel and Skord were sitting near the fringe of the forest, by the edge of a plot called the Burntland. She was chatting with him, but she was also doing other things. She had put some little twigs into a fir cone. Once in a while, she would look down towards the farm, where people and animals went to and fro on the worn, sun-scorched grass. Then she found more twigs and put them into another fir cone. Skord felt sad when she smiled at her arrangement. He could not understand what pleased her so.

Now a man emerged from between the houses below them. He was walking heavily and leading a bull by the ring through its nostrils. It was a small, short-necked, long-haired bull with a white blaze on its forehead. The farmer was standing by the wall of his house, holding a cow by its bridle. She arched her back and looked round for the bull as it came closer. They could hear the men shouting in the still warm haze, their voices harsh and impatient. In the end the bull mounted the cow, clasping her with his forelegs, in the way that the elks did at the time of the year when they were rutting and digging their reeking pits. Bodel gave a little laugh, and fiddled with her cones. When Skord looked, he saw that she had put one of the cones half leaning on top of the other.

Then, finally, he understood. He looked away from the cone with the twigs, and observed the bull down below. He watched the cow, and then looked at the other fir cone, stuck through with the same number of twigs as the first one. Now he started to laugh. He laughed so hard he had to roll over and over on the ground.

Suddenly, Bodel separated the two cones. At the same time something changed in the village. The bull pulled away from the cow, and they were both led off.

She made images! At last he understood what she was up to with the things she had spread out on the ground in front of her. She fashioned houses from rows of sticks, she built well-heads with stones, made meadow fences from twigs and created cows and horses using cones. She was making a likeness of the whole farm, though much smaller. She took a delight in that smallness for its own sake, and Skord felt just the same, now that he had finally understood. He also got some kind of idea of why they all seemed to enjoy stories and images so much. It was not just the craftiness. It meant power.

She invited him to join her as she carried on building the whole village on the ground in front of them, but at first he was poor at handling these small things. They broke or got stuck under his nails. She taught him how careful one had to be.

They could hear the farmer's voice from down there by the outbuildings, and watch the people bend over the tasks he gave them. But up here by the Burntland sat Bodel, and, little as she was, did as she saw fit, moving his goats and his cows, raising water from his well and stacking his logs.

Towards evening, they saw the farmer strike Erker with the shaft of his spade. They watched Erker stumble and get kicked for good measure, and start walking back to the Burntland without having been given anything to eat.

Then Skord picked up a stone and let it fall on the farmer's house. Bodel licked her lips, but said nothing. Next, Skord grabbed a whole handful of stones and held them over the farm, over the cattle and the well. Bodel stared hard at him. It seemed her turn to listen now.

He who is up there in Heaven is a great destroyer. Skord could tell Bodel about that, now that they had the village spread out below them.

Everyone can hear when His footfalls rumble over the hillsides. The clouds are made from the dust billowing as He swings His huge shanks. Watch, Bodel. He makes the water spill out so that the well runs dry. He allows the streams to drain away, leaving only gravel in their old courses. The hops stop climbing up the farmer's poles and die. The mountains and rocks and shaggy rolling hills are all in fear of Him. When He rages, they bend their backs, and terror makes the bogpools fathomless.

Watch, Bodel. I drive a stick into the fathomless depths and it vanishes.

This is the fear instilled by Him, who walks over the mountains as if they were an even floor. God Our Father in Heaven.

When He gets angry, He lets the fire loose. He makes it shower down over the houses.

Watch, Bodel. Watch. He destroys the farmer's house, and those inside it too. The house-people are lying in there, twisted together like creeping heather and whortleberry runners. When the fire comes, the juices leach out of their bodies and they burn like dry kindling.

But the farmer himself will escape for a while yet. Here is a little stick which he will use as he walks the roads. I have peeled it myself, using my nails the way you showed me. His tightly swaddled children in their birch-bark cradles will get their skulls crushed, so hard that their eyes are forced out of their sockets. Their legs will be pulled out of joint by traps and wire-gins and loops made from tough willow saplings. The farmer will walk about in ragged clothes, staggering as if drunk on strong beer. The foxes will get in and break the necks of his hens.

Here comes the fire! Farmer, water will not help you! It will turn to steam as it meets the blast of His breath. And as for you, maggots will burrow inside you and eat themselves fat on your body. When they are ready, they will grow wings and fly away with you and then nobody will know where they have taken you. Farmer, you will be destroyed. Destroyed by Him who lives high up here, with the mountains as a floor under his feet. He has let the fire loose over you, and the stones and the water too. He will extinguish you with a fiery blast of His breath.

Bodel looked at the devastation of the stones and the broken twigs, the crushed shells and blackened soil where the village had been. She looked scared, but also close to laughter.

Now Erker arrived and said he had ruined the edge of an axe belonging to the farmer, and they had to move on. But he found it hard to walk because his back hurt. He said little about the broken-up village at the edge of the Burntland. He just glanced at it.

'You little ones, you just play.'

He grew older every time he was beaten.

They left that evening, and slept in the forest. When they started walking the following morning, Bodel was sure she could smell burning and smoke. Skord hurried them on. The smoke became heavier, and smelt of frying fat. It came drifting up from the village they had left. Erker thought that it was odd that the people in the village dared to clear forest by burning on such a warm day. By evening, the smoke was cold and had sunk to the ground in the forest glades. When brother and sister had fallen asleep under a fir

31

tree, Skord climbed a rock face where the ravens nested. He reached a place high enough to see out over the forest.

It was a fine evening, with sunlight touching the tops of the firs. Far away, he could see the clearing in the forest where the village had been, and where Erker had been beaten. The blackened earth was smoking. The village looked small from up there on the rock. The houses and cabins had burned down, and the remains looked like broken sticks, crushed shells and black, smoking soil. He observed the ruins for a long time. When he climbed down again, he had decided not to tell Bodel and Erker anything about what had happened.

Brother and sister had become braver now that Skord walked with them through the forest, and would strike out towards distant villages. It was summer, holy Mary's gentle season. This is how they always walked: Erker first, carrying his bundle on the end of a stick, then little Bodel, her bag tied across her chest, and Skord last, carrying no burden, leaping around on his mucky feet into every bog-hole, sometimes singing like a swan, sometimes chirping like a fieldfare. He pleased wild animals by treating them with respect and addressing them using nice names: good Honey-Paw, Silver-Foot with golden nails and little Silky-Snout. In the clearings, they found trees in full leaf and resounding with birdsong, and when they went angling in the streams, they caught shy grayling with leaf-caterpillar bait. Skord found honeycombs inside old trees. Bodel and Erker turned away while he picked out the larvae and ate them. But afterwards they sucked on the waxen combs, for inside was a strong, brown honey, which ran down over their fingers.

They walked as far as Skule forest. Bodel told the story of how Satan, who lived in the underworld, had put his black thumb mark just to the north of Skule forest. He did that when he tempted Jesus by showing Him a map of all the countries in the world. It followed that north of Skule lived all the worst people on Earth, murderers, rogues, whores and outlaws. They had practised every evil and sinful act under the sun. They were like swine, bristles grew on their necks, their teeth were like boar's tusks and they foamed round the mouth when they spoke.

When the children had reached the last village before Skule forest, they saw a coarse, horrible rock towering in front of them. Bodel said that high up there were outlaws carrying spears. And Erker said, he once met someone who had seen two such outlaws hanging by their necks. One had had a hole straight through his head and the other one had had his teeth knocked out, and both were deader than dried codfish.

That summer they walked westwards, further than they had ever been, until they reached a long lake, a gash cut into the marshland. There was a market being held on a tongue of land sticking out into the cold, sky-pale waters, and crowds of people had come in boats or pulled by harnessed horses and reindeer. They traded skins and honey, and also salt, leather straps, knives and kettles, and drank beer and lit fires and sang and shouted and fought each other with their newly bought knives. The beer made them generous, and so quite a few of the bag-people had turned up. As the evening drew in, these dared approach even as far as the fires. Erker and Bodel went there, and Skord too, though he kept within reach of the forest. They sat down and listened, and if someone was telling stories, they moved a little closer still.

Many of those who had come could perform feats so peculiar that others would put food into their bags in return for letting them watch. One man had lost a foot and no one could work out how he could cross the marshes. But he could whistle the way grouse do, and hoot like an owl and warble like a starling or sound like whatever anyone might demand. And another one said his stomach was full of frogs, and invited bystanders to put their ears close to his belly and listen to the croaking. Then the people at the market forgot the starling-whistler, who hopped away from the fire leaning on his crutch. The knives were passed around, handled and had their edges tested on single hairs. This was when it occurred to Skord that he would do something more unusual than anybody else had dared. Whistling like a grouse was easy for him. But then, it had been done. Swallowing frogs whole did not seem to him a trick worth boasting about, even if both your feet were missing.

He reached for one of the newly sharpened knives that were handed round and said he would cut off one of his fingers. All the faces, flushed from the fire, turned towards him.

There and then, he cut the little finger from his left hand, just as you would cut a twig off a branch. Though it hurt. He had not expected that. Nor was it as quick as he thought it would be. Nobody said a word except little Bodel, who screamed as if she was the one who was cut. She tried to push her way towards him to stop his act, just as the finger came off. Skord made an ugly face.

Now everybody was laughing and shouting at the same time – all except little Bodel. The frog-eater shuffled away. As a reward, Skord was allowed to keep the knife he had used. There were enough people willing to put up the money to pay the owner back. The grin on Skord's face grew more and more rigid as the blood gushed from the cut stump, which hurt with a throbbing pain. Bodel pulled him away to put a rag on the wound, and scolded him and wept. During the night, she came back after having begged more cloth. She bandaged the wound tightly, but the stump kept bleeding and aching. Skord had not expected this misery. He was pale and covered in a cold sweat. An ague shook him, and he was thankful no one but Bodel could see him now.

He had thought the finger would grow back again, but it did not. Nor could Bodel stem the flow of blood. When the morning dawned, she made him come to see an old woman, who lived in a tent made of skins. It was said of her that she knew many kinds of witchcraft.

'Can ye stem the bluid?' Bodel asked with tears running down her cheeks.

The old woman, whose skirt was decorated with silver clappers, and who wore her jet-black hair loose under a leather cap, could not understand their language. But the words were repeated in another language by a young girl, who was dressed the same way. Then the girl explained that the wise woman wanted payment for the service they wanted, and asked them what they had to offer. Bodel loosened the ties on their bundles and showed her: two pieces of bread, the skin of a hare, a couple of feathers from a jay and some fir-tree resin wrapped in a leaf. The crone grabbed the lot with her brown claws, and then asked for Skord's name. He said his name, and the crone repeated it while she scratched her neck, which had wrinkled, folded skin like a frog's.

'Go to bed now and sleep,' the girl told Skord, 'When you get up the bluid will have stilled.'

'Good mother, we thank 'ee kindly. May Our Saviour grant ye gifts in return for what you have done,' Bodel said.

The old woman spat and went back into her tent. And Skord lay down under a fir tree and slept till the evening, and when he woke the bandage round his hand had turned brown and stiff with dried blood. Bodel removed the material carefully, and they could see that the wound had got a whitish crust and the edges of skin round it were pulled together it as if the crone had sewn it in place. It was the louse-killer he had cut off, the smallest finger.

Afterwards, Bodel often spoke about the crone with the leather cap and the very great service she had done Skord. He was less convinced himself. He had become thoughtful after the incident with the knife cut, and kept uncommonly quiet. He stayed in the same place under the fir tree, his wound covered with plantain leaves. He put one leg over the other and waggled his foot to and fro. This is how he was lying every time Bodel crawled in under the fir branches, which dragged against the ground like a full skirt. She was baffled and scared by finding the hare skin back, when she came to put a piece of bread in her bag, which he had been minding for her.

'What have you done?' she exclaimed.

'Not much,' was his answer.

She said he would meet with great misfortune for stealing the hare skin from the crone, when they had given it to her in return for the good deed she had done.

'I'm not sure about any good deed,' said Skord, 'and I can't help it if the skin came running back to us.'

'Skord, Skord, what have you done?' Bodel was weeping now.

'Nothing. Well, maybe I whistled for it a little,' he said.

Bodel said they had to leave straight away, because as like as not the crone would destroy all three of them.

So once again they plodded across the marshes. Skord stayed silent and the midges were really bad. It became a gloomy walk. Erker said he was too old now to carry a bag. He planned to get to stay somewhere, chopping logs and making ties for fence posts. Maybe they would let Bodel herd the goats. Then they could both stay in the same place together, get to sleep indoors and eat cooked porridge oats in the morning. He did not mention what Skord would be doing.

The children arrived at a solitary farm in a clearing one evening soon after the feast day of James the Apostle. They had been walking through dried-up forest, avoiding piles of dead branches, and in order to drive way away their fears, Bodel had been telling them about James of the Wet Hat. He was one of the sons of Zebedee and had followed Our Saviour on his bare feet through much worse undergrowth and skree and sour-bogs than this. Then the Lord Jesus Christ had been killed by the Jews and James had walked on all alone until he ended up in the country called Hispania. In that country they had marble lions and leaping springs made by human hands. Anyway, they buried him there, and ever since pious and wealthy people have walked to his grave to pray, and when they return, they have shells sown on their hats.

A strange story. Plod on. Plod on. In the undergrowth, paw and claw and jaw of wolf. Who walks barefoot all the way to Hispania to pray next to a cadaver? Better just plod on. Skord would have preferred to enter a crow and fly. But Bodel kept on telling stories and that held him. They walked past small overgrown forest plots with stone cairns, left from the time of the slashers-and-burners. The plots were abandoned now. Wolves or hunger had driven the people away.

That evening, they smelled smoke and caught a glimpse of grey houses between the tree trunks. Skord had planned to stay behind in the forest cover as usual, when they were surprised by an old woman who came up behind them, returning from collecting a skirtful of branches. She herded the children in front of her with pitying words, and Skord did not dare step aside, frightened as he was that she would do horrible things to him. Jostling for attention inside his head were images of all the things humans could do: traps and snares, unnatural leaping springs, sticks that sprouted fire at one end, cutting irons, hats made from dead squirrels. Anyone with enough power to destroy a roaring lion, a creature worse than a bear, and turn it into a marble effigy in front of his house, could easily transform and magic away a thin body like his own. Which is why he did step across the threshold of the house where the people lived, though he stopped in the porch. He shook with fear when he saw the ceiling over his head.

He heard Bodel's clear voice ask that, for the mercy of Jesus Christ, they should be given something to eat and have something to put in the bag as well. Skord pressed himself close to the wall and probed the moss-filled cracks to investigate whether he could get out. The old woman had put a bar across the door and he had no idea how to remove it.

From inside the cottage came the noise of people speaking and of iron cooking vessels and chains and wooden spoons scraping, and the smell of porridge, sour wool, goat fell and chopped juniper. The door was pushed open, and the housewife stepped into the porch, with a great smell coming from her skirts. Skord hissed.

'You poor creature, so you're hiding out here,' she said. 'Just as well, you look right louse-ridden. Just stay here and we'll give you something to eat too.'

She had keys dangling from her belt, and using one of them, she unlocked the door to a room forming the other half of the porch. In there, she kept cheeses and loaves of bread. She picked a piece of bread and a cheese wrapped in a damp linen cloth, and went back into the cottage again, without closing the door behind her. Across the high threshold he could see the people sitting at the table eating their evening meal.

It was the first time he had seen people eating at a table. They did not seem truly famished, he thought. Rather, they were playing with the food and seemed to be trying to increase their pleasure or interest by employing strange practices: picking at the food with their fingers, cutting it into pieces with knives, chewing for ever and waiting between each new helping into the big dish. Skord started to growl. A man got up to kick the dog out, but returned laughing, saying that there was a scrofulous and louse-bitten laddie outside. While the man was in the porch, Skord had kept hissing until hoarse and dry-mouthed. It was as if he thought he could hide himself inside his own spittle, like frog-hopper larvae.

Erker never said much. Talk was always rippling between Skord and little Bodel like a stream between rocks, but Erker just listened and stayed silent. Once, he too had tried to excel in a group at a marketplace fire. The people had become drunk on the beer, and Erker had wanted to tell them of something he had once heard, sitting at another fire. He had shown them a small earthenware flask, closed by a wooden stopper and sealed by fir-tree resin.

'In this flask of mine there is a stronger drink than beer,' he said. 'It is the strongest drink on Earth.'

They wanted him to pull the stopper out and let them taste it. All would have gone well if Erker had just copied the man he had heard tell of the strongest drink on Earth the first time round. But he had become greedy and demanded cheese and dried meat in exchange for the flask. When he had eaten all they had given him and licked every crumb from his fingers, they asked him to pull out the wooden stopper. He did as they wanted and handed them the flask to drink from. They smelled it and they tasted it.

'But it's just water!' they shouted. And then they beat him up. Erker tried to shout back all that he had heard about how water truly was the strongest drink on Earth. It could pull bridges away and whole houses too. It made the millstones go round, and carried ships as large as churches. But in return for that information, they split his upper lip and tore out great tufts of his hair.

Since then he had not tried to draw attention to himself by talk. But when just the three of them were together, he would sometimes break his silence and ask questions that left little Bodel at a loss for an answer. One evening she had been telling Skord how God, the Heavenly Father, had made the Earth and everything upon it. Afterwards, Erker asked, 'What did he make it from?'

Bodel fell silent at that. But Skord said, 'He made a big heap first.'

'How did he do that?' asked Erker, and Skord answered, 'Shitting.'

Bodel slapped his face and told him he would suffer for saying such wicked things.

It is the first night he has slept in a house. Though sleeping is hardly the right word. He is confused by all the many things. They glitter and shine and change their shapes. The old woman, whom he saw working by the hearth all evening, has now put the pans to the side. She used a rake to push the ashes over the embers. The scraping of the rake was the last awake sound. Then the night sounds began, moans and sighs, rustling of straw, snores, farts and squeaks. His neck aches when he is lying on his back, and his hip aches when he is on his side. He does not dare sleep. Grey light enters through the hole in the roof, but the cottage is filled with dark shadows. It smells of soot and cooling ashes. He hears a faint noise and sees one of the black cauldrons come to life and move across the hearth. Terrified, he observes it fold its legs underneath its belly and settle down. His mouth feels dry.

There is a rustling noise as a large rat runs in the straw on the floor. The bedcover rests heavily on him, and he is afraiad to move because of the stiff, crackling sound it makes. He fingers a corner and feels something rough poking out of it. It is stuffed with the flower heads of reeds.

It is all confusing. Covering oneself with bags of cloth stuffed with reeds. Cutting down trees, peeling off bark and twigs, and raising them up again, plugging the gaps with birch bark, hammering nails into planks to make a door, locking oneself in. A fox would have at least two ways out of his lair. Here, the only door is closed and kept shut with a bar.

The cottage breathes and squeaks. One of the cooking pots moves deeper into the cooling hearth. Skord is retching from the stale, greasy air. His fingers keep picking away at the reed stalks poking out through the bedcover. Too many smells, too many things.

He thinks: it would be a mad fox who collected everything he could find and dragged it into his lair. Maybe biting mad, impossible to frighten off. A mad fox, its teeth biting into a leg, its yellow eyes shining, foam standing round its mouth. The man sleeping in the big bed there must be mad. He is naked but for the cap on his head. His shoes are standing under the bed. They do not look like feet, but like jugs with spouts. The vixen sleeps next to him, and she too is naked. Folds of skin cover her yellow eyes.

They have dragged them here, all these things visible now in the grey light of early morning. Here they sleep, surrounded by all the things they have got together, and they have barred the door, so that no other mad fox will get in and pull the prey from their jaws.

There is a sour smell of anxiety lingering around them as they sleep.

At last, morning comes, and the sky over the hole in the roof turns white. A blackbird starts calling in his familiar voice. It is tempting him outside, to the water of the lake and the damp greenery. Then a gust of wind blows in through the smoke-hole, causing the ashes on the hearth to whirl. The embers flare, and the cat gets up and jumps down into the straw on the floor.

The old woman has woken up in some corner and walks over to the hearth. She puts kindling on the embers, and the fire starts sparkling. It gives off clouds of white smoke. Every so often, puffs of smoke spread through the cottage and Skord sneezes. His eyes start watering.

Now the master of the house turns heavily in his bed and breaks wind. The mistress stretches out a white arm and grabs her clothes. She gets dressed and joins the old woman at the hearth. Without speaking, she opens a bread bin and cuts chunks off the black bread. Her husband gets out of bed and pulls back the bar. The morning air flows in when the door opens. Shaking, Skord breathes it in. He is alive again.

One after another, the people in the house go outside to relieve themselves. Every time the door is pushed open, the scent of morning dew on grass reaches him. He can hear a goat bleat.

Far away on the mountainside someone has spread out a small square covering of gold. It lies there, shining among the rough firs and the skree. Sometimes it moves. Sometimes it fades.

High up in the coarse rowan tree, which has flowers smelling of fish gone stale in the summer heat, three golden leaves are playing. Sometimes they fall silent. Then the only sound is the whining of the gnats.

Deep down underground, there is a small stream of the finest silver, rushing between cold stones. It makes the ground ring. Then silence.

Silence in the ground, and silence in the treetops, rugged greyness over the hillside bogs, sour and evil and wet, when you plod with human feet.

A human being comes out the same way as a fox cub, and little Bodel can say what she likes about souls. The small human suckles like a fox and shits yellow like a fox. There is no difference.

But when the priest has breathed in her face and put salt in her mouth and said 'Effata!', then there is a difference.

That is why they swaddle her, making her as hard as a board. When she is no cry-baby any more, she has to work.

Then she eats of the salty and the cured, and wields a spade or spins a thread full of knots and tows.

Skord works no more than a magpie does, or a fox. When the fox has filled his belly, he lies in the sun. When he is hungry, he tramps about and takes what he can get. The fox can lose his leg in a gin, and something similar could well happen with the fingers Skord has got left, if he is too greedy. This is a hard lesson for him. Even though Bodel is weeping with hunger, she throws away the tit-bit he brings her. She says that he has been in the larder and pinched it from the crock where the farmer's wife keeps her cured meat. He does not argue with her.

He ambles around the houses the way foxes do. And so he hears many things that are not for his ears.

One day they arrive in a village where the people are harvesting the barley. There they go, backsides in the air, cutting it with curved iron blades. The blades whine and whistle through the barley stalks. The children hide in the forest, waiting. It is not worth angering the people by wandering along, free and easy, while they are working. But Skord sneaks off down to the houses, where he watches and listens. There is just one old woman alone at home. She is preparing food for the harvesters, and talking to herself.

When at last the barley is stooked and the corpses of the voles are scattered among the sharp stubble, the people walk back home for their evening meal. The children wait for a while before coming forward. By then, Skord has joined them. He is wearing an old hat made of hareskin, which he picked up somewhere. It is yellow and tufty and practically bald on top. They are allowed to come forward when the people in the house have finished eating, and the old woman, who is the grandmother, pours them helpings of sour milk. They notice she is watering the milk, but then she did the same for the other people. The wife has no say in this house. It is the grandmother who cuts up the bread. It is mouldy, but the people have been eating from the same loaf. The children hand the bowl between them and drink the sour and watery milk.

'Quiet now!' says Skord.

He is addressing something under the table, and everybody wonders at him.

'Who is it you are talking to?' the husband asks in a hard voice.

'Oh, it's only my soothsayer,' Skord answers.

Everybody wants to look under the table now, but no one can see anything except Skord's bald old hat, which he has put under one of his feet.

'Now, keep quiet!' he says and stamps on the hat.

'What does he say, what does he say?' the maidservants are murmuring. They all think anything to do with soothsaying must be about love and betrothals.

'He's speaking through his hat, as usual,' Skord says. 'He's telling of a cock having got himself locked up inside the window seat.'

'Then we would hear him, for sure,' the husband says. 'Shut your trap now and eat what's been set in front of you. Afterwards you'll have to be on your way.'

'But open up the seat!' the serving girls exclaim. 'Just think, the red cock may be lying there inside it! He may be out cold.'

'Shut up!' Skord shouts. 'You'll get me into trouble!'

'What does he say? What does he say?'

'He says that if the cock is out cold, it's because it got too hot for him,' Skord says. 'But that tittle-tattler under the table must be quiet. I can only ask for your forbearance. Besides, we've got to leave soon.'

The maids ask yet again for the seat to be opened but the grandmother tells them that they're not to bother about it. Because there's only some uncarded wool inside the seat.

'Quiet!'

'What did he say now?'

'He said cock-a-doodle-doo,' Skord says.

At that, a large girl stepped forward and lifted the top of the seat with her red hands. Inside was a roasted cock, a loaf of fresh crusty bread and a pottery dish full of milk so rich, the surface had a thick creamy skin.

'What in the name of Jesus Christ!' shouted the wife. 'How come there's food inside the seat?'

The grandmother had to share the food out between them all, and everyone wondered about what had happened. But the husband kept exchanging glances with the old woman, and then said to Skord in the mildest of voices that he would quite like to buy the hat from him. Though that would be on condition that they left the house promptly. They were given half the loaf of bread and the wings of the cock in exchange for the hat, and so they said thank you kindly, and got out of the house as soon as they could.

Little Bodel kept looking curiously at Skord as they walked along, but she said nothing. They sat down for a while when they had reached the edge of the forest. They were full up and their stomachs were heavy. Skord was sniffing the air. A black greasy smoke was coming out of the roof-hole of the main farmhouse.

'That's strange,' he said. 'When I arrived in this village the smoke smelled of roasting cock. But now it smells as if they are burning old hare skin. These people have strange eating habits.'

Then Bodel thought they had better be on their way.

Sometimes they worked for their food. That is to say, Bodel and Erker worked. Skord grew very long legs whenever someone tried to put a spade or a fork in his hand. But he had suddenly got hold of a stick, which he carried around with him everywhere. It would get up to tricks, like pointing to people in the farmhouses, and then he would try to force it back towards the floor. It always rose again.

'I can't control it,' he said. 'It's my sight-stick.'

They wondered what it was the stick was seeing, and he told them it could see who would die that year, and point out him or her. They would ask him to get packing as soon as he could, and put food into the children's bag and shoved them out through the door. Skord would fight the stick, which kept trying to rise, and managed to get it out through the door before it pointed at somebody.

One night they were in a cottage with people who lived on their own by a plot of land they had got by burning the forest. They were talkative, because they rarely had visitors. The husband was holding forth the most. He was saying how they had moved deeper into the forest because they had got so tired of other people. Suddenly a bell started rattling and ringing, as if a goat had found his way into the cottage. When it stopped, the husband went on with his tale, saying how well off they had been when they lived on the coast, and how many lads and girls they had in their service. Then the bell rang again. He asked what all that was about.

'It is my goat bell,' Skord said. 'It rings unaided.'

The husband wouldn't believe it. But Skord stood up and stretched out one arm, with the rusty bell hanging from his wrist.

'Bodel, say that you are wearing an underskirt of silk,' he said.

'That I do not, nor will I in my entire life,' Bodel said. She was never good-tempered when Skord made a spectacle of himself in the farms.

'But say it anyway, and then the bell will ring,' he said.

But she stayed silent and turned her back to him. Then the only daughter in the house offered to say it. She was a louse-bitten creature in a torn overblouse made of coarse cloth. But she said what Skord wanted, and straight away the bell started rattling and ringing, as if he had used his hand to make it.

'That's a strange bell you've got,' the farmer said.

'But why does it ring?' the daughter said.

'If I only knew,' Skord said.

Now, the farmer had told them that Erker and Bodel, and yes, Skord too, would have to work for the food they had eaten. But seemingly he had changed his mind now. They had better leave straight away, he said. His wife pointed out that the children had eaten a great deal. But the farmer wanted the bell in return. Skord did not want to hand it over. He said that, old and battered as it was, it meant a great deal to him. He thought it might come to him soon what made it ring, and then it could be of great use. In the end, however, he agreed to give up the bell in exchange for a piece of butter, and for all of them to be allowed to sleep under a roof that night.

'We've not churned the milk yet,' the farmer said.

The bell started ringing, and made quite a noise.

'I cannot understand what the matter is with it,' Skord said, 'but I'll find out soon enough. Pity about the butter, because that is what we like best. But I'm just as pleased to keep my bell.'

But the farmer remembered there might be some butter left in the stone cellar after all, and he sent his wife to bring it up. Afterwards there was an exchange. Skord got a lump of butter, about as much as he could hold in his hand, and the farmer got the goat bell. He seemed very pleased with the bargain.

When the children were back on their own, they spread butter on crusts of bread and ate. Little Bodel was wondering if what they had done was right. Skord said it was, because the farmer was pleased about getting the bell. But they never heard it ring again. In the morning, the farmer said he had chanced to drop it in the well. There it stayed, in silence.

Skord had observed that people found great joy in each other's company. They clung together like young grass snakes in a dungheap. They would be very close when they spoke to each other, so eagerly that their breaths mixed, and at night they would rub against each other's naked skins. When they were feeling tender and loving, they picked lice from each other's scalps. They drank from the same jugs and ate from the same dishes. Around them hung a scent, powerful and mysterious, which they seemed keen to protect. They did not go into hiding like badgers, and they never hunted alone like owls. There were times when the sight of a short-eared owl gliding along, its wings slicing soundlessly through the grey night air, was all Skord needed to fall prey to a great longing to get away from all this human crowding and kindness towards each other, which could also mean bruises and grazes and taunts.

When the children returned again to the village at the edge of Skule forest, he slipped away like a weasel. He thought he would like to see the mighty forest, even though it could be an evil place. But it was anything but that. He stepped into it as into a great hall. The ground was covered by the most delicate grasses, woven through with flowers, twisting in and out like bright threads of wool in a girl's hair.

Tall serious fir trees stood there, the evening breeze toying with their branches, and small squirrels with claws like hooks were rattling up and down the trunks and observing him with their bright eyes. There were noble trees with golden leaves playing in their canopies, and there were creepers, smelling strongly of fresh cheese and honey, twisting over the moss-edged rocks. He climbed steadily upwards among the spires of the ferns, and finally reached heights where the forest thinned out and the sides of the mountain showed through, crusty with silver lichen. There he came across a great bowl, carved out of the hillside, and in it was the clearest water he had ever seen. It was deep, but he could still see the bottom where the stones blazed, reflecting angled shafts of sunlight, and where soft green stalks swayed as the Earth breathed.

He climbed up on a stone next to the deep tarn and settled there, looking down into the water. Then he noticed a bird floating in the depths. It had a large wingspan – it was a buzzard. It was caught in the clear lake water, needing only to flick its wings almost imperceptibly to keep suspended between the bottom of the tarn and its smooth surface. Skord wanted to get down there and join it.

He took off his ragged clothing and put it in the grass. He, who had never willingly washed or bathed, now lowered himself into water as cold as liquid ice. He rolled over on his back and gently flicked his arms as if they were buzzard's wings. Then he saw the buzzard floating in the sky above him. Suddenly, he felt cold, so cold that his blood froze to stone in his head and stomach. He leaped out of the water.

The buzzard in the sky was just a buzzard. But the bird in the tarn had been an image, and it had great power over him.

Images were not always created by human beings. Sometimes images just turned up. He saw, and tried to understand. If the image caused his soul to soar, if his spirit floated upwards like a buzzard's feather in warm air and left his body behind on the hillside, a shrunken cast of snake-skin, then he had understood it right. He had seen what it really meant.

To someone who had really seen, words mattered no more than the chatter and whistling of starlings.

Skord walked back down the hill. Darkness was falling quickly and under his feet the fir-tree roots were like the fleshy backs of snakes. Melancholy overcame him, because he realised that he had brought the human world with him into the forest. It was inside his head and kept pushing its way out. He had wanted to lose it, but could not.

The Moon of Illyria

S ir Hinrik came and took the land below the mountain. He sent his people ahead to build houses and farms. They had to ride hard and work hard. They spent nights without sleeping, worrying about each other and the animals. Nights harsh with frost and nights lit by a pale sun. It was a strange land. During the darkest time he would stand there, trying to see the fringe of the forest, his squirrel-fur coat against his cheeks, stiffened by his frozen breath. The built-up area reached all the way to the forest, but he could not see the houses. They were swallowed up by the darkness. It was as if he had built nothing at all.

But by the third year, he became aware of how green the pelt of grass was in the late summer. It was growing back strongly. The sheep were grazing there, with yellow milk in their udders. He walked in the chicken droppings. This was rich stuff and should be swept up and spread over the turnip rows. He watched the flies crawl over the cleaned pike carcasses nailed to the wall. The forenoon was grey. Mists and vapours were rising as if from a stockpot. There was a shiny lump of lard behind the thick haze: the sun. He walked on past the baking shed, stopped for a while and stood there in the smell of freshly baked bread, watching the fleshy buttocks of the women. They spotted him but kept clattering with peels and rolling pins, blushing up to their ears and giggling. But they did not dare offer him the squashed leftovers, since he was more special than other passers-by. He continued through the steam, the heady mixture of summer and hard work, of meat, skins, logs, timber, tar, wax, wool, grain, straw, flax and cheese. When he came to a halt in the doorway, he noticed that the foreman had sent a boy with a limp to sweep up the chicken shit.

He would remember this forenoon, sometimes in surprise.

Why, out of a life that normally moved so swiftly, would it re-emerge with its calm, its smells and dull noises?

Gentleness and forethought were not for him, then. He was young when he stood in snow-slush, having returned after the last contact for that year with the country to the south. Red frothing lung-blood flowed from the muzzle of the horse he had ridden almost to death. A raw chill crept up his legs, and he felt a lurking wonderment, like the first shiver of fever.

What was the point of all this?

The new horses were neighing in their paddock over by the pine-wood. Sir Hinrik had to ride on. He was following a call, composed of fever and wonderment.

He was in the prime of life; the short black beard had not a single white hair. His lips and cheeks were red, his trunk sturdy and his legs powerful. No sinews ached or vertebrae creaked. This is how he was when he arrived in Tjärr: full of life and vigour.

It had all started during a hunting trip. He was sitting in a house, sharing a meal with the owners. They were well-to-do farmers, though not members of the nobility like Sir Hinrik. The housewife had eyes like slits and a big fat behind. Her origins were uncertain or, at least, not mentioned.

They had lit many candles. It was late afternoon in winter, and the windows looked dull. There was no change in the light penetrating the sheets of skin covering the windows. Then the door opened, and two women helped someone across the high threshold. One of them supported the creature, the other unwound her layers of shawls and veils. She spread out her arms as if to free herself from their help and care. She was so small that had Sir Hinrik got up from his seat, she would only have reached halfway up his chest. Her legs were outlined beneath her skirt, the long bones of shin and thigh. Her kneecaps could be seen through the cloth, as could the balls of bone at her elbow and shoulder joints. Her tense ribcage showed, the vessel of her skull, which rested on the curved stalk of her neck, contained deep-set eyes, and her hipbones formed a shallow bowl. When she moved across the floor, her arms kept straight along her sides, he thought he could see the leaden grey of her gaze. The taut skin across her jaw held shadows. Her teeth were close to the skin of her lips. Her hair was thin and the colour of ashes.

Sir Hinrik had been about to take a drink, but when she entered through the door he put the goblet down. His lips felt dry. The creature walked across the floor and disappeared into a bedroom which must have been chilled through, because a cold current of air was felt when the door opened. Then the women came back and the door was closed behind this rare being. The farmer said that she was his daughter.

Sir Hinrik returned to Tjärr many times. He wanted to see her. She was very pious and hardly ever ate. He sat at the table and watched her walk through the house. She held her fingers straight and aligned with the folds of her dress. The person sitting next to him whispered that she came from the privy where she would sit in the cold for many hours. He would have liked to dare touch her hair. Maybe it would fall out.

When the door to her bedroom closed behind her, her mother and the maids would start rushing about with dishes and bowls. The house would fill with the smell of food, the stench of burnt fat and singed meat. He thought that it was as if the pieces of meat had been roasted with bits of hair and fur left on. He retched then, and did not want to eat.

The daughter was eighteen years old and no bigger than a child. Ever since she was little, she had longed for Heaven, and for longer and longer periods she fasted on bread and water so that she would get there. When she grew older, she put her linen dresses away, and wore rough leather straps and horsehair next to her skin. In the evening, she pulled all the bedclothes off her bed and lay down on the wooden boards. Later, when she had become too weak to lift anything, she would pray till she fell asleep on the floor. Her mother would make one of the maids cover her with a light blanket. But if she was woken by the morning chill she would throw off the coverlet. She preferred to sleep with her arms stretched out and her legs so tightly together that she formed the shape of a cross, and she also said her prayers in this position.

Starvation had dried her and made her look like a shrunken old woman as she moved about among the others. It was as if a small skeleton walked there, the image of death among the living. She seemed to want to say to them: look at what you have got now, all you fat-bottomed women and hard-bellied men. Look at me, here

I am, small, grey and wicked. I can be like a swollen mass of pus in your groin. Watch me!

As a child, her piety was much spoken of and praised. But as she grew older, most people thought her mad. There were tales going around of how she saw spiders and rat droppings in the bowl of milk her mother prepared for her, and how once she had said that a chopped-off paw of a dog had turned up in her porridge.

Her parents had finally decided that enough was enough. They forced her to eat, so that she would not die. She vomited afterwards. She had visitations from the Devil, who possessed her and made foul language pour out of her mouth. He yelled at the mother that she was greasy sow and a cow in heat. The Devil let out an evil stench like burning marsh-gas, and screeched abuse in the voice of a virgin.

Sir Hinrik came to visit her, but she had become too weak to leave her bed. She had dirtied herself and the room smelt of it. She had scratched her cheeks till they were torn and bloody. He greeted her but seemed shy, which was unlike him. After standing for a while at the door, he turned and left. He rode off home and they did not expect to see him again at Tjärr.

But he did return and asked to be allowed to speak to the young lady. There was only an old woman in the room. She was carding wool. Afterwards they asked her what those two had spoken of together. She said that she had not understood it, but that she believed they had been talking of Heaven.

When the first snow of winter had settled, he came back again and brought with him a priest, who talked to her sternly. He urged her to get up and carry out such services as she could to help her mother. She had to eat and drink and look after herself in order to gain strength, and she must not pray except for morning and evening prayers. He told her that her soul was filled with selfishness, and that it was a sin to be disobedient to one's parents. Then he prayed for her, and that made her scream and back away until her head hit the timbers in the wall. This happened over and over again, so that her mother had to put a pillow behind her head and get two women to hold on to her. The priest left. She shouted after him that she had seen a large vole leap out of his mouth.

By now, people were laughing openly at her attempts at

holiness. After the priest had visited, nobody took her visions and penitence seriously any more, even though she was becoming frailer and frailer, and was bleeding copiously from the nose. No one thought Sir Hinrik would bother with her any more. But he did come back and asked to speak to the young lady alone. No shame in that, they thought, since she was as weak as someone who had suffered from the cholera for weeks. Nor was it easy to deny the great lord anything.

He sat with her from noon till twilight, and when he rode off on his way home, he had given her a book with covers of carved wood. This frightened her father, who rode after him. Her father said that he would like to return this book which my lord had left behind. In reality he believed Sir Hinrik had gone mad too. The farmer was afraid of having such a precious thing in his house. The lord's high-up relatives might arrive from the south to look into the matter.

Sir Hinrik refused the book. He said it was a gift for the young lady. Her father countered by saying that she might dirty its pages and tear them during her times of possession. But the great lord insisted, and they had to return the book to her. To their surprise, she did not tear it apart. She asked to be given a small hand basin for washing in. She wanted to wash so as not to sully the book. She could not read, but Sir Hinrik returned and read to her. They conversed. She became less feeble and promised to take some bread, and milk mixed with water.

At Easter-time, Sir Hinrik asked for her hand in marriage. He asked without an intermediary, and wanted to betroth her that same evening. He said a profound friendship and love had grown between himself and Lady Ingilike. The father felt ashamed when he heard the great lord talking like that, and was still afraid of the relatives. But he did not dare argue, and could not refuse to marry off his daughter.

The wife, who was a capable person and made her mind up more swiftly than her husband, asked to be allowed to speak openly with Sir Hinrik. They met by the hearth, their backs towards the room. The wife said that Ingilike had become sick in her body and her blood through her piety and penitences – for she could not describe the excesses of her daughter otherwise in his presence. The young lady was still like a child. When he seemed to take no notice of this, she said straight out that her daughter had not yet had a monthly period of cleansing. Sir Hinrik shook his head impatiently and wanted the talk to be over with. When she held on to his arm, he freed himself and said, so crisply it was obvious that a fine gentleman was speaking, 'Can't you understand that the young lady and I are deeply attached to one another, in friendship and love, for the sake of Christ Our Lord!'

That evening, he became betrothed to the virgin, who, for the occasion, had agreed to a wash in the bath-house and put on clothes made of linen. When he rode off, they all felt it was more like a dream or the tale of a passing storyteller. The man to whom Ingilike had been promised was of noble family. He carried a sword and had been to France as a young man, he could read and his chests were full of costly clothes. They thought there would be no wedding, but they were wrong. No relatives arrived from the south to end the betrothal. They were married by the priest who had told Ingilike to eat and work.

When she had settled in Sir Hinrik's house, she became prettier to look at, ate her bread with pleasure, and drank milk, though just a little. There were no further visitations by the Devil, she stopped smearing herself with excreta and screaming towards the ceiling in anguish. Though she was still thin, broken by fasting once and for all and as fragile as a stalk of angelica.

They did not have children, but nobody had believed they would anyway. They seemed to find all their pleasure in talking together at length and in deepest confidence. But no one knew very much about it, because the talking took place in the bedroom, which, in the manner of fine folk, was separate from the main room of the house.

During the time Sir Hinrik had been visiting her in Tjärr, he had turned thin and restless and allowed the foreman to manage most things on his farms. There were many who thought he would be drawn into her madness, but it was not to be. Soon he became the same strong man again, red of face and black of hair.

At Hinrik Turesson's farm there is a timber-framed shed, where one can go to be alone behind a locked door. Along the wall runs a high bench with a hole cut out of it. There, with his most secret and delicate body parts exposed to the March wind, which is pushing its way through the hatch at the back of the house, sits the Reverend Magister Ragvaldus Ovidi. He has a bladder stone which causes him much pain. His eyes closed, he is trying his best to avoid the pain but also to get on with what he has come for. Then he hears a voice saying, 'Terporobem terraromsangta! Konfitetor ecklisiapatrem! Immensia majestatis venerandom to-om verometonikom filiomsangtom kvockve! Para-kletom spiritom!'

It takes quite a while for the Magister to sort out the sounds in his head and just as he has managed it, this is the next thing he hears: 'Tu Rex Gloriae Christe, Tu Patris Sempiternus et Filius, Tu ad liberandum suscepisti hominem, Non horruisti virginis uterum.'

And soon afterwards: 'Todevikto morrtis! Akooeloo! Aperrois-sti kredentiboss! Regna! Saelorom!'

The voice continues to speak. One moment it rambles on, producing a flow of senseless syllables, the next it praises God in good Latin. It depends entirely on how Magister Ragvald adjusts the ears of his mind.

He applies the sphagnum moss, which is kept in a box on the wall, straightens his priestly garments and steps quietly down onto the floor. The wall has a wide crack. Looking through it, he would not have been surprised to see the Devil on the other side.

'Oofons blandosiae!' cries the voice. 'Splendiddioor vitroo!'

The Magister blushes, even though he is quite alone. It is no longer a matter of praising God, but instead a spring in Blandusia with water as clear as glass. A sigh follows, and then the voice declares that the soul stays where it is in love, rather than where it breathes. Afterwards, the glorification of the Trinity continues.

'In te Dominae speravi: non confundar in aeternum.'

And so the Magister recalls the summer. He can smell the wormwood heated by the sun close to the wall of the house. He sees Mistress Ingilike's yellow face, her eyes closed and her hands crossed on her chest. His own voice is reading. Somehow, in some satanic, magic way, it has been preserved during the winter, like sour cabbage in a crock. The voice has echoed, going out through the window in the great hall and hit the wall timbers. It has bounced back now, eight months later. It exposes him. But only to himself. Nobody else around here knows any Latin.

The dark windy winter's morning is interwoven with voices stemming from within his own voice, speaking to him from far away. Not long ago, the pain caused by stones lacerating his bladder had prevented him from pushing to start a bowel movement. It had seemed to him then that God gave life to man only in order to let him sink into a bitter and cloudy brew of suffering and tedium. Now a voice echoing his own is speaking, emerging from a summer which has been dried and preserved like bunches of buttercups, glowing above a doorframe. Plaited into it are other voices, like flowers mixed into straw, and within them, yet more: the chatter of Lalage, the careful mumbling of St Bernard, the clear voices of boys resounding under the vaults, the laughter of girls, and the hymns to the blessed.

The Magister becomes distracted and powerfully stirred. But still he remains the Magister of the Faculty of Arts and a Bachelor of Theology: he starts thinking. The presence of this voice with other voices whispering inside it, just outside a privy in this wilderness, may be interpreted in three ways, in accordance with the teachings of Origen, Father of the Church. But the Magister senses that the anagogical and allegorical methods are getting mixed up. He is very eager. It is clear, in any case, that we live imprisoned in a world of foulness and impurity, immersed in the suffering and grief of things temporal – as if in a privy. However, Heaven is close by and resounding with the voices of angels.

Then, of course, there is the moral interpretation. Indeed, this was the first one that occurred to the Magister. During one hot summer afternoon, as he was reading to Mistress Ingilike, who is pious but ignorant of Latin, he added readings from worldly poets, praising spring water, women's bodies, leafy trees, wine and flute playing, and also a sigh from Clairvaux. But that sigh had been secular too. For when he had spoken the words about how the soul would rather be where it loves than where it lives and breathes, he had been thinking of Linköping and not of Heaven. But God hears, remembers and recalls.

Then the Magister realises that he is in the same delicious and painful turmoil as Augustine was when he heard the voice of a child say, 'Tolle! Lege!' For what he is hearing is in fact the voice of a child, a small boy! He advances on the crack in the wall and looks into a shed with logs stacked along the walls. Unlike the half he is in, this woodshed has not been sealed with moss. The snow has got in. Two bundles of cloth, possibly children, are sitting on the floor, and a monkey is sitting perched on the chopping block. The monkey is the speaker.

He saw monkeys in Paris. Unlike the ignorant, he does not believe that they are demons. But he might be confusing them with little boys. He keeps observing the creature who has clambered up on the coarse tree stump, and sees more and more human features. It must be a boy with a black tussock of hair.

The Magister leaves the privy and swiftly steps into the woodshed. The voice falls silent. The two bundles come to life and creep into a corner. The monkey-boy cautiously climbs down from the chopping block. His eyes gleam watchfully. Now he seems more like a fox looking for a way out of a trap. Then the voice of a girl comes out of one of the bundles by the wall: 'For the sake of Our Lord! Forgive him!'

The Magister puts his hand on the boy's arm. It twitches. It is as thin as a stick, as the shank of a fox.

'Quiet,' he says. 'Come with me.'

So it came about that Skord met Magister Ragvaldus Ovidi and became his familiar.

Great lords might keep malformed creatures for their amusement. In such cases, the creature's head would be shaven, and it would be decked out in brightly patterned clothes and made to carry a rattle. If it was a dwarf, all it had to do to raise a laugh was to climb up on a chair. If it had a hump it might be useful to touch it. During his travels, Magister Ragvaldus had seen many palace fools, squinting, grinning, chattering, playing instruments, doing cartwheels. After the banishment of King Magnus, the spirit of the times had been such that even the Bishop of Linköping had kept a fool. He had also a retinue of heavily armed courtiers and pageboys, fine hounds and horses.

Ragvald also knew that there were fools who in exchange for the extinction of their wit had been granted one extraordinary talent. At the court of Neapolis in the Kingdom of Sicilie there was one such, who could play the harp. He could do nothing else. His mouth hung open like a cow's, and he had never learned to speak. In Flanders, the Magister had met a wealthy cloth merchant who kept a snivelling idiot who could remember every number he had heard, and could add up in his head any sum, however large and long.

Now I have got a fool of my own, Magister Ragvaldus thought to himself. A chattering idiot who can rattle off anything I read aloud. But he must be kept on a lead, or he might escape.

The tussock of black hair on Skord's head could not be combed, so the Magister tied him to a chair and shaved it off. Afterwards he realised that the monster was afraid of knives. He had sat stock still, and he breathed without making a sound. When the Magister had tidied him up and changed the stinking rags he had been wearing for clean if somewhat oversized clothes, he told him to say again what he had been declaiming in the woodshed. Skord looked blank. The priest put a bowl of porridge close to him, but shortened the lead so the bowl stayed out of reach.

'Read now, and then you will get something to eat,' he said.

Then Skord read:

> 'Arve Marajve
> Grassera Pina
> benkie denkie
> in Mulleribuss.
> Dunkerie stoom,
> bullerie doom.
> Litti lirum.
> Mobbeli poss.
> Sat Goss angel
> red in the book.
> Cross a cross.
> Matti torum.
> Amen.'

This was poor stuff, the Magister said. This was the kind of thing the peasants would say secretly to ward off adder bites and toothache. There were strict punishments for those who defiled holy words.

'Read the things I heard you read to the two children in the woodshed.'

But Skord seemed unable to remember. The Magister put a lump of butter on the porridge. Skord watched it melting. Then he opened his mouth and said that once, he had seen the eastern clouds translucent, limpid with light from the other side, like the petals of a wild rose, and the sun had risen in a sweet and silver-bright haze, which had made it possible to bear looking at her face. In the same way, a woman had appeared to him, and light clouds of flowers kept aloft by the hands of angels had been floating around her, who was clothed in veils and a dress as white as snow and as red as scarlet and as green as fresh leaves.

This was all uttered in the Italian language, and the Magister started weeping so violently that he let go of the lead. Then Skord got at the porridge, which he shovelled into his mouth, with his face close to the bowl. He ate like a dog.

It was not only speech that Skord could imitate. The Magister soon taught him to eat without getting his face mucky, and to sit on a bench with his feet on the floor. He would sit there in front of his master, listening. If he heard verses being read, he repeated them. In this way, after six years of harrowing solitude, the Magister could listen to the voice of a cultured human being, and to the languages spoken in countries without fir-tree forests. He was playing a trick on himself, and knew it.

Where people are not slashing and burning, the forest takes over, with its uprooted trees and piles of broken branches, its undergrowth and darkness. People do not create the music that plays in linden trees, nor the sweet flowers in the meadows and the soft grasses covering the sheep hills, but their presence is essential. Once in a while, as the Magister reluctantly carried out the priestly duties forced on him by his office, he would ride through more open countryside. There he thought he saw meadows, partly hidden under light mists, and leafy trees and dancing white-water streams. Here and there in the grass grew plants covered in white blossom. Riding through such landscapes, he would half close his eyes, so that the images would stay with him for as long as possible. At the same time he knew full well it was all a trick. These shadows were not cast by hazel and linden trees, but by rock-willow and scrub birches, crabbed and covered in witches' brooms and black lichen. Fungi were feasting off the wood of dead trees. The meadows were really bogs, and the grass, tough marsh reeds. The horse would be labouring to pull his hooves out of the sucking wetlands. These were not lilies in the grass, but the tufts of bog-cotton. This land was sodden and treacherous, and there were cold streaks of fog wavering over the wet marshes, where the horse might at any time step into a black, bottomless hole. The Magister had just been playing a game for a little while, and now he was playing another one, with this little boy who could imitate poetry and prose. But the game took him a long way, further than he had ever been since he went into exile.

Who plays the game? Is it the hand inside the puppet, twisting and turning the soulless manikin, making it seem funny and enchanting? Or is the manikin controlling the hand? Sometimes the Magister wanted to end the game, and send the boy back to begging. But then he would be alone again. Hour after hour, alone with the chilly mists on the marsh, the whining of the midge swarms and the rasping song of the bramblings.

He was gripped by a burning desire to tell his own story to the page sitting there opposite him. Somehow, by half closing his eyes, he would have to filter out the coarse clothing and the woollen cap, which he used to cover up the boy's shaved skull with its black stubble. He asked him to put his crippled hand inside his blouse. There was no need to filter out the eyes, or the thin nose or that mouth, when it stayed closed as it had been taught.

As a very young man, Magister Ragvaldus had been much in love, fervently so, with the Holy Virgin. He had desired to carry out wondrous deeds in Her honour and often these plans had sent him into a feverish state. But he had had to make a living, using his fine mind, and had been taken into employment. Concerns and regulations turned him away from Her service. And, to be fair, he had enjoyed many of his tasks. But he still wanted to live for Her, and though there never seemed to be time enough, he often wished himself in a desert cave, where he might be in communion with the Gentle One. He had been in the habit of praying, intensely and impatiently, as his temperament bid him, that he would be taken away from the world of people and work to a place where he could dedicate himself to Her.

For a long time, he thought his journey to the north might be an answer to his prayers. A mocking answer, as his thighs and buttocks became tenderised by the riding, his back bent and his face swollen from the midge bites. It was not easy either to regard his blood cousin, the Bishop of Linköping, as God's guiding spirit. As easy as believing that a goat was God's messenger. But the thought stayed with him.

He was expecting a wilderness and the peace of the void. But the backwoods of the Christian world were quite densely inhabited. It was July and the insects did not leave him alone for the whole journey. He bumped along with his sack of books and chest of clothes, always bitten, blistered and swollen. The horses got smaller and rougher at each change. On their flanks, the ribcage would show, like sets of strings on an instrument. He and the two soldiers spent the nights sleeping in barns. If he once in a while bought himself a place in a bed, it would be seething with lice.

The Sub-Deacon who was to keep him company fell ill two days north of Uppsala and had to be left. The soldiers were in a hurry. That evening, the Magister sat by a stream and wept for his loss. Then it struck him how absurd this was: he had conversed with learned men at the court of Queen Giovanna, yet here he was, weeping for the company of a beer-bellied Sub-Deacon who could barely read. He laughed. The laughter shook him and reverberated from the rocks. He could not stop. The soldiers kept staring hard at the fire, and the horses became restive. But Magister Ragvaldus did not stop laughing until exhausted. Even as he slept, his hands were clutching his midriff where the demon laughter had ridden him as hard as a man rides a borrowed horse.

He had no memory of ever laughing since then. Now he was sitting opposite this thin-nosed boy, whose upper lip formed two delicate arches. The colour of his eyes was shifting and composite, like that of gravel in a forest stream, seen though the clear flowing water: glittering grains of quartz, flakes of gold, rusty bog-iron, and whirlpools stirring up charcoal-coloured mud. The irises were ringed in black, and the pupils dilated in the twilight of the spring evening.

His face was baffling. Sometimes it reminded the Magister of figures seen in the murals of the grandest palaces, and at other times of agile, cunning and predatory animals, like ferrets or stoats. His hair had been a coarse tussock, but his eyebrows grew in precise curves, as if they had been plucked.

As a grown man, the Magister had never been given to speaking about himself, partly from lack of interest and partly from caution. But now he felt a hot, almost sickening desire to tell at least some things, like how he came to be the priest in a church which was no more than a rickety hovel, stinking of tar inside and out. It was the voice that tempted him to confide, that voice which could respond with a canzonetta.

But to what end served his talk? Would it not have served him as well to polish a pewter jug until it shone, and to speak and speak and speak to the distorted image captured in its curving side?

After learning the boy's name, he called him his princeps scordiscorum. But what did he who looked like an Illyrian prince understand of that? Speaking of the rich earth of Östergötland, where he was born, the Magister realised that he might as well have said Picardie or Hesperides, for all that it meant to the boy.

And rich earth – what does that mean to someone who knows nothing other than the thin, brown soil pared from between the stones and stumps in burnt forest ground?

Skord seemed really to enjoy the stories from the Cathedral School in Linköping. But could he tell the School apart from the Linköping Collegium in Paris where the Magister had studied for his degree? Doubtful. Anyway, he listened. When the Magister told of how he had returned and made himself useful while he waited to apply for the post of the old Canon of Lincopia, the boy's eyes looked empty.

But he was immensely amused by the stories of how Magister Ragvaldus, on the strength of his skills with languages, had been allowed to join the embassy set up by King Magnus to deal with the Pope in Avignon. It was the story about the fur coat he liked best. The King had equipped the Ambassador with this special fur coat, made from the joined skins of hundreds of ermines. When the Ambassador moved, it looked as if the white animals with black-tipped tails were alive. He wanted to hear about this again and again. Perhaps he believed that the coat was actually made from live ermines, which had huddled close to each other? He cared nothing for the other grand garments, the silver chains, the bell-edged belts, embroidered gloves and tall velvet hats. But as they settled down in the evenings, the Magister in his wooden armchair, with Skord in front of him on the bench, and the question of which story he wanted was raised, Skord would say, 'The one about the stoats in King Magnus's coat. And the story about the white falcons that were presented to the Pope.'

There were stories Skord did not mind listening to from the long years when the Magister had been negotiating – mostly for loans of money – on behalf of King Magnus. But the episode from the life of the Magister that pleased the boy more than any other was when Ragvaldus Ovidi finally met his cousin the Bishop, in the meadow behind the Bishop's Residence in Linköping.

It happened on a summer's morning, before the cocks crowed. The Magister had been hauled out of the dungeon of the Residence, where his cheeks had become sunken and his clothes had started to stink. Hatless, hands tied with rope behind his back, he stood there, waiting for the Bishop's soldiers to finish their preparations. They were building a platform from roughly hewn young birch trees. The Magister was meant to step up on it and put his neck in a hollowed-out trunk.

Skord understood the idea; he had watched cockerels being dealt with in this way. He would often stare at the Magister's thin neck, where the hair came to a point in a soft black whorl, and at times he would smile. Once, he touched it with his index finger, and caused a strange sensation in the Magister's groin.

To be seen is a strange thing, and no stoat or peregrine falcon longs for it. For many long years, that whorl of black hair in the hollow at back of the Magister's neck had remained as unseen as the tip of a live stoat's tail, or as the tuft of feathers on the ears of an owl. Now it had become a sign, a part of a narrative already begun and a cause of smiles.

'Tell the story of Ragvaldus Ovidi!'

Ragvaldus Ovidi was standing with his hands tied behind his back in the meadow behind the Residence of the Bishop in Linköping, waiting for the soldiers to finish building his executioner's block. They had just woken him from his sleep. His head was empty. He did not even pray. Perhaps his body was too strong and too young. It had no flaws for Death to grip hold of, no fistulae and pus-filled abscesses. He was smooth. Death could not reach his mind. His heart echoed, like a great hall standing empty during the summer months. He did not have visions of the Virgin. He had no visions at all.

You can be very candid when you speak to someone who cannot understand. It is like talking to your dog or caged goldfinch. But it is not like talking to yourself. Somehow, there is someone else there. And it is as if you are telling a story.

And so Ragvaldus Ovidi hears the barking of impatient hounds and the thumping of horses' hooves hitting the ground; suddenly – video archivechiam venire! His cousin, the Bishop! On horseback. He is going hunting, wearing deerskin leggings which are already damp with dew. 'From where I am standing, I view him from below and can clearly see his belt and the ties holding his leggings in place under the jacket tails. It does not matter to him. But he is seeing me hatless!

'He stinks like a billy goat, but that is how he likes it. The hounds are restless, pulling on their leads and whining.

'"Well, Ragvald Övedsson," says the Reverend Goat, "fancy

finding you here." You see, Skord, his slow, cunning mind had already got it all worked out. But I did not realise it at the time.

'It is true that my mother spoiled me. I was slight of build but had – I have to admit it – a good mind. My cousin was called Kettil and grew up with us. He had nursed his hatred towards me ever since, on account of my brain, and now he seemed determined to separate it from the rest of my body.

'"Puto me non hoc meruisse!" I cried, hatless and fettered.

'"Putt, putt, putt," said the Bishop and pursed his lips. It still annoyed him that I could speak a language which he barely understood. When I returned from abroad, and King Magnus was in exile, this halfwit had succeeded the old Bishop of Linköping. Do you see, Skord? The good times had come to an end. Bishop! His entire life had been spent drifting about on horseback with a gang of armed men. Still does, for all I know. He had invited me to his Residence, and we conversed about matters spiritual. I might as well have been talking to the fireguard for all I got out of it. At the end of the conversation, I was thrown straight into the dungeon and was left there waiting for my sentence. It took him some time to make up his mind about which of my ill deeds was the worst. Possibly heretical thoughts along the same lines as Origen, Father of the Church. Origen! He had never heard the name before I mentioned it. Or I might have been conspiring in foreign countries against our legal ruler, Albrecht of Mecklenburg. Duke Albrecht! The very duke whose father had obliged me by lending thousands of silver marks in support of my master, King Magnus!

'I tell you, Skord, when I returned the country was like a farm where the wolf has become foreman, the fox minds the flock of hens, the rats carry the flour to the bakehouse, and where the goat himself says prayers to thank the Lord for blessing the food!'

At this Skord laughed so much, he had to roll off the bench and tumble about in the straw on the floor. When he had finished laughing, he repeated everything that had been said, word for word.

However, while the morning was still fresh with dew, and the soldiers were getting their birch-wood contraption set up in the approved manner, the Bishop started bargaining.

'You have such a good head on you, Ragvald,' he said. 'Maybe we should let it stay in place, for the sake of your dear mother who thought so highly of it. We will send you off as an ambassador instead. It seems you can speak all the languages there are. We shall dispatch you to sermonise to the Lapps on the teachings of Origen.'

He laughed heartily at this. But there was a condition for allowing the Magister to keep his head in place and become an ambassador to the Lapps. He had to write a deed of gift for the farm inherited by the sons of Öved. His brothers had already suffered the same fate that now threatened Ragvald. But at least they had joined bands of armed men. The Magister was no rebel. He was a linguist, a great scholar. When he argued this case, his cousin smiled and said, 'Still waters run deep.'

As luck would have it, he just happened to have brought a deed of gift, already drafted. He handed it over. The Magister had time to read only the first sentence before a quill and ink was handed to him. His cousin was carrying some mighty odd hunting equipment. Ragvald signed the document, a well-prepared calfskin with traces of other writings, which mattered as little to the Bishop as did Origen. Then the Bishop gave Ragvald's hatless head a friendly slap and dug his spurs into the flanks of his horse. The hounds ran ahead, barking and whining.

The Magister had hoped that once he arrived in Uppsala, he would be able to persuade the Archbishop to countermand his forced exile. But this did not happen. He got the Sub-Deacon for company, a pale and rather plump young man, who had been pulling gold threads out of the vestments to get money for beer. They were sent on their way up north with two soldiers as guards. The Deacon wept openly, and Magister Ragvaldus sat there remembering how once, when he had come back home from the Cathedral School in Linköping, he had shamed his boorish cousin Kettil by talking to him in fluent Latin.

During that northward journey, he often recalled the Roman writer Lucian's mockery of the gods of Olympus and their animalistic subordinates: rams, satyrs, half-human horses and women with snakes for hair. In these northern lands, the creatures appeared to be somewhere between god and demon, between animal and human. A snarling Anubis would be standing there on the grassy slope outside a rough timber cottage, which might have been the home of other marsh gods: cat, snake, sharp-beaked bird – what did he know? He giggled, because he felt creative. His brain was sparkling. The soldiers scowled at his outburst. The corner of his mouth filled with spittle as he chortled. Something was out of true with him, oscillating around its proper centre. He closed his eyes, and the hard back of the horse carried him on, through the outcrop of a bog which reeked of stagnation, damp, rotting matter and a faint acidity. It got worse. Disorder and dirt were forced on him. The demons changed their animal forms, now with jaws like foxes, ears like lynxes and paws like wolves, growing fur like bears and mouths like badgers. He choked back speech, and instead of words, a mishmash of images simmered inside his head. Lucian had nothing to say about this muddy chaos.

With his sack of books, his pans and clothes, the Magister was to be left in the last village before Skule forest. It was at the foot of a steep hill which sloped down to deep sea inlets. The first person he saw in that village was an old woman, stirring an iron cauldron. He thought the contents stank of goat fur, dog piss and fish guts. She kept boiling and stirring, and the concoction was becoming an ever deeper brown, and the rank smell more powerful. Standing there, he had to fight down nausea and stop himself from vomiting by trying to imagine an apple cut in half on a clean linen cloth.

He was told that she was cooking something from goat's milk. She had sieved the lumps of cheese from the milk and was reducing the whey to a rust-coloured mass called mese.

By now, seven years later, he could eat mese, and would carve slices from the dark-brown, porous, matured cheese and taste them thoughtfully. Other senses had been alerted. To be sure, he had broken his nails and cooled his ardour in this village, and he wore a rough woollen cap on his head, rather than the hat that once had been knocked off his head in the Bishop's Residence. But he had learned to determine the goodness of a dried, blackened reindeer heart by cutting it, and the ripeness of the sour-herring in its barrel.

There was still no time to live for the Virgin alone. In the beginning, he thought he had better stay in his house, away from midges and horseflies. But he had always been an enterprising man, and could not stop himself now. Anyway, the first thing he had to do was to bury his predecessor properly. He was resting in shallow soil under a mound of stones. It was a temporary arrangement, caused by the ice-hardened soil at the time of his death. When the Magister saw the dried remains of flesh on the ribcage and skull, which was all that the foxes had left uneaten, he decided he must return down south alive, if only to get a decent burial. He made a sacred promise to himself.

The Virgin ruled up here too, but a fetid odour followed her. He would see her sometimes in his dreams. Her eyes were wild and she held bunches of snakes in her hands. She killed her enemies by screaming.

In the daytime, when the sun shone, he would be very active. For a while he might catch a little warmth by leaning against the cottage wall, but then he would be bumping along on his horse with his books about stones and herbs in his bag. He had brought them with him, but found that a sharpened knife was of greater use. He taught himself to lance boils. It was necessary. If not, the peasants would open their doors to the Lapps, whom they believed able to cure abscesses and fever by reading over them. The Magister detested Lapps even more than lemmings, those repulsive little animals which, squeaking and barking noisily, would attack the wanderer despite being as small as voles. He had seen a Lapp roll across a cottage floor in a trance which he had brought on himself in order to reach his animal gods. The Magister ordered the dragon heads to be chopped off the beams of the church roof, and then burned the heads on his hearth, so that no Lapp nor anybody else would be able to practise spells with them. He sat on his stump-stool, watching them burn and vomit fire from their blackened jaws.

As soon as the first dizzying attack of fear had died down, he realised that the people round here were no different from anywhere else. They were kind and cunning, cruel, thoughtful, mean, evil, wasteful, noisy, wise and jovial. There was someone who was just like the present Bishop of Linköping. In a small forest village, he came across a man who reminded him of a prominent money-lender in Florence. However, the people he met mostly reminded him of the poor and ignorant peasants of Picardie and Tuscany. Here they seemed to be ill more often, though. He could not be sure, because he had had nothing to do with peasants in the past. Certainly, these were often sickly, and prone to accidents and disease. His predecessor had written on strips of birch bark words that the sick and afflicted had believed to be powerful incantations. But the text was really about cures and interventions which had been known to or learned by the priest. The first time Ragvald flicked through the advice on the bark strips was when they came carrying a screaming man. His shoulder had been dislocated after he got caught in an elk trap and his prey had run off, pulling the hunter along.

He had nobody to talk to. Until he found this boy who might or might not be a fool. Had the Creator happened to give him understanding, or was his wit pure illusion? Either way, he was a famulus, a little pet dog, a cheerful and colourful parakeet who would not stop talking.

Certainly, Magister Ragvaldus was good to him. Especially so, since this familiar refused to work, at least with spade or axe. But he travelled with his master on priestly errands. He would sit in the saddle in front of the priest, with his small buttocks squeezed down tight between the butt of the saddle and the Magister's most tender parts, which at times were still overcome by pain caused by the stones. So they rubbed along, chatting like parrots in a bright heathen wood. No one understood a word they said to each other.

Although seven years had gone by, the Magister was still frightened of the farm dogs when they came galloping over with tails bolt upright and lips drawn back to expose rows of yellow teeth. But Skord would hold out his small brown hand and say, 'I bridle you, tooth and tongue, liver and lung, by the names of the tri – amen! Stay still!'

The Magister was touched by the boy's wish to go in first and protect him. Nonetheless, he felt he must forbid this formula being read.

'Don't say these things. They are evil. It sounds like the gabbling of the Lapps, and must be condemned. This can end in Hell.'

'It's the Virgin who is clamping the jaws of the bitch,' Skord said. 'She is the most powerful being in the world. By the tri names. Amen.'

They were walking past the bitch, who had settled down on her rump. The Magister kept his hand on Skord's hair, which had grown back and been cut squarely. It looked like a small, shiny cap.

One evening, the Magister had been given a chunk of butter after having read over the dead husband at a farm. Riding away, it turned out that Skord carried a whole wheel of cheese. Ragvald questioned him, and the boy answered that it came from the widow, in return for a string of woollen yarn with four knots in it.

She had four sons and she worried about them, now that her husband had died. She feared that they would go and get married to lazy and careless women, share the farm between them and put the mother in an outbuilding. Skord had fingered the woollen string and told the widow to ask where her eldest son was.

'Whereabouts are ye?' she called out.

The knot had answered in a shrill voice, 'Mother, here I am!'

Then he had described exactly where he was and what he was doing. Skord had assured her that the knots never spoke an untruth. She had become very eager to have the string and had given him the sweet cheese from sheer gratitude.

Usually, the Magister would have made him return the gift, but this time he let it be. The lump of butter had been quite small and besides full of cow hairs.

'If she wants to believe in these childish games, let her,' he said. 'I suppose you would rather not come along the next time, when the corpse is due to be taken from the house.'

Skord, his fingers busy with the cheese, did not answer.

This is how the sunny days passed. Well, the sun did not always shine, although it was a day under the sign of the sun. Good rain might be falling. All creatures would give birth to twins. As bright and lively as squirrels, a priest and his familiar would travel between the villages. It is true that the priest practised the skills of a barber, lancing boils and reading urine. He ought to provide a chamber pot in the churches, he told Skord, wryly though without bitterness. The pot would be a greater attraction than the cross. They talked freely together. The Magister spoke as if to another scholar, in a way that the ignorant must not hear. Openly and sunnily.

Back home, they would line up their gifts every evening. Cured saddle of elk, glittering with grains of salt. A big-jawed pike, cleaned and dried. A wheel of sweet cheese, fat and brown. They would look at each other almost as if they were two cheerful thieves. The Magister could speak openly to Skord, and only to him. He had confessed that he was as poor a priest as he was a surgeon.

Then they would eat and rest in front of the fire, warm and tired. Skord would stretch out on a sheepskin, and the Magister sweep up the crumbs, pike bones, bits of bark and needles. It must be understood that a prince of the heralded Scordisci tribe could not possibly wield a broom. Afterwards, the Magister sat down in the stump-chair, with the intention of reading aloud from a book or speaking from memory. Often Skord asked, 'Tell me what it was like in this country when you came back from France.'

'Oh, it was utter misery.'

'How was it miserable?'

'Well, it was miserable because the water was flowing backwards up the rivers, and the millstones ground flour as black as soot.'

'Who was king?'

'A cabbage caterpillar.'

'What did he have on his head?'

'A cap of perch skin.'

'Did the spikes point inwards?'

'No, outwards. Like a heron. Ypp! Ypp! Ypp!'

'And when you arrived at the court of the Bishop, what happened?'

'Bad things happened.'

'How bad?'

'Oh, you see, I lost my head, and since then I've been carrying this crock on my shoulders.'

'What's swimming around inside the crock?'

'Tadpoles.'

'Are they wearing leggings?'

'They certainly are.'

'What are they up to, these little bulgy-bellied tadpoles?'

'They are telling me about what is going on at the court of the Bishop now.'

'What is happening?'

'The Queen is visiting.'

'So let them tell the story, and let's not interrupt them,' Skord begged.

And so they would listen to the story of the cunning yellow-toothed old vixen, who has become Queen after the lovely Blanche. The bitch ate and drank everything that the Bishop offered her. Then she felt sleepy, scratched her belly, yawned and produced some flatus. Yes indeed, she could play the flute per rectum! Quite in tune with the pipers and whiners of musicians, which the Bishop had placed on a platform behind the table. They were grasshoppers and young shrews. The Bishop was an old badger hog. He had been eating a goose, and now his belly was ready to burst. He had to play the flute as well, in chorus with the Queen. It was an old French song: Prenez-la-garde! Prenez-la-garde! The Canon and the Deacon had long since fallen asleep with their beaks in the soup. Scolasticus and Economicus were quarrelling. The former was an elderly vole, and the latter a copperhead grass snake, whose legs dropped off when the Queen kept sniggering at his being a redhead.

'So you see, Skord, it is all as usual among the nobility,' the Magister said, 'and we should be pleased not to be part of it all.'

Skord too had no wish to be anywhere else.

These were the sunny days.

There were also days in the sign of the moon, when thoughts moved as slowly as crayfish across the bottom of deep pools. They would hear the howling of wild dogs, unsure whether it was not just the wind in the smoke-hole. On such days, the Magister was utterly bored, and paced up and down. During moon days, he could see only the monkey in Skord. Absently, he would grip the boy's neck. His thoughts moved along strange paths. He could not sleep because of the fusty air, but had to keep the boy close in the bed, with the lead wound tightly round his wrist. If not, Skord might run away, because he was in one of these moods. He was restless and foxy. He smelled more pungent than usual.

The Magister pulled him close, put his cock between the boy's legs and spread his seed over the boy's cold thin thighs. It was apparently accidental the first time it happened. Then he became more cunning, and found other ways of getting what he had been looking for. He slithered between the sweetness of the pleasure and the nausea of his torment. He wanted the boy to like it, but

Skord's eyes turned black and cold like a weasel's. The bed was stale with sweat. They fell asleep locked in each other's arms. The rein round Skord's waist would wrap itself round them both.

Magister Ragvald's mother had been very pious, and so weak from her fasting that there was not enough milk in her breasts for the newborn boy. She had had to find him a wet-nurse, to make up for this failure. It was not in order to get rid of the child and keep her breasts from becoming slack and suckled dry, as was the case with many women. The nurse was a lusty wench, like most of her kind. The child knew and spat out her teats, as if they had been smeared with excrement. He would suckle only at his mother's breasts, little as there was on offer. The trickle of milk made his limbs grow thin. He stayed that way for the rest of his life: slight and impatient, swift-moving and shorter than most. His mother was convinced he would become a holy man, this child who had sensed the bitter taste of lust and spat it out.

But now, what coarse teats did he not suckle, and how loathsome was the milk! She was dead and had turned to ashes. Her hopes were buried too, and stank of death. His mouth filled with self-disgust.

He woke, and the scent of young birch leaves came in when the maid opened the door. He carefully unwound the rein and looked at the sleeping child. It seemed to him the boy looked like the ill-treated young reindeer – little more than a calf – which he had once found abandoned after it had been flogged and driven to death by a Lapp.

No absolution was to be found here. The Sub-Deacon who was to come with him had been left in Gävle, coughing blood. He was probably dead by now. No voice out of the darkness, no te absolvo. He would have to live with his sin, like a toad in his slime.

Then, surrounded by the scent of birch leaves, he turns towards the boy and, looking at the slender body, is about to say what he has said before: what we did last night, we will not do again.

Instead, silence. It must not be said. He rolls the boy over and releases the rein.

'Get up,' he says.

As usual, the boy is instantly alert. When he realises that the lead has come off, he becomes watchful and ready to leap.

'Skord, you must be free,' Ragvald says. 'Stay with me, if you like.'

He had been about to add: I can give you milk. You can have more letters too – all of them. Even the Greek ones. But he holds back. He does not want to open any negotiations. Does not want to buy, or urge or tempt.

'You can stay if you like,' he says.

And then he walks away from the bed. He takes his shaving things from the cupboard. There is a rustling noise from the straw on the floor behind him. When he turns to look, Skord has already left the cottage.

Luxuria had been riding him, spreading her legs as if he had been her goat. From where the Magister was, she looked like the women you might see in the twilight of spring evenings, sitting astride the fences, their hair loose and belts undone, and their twisted smiles looking like squints.

Now Acedia had arrived. She did not ride. She did not even take on a shape. She couldn't be bothered. She got into the blue milk and the rancid fish, and said: Your life smells of carrion. Never mind. Turn your back. The twilight will last for a long time. The evening will take an age to come. Why go outside? To see the coltsfoot growing in the melting snow? What's the point? In the end, all you can do is return to your own bed straw.

Acedia got in everywhere. She creaked in the wall timbers and dripped on the birch-bark roof. Because the Magister was staying in and keeping the fire going all day, the warmth in the house woke the death-watch beetle. But when the black one sneaked out of his crack in the wall, he was crunched under a thumbnail without having time to deliver his message.

During this time, Magister Ragvald would come and put herbal mixtures on swollen and sore bellies to draw out the pain. He would blow on the faces of the children brought to christening and read over the dead. But the hand that was held over children and corpses was not his. His own hand stayed in the bed straw.

One morning he was staring at the crusty, corroded snow, decaying in the sunlight. An insect, an elongated thin-winged fly, moved swiftly across the surface of the snow. It seemed to be searching for something without knowing what it was. The Magister asked himself if it might have something to tell him. After all, it had come out at the wrong time and had attracted his attention the way few things had done for a long time. But what it was telling him he did not know. Standing next to him was the farmer, holding the bridle of a horse whose saddle-packs were laden with the Magister's medicaments.

'Do you remember the boy I used to bring along?' he asked.

'Him Skord, ain't that right?' answered the farmer, smiling as if recalling a puppy or a piglet.

'When was it? This last autumn?'

The farmer stared at him then. 'This mare here was a foal,' he said. 'And she com' from that red mare of mine.'

'That's right, I bought her of you.'

'She be a good horse,' said the farmer, as if he was pleased to get away from the first question. 'Worth yer pennies. As it were.'

He helped the Magister up in the saddle. The mare started walking. She was no longer young. The Magister was thinking: Skord, the parrot-child who looked like an Illyrian prince, must be a young man by now. A crude, spotty youth with red hands. Why am I thinking of him? The strangest things emerge from under the snow. Senseless things. The hand holding the reins was not his. That hand belonged to nobody. It was twitching. Obeying a spasmodic will. Whose will? Come on, Acedia, let's go home. You have taken on a shape for me now. The shape of a broken old nag. Footfalls in sodden snow. Home to the bed straw. Jaws grinding in the stable. Shifting of hooves in straw full of shit. Falling asleep standing.

The summer had been cold and rainy, and a winter of hunger had followed. He had not been able to get wax candles for the church, and had to use tallow ones, which reeked with a different, soulless odour. The church was cold and full of smoke. The sacrament was miraculous, but the chalice he held did not even contain wine, only much diluted grain spirit.

His thin hands fluttered over pyx and paten like those of a buffoon or trickster at a market. The tar-soaked timbers creaked and the wet snow slid off the roof. The Magister felt the flowing wetness would just cause rot and decay. But those who knelt in front of him fixed their eyes on him trustingly from under their fringes and shawls.

The miracle happened.

The mouths gaped open. It had taken place. Not even the crudest of performers can create without inspiration. If it was not his hand inside the hand holding the chalice aloft, whose was it? It had really happened. He was shaking as if in a fever, and spilled the bloody fluid on the white linen cloth. Who was he who had come down to them in the midst of the tedium, the indifference and mockery?

But after that it failed them, and did not happen the next time nor the next nor the one after that. Much water was pouring off the roof and the leaves were rotting. The Magister ought to have changed his bed straw. Once, he asked the girl who cooked his food and milked the goats, 'Do you remember when I spilt the wine in church?'

'Yes, I do.'

'When was that?'

But she could not remember. 'Maybe before I was born,' she said.

So she had just heard the tale. He suddenly felt like hitting her across the mouth.

Time is such a minute movement in such a large space. An old nag on a horse-drawn mill wheel. But the mill is roofless and without floor or walls.

Skord arrived one summer afternoon. It was hot. The Magister had holed up inside to shelter from the insects. He heard the door squeak and turned. The boy was standing there, having stepped across the threshold. He was as slight as ever. A child.

'This is not possible!' said the Magister.

Skord, tight-lipped, smiled briefly. 'It is,' he said. 'Come with me.'

Magister Ragvaldus followed him. The mare was standing there, her head casting about to scare off the clegs. The boy had led her out and saddled her.

'We are going to Sir Hinrik's farm,' he said. 'Someone there has been taken ill.'

Ragvald obeyed, not knowing whether he did so from surprise or fear. He hung his medicament bag on the saddle, and Skord climbed up in front. The way it used to be. The Magister could smell his skin: sunny hillside, fresh fir-tree shoots and ants' piss. They rode on, enveloped in a cloud of insects. It looked like an emanation of themselves. A soul. A united soul.

It was evening when they arrived, but the sun was still in the sky. Skord jumped down, took the reins of the mare and led her down a path towards a barn. He tied her to the wall facing the forest. It seemed that he did not want them to be seen. The Magister fumbled with his bag and worried about stepping into the nettles, which were sprouting in the sunny spot along the wall of the barn.

The boy showed the way up a ladder to the loft. It was grey with age, and the rungs were covered in lichen. He was not sure if he dared climb it, but Skord pushed him from behind. Finally up, the Magister realised that two rungs had broken under his feet. Laboriously he crawled through a small hatch, head first. Once through, he was dazzled by the light and then he sneezed several times.

Looking up, he saw a young maid sitting in the middle of the floor. Around her the air was filled with a golden dust, suspended in the strong light from the hatches.

He was lying on his belly at her feet, but pulled himself up to rest on his elbows. His body recoiled, as if he had suddenly received a blow. But he felt no pain. The whining of the midge swarms filled the air over the late summer grasses. Rats scuttled in the straw. He could hear a blackbird starting on his intricate and sweetly persuasive loops of sound from a treetop. His fingers touched slippery barley straw and the flying chaff made him sneeze again.

She sat leaning against a timber beam which acted as a buttress for the roof. Her head was covered by a veil, held tightly in place by a strip of twisted cloth. He could see two thin strands of hair which swept over her fragile white temples and disappeared in under the veil. Her forehead was as round as a child's and her eyes grave. When he saw her lips, transparent and thin as flower petals, he involuntarily touched his own and realised how coarse they were.

Her hands were resting in her lap, one put weightlessly on top of the other. They were coated by a thin layer of golden dust, which had settled from the glowing air around her.

By now, Skord too had climbed in through the hatch, and gone to stand next to the maid. He was small enough to stand upright under the roof. His weight rested on one foot, and he was smiling. The Magister thought he looked wicked and beautiful. When

Skord looked at him, with a smile that may or may not have been mocking, Ragvald unclasped his hands and began brushing off the dust and chaff. While he was trying to get into a new position without hitting his head on the roof, Skord kneeled next to the maiden. He lifted her skirt to show her legs. One was white, with a round knee, but the other was lying there like a rotten tree trunk, swollen and bluish black.

'Bodel has been bitten by a snake,' Skord said. 'You must cure her.'

When her leg was bared, the maid bent her head and looked down.

The Magister had recovered. He felt the engorged leg and the maid's forehead, which was covered in cold sweat, and ordered that she should be brought down to the farm. There was a staircase and an ordinary door. He could see no point in using the hatch and the ladder again, or any secret routes at all. Skord had always been suspicious of the people in Sir Hinrik's house, and especially of Mistress Ingilike. However, the Magister saw to it that Bodel was brought indoors, wrapped in sheepskin blankets, given fresh water to drink, and put on a bench by the window in the big hall. He placed a poultice of herbs on her leg. The lady of the house, supported by two maid servants, came into the hall to find out what caused the commotion. The Magister explained that he saw it as a God-given opportunity for her to practise charity towards this poor girl, who usually milked Sir Hinrik's cows and herded his goats up on the hillside. He strictly forbade any heathen runes and magic words to be said over the leg, and ordered that all the people in the house should gather before him. He started speaking in thunderous Latin, and soon they felt uplifted and purified.

It was late evening now. Inside the house, the spirit was so strongly felt that some of the people fell asleep before they could finish their evening porridge. They slept from utter exhaustion, and their heads were ringing with holy language. No one had seen the priest like this for years: powerful, strict and dominant.

The following morning, Bodel's leg was less swollen, and even though she had not been able to sleep much because of it aching fit to burst, she felt much better. She smiled gratefully at the priest but did not dare speak to him. She had not seen him since childhood, the time he had been listening to Skord's reading in the woodshed. But he remembered her voice asking for forgiveness on Skord's behalf, and he wanted to hear it again. He asked her many questions, but received no answers. She only put her hand to her mouth. He could see the smile in her eyes. Then he rode back home again, after a conversation with Mistress Ingilike about spiritual matters. He had emphasised the importance of charity. Skord came along for part of the way, sitting perched in front of him in the saddle as before. When they got in under the fir trees, he stopped the horse by pulling in the reins. He slipped down and asked the Magister to follow him into the forest.

Magister Ragvald followed, but with distaste. He was always unpleasantly affected by the piles of broken branches and fallen tree trunks in a large forest. Just now, he would have preferred to ride on and recall the spaciousness and solidity of Sir Hinrik's house. He wanted to think of sheepskin blankets with bright borders, fluffy skins on top of linen or woollen sheets, pewter boxes for bread, and good birch logs for the fireplaces. He had no desire to get back to his own cottage, nor to the holy hovel where the rats supped off the tallow candles.

'This is him who bit Bodel,' Skord said.

A massive adder had been speared on a barked birch branch, with a point as sharp as the tip of a knife. It slithered and twisted to get away from the ants which had discovered it. The Magister wanted them to be on their way. He thought it a disgusting sight. But Skord bent down, quickly got a grip on the snake by its neck and raised its head to his lips. Then he hissed a puff of air over it. As they went back to the tree where the horse was tethered, Skord practically walked backwards in order to keep watching the snake, twisting round its stick, for as long as possible.

The boy did not come with him all the way home, but a few days later he turned up and said Bodel had got much better, and the lady had been very kind to her. She had promised that the girl would be allowed to become an indoor maid, and learn baking and other clean skills.

Skord himself seemed to give no thought to finding farm work. Besides, he was of such small stature and so thin that no one would have employed him for anything other than herding goats. He claimed he had worked as a shepherd once, but the Magister did not know what to believe. He said, though, that when the

82

shepherd and the wolves agree, the farmer is likely to lose his herd. Skord grinned at that.

He was kitted out in the strangest manner. He had a leather cap on his head, so worn it shone, and he had decorated it with two blackbird wings, one by each ear. Round his waist was a rope hung with bone pipes and other odds and ends he had made. The Magister asked him if he sold these things, and Skord admitted that sometimes he would get a couple of eggs or a fried cockerel wing in exchange for some of this rubbish. Ragvald suspected he got more than that, and got it because he spoke for his wares and insisted on their strong powers.

His hair was no longer cut straight across to look like a shining helmet. It had grown and hung in loose ringlets to his shoulders. He said he had been wandering far and wide meeting all kinds of folk, but always returned to Sir Hinrik Turesson's farm to keep an eye on Bodel's fortunes.

'Why are you so small, Skord?' the Magister asked anxiously, and felt the thin arm. He had seen dwarfs, but they were sturdy and had crooked legs. Their faces aged. But nothing in Skord's face had grown coarse with age. It was thin-lipped and the yellowish brown gaze was swift. All his movements were still those of a child. His mind was childlike too.

'Tell me about the stoats that went to meet the Pope when he lived in France,' he asked. 'Tell me how they travelled in King Magnus's coat. Did they wear gold chains round their necks?'

'You tell the story better than I do,' the Magister said smilingly. 'But it is true they wore gold chains round their necks, and each one had a silver bell in its mouth, which tinkled when they heard something they liked.'

Skord sighed then, and curled up to listen.

It was late summer now. The farmers were cutting the barley, and the cool, damp air smelled as if it came fom a spice chest. Gnats and midges, flies and clegs and other insects were insensible with cold. People dared breathe deeply and could stay outside. The thick coarse grass round the Magister's cottage had turned yellow, and the nettles had withered. He felt ashamed to see that they grew most strongly where he had been relieving himself. He had always lectured people about doing this somewhere away from their houses. Now these poison-blooms of the devil were giving him away, by telling of his apathy and indifference over the past years.

Skord turned up more and more often as the evenings grew darker and the air cooler. He said he wanted letters to carve into his sticks. The letters gave them great power, and people would buy his sticks. The Magister did not approve. But he had always allowed him these childish pranks, from way back when Skord was living with him, tied by a rein and sharing his bed.

'Dear father,' he would ask, 'what is this? It looks like dung-beetle with his legs sticking out of a soft cowpat.'

If the Magister had been in a good mood, he might have said, 'That is an A. She is the amanuensis of all, always ambling around and about.'

Then Skord would carve the letter into his stick, and so it would become his. One day he asked about something that looked like a wide-open crow's beak, and was told that it was like a kettle in the kitchen, and could keen like a kicked kitten. He carved that one as well. On good days he would collect rows of these creatures on his sticks. There were some curved ones which were hard to shape with a knife, but instead he burned them in, using a red-hot nail.

Now he would turn up in the evenings when the Magister was sitting there over his books, and want to start up the old game again.

'What is this kind of creepy-crawly then?' he asked, though he knew full well that it was an A.

'That's an alapa,' the priest said.

'What's an alapa?'

Then the Magister hit him across the cheek with the flat of his hand. It stung, and Skord went head over heels.

'Is that a forbidden word?' he asked.

'No, I just gave you an alapa to show you. It is what the master gave the slave as a sign that he was free.'

'I'll carve that,' Skord said, and with one cheek glowing red, bent over his stick.

'Alapa amburat,' he muttered, and that was the first time the Magister heard him speak Latin, not merely imitating.

The Magister did not like it when Skord made sticks with signs on and sold them to gullible and superstitious peasants. Instead, he made him a writing-board covered with a layer of wax and cut a bone stylus for him. Soon the boy was leaning over his board, where the letters could be erased, and competing with the Magister for the light from the fireplace. This carried them into winter without either noticing. That year the Magister thought the first snow smelled like a length of linen spread out on a leen to bleach. He did not have a Donat to encourage Skord's struggle with the grammar. They had neither Doctrinale or Gaecismus, but even so, as the boy studied, the Magister remembered the Cathedral School. Apart from that single blow which made his cheek burn, the pupil was not slapped or caned, nor did the Magister have a belt made for striking him. As a schoolboy he himself had often cried bitterly, because it was so cold and hard to sit there struggling with the Donat, and so grievous for mother's pet to be punished.

But Skord enjoyed himself like a tadpole in a nice warm puddle. He had already read the hymns by Prudentius and started on Horace, whom he knew well from his time as a parrot. By now, he had almost finished the Magister's books. They had to start reading the book about stones, and the one about the properties and preparations of herbal remedies. Both were so worn from use that the Magister had to make them new covers from eel skin.

The Magister had many plans for when the first winter snows had settled. He felt it was time to return to more humane regions in the south, and not just wait until his funeral. There were good reasons to hope, indeed to believe, that the time was up for his cousin's bishopric. Ragvald realised that his exile would never be revoked if he arrived as a beggar dressed in a worn cloak and a woollen hood. He had to bring the Church a large gift to have any expectation of success. It followed that he would have to persuade somebody to donate their property to the Church for the salvation of their immortal soul.

To the north of the forest lived a great lady who had lost her husband in a terrible accident: three horses, with men and luggage, had fallen when a riverbank collapsed during a thaw. The wife was a tough and enterprising lady, who had no wish to contemplate her own death. The Magister started journeying to see her, in an attempt to turn her mind away from worldly things. But he only began to get somewhere with her after a winter when she had been stricken with illness.

He had been warned not to ride north of the forest on account of the outlaws. But when spring had come, and the paths had dried after streaming with thawed snow, he went anyway and took Skord with him. They did not carry any bags on the horse, and so he assumed that they would be left in peace.

During the last visit, which had taken place the previous summer, they had not only spoken of death and heavenly bliss, but also occasionally about hell. Skord, who had begun to grasp the Magister's plans, asked if he could help by frightening her enough to sign the deed of gift there and then. This caused Ragvald some disquiet, and he said he would not tolerate any trollish tricks.

It took her two more years to decide, and he had to leave her in peace during the coldest part of winter and the treacherous snows of early spring. But when the cattle had been let out to graze in the second year, he rode north with Skord, taking the deed of gift in a carefully folded leather pouch. The widow had sent a message to say that she was prepared to put her sign on the deed.

Skord had inscribed the deed to the Magister's dictation. It was beautifully written, evenly and as intricately as the tracks of weevils on the inside of a sliver of fir-tree bark. It began, 'I, Margareta Ambjörnsdotter, greet in the name of God all those who come to hear or see this letter. Here I announce that my property in Vässle is donated to the Cathedral Church in Uppsala for the sake of my soul, so that it may blessed in eternity.'

They had left a space for the figures stating the amount in square perches and acres, should she prefer to give less than her all. Also, they had given her room to add that the Cathedral Chapter had to lease the property to her sons Ingolf and Ypper for as many silver thalers as she would decide.

Skord had made the capitals look like millipedes and dragon-flies, and the Magister was a little concerned they might not be rightly understood. The deed ended by saying that it had been written after the Birth of Our Lord Jesus Christ, but Skord had left the year out. He said that if she sent them back home without her putting her sign on it, they would have to alter the year. The Magister agreed the Chapter would be suspicious if something on the parchment had been scratched out.

What Skord had feared happened. This time too they had to return empty-handed. She had changed her mind. But still, it was on her conscience that she had made the priest ride so far, and she sent along as much food as the horse could carry.

Skord said eyes watched and ears listened for them and that this was the case every time they journeyed through Skule forest. They tried not to think about it, and when riding along in the middle of the gorge, they avoided looking up towards the cave of the outlaws high up on the hillside. Skord fell silent, but the Magister told him to chatter away as usual, for Christ's sake. He had made a small switch from a willow branch and used it to goad on the horse, which was old and preferred its own pace to anybody else's. Dangling from the saddle was a side of pork, wrapped in a linen cloth to keep the flies off. They also carried a pot of lard, a whole roasted capercaillie stuffed with fried innards, onions and song-birds. Finally, they had pig's trotters and honey. All this had been sent with them to salve the bad conscience of the widow of Sir Ingolf in Vässle.

The path wound its way back into the forest. Here the firs looked like weird harps, with bare, dead branches for strings. Moss grew on the fallen trees. Dead birches were still standing upright, their trunks covered in wood fungi and banners of black lichen on their branches drooping in the still air. All was in a state of transformation, which made the Magister ill at ease. For a few moments this forest had looked like a cathedral, with tall columns, stringed harps and narrow windows filtering the sunlight like pale meat stock through muslin. It soon changed: the strings on the harps burst, the lights in the windows were extinguished and the stone-falls made it look as if the church floor had broken to expose the dead.

In front of them stood a horse carrying a man with a grey hood pulled so far down that his eyes were barely visible. The horse blocked their path. The Magister pulled slowly on the rein, and for a while all was still. Only a long, brightly coloured feather in the man's cap flicked from side to side.

He had a spear.

During the silence Ragvald believed that the spear would turn into a fir trunk and the legs of the horse into an elk's, and start running away. Then everything would be as before. Appearances would shift and the man disappear.

But the feather kept flicking, and the spear pointing.

Pax tecum, was what the Magister wanted to say but he could not utter a sound. Somehow he lacked breath. The man made the horse a take few steps forwards and then pushed the spear against Ragvald's chest. He pushed, just lightly, and the Magister fell like a ripe plum. Then the man with the almost invisible eyes under the hood made a sign, and Skord took over the reins. His gaze had become as hard and black as a stoat's. It was strange how well the two of them understood each other without words. All that was heard was the brambling whistling stubbornly its single piercing note, over and over again.

The large grey horse edged towards the Magister. It rolled its eyes and flattened its ears. The man pointed at his body with the tip of the spear once more, and the Magister understood. He started undressing. The man was not content until the Magister was naked. Then the spear pointed at the pile of clothes, and the man nodded towards the fat little mare. The Magister picked up the clothes and put them in the saddle in front of Skord, who was sitting there silently, thin-lipped and alert.

The man in the grey hood with the long pointed feather rode up to grab the mare's reins, and swung his spear. The Magister thought it would be thrown at him, and that he had been made to undress to avoid the clothes being cut in the kill. Ragvald turned, hunching his thin shoulders and his bent white back. But the man only inserted the blunt end of the spear between his buttocks and pushed. The Magister fell forward on the path. He did not take in the departure of the horses nor the direction in which they went. When he had crawled to his feet, he was alone and only then did he hear the whistling that had filled his ears all the time – the harsh, unchanging note of the brambling.

He wanted to take cover. He wanted to hide. The forest is a thick fur, but not for the skinless. He wrapped his arms round his body.

Death could not be more bitter than this.

He dared not sit down, nor lean against anything. He curled up and thought of the forest all around him, how wild it was and how full of precipices and fallen trees, of slopes covered in scree and boulders, of bottomless marshes and cold tarns. How undergrowth and dead branches made it impenetrable, and how the hillsides were silently stalked by a spotted animal, swift of foot, with black, tufted ears and yellow eyes. He thought of the shaggy brown one, whose paws are full of claws, and of how these claws would feel like nails in the skin of his back. And he thought of the grey one, of the stinking mouth, the tall legs, with ears like a dog and a nose that might already have caught the scent of his body. As all this passed through his mind, he got up and started stumbling onwards, his arms clutching his body.

The air grew cooler. The insects emerged. The forest was silent. A high wind moved through treetops and droned like the sea. He wanted to pray, but found no words – only visions. He wanted to reach out with his hand and break a twig off a wayfaring tree to have something to use as protection against the midges. But he dared not touch anything. He kept stumbling on.

The forest did nothing. It sent neither bear nor wolf to him. It allowed the brambling to go on whistling and the water of the streams to go on rustling between the stones. The Magister was left to sink deeply into his pain and his visions.

For as long as he had lived, he had been aware that he would die. His soul would then be liberated from its shell and leave it behind somewhere, on the ground or in a bed. Whatever happened to his body, whether eaten by the ants or the worms which feed on corpses, would be immaterial to his soul. But what was happening now frightened him. So many of them wanted to eat him already. He was swelling up with their bites. They were wanting to get into his body and dissolve it while he still lived.

All forest things were impure and dissolute. They wanted to merge with one another. Fluids seeped and penetrated, tissues ruptured and roots worked their way through the torn fibres. The ground wanted him to lie down on it. If he did, his body would dissolve while he was alive. His soul would disintegrate, and when he had liquefied and been transformed beyond recognition, there would be nothing left to rise upwards.

He did not dare look up. He ran on with his back bent, not daring to scream. He sounded like a puppy bounding along, whining as it went.

Arguably, nothing very bad happened to the Magister. He got a spear up his rump, was bitten by insects and became very hungry. The soles of his feet swelled and his body was chilled to the bone. But he did arrive. He came out of the forest.

However, he felt that he would never be the same again. He realised that most people who say this stay sadly unchanged. He too did not seem to alter, and kept quiet about his experiences. This was how much wiser he had become since the time when he had sat with his cousin, the Bishop of Linköping, holding forth about the existence of the soul before birth.

There is a darkness out of which images emerge. These are neither good nor evil. They hold secrets. Occasionally it is possible to hint at what they are like. Mostly, one keeps quiet.

He had arrived at a grazing leen. White cows with bulging crowns like birch fungus raised their heads and flicked their black ears. He could hear the low, rumbling noises coming from their insides as they ruminated. The buttercups were still flowering in the meadow and nodding in the evening breeze. A girl came out from the cookhouse, and he heard her call to a herd of sheep partly hidden by the forest above him.

'Come, little ewies! Come, come!'

When the sheep hesitated, she observed the forest more closely and spotted the Magister. She swiftly went back into the house, and came back out with a kerchief over her hair.

The priest was hiding behind a small fir. He shouted to her that she must not be afraid of him, and bring him something to cover his nakedness. By now, he had recognised her as Bodel. She brought a patched sheepskin blanket, led him into the house and sat him down next to the hearth. She got the fire going with birch-bark scrolls and twigs from dry-firs.

He was exhausted and dozed off. When he opened his swollen eyes he saw her pouring milk from one bowl into another. Many times over she poured it back and forth between the bowls. He asked her why. She smiled, and said she had made the milk too hot and this was to cool it. Then she handed him the milk in a ladle, and it was warm and sweet and clean.

He was to stay with her until her brother Erker was due to come up to the leen. Usually she would have had the other maid for company, but she had been taken poorly and gone back with her brother last Sunday. The priest asked if she was not frightened of being alone. This time she answered almost all his questions. It was as if she were less shy now that she had seen him without clothes.

'I have the cows around me. They're such dear things,' she said. 'And the goats. And the ewes and their lambs.'

Then she blushed deeply, and he got not another word from her for a long while.

He followed her around for four days, wrapped in the sheepskin blanket. She busied herself always with separating one thing from another. She sieved the milk through fir branches to remove flies and dirt. She spooned the skin of cream from the milk in the bowls, and banged hard with the paddle in the churn to separate the lumps of butter from the buttermilk. She heated the milk with rennet in a copper pan until it curdled. Then she squeezed the mass of cheese and packed it into the moulds. Finally she boiled the whey until it turned brown. The mese smelled sweetly, like clover. She kept smiling and stirring. In front of the hearth stood a bench so old that the wood was silver grey. Letters were carved into it. They formed the name Bodel and other words too, which the Magister preferred to overlook. But he realised Skord was behind this.

Until Erker arrived, the Magister did not tell Bodel quite how bad was the bad thing that had happened on their way back through the forest.

'Skord had been taken by the outlaws,' he said.

All that remains to be said about the Magister concerns his old age, which began in the autumn of the year in which he and Skord were separated from each other in Skule forest. One morning when his maidservant arrived, he was still in bed, unable to speak or move. It took some time for him to get back on his feet and make himself understood again. He still had difficulties with his right leg when walking, and was not able to push his pen as smoothly as before. However, when spring came, he was riding about almost as usual. With the help of his old mare, he travelled up to pray for the animals by the cattle sheds on the high leens. This he did to prevent the widespread heathen practice of screeching like peregrine falcons to ward off wild beasts. He continued with these journeys into high old age. Two summers after Skord's disappearance he went into Bodel's house and noticed that new letters had been carved into the bench. He did not ask her about this, but their eyes met and afterwards the Magister never again spoke about Skord or grieved for him as dead.

By now it was clear to him that he would never travel back down south alive or, in all probability, as a corpse. He would not have been able to tell – had there been anyone to tell after Skord was taken – whether this caused him much grief. A great calm had come over him, or rather, an indifference to the external world and all its activities: living and acting, eating and keeping house, coming and going, falling ill and getting buried. Internal matters troubled him as much as ever, indeed more. One winter's night he experienced something that would continue to preoccupy him for the rest of his life.

He woke with a strong urge to go outside, even though it was so cold that the timbers creaked and moaned. He pulled on his shoes and his thick felt cloak. Stepping out on the porch, nails of cold pierced his lungs. Above the fringe of the forest the sky panted and shifted beneath veils of light. It was the cold glow of the northern lights. A huge creature was breathing, and the sky was sifted through its gills, undulating and shivering with each breath. As he watched, the colours solidified and the misty lights coalesced into one large glittering circle. At first he thought it would turn into a face like a human being's, but then it became clear it was the face of a clock. All the time the outlines of the shape hardened in the cold, and he could distinguish seven crystalline spheres enclosed within the clock, and within the spheres, small moving figures. A large precious stone gleamed in the nave of the clock wheel. Although it was becoming more and more transparent, it was so many-faceted that he could not see if there was anything moving within the innermost sphere. He could hear the movement of the great clock through the silence of the winter night, deep rumbling chords sounding as if they came from the heavens above and the depths below. In the end, the light of the spheres faded, and veils hid the clock face which sank into the darkening sky.

When all was extinguished and silent, a frozen and shaking Magister Ragvaldus found his way back inside the house, and with stiffened lips blew a glow back into the embers on the hearth.

Over the time that followed the great clock was incessantly on his mind. He tried to draw it, first on pieces of birch bark as small diagrams of circles, later on parchment which he prepared for the purpose. He added the names of the seven planets to the inner spheres, and then inside them, the names of the saints. He became convinced that he had also seen the clock face divided into twelve sections, one for each of the creatures of the zodiac.

Then one night the vision of the clock returned. This time it was in his dreams. He could see the spheres rotating lit by a strong light, as if from a fire. Inside them pulsed the smaller spheres, each containing its creatures. In the dream he approached the great face of the clock. Walking through the ether or empty space towards the fiery circle, he was all of a sudden so close that he could see a door next to the nave. It opened, and he stepped inside. Somehow he understood that he was about to see the mechanism at the back of the large clock, and its cogwheels, pinions and chains.

It was dark, and all he could see were bundles of rough grey strings, like those of a huge harp. There was a sound of wood grinding against wood, a toneless droning and, it seemed, the desolate noise of water breaking over stones. As his eyes got used to the gloom, he could see great roots twisting around each other. Whichever way he looked, there was nothing but undergrowth and heaps of dead branches, twisting roots and screefalls. He woke up in the middle of this vision.

The parchment version of the clock of the world was never completed. He started pondering the dream images. The devil must have sent the dream to ruin his attempts to record the first vision. Then the thought came to him that both visions were the work of the devil. He realised he was a useless and profoundly sinful priest, and that it was more likely that he would be punished in hell than that he would be allowed to see the great clock wheels which drive the saecula saeculorum.

The clock of the world must have been a mockery. In the end, he clung to the notion that his dream had been sent by God. It had revealed the first vision as a satanic impulse, by letting him enter the inner chamber and find it a maze of creeping roots and piled with dead branches.

Mockery took over. His parchment drawings become ever more warped. Absentmindedly, he drew small figures with tails on the perimeters of the circles listing the holy men and women of the Calendarium. A whimsical jumble of ideas took control over his pen. The clock face became less and less like what he had seen that winter's night.

Finally, he could no longer bear to see the miserable results of so much pointless effort, and hid the parchment in his cupboard.

Other strange things happened, which he wrote down on pages of parchment from which the instructions for curing stone pains had been scraped, since he knew them by heart. Thus, Sir Hinrik had told him what had happened to his wife. The Magister had realised that during her fasting, the lady would eat at times when no one was watching. She would first fill her stomach, and then vomit. The farm dogs were her best friends, and followed her whenever she went outside.

But after her marriage, she stopped eating on the sly. Sir Hinrik respected and honoured her. She wanted to deserve such respect and honour, and so she no longer sneaked food into her mouth when she was alone, and stopped vomiting. There was a stillness around and inside her. Out of the stillness came light, and she could hear pious and ardent words. Her husband told of this. She no longer saw the devil rooting around with a dung fork in her own flesh. She did not tear open wounds in her skin or smear herself with excrement, and she ceased having visions of Christ with broken limbs and blood pouring from His forehead. One day Sir Hinrik had put his hand on her forehead. He leaned down to her and in a whisper asked her what she had seen during the long Christmas night, when she had been lying quite still with her eyes wide open.

'I saw light,' she whispered back.

He asked her in a low voice, his mouth close to her ear, what she had heard during that long night. She answered that she had been listening to words full of sweet ardour. She could not express the sounds. These were words different from those which she and her husband used together. They could not be repeated. They came from the innermost source where the light was.

Sir Hinrik knelt down and wept.

Magister Ragvaldus could not fathom which parts of all this were holy, and which were unholy nonsense. But he wrote the story down in his book, and often brooded on it. Everything he had believed and hoped for in his youth seemed distorted. It slipped and went off in an unexpected direction.

As for himself, the passing years did not make him more pious, but rather he became more anxious and hot-tempered. He often retraced in his mind the journey he made through Flanders during the plague years. He saw how the sea had reclaimed the land which people had turned into fields and meadows. In the plague years, the villages were silent. Flies crawled on the sun-baked walls. Shrubs and coarse grasses invaded the cultivated fields, and the sea could be heard advancing and soaking the land in corroding salt water. Sucking and slapping, wave after wave hit the soil and left it sodden and tainted with salt.

Skord returned one summer's evening. The Magister had not heard the horse's hooves. There was a light knock on the door, and at once he knew who it must be. A smiling Skord slipped through as soon as Magister Ragvaldus opened the door a crack. He was as slight as ever. His arms and legs had perhaps grown longer and more wiry. But his face was still that of a child. The Magister touched it with his fingertips. The skin was unscarred, smooth and fresh. He cried and stammered. Skord laughed at him.

But should he not tell the tale of how he had been since they parted? Had he been maltreated? Well, so, so. Not more than the others. What had he been doing in a band of outlaws? This and that. What had to be done to stay alive.

'For the sake of Our Lord, Skord, surely you have not caused yourself to be damned?'

Well, now – you don't go to hell for stealing hens. Now they must talk about the Magister. The Magister! No one had called him that since this boy had disappeared.

'Skord, how come you don't grow?'

But he had grown. Just feel his arm now. And maybe he was right. He had got a bit taller too. Now it was the Magister's turn to talk about himself. Skord had already heard about all the everyday things from Bodel. But what of his inner life, his battles with himself, his restless dreaming, the acedia, the doubts and the questions? The Magister said he had realised he would never return to the south now, and also would never be allowed the sight he had imagined so many times riding over the damp marshlands.

'What sight?' Skord asked.

'The sight of a meadow in flower, surrounded by playing linden trees and by flowering hazel and sloe and guelder rose.'

'I can take you there tomorrow,' Skord said. He was poking his teeth with a twig after having eating some of the Magister's cured meat.

'Don't mock me,' the Magister begged him.

'Tomorrow,' Skord said. 'But the sloe is not in flower. It's too late in the year.'

Early the next morning before anybody else was up, he put the Magister on the thin, pied grey horse which was tied up in the barn. They went into the forest to avoid being seen. The Magister, who was very thin now, sat in front of Skord. They rode through the same rough fir-tree forest as before, heard the same brambling whistling and the same stream rustling over underground stones. They did not ride southwards, but straight into Skule forest. The Magister could see no point in it, but assumed that Skord had found a place where at a distance the lichen-coated birches looked like young oaks, and the marshy tussocks lit from the side by evening sunshine, like a meadow with hazel and guelder rose instead of dwarf willow and crowberry shrubs. His weak back made sitting upright hard for him, and he leaned against the boy. He slept for while in the end.

Skord touched his arm lightly and said, 'You must open your eyes now and have a look around.'

He found he was in a forest of linden trees in flower. Skord slipped off the horse and helped the Magister down into the soft grass. He weighed no more than a sack of kindling. The earth did not give under his feet and did not smell of marshdamp. Bumblebees and butterflies hummed and flitted among the flower petals. He reached out and touched the leaves on a hazel. Clusters of green, still soft-shelled nuts hid among the rosettes of leaves.

'Is this foolery?' he asked.

'No,' Skord said. 'We are deep inside Skule forest. Here grow linden and hazel, and all you asked for. What you longed for was here, all the time.'

'It is truly so?' the Magister asked. He went down on his knees on the dry, firm ground to thank God. Skord sat next to him on a stone, paring his nails with a knife. While the Magister finished a long complicated conversation with his Lord, conducted partly in Latin, Skord picked a handful of wild strawberries for him to eat. They stayed until late in the afternoon, when it started raining. It was this wet and completely real rain that convinced the Magister that he had not been fooled, and that the meadow with its linden trees and hazel bushes was hidden deep in the terrible forest of Skule.

They made their way home. The Magister had to walk the last bit down to the village, because there were people about and Skord did not want to be discovered.

Skord returned to the cottage a few times after that, and found Ragvald weaker of body but as vigorous of mind as ever. There was something he must tell Skord, come what may, and this was what he said: 'All things are in everything.'

Skord scratched himself under his breeches, and said that the damned fleas were round 'n aboot everywhere for sure. But Magister Ragvaldus did not hear.

'All things are in everything,' he repeated. 'Even in this place where nobody has got so much as a ragged piece of cloth from Flanders. Look at this, Skord.' He held out his hand. 'This is the hand that held one of the white falcons sent by King Magnus in front of the throne of the Pope in Avignon.'

Skord held the hand. It was thin and bony like a falcon's claw. The back of the hand was white, and the nails curved and sharp-tipped.

'Tell the story of King Magnus's coat,' he asked.

This wish worried the Magister. Was Skord still a child, with childish desires? How would life treat him? Would he end up as a poultry thief, or worse?

'A finger has been cut off your hand, Skord, take heed.'

'I chopped it off myself.'

'Take heed. The thief cuts off his own fingers.'

He looked at the boy, who wore a long, pointed feather in his cap.

'You, who read Lucian,' the Magister said. 'Or have you forgotten it all?'

Skord then read him long and beautiful passages. It did not soothe him, or stop his worrying. How could it be that a flea-bitten poultry thief with a mutilated hand stood behind that boy, who was sitting straight-backed in the chair and reading in a language so beautiful and virtuous?

'Well, well,' he said. 'There is always somebody else standing behind. Remember that, Skord.'

Behind the wise Solomon in all his glory stands a dwarf with crooked legs, squinting, grinning, farting. For every word of wisdom that falls from the sweet-smelling mouth of Solomon, the dwarf has a crude and lurid gibe. He grows bristles like a swine where Solomon has a plait bound with silk, and his feet are like cloven hooves deep in dung. There he stands, lurking behind the back of the wise and high-born king.

As Queen Semiramis is taking a stroll through her garden in the cool of the evening, she is followed by an old wifie with a can full of dunghill soak-away water. The mirror held up to the pale face of the Queen of Sheba reflects the grin of a toad-skinned witch. The angelic boy praising God's salvation cannot hide the sharp-toothed animal sneaking behind his back. It is a stoat, with shining, soulless eyes.

'Skord, oh, Skord, there is always someone behind, lurking in a dark corner. Nobody is his own master and nobody is safe and sufficient unto himself.'

Then there was a long silence, broken only by the hissing of the birch logs in the fireplace. Shadows chased each other round the timbered wall of the cottage. At one point the Magister seemed to have fallen asleep. But his lips were moving, and when Skord leaned over him he was speaking.

'Nobody is made up just of aching limbs, sore eyes and an empty soul. Nobody is abandoned to himself. Someone else is standing there, ready to step inside.'

'Who?' Skord whispered.

'I do not know who He is,' Magister Ragvaldus answered, so quietly that his words were barely audible.

Next time Skord turned up, the Magister was worrying again but hiding it with jokes.

'Hail, he who has descended from Scordus, the Illyrian mountain, in order to visit an old outcast like myself. Here I stay, slowly simmering and turning into vapour, in my flea-ridden rags. Illyrian prince, what do you bring me? Absolution? No, it cannot be. That you cannot bring.'

'Do you want a priest?'

'Do I want a priest? Oh, Skord, Skord . . .'

'Would any shitty old priest do? Sinful, bitten by fleas and short on learning?'

'Anyone. He would still be the successor of Peter.'

'The last part is beyond me,' Skord said. 'But would you still want the priest even if he – well, has done things we would not speak about or care to remember?'

'You're so good to me, my dear boy. But not even you can get me a priest in this place, no matter how flea-ridden or sinful.'

But Skord did come back with someone he claimed had been ordained. He was a thin man, beer-sodden and shaky on his pins. They arrived in the night. The beer-priest was cross-eyed with fear. He was weeping and begging to be spared. It was hard to see how, but Skord had a hold over him. Perhaps it was due to something that would not be spoken of if the priest obeyed him.

'Here he is now,' Skord said, 'An outlawed priest. He has

forgotten most of his Latin, but he is surely able to hear your confession and say, "Ego te absolvo."'

Skord had no idea what all this was for. The Lapps wanted to have somebody lying on the ground in a state of delirium to read over them and free them from animal shapes, wooden breeches and lichen caps. The Magister wanted a shaking, dirty priest, who was without any doubt a utter scoundrel, to listen while he told of how he once a long time ago had put his penis between Skord's thighs, and so on and so forth, all said in Latin and with much mumbling. Skord shook his head and smiled at the thought that this priest was supposed to forgive the Magister his black deeds. It was with mild humour that he recalled how the Magister rubbed against his body. Any distaste he might have felt had been worn away long since. He had been ground smooth by so much else that he had seen and heard and been part of. Not least by what had been done by the crooked priest who was sitting there now, his eyes rolling in his head. He had violated, humiliated and dirtied until only the killing was left to do, putting out what light of life still remained in the being who had watched him with eyes that remembered.

The shambling priest reached out his hand and said the words. Liberated, the Magister reclined into the bed straw. His face looked smooth and his eyes bright.

'Get off with you,' Skord said, and put his knee into the rump of the worthless priest, who was out of the cottage and astride the shaggy horse with cloth-wrapped hooves as quick as quick could be. He disappeared into the night as silently as a moth. Skord felt ill at ease when he saw the clear gaze in Magister Ragvaldus's eyes and sensed his peacefulness. He thought the Magister had been cheated. He was an innocent after all, who had never dealt with criminals worse than his cousin, the Bishop of Linköping. Perhaps Skord should have read out the list of things for which the shambling priest had been outlawed? But he realised that Ragvaldus was quite satisfied, and took no interest in what his confessor had been up to since his ordination.

Skord could not ride down to the village during the winter. When he returned the next year at the time when the buds were opening, the Magister had died. The old maidservant who used to help him had burned all his books, together with the bed straw he had died in. She believed that they contained strong magic which would be let loose now that the Magister was no longer in charge. Skord made his way into the cottage late one night, and looked in the grey light for books and parchment. He found nothing. Ragvaldus Ovidi had left no trace in his house. The ashes had been swept from the hearth stone. Wasps had started building a byke in the window. He searched the house for his writing-board and the bone stylus, but found nothing.

Baldesjor

The latch on the door was missing. Nobody had replaced it. Kicking the door open worked well enough.

It was a grey morning; dull, silent and still. The clouds hung low over the mountain ridges clad in soft furry coats of forest. When he had picked enough dry-fir twigs, he shuffled back inside the shed. In order to open the door he had to plunge his knife into the wood and pull. He busied himself for a bit with closing the door, and then set to work building a fire in the hearth. It caught and began to glow. He could see the patch of sky over the smoke-hole slowly changing colour. It shifted from deep grey to blue.

The moon was in its first quarter. It was just a thin sliver, jagged round the edges like worn linen cloth. A woman, now dead, came to his mind. She was called La Guapa. For her, the moon recalled and explained her pain. She said that the moon was evil and a reflection, as white as bone, of Death the Tormentor.

'Moonlight is the sun's image seen in a black mirror,' she said. 'The day can look at a keepsake of itself.'

Now it looked like a nail-paring against a sky growing an ever brighter blue, a memory of a memory. La Guapa had watched it, and it had helped her understand and put bad feelings to one side. She had died, but the moon remained.

Skord sat next to the hearth, close to the burning dry-fir. He was waiting for the sun to rise and for someone to stir.

During the winter, the outlaws dug themselves into the snow like black grouse. Their blood was thin and their lifelines always close to breaking. Sometimes one of them would fall asleep and never wake. In the cold of winter, dying from sheer lack of enterprise was more than possible. He listened tensely for sounds of waking in the bitter cold of the hovel.

Blood and stomach sense the sunrise first. As always, he had woken up a while before dawn. All was still. Now he could hear the call of a crow and the voice of the wind, which was getting stronger and lifted the light snow cover to join the billowing smoke.

When he went outside for the second time, the crow flapped away from the roof. The air was greyer than ever and full of small grains of snow. The cold was calm and cruel. Was this the same morning? He had to turn and check his knife marks in the door. Had another day passed?

He had woken to so many dawns up here. Not just in this hovel. The outlaws drifted from one to another. Some had rotted and crumbled as time passed. There were countless knife marks in the door. No, they could be counted, but nobody did. There were times when he longed desperately for letters and numbers, for the bone stylus, the waxed board and the chair made from a tree stump. He would also long for chopped, seasoned logs, for care and forethought. For pancakes.

The clearing sky made the dawn colours fade. The blue shaded into sulphur yellow, with faint outlines of flower-petal red along the mountain ridges. There was a zone of blended colour which was neither violet nor green, a pale border of an unnameable shade. Why should anyone want to name it? Up here, he had lived the life of a true outcast for such a long time. Always under this huge sky.

Now it had faded. Except for the zenith, the blue was no longer blue. The border of rose and yellow was narrower and paler, but there were long lines of cloud in strong blue and violet gleaming over the forest to the south-east. Then they changed into pale red. The crow cawed again. Was it the same crow, though? Maybe its offspring, or its offspring's offspring. He recalled the swift movements of people. Riding. Hacking at each other in order to kill. Did anything happen yesterday? Or was the new knife mark in the door all that occurred?

The nearest dry-fir was far away. No outlaw ever collected and stacked wood for seasoning. He would grab the nearest dry branch after having been out for his piss in the morning.

Yesterday, no one had been awake. Only Skord. Left on his own, Skord is not much like a human being. His memory sleeps, and the knife marks grow in number. He hangs on during the winter, jaws biting into the fur of the mountain, and is never quite sure whether he is completely alone. Anyway, there are tracks of a marten chasing a squirrel in the new snow cover. He has not seen a fox since the autumn. Everything stays silent.

But the mountains of Skule have not rubbed the fleas from their backs. The outlaws are hanging on. They live in an old shepherd's hut, which the farmers have been forced to abandon. These huts are useful. At first there is cheese and meat and the warmth of women to be had. Later on, when all has died and been eaten away, when the embers in the cooking shed have grown cold and the cowdung smells harshly of dust, they move in and live there. They burn the milking stools and wooden buckets and cupboards until it is time to get back to gathering dry-fir again. High up in Skule forest there is a borderline above which the farmers give up their shepherd's huts to the outlaws. Up there, the leens are overgrown with tall wolf's-bane, dirty blue and poisonous. Up there, the doors get marked with cuts from a knife held by a thin brown hand.

Rimer was the outlaw who once had come across the priest and his familiar with the shorn hair in the gorge. He had noticed Skord's mutilated hand and believed that the boy was one of them, a punished thief. The villagers never let go easily of one of their kind. The Skule outlaws were always forced to leave something behind – a couple of fingers, maybe, or the skin off their backs. Some lost their tongues. But Rimer did not spare the boy out of sympathy. He thought he might come in useful. Thin bodies get into hencoops more easily.

At night, two men would wait at the edge of the forest, their horses snorting in the darkness under the trees. Skord could get through the narrow openings high up on coops and sheds. They told him to get into the fenced meadows and take lambs. He would put a lamb across his shoulders and run back to the horses. The ewes would bleat and run around on thin legs, their easily aroused fears filling their heavy bodies. The farm dogs would bark furiously. But by the time people had lit their torches and were stumbling out of their houses, the outlaws had got away. Villagers did not dare pursue them in the dark. The outlaws would ride through the forest with their hoods pulled down over their faces.

Even so, a sharp branch of a dry-fir might rip out an eye. Many such things happened. Outlaws never lived for long. They stole horses in the summer, when the villagers had let them out to graze, or when travellers went to the regions north of the forest. They lived in shepherd's huts and forest crofts. If anyone attacked them, they would retreat to the cave and roll stones down on their attackers.

Every little lad at school can list the names of the kings of Sweden way back from the age of Olof Skötkonung, the first king to be christened. But for every king there are several robber chieftains, remembered by nobody. The name of someone like Byrd might live on for some time because, like King Edmund the Coalburner, Byrd took pleasure in fires and burned down a great many barns and houses. Twice his men reduced an entire village to ashes.

But the robber chieftains will not be remembered by villagers because they looked after their men, like King Stenkil who took such care of the Western Goths, or because they were courteous and amiable, like King Halsten, brother of Inge, who never broke up a gathering. A chieftain might be remembered because one of his ears was torn off, or because he thought it good entertainment to break a captive's arm. This was true of Knut the Kettletinker, a small man, black and bent, whose strength nobody reckoned with until subjected to his sense of humour. Still, there were chieftains who did care about their men and kept good horses without breaking them. When Rimer brought Skord to Skule, the chieftain was called Iwan. He saw to it that his archers were well trained. They wore strong salmon-skins to protect their forearms against the whiplash of the strings and practised on targets he had put up among the firs. Iwan wore a short coat which he had stolen from a Lapp. It was richly embroidered, and had a many-coloured front: the feathered skin of a loom, sewn on with silver wire. Iwan died in the same way as King Sverker the Old. He was murdered by his groom after setting out for Christmas Mass. He had been making his way down the hill with his men to rob the people on their way to church.

Sverker the Old was buried in Alvastra. The grave of Erik, twelfth king of Sweden, is in Uppsala. King Knut, who took the lives of King Koll and King Byrisleff, and won the Kingdom of

Sweden by the sword, is lying under a stone in Varnhem. So is King Erik, the seventeenth to rule all Sweden, who gave the land good harvests for seven years running. Their bones rest in Uppsala, Alvastra and Varnhem, and God will save their souls and people their memories. But the remains of Byrd lie in the cleft in the Slåttdal rock. If one leans over the edge, his bones are there to be seen. Iwan ended up under a pile of stones, which were thrown by the villagers over his stinking carcass when it emerged from under the snow. Knut the Kettletinker was speared on a branch. It was part of the skeleton of a dead fir tree, and pierced him when he was riding through the darkening shadows. His body hung there, banging in the wind like a clapper, until clothes and flesh fell off. No outlaw would ever go that way again. Everybody forgot about Knut the Kettletinker except those whose arms he had broken. When they died he was gone. Nobody preserved his memory, and if God saved his soul, then God is great indeed.

The snow is cold and bright blue. The pawmarks of the marten look darker and deeper in its soft new top layer. Not much light is left outside. Skord follows the frightened leaps of the squirrel until the snow under the firs becomes too deep. He ought to bind skis to his feet, but cannot be bothered. He has still got a piece of frozen black grouse breast. It is enough, as long as nobody else wakes up.

Perhaps, finally, he is alone.

At the time of the Great Death, the people in the villages woke to silence, as he does now. The forest invaded many villages. Scrub birches were the first to arrive, and after them came aspen saplings. Here and there, the pointed tops of fir trees protruded through the dense pelt of crane's-bill and meadow-sweet. The aspens at the edge of the forest sent out their strong roots and anchored them in what had once been ploughed and hoed ground. Many people were left alone, and some took to the forest. For them, Death was often mean and slow. He sucked them dry and left them to starve. He could also be swift and sinewy, striking in the heat of noon and bending a strong man over the back of his horse. Another kind of Death, known only by rumour in these northern parts, had become bloated after feasting on corpses. It seemed that God had finally tired of greed, treachery, whore-mongering and war, and now he was letting Death have his fill. There were those who knew of no Death other than the kind which kills by means of grossness and indulgence. Following in his tracks came clamouring hordes of lesser kinds of dying: death by roaming soldiery, highwaymen, feudal lords or their mercenaries. These brought about their effects using very human devices, unremarkable inventions which proved their worth in the long run, and fed the earth. Sometimes Death took a rest and withdrew to the forests. He would take the lives of a few outlaws now and then, like someone picking fleas out of a fur coat. Break a neck. Send a winter chill which would finally put an end to a stubborn, hacking cough. Erode a body with starvation and tedium. If the outlaws had taken a woman after an ambush, Death might first put an end to her wits and then to her life.

Skord could remember only one woman up here who had died from old age. That was La Guapa. There had been nothing wrong with her wits. The men had ridden her for many years. Becoming dry and ugly enough to put them off had freed and cooled her, just as reaching the snowfields at last soothes the reindeer cow and frees her from the stinging clegs. They could have sent La Guapa out on the roads, but did not. The secret that saved her was wrapped in a small piece of silk. She kept it, tightly bound, close to the wrinkled brown skin of her chest.

She had never known Skord's secret, but being so long-lived, she may have guessed it. Outlaws never lived for long and their memories did not last. There was no one now who could remember when he had joined them. He was still a boy. Maybe he had become just a little taller and thinner, and his face more tightly drawn around the eyes and cheekbones, but he was a young lad.

Towards the end, La Guapa had been reduced to dry, dark yellow skin, stretched over her skull and fragile bones. Below the bars of her eyebrows, her eye sockets held two black globes. She coughed a lot, and then she died. But before that, she had called for Skord and given him a parcel. It was wrapped in a piece of silk and felt as if it contained a small book. Skord realised that it was the cards she used for telling the future.

'You have the gift,' she said.

Afterwards she lay there, eyes dulled and jaws working. It took a long time for her to die. As soon as they had been left alone, he spread out the cards. She told him what they were called, but wanted him to describe them first. This was because she could no longer see what card he was showing her.

Twenty-one powerful beings ruled the lives of men and women. These beings existed in the heavenly worlds of the planets. When people fought, large shadows fell over them because these beings were also fighting each other. If two people drew close and held one another tenderly, it was because those up there had done so first. No one could stir the pot without a great hand having stirred another enormous pot.

Skord asked if there was nothing people could do of their own free will.

Nothing. The great ones ruled. Now he must learn who they were. He was to hold up their images, one after the other, and tell her what they looked like.

'A man with a churn on his head,' Skord said. 'He holds the paddle-stick in his hand and is handsomely dressed.'

'That's the Hierophant. The Pope in Rome can make no move unless this being has made it first. What was on the card you just put down?'

'An old crone what reads a book, with a pot on her head and a fluttering cloak. Maybe she is sitting in a draught.'

'You should watch yer gob, Skord. That was the High Priestess. She is my card.'

'On this one they have hung a poor sod upside down by his feet and emptied the money from his pockets.'

'That's the Hanged Man. Look at him closely. Maybe you will hang like him one day.'

'This 'ere one is a fine lady with a crown on her head.'

'The Empress.'

'This lady I like. She has great wings and a flower in the middle of her forehead, and she's pouring water from one beaker into another.'

'That is Temperance.'

He also saw a sturdy lady holding scales in one hand and a sword in the other. That was Justice. Then there was the Emperor, with elegantly slashed breeches and a cap with a golden wreath.

'Here comes a reel,' he said. 'There are three monkeys climbing on it. The one at the top wears a crown and carries a sword.'

That was the Wheel of Fortune.

'This is a virgin who is locking the jaws of wolf or a lynx with her hands!'

'No, it is a lion whose mouth she is forcing open with her delicate hands. She is Strength. You find it where you least expect it.'

'Here's a creature who's flying through the air and firing arrows at three others, one male and two females.'

These were the Lovers, La Guapa said, and a difficult card which he had better not use. He was too young to understand it. Then the beautiful one turned up again, the figure he felt so fond of. She had lost her angel's wings this time and was quite naked. She was sitting on the bank of a great river pouring the clear water from her two beakers. A star shone above her, and that was how she was known: the Star. After her came Death, with his skeleton hands clasping the shaft of his scythe. The blade of the scythe had cut off hands and heads, and these were scattered over the black earth.

'He is after me now,' La Guapa said. 'I can hear the blade slashing the air.'

'Here's someone sitting in the sky, blowing a horn for a lot of naked folk.'

'Skord, these are people who have risen from their graves. This is the Judgement. It's no concern of ours, though. We are bound for Hell.'

'Here's moonlight, and a heavy rain falling as well. Two dogs are howling and not a human soul anywhere. Deep down in a pond walks a crayfish with long claws.'

'That card is known as the Moon.'

'This figure looks like someone I used to know. He's wearing a long cloak, and he walks leaning on a stick and lights his way with a lamp.'

'That's the Hermit. He's a wise man.'

'Now, on this one there's sunshine even though the rain is falling here too. Two boys are patting each other.'

'That's called the Sun. It's a very strong card. And a good one.'

'Here they have built a high building, but it has been hit by a flash of lightning and the roof has come away and the men are falling headlong into the mud.'

'That's the Lightening Struck Tower. It represents all human endeavour.'

'Now, then, a quick-fingered one is coming along and he's fiddling with something at a table. He's wearing a big hat and has a wand in his hand.'

'The Magician, that's who he is.'

'Here's a naked female inside a wreath. She is guarded by an angel, an ox, a lion and an eagle.'

'She's the World.'

'Afterwards comes the Devil with furry legs and wings like a bat. There are small demons busying themselves all around him, and they are tied by ropes round their necks.'

'He's not as powerful as they say,' La Guapa said. 'The Other One is worse. The Devil is nothing but his servant. Carry on.'

'Here's a fine young man in a carriage. It's drawn by two horses.'

'That's the Chariot. Well now, you'll be travelling soon too, won't you, Skord? But do you think that young man is steering himself?'

'You said there were twenty-one cards. But here's one more.'

'The Fool.'

'Who's he?'

'He's someone who's forever running about among the rest. He's powerless, yet he has more power than they have – because he has the ability to turn things back to front.'

'Is he the Other One?'

'You must be out of your mind, Skord.'

'Who is the Other One?'

'He's the one who moves all the Beings.'

'Why does he do that?'

'Nobody knows.'

'Will He tire of it?'

'Nobody knows. You take them now. Gather up the cards and look after them well.'

The moon rose in the middle of the day, ascended the sky and at the same time moved first southwards and then towards the west. By the time the long blue evening shadows were turning black, the moon stood in the north. Skord woke up in the night and through the smoke-hole could see the half of him, looking cold and evil. He wanted to cover the hole against the stare of this barren thing, but there were no pieces of cloth that he had not already wrapped round his body to keep the cold out. He must go to sleep now and wake later, but he did not want to be the only one awake. A new day would dawn, a death day, a birthday, uneventful for badgers but perhaps of great importance to redpolls among the last cones in the fir.

It turned out to be an unusual day. The sun only came out for a moment: a sharp edge, glowing with white and blue flames. It was soon hidden behind a smooth, solid bank of cloud moving in from the south. The wind was in the south, changing to south-east and building in strength. He hurried back inside quickly, wrapped himself in his rags and listened to a growing roar. It was a blizzard, a dense, dark mass surrounding the hovel. The air was howling. The south-facing wall was as cold as ice and the west-facing one not much better. He moved about in the darkness, bumped into a bundled-up body and pulled back. He did not want to wake up next to someone dead – if it had come to that.

Where had the redpolls gone now? Where were they all, the marsh tits, great tits, blue tits, the grey-headed woodpeckers, the jays? Had they crawled into lee somewhere? Maybe they had gone to ground in the old milkstore, with its holes packed with straw and cracks between the stones. Or in the hollows inside the trunks of dead fir trees.

Howl away, you horrible wind. Push my face against the darkness. Earth and sky have joined in a whirling black tumult.

There are no human beings here; no one to talk to me about the heavenly paths of the planets, the seven crystalline spheres and the great unchanging Order.

Howl and roar, you wind. Rattle the birch-bark rooftiles, plaster the flying snow against the timber walls, screech in the smoke-hole – tell of the Great Disorder! Break the branches of tall pines, pull this shed up by its very roots and shake us like bits of cloth! Terrify us out of our senses – but do not leave me alone!

After many hours, during which there was no telling day from night, dawn from noon, twilight from evening, he crawled outside and found that the storm had reshaped the world and scoured the sky clean. Radiating from the meadow in front of the house lay sloping drifts of snow, with blue crests as sharp as knives. The firs were so laden with snow that their branches hung down like heavy white bell clappers. Young birches had been bowed by the storm into arches, anchored to the ground by the grip of packed, ice-bound snow holding on to their branches. The crust of the snow was strong enough to bear him, but he had nowhere to go. The snares and traps were buried in heavy whiteness and impossible to find. He had better go and set up more traps. First, he climbed the walls of hard snowdrifts and looked for birds frozen to death in the lee of the icy crust. He did find a few small carcasses. If the storm had come from the east, the heavy snow would have barred the door to the shed and it would have taken him several days to dig his way out. Still, the outer door opened inwards. A thought about farmers, of whom he knew little, suddenly came to him. He considered their careful positioning of doors, and their way of building hillside cottages with the entrance facing the east, which in this area rarely was a source of storms.

The outlaws cared little for such things. They regarded attempts to keep the draft out as something for old women, and putting a catch on the door as slave labour. Kicking doors open seemed a suitably dashing way for outlaws to go about things. This doorframe had been badly seated for a long time. A farmer would have driven in wedges to stabilise it, but here someone had just packed the crack with rags. Perhaps an outlaw had been old-womanish enough to foresee a long winter, and on the sly tried to prevent the door from coming off and hitting his head every time he pulled it open. Skord pulled out the piece of rag and looked at the fine stitching on it. He recognised the stitching.

Women were able to write in a special way, using threads pushed through the eye of a sharp needle. Bodel had owned a needle. It had been her most cherished possession, and she had used it to write on linen cheese clouts and other bits of cloth. She wrote down the flowers outside the house, one by one. This way, flowers became more than just tufts of sweet-smelling stuff, nodding in the wind above a mat of cow grass. She wrote them using linen yarns, spun with double threads which had been dyed with birch leaves, reindeer lichen or the bark of aspens. She did not write them as they were. They could not have been taken from the linen clout and put back into the grass. She turned them into signs. Skord had looked from the grass outside to the cloth with its simple border of flowers, and then back again. He had realised that each herb and flower had its own special character. Bodel had teased this out of them and put it onto the linen with her sparse stitches.

She had made tablecloths from worn, washed-out and over-mangled material, which she had mended and hemmed. Skord had wanted to mingle his own writing with hers each time he was served a bowl of thick and slightly sour milk on a tablecloth decorated with the delicate outlines of rock roses drawn in thin thread. He had wanted to join his signs with hers, the way two chanting girls in the forest would call the cows by joining intricate whorls of sound. He carved the initials of her name – B K D – into the bench in front of the hearth, and she copied the letters in stitching among the flowers. But she felt ashamed at putting on such airs. Writing flowers was something that just came to her naturally. All she could do was to use her skill as well, and as prettily as could be. The glory was God's, and did not belong to Bodel, Karl's Dowthir. Then he carved Glory To God into the hearth seat, and she sewed the letters beneath the initials of her name.

He knew there were many different kinds of writing. The signs carved by the chiselling jaws of the weevils on the inside of the bark of dead fir trees were as orderly and beautiful as the Greek letters inside the most precious book owned by Ragvaldus Ovidi.

But the weevil tracks meant nothing. Or rather, they signified no more than eating, crawling, giving birth, laying waste and killing.

Sooner or later, all Bodel's tablecloths had been turned into rags for wiping cow's udders. Now and then he would find them, decaying but with some faded stitches still showing. Then these too vanished. She might as well have been writing on water.

He had been living for such a long time, long enough to see them go. This was his fate, and although odd, he scarcely gave it a thought.

Those who visited the villages had to be able to give their names and describe where they came from to everybody's satisfaction. People would remember. If Skord returned to a village, most of the people he had met had normally died, but there was occasionally some old person left who might remember him, and that was dangerous.

But the memories of the outlaws were short. Their lives were short. After Erker died, Bodel had been the only one who had known his secret. She did not refer to it – except once, when she made a joke which was unusually crude for her. She was making a felted cap for him and needed the usual fluid for wetting the wool. She had turned to Skord and asked him to go outside and fill the pot, ''Cause troll's piss is stronger.'

Then she had caressed his cheek quickly with her hand, which was becoming rough and thin. It was as if she regretted her words.

He knew that Bodel had desired to do things that would have displeased Sweet Jesus and could not be sewn into patterns in His Glory. Once she had told him that she could hear a voice whispering to her that she should sew with twisted and ugly stitches and make scratch marks with her needle like those of a hen's claws in farmyard muck. 'Sew prickly plants and stinking blooms, Bodel,' the voice whispered. 'Come on, do. Make knots in your sewing thread. Sew a snake.'

She never did.

Bodel grew older but no man cared for her.

'I think you must have played a trick so that no man can see me,' she would say to Skord. She never got an answer to that.

When she became old, she was set to look after the fire in the house of Sir Hinrik. It was her task to cover the embers with ashes each night. In the morning, she got up before everyone else and blew into the fireplace so that the flames caught the dry twigs and scrolls of birch bark.

'Here I am, sitting by the ashes in the hearth, and that's all I'm good for,' she would say. In fact she trotted around with all kinds of bundles and bags, giving clothes away to those who had none, and helping the sick by placing poultices on their swollen bellies and applying salves to their wounds. When she had grown too old to journey to the hill leens in the summer, she would meet Skord in the meadows where she collected herbs. She told him about Mistress Ingilike, who was becoming frailer and more pious with every passing year. It almost seemed that she might be swept up and out, the way spring breezes clear the spider's webs from dusty corners. But she was curiously tough, whether from sanctity or some other reason. Bodel would offer no opinion on this.

Once, lying among the small birches on the slope above the farm, Skord saw the great lady escorted to the privy. She was as pale, trembling, fragile and weak as ever. It was as if she had not aged since the time Sir Hinrik discovered her in Tjärr and everybody was laughing at her. Bodel said that according to the maids who accompanied her, if her bowels yielded anything it was only tiny hard balls, which clattered on the wooden staves. God had not blessed her with ease, but made her show her piety by putting up with hardness and all the suffering that went with it. On the other hand, the maids who supported her, who sinned and enjoyed it, at least in summertime, were able to shit freely and copiously. Bodel said this showed how mysteriously things were ordered, when a sluttish farm maid, who knew nothing, could have a gentler time of it than a fine lady.

In old age, the spouse of Sir Hinrik fell ill with a sickness which drained her of all fluid and ended her life. This happened one summer, when the maids were having a fine time and their wee cry-babies were rocking in birch-bark cradles hanging from the branches of the birches, while their mothers raked up the hay. Dark-green hops climbed the posts, their leaves rough and vigorous, and the air was full of the sweetness of clover and the murmuring of bees. Mistress Ingilike was propped up against her pillows. Her breathing was rasping. Old Sir Hinrik was at her side, sitting on a small chest by the bed.

'Do you remember that chest, Skord?' Bodel said. 'She brought it with her from Tjärr, a plain farmhouse chest with iron fittings and a small lokkit drawer inside. It has stayed where they first set it down, because she got so rich when she married, there was no need to unpack the linen from home. You mark my words, she'll be leaving us soon, and none of her wealth can she take with her. And she's been suffering with a sore stomach all her life as well.'

Sir Hinrik would lean forward, whispering in her ear, and no one ever found out what he was saying. Until the last words, which he shouted. Once they had heard her answer him, saying in a whisper: 'My dearest one, I have drawn warmth from your breast and sweetness from your words.'

When she stopped breathing, they heard Sir Hinrik cry out, 'I would rather die than be apart from you!'

Everybody in the main house wept, and likewise in the house of the factor: hot salty tears flowed for the sake of Mistress Ingilike. For one whole day, people beat their chests and wailed.

Skord had found the words of Sir Hinrik so remarkable that he wrote them down. Using a sharp needle, he scratched on the inner surface of a piece of fresh birch bark:

Ich wolde rather dayen than ben apart fram thee.

It seemed miraculous to him that two people could share a secret, unknown to everybody else and never spoken of, which could be so precious that they would lose their lives to keep it, and indeed did so in the end.

He realised that Sir Hinrik had spoken the truth, because he was not really alive after her death, at least no more than a hoof fungus growing on a dead birch stump. He was there, and maybe he was breathing. But he was withdrawn, grey and hard. His brother's sons, Styrbjörn and Ingelfast, had come up from the south many years before, after it had become clear to everyone that Sir Hinrik would have no descendants of his own. They shared out the farms while he still lived, if you could call it being alive.

Bodel also died. She passed away on the day of the great lady's funeral. For a second time, the priest at the head of the procession had to ride up to the farm with the sacraments in a bag made of silk. Skord had planned to meet Bodel in the hill meadow to give her a couple of bunches of saxifrage and angelica which he had brought back from the mountain. But she never came.

He had never thought of Bodel dying. He stayed up there in the undergrowth, looking down on the farm as they carried out the body of Mistress Ingilike, clothed in her finest things, and put it on a horse-drawn bier. He thought that Bodel might be busy with bunches of herbs to place under the cover of the bier, so he waited. But she did not come out of the house. When the crowd moved off, following the bier to the church, she was not among them. Nor could he see her grey, shrunken figure among those lining the road, kneeling and raising their clasped hands in prayer as the body passed by.

Bodel had planned to see the great lady's leave-taking. But first she went back to rake ashes over the embers. It was so easy to forget the fire on a hot day like this, especially one also filled with sobs and lamentation. As she bent over the fire, Death did his work. Not much violence was needed, hardly more than it would take to kill a redpoll.

The priest had brought three kinds of oil from the chrismatory to Mistress Ingilike, so that he could anoint her eyes, her nose and lips and her hands and feet. Her stiff fingers had been given a candle of death to hold and her eyelids had been closed. When Bodel died, one of the maids clapped her hands together when she came into the room and realised what had happened. That was her ceremony.

Of course, the priest was hastily called back to read over her body. They had laid it out on the table. This way he would not have to make that long journey again. Skord watched from the hill as the procession stopped between the faded flowers which covered the banks along the road. He watched people milling about in confusion. Finally the horses were turned around and the bier returned. It all looked like a lot of trouble. The dogs were barking hoarsely in the shimmering heat between the buildings, and through the air above the swallows were diving with long, piping whistles. The funeral procession did not start out again until the evening, and by then there were two biers pulled by the patient, ignorant horses. When Skord saw that the second body was barefoot and small as a child's, he realised what had happened.

There was quite a crowd following the first bier to the grave in the yard next to the new stone-built church. Sir Hinrik sat slumped in the saddle and let his horse find its own way along the narrow path. In the end, they had to put a young lad behind him, to hold the reins and prop up the old man's body. After the priest came the factor and the nephews on horseback, but the other members of the procession were on foot. When night fell, the procession came to a halt and fires were lit. The other bier, carrying the shoeless body, soon caught up and the sobbing and screaming started up again. It had ceased during the difficult journey.

Skord followed at a distance, staying inside the forest. He could smell the smoke mingling with the strong scent of the meadow-sweet and wild valerian, which glowed in the twilight. Sometimes the heavy insect-laden air also brought a waft from the great lady's body.

During the bleakest hours of the night, the people round the fires took turns to sleep and lament. Then they got going again, the biers bumping over roots and rocks. Tall brush-like tufts of overgrown grass scattered late summer's dew over the two bodies, soaking the shrouds. When Skord caught a glimpse of the stone church, he stopped following the people and retreated into the forest. He did not want to see them throw gravel and earth on Bodel's face.

That was what they did, though: they threw coarse gravel, stones and earth all over her eyes and cheeks and her soft lips. They covered her body and as they went about their dirty work, they thought they heard a wolf howling in the forest.

That was a long time ago now.

It was long ago, but he would never forget. Thinking about it brought a wave of hatred against the gravel-throwers and bier-pullers, against their submissive sobbing and their awkwardness in the face of the Tormentor. When this feeling came over him, he would start throwing his knife towards a mark on a pine trunk, and if nobody was watching, he would call the knife back after each throw.

This was what he thought about as the outlaws were attacking and looting: the gravel-throwing and wet shrouds, the wailing and the humble plodding along the paths. He would use his knife and shout, and the highwaymen would laugh at him, and grab the twisting body of the boy the way one holds a slippery fish.

The long clouds were the colour of clotted blood, but their tips were touched with brightly shining gold while Skord was breaking dry-fir branches over his knee. He could feel his heart beating. So many dawns had been nothing more than greyish things. The bleak light would wax cautiously and soon wane again. The greyness would turn a lighter grey, no more than that. Grey time. Rat time. Ash time. When the sun had finally risen, all you could say was: it's done. As one might after having lanced a boil on somebody asleep, drunk or clubbed unconscious.

While he was indoors kindling the fire on the hearth, the clouds dispersed. They drifted away over the sky in the east, which was covered in a yellow glow. Then the yellow darkened and shaded into red. On these, the shortest days, the sun rose between two mountain ridges running down towards the sea, shaggy with firs and dappled with snow. A pool of gold formed there. Then the light intensified, as if drained away from the rest of the sky by a cupping-glass. The pool of gold grew redder. No eye could bear looking at it for more than the odd brief glance. The crest of the mountain became outlined by a narrow gilt border. A heavy bank of cloud floated past, looking like an unreal and fantastic mountain. Then the sharp edge of a disc emerged in the golden glow. Drinking it in, eyes blinked; it hurt. The edge stayed there for longer than usual. And then it rose. It became a sphere. Shadows fell on the snow. Light, the colour of roses, played over the long ice crystals in the pines. He could hear birds twittering, and pushed his feet into the leather straps of his skis. Then he slid along on feather-light powdery snow which had fallen overnight.

Sun on the snow. The violet mountain of cloud dissolved like a receding headache. His heart was still beating hard, and he was getting hungry. It was not like the old famished pain in the belly, burning and noisy. This hunger felt good.

He found his new snares under the scrub birches where the black grouse would go looking for buds, and they reminded him of the blizzard. But he could not remember if it happened this or some earlier winter. He was thinking clearly. His thoughts were as precise as the blue tracks of his skis behind him in the snow. Inside his head, he said to himself: I'll wake him. I'll make him come alive. Then I will have company and someone to talk to. We will speak of time. We will mark the days with little lines and count them. To do that we will put ties around each little bundle of days the way sheaves are bound with straw twine.

He found a hen bird, beady-eyed with fear. She flapped her wings and clucked when he grabbed her round the neck. It seemed to stretch and grow slippery under his fingers as he twisted. Feathers and skin slid stockinglike over the spine. He could not stand it any longer. Feeling the warmth of the bird's body had turned his good hunger into a frenzied ache. He flicked with the tip of his knife next to the anus, got hold of the flaps of skin and pulled the whole thing inside out as far as the tips of the wings. It was like pulling off a damp and dirty sock. The breast meat was pink and almost transparent. He did not touch it. Instead he pulled out the long grey and yellow strands of gut until he got to the heart and liver. He put them in his mouth and tears came to his eyes as he ate. It was so warm and strong that he felt it glow in his mouth, and it warmed and excited his stomach like the wine that Magister Ragvaldus Ovidi had spoken of so often.

He cut the wings, head and feet off the bird and put the body inside his leather jerkin. It warmed him. He found a dry-fir, broke off the biggest branches he could manage and dragged them to the house. There was still a red sun-glow around him and birds moved among the firs.

When he got inside, he stoked the fire until it roared in the smoke-hole. He would cook now, and wake the sour-hump in the corner. God help them both if he had gone and died! Now, this was going to be done the proper Christian way, the bird fried in a pan, carved and eaten, if not at a table – it had been used for firewood – then on the chopping block. He had had no lard for many weeks. Butter was not to be thought of. But eating birch buds had fattened up the grouse hen and he pulled yellow lumps of fat from around her rump and melted them in the pan. He halved the bird and put the pieces into the spattering fat. Soon a smell of browning meat filled the room.

Skord watched the blanket heave. The smell of frying was strong. It slipped in under the layers in the heap of cloth. He heard a long growling sound and could not work out whether it came from a stomach or a windpipe. The bundle of matted yellowing sheepskins rose, and the skins fell apart. But what emerged was still wrapped in skins and rags, a huge pile of flesh and bones, with a reddish beard spread over the front like a thicket and a hood pulled down to where the beard started on the cheeks, leaving only a crack through which two small blue and red-rimmed eyes peered coldly at Skord.

He tried to scratch himself with his wrapped-up hand. It appeared to feel around for a huge groin. But Skord knew that there was nothing supernatural about the bulk. The being in the corner was no creature of the night and the forest. It may have been made larger by beard and flea-ridden skins, but it was truly human.

Baldesjor was the name of the last outlaw in Skule forest that winter. The band had started losing members in late autumn. Those who were left did what bears do during their long sleep: they suck their paws. Skord could hardly be bothered to look out though the window at the steady snowfall, grey and ceaseless. His nails and hair grew longer; he was lying fallow. Christmas was coming. The outlaws, except for Baldesjor, who was a great sleeper, went down to the villages. Dizzy with starvation, they had lost their grasp of what might happen to them down there. Two of them had died of a feverish cough, and one after the last round of stabbings. The fight had flared up from some smouldering old grudges. No one could remember what it was about. By now, they had all died, apart from this last one, who was sleeping so noisily that the wall timbers rang.

After the others had gone, Baldesjor turned his back to the boy and the hovel, and slept through the nights and days of piercing cold. Now and then he would wake up and grab a piece of bird carcass to eat. He drank from a bowl of melted snow that Skord had put close to him, and pissed into a milk crock. Once, when the bird had been badly plucked, he happened to chew on a feather. Skord had caught a glimpse of his sour eyes above the sheepskin cover. Then he spat and wiped his mouth with the furry back of his hand.

'That's life,' he said; only that. He laughed nastily for a long time afterwards, before turning his back on the room again and going back to sleep. Skord stayed awake, bored and famished.

But now he had got a bird and they would eat it sitting facing each other. He arranged the black grouse neatly on the chopping block and was cheered to see Baldesjor come crawling out from under his covers and shaking himself awake. Skord quickly pushed forward the milking stool, the only item of furniture which had escaped being burned, and sat himself down on the hearth. Then they ate. Baldesjor grabbed a thigh and started chewing cautiously with his sore tooth stumps.

'Now then,' he said. 'Yes, yes. God almichty.'

He looked ready to fall asleep again and Skord could not think what to say or do to make him stay awake. But then the outlaw himself got an idea.

'Now, there's something called pipper,' he said. 'It's strong. Michty me. But we haven't got it.'

Skord had heard about it. It was also called pepper. As costly as pepper, people would say.

'Not to speak of salt, now.'

Baldesjor looked at the wall as if he was trying to see straight through the timbers.

'Now then, Skord, you could go down there and steal some salt,' he said.

They sighed. Neither felt the need to say anything, because in their mind's eye they both saw the tracks of skis in the snow, gleaming blue in the moonlight and outlined in black shadow by the sun. They would be found, clubbed and dismembered.

'Aye, well,' Baldesjor said. 'Winter is a damned time o' year. And how many winters have we been holed up here?'

He stared at the wall again, but could see nothing except the tinder-dry moss in the cracks between the timbers.

'How old are you, Skord?' he suddenly asked.

'If only I knew.'

'There you are,' the outlaw said. 'I wouldn't rightly know myself. When I got to the convent of the Dominican friars in Kalmar, they wanted to know how old I was, and I said I'd ask my father next time I was home on leave. Father and I judged my age by the pied horse he borrowed for the autumn ploughing. We counted back over the fallow and the growing years, and worked out how old the horse was from how long he had been helping with the ploughing. We reckoned fourteen years seemed a fitting and proper figure. I may have been a bit older.'

He sharpened a broken bit of fir twig to a point, and used it to search between his tooth stumps until he found a small piece of bird tendon to chew on.

'I would have been a clodhopper, plain and simple, if the Lord and his gift of a good head for learning hadn't taken me to the Friars in Kalmar,' Baldesjor said and used the sharpened twig to scratch the rind that covered his good head.

Skord was pleased that the outlaw had started speaking about himself, because he would stay awake for as long as it took. Everything he was saying he had said not once but several times before. But for someone who had gone for weeks without the sound of a human voice it was still cheering to listen to. He was not a gloomy soul, for all his sighing and muttering. In spite of his less than splendid situation – the last outlaw left that winter, horseless in Skule forest – he always started his tales by pointing out how well things had turned out for him.

'Now, if I hadn't got a head for learning I would be shovelling shit today,' he said. 'Instead it so happened that I was the one who got to go to Cologne with Brother Anselm to visit the Studium Generale of our order. Did I ever tell you about that?'

Skord smiled but did not speak. He waited.

'I accompanied him on the way home, and on the way out the next time he went. We walked to Paris and the university there and it took us many weeks. Paris is a very large city, then as now, but at that time many of the inhabitants had died in the plague. We got to the college and it turned out to be a stone-cold house with straw on the floor. Two learned magisters were fighting, using knives with very long blades, over some matter to do with their lovers.'

Baldesjor fell silent, as if he could see Paris with his inner eye.

'Aye, well,' he said after a long silence. 'It was a time for learning. But not in the college. Plague and poor harvests and warfare had made some people indifferent and turned others into hotheads. Just as bad, either way. Some were chasing women and some were after property. Some wanted to rape and loot. The indifferent people still tried to get as much food and drink as possible.'

Skord thought that there was nothing as pleasing and interesting and instructive as listening to someone who could speak beautifully. Baldesjor was very eloquent. He knew French too, but had forgotten his Latin.

'There you are,' he said. 'My Latin I forgot in the inns of Paris,

127

but I learned French there all the better. It's a gentle language to the tongue.'

This meant that it was time for him to tell the tale of how he learned French. Skord enjoyed it, because songs and jests and fables would pour out of the hole in the greying red beard as Baldesjor grew enthusiastic. But on this day there were no songs. Baldesjor picked his teeth and sighed long and heavily. Of Paris he only said that he had been left behind when Brother Anselm had set out to return to Kalmar.

'It was wintertime, you see. Yes, I remember well enough. I remember the afternoon when we said goodbye.'

'And what happened?' asked Skord, hoping to hear of a huge fight, or a great row or a fire, of tears and screams and running on the stairs and maids fainting with pleasure and a drunk priest who could sing the Te Deum backwards.

'I owned nothing then, except a small brown cheese and a dagger,' Baldesjor said. 'After he'd left I just sat there, clutching the dagger and full of dread.'

He stared hard at the wall again, as if the scenes he described were happening there, in front of his eyes. Skord too stared, as if expecting to see them on the wall: Baldesjor, young and with a mouthful of healthy teeth, and Anselm, the Dominican friar, bags at his belt and sack on his back.

'Yes, I was frightened. But I did not follow him. I went to the inn. I knew songs and stories in the French language. They paid me when I sang – in beer or soup. My head was whirling. Being able to write was a good thing. The times were bad, and there were many marriage contracts and wills to draft. People married in order to get hold of property. One single unprotected woman might be the sole inheritor of a whole family, which had died in the plague or in the war. I knew the art of writing and could support myself with such things.'

By now all the meat on the bird carcass had been eaten. Baldesjor turned the legs upside down and poked about inside them, but found nothing. Skord took a thigh bone and cracked it neatly with his teeth. He handed it to the outlaw, who closed his eyes and sucked to get at the reddish-brown marrow. Skord did the same with the other leg bone and handed it over. When he had finished sucking, Baldesjor still would not speak. He was leaning dangerously far back on his stool and his eyelids were drooping.

Skord, who realised that he was about to fall asleep again, kept asking questions about Paris and the Parisian way of life. Nothing helped, not even whistling the tunes of Baldesjor's jolliest French songs. The outlaw had gone back to sleep. After a while he fell to the floor and, without waking, started groping for his covers.

S kord had lived in the world for long enough to understand that human life was a sad and long drawn-out affair. People caught colds, endured corns and saddle-sores, and their plans either did not go very well or failed altogether.

But the stories they told about their lives were very different. These were often very cheerful, and, if not, then at least things happened more quickly than in the dour, tedious reality of the people who told them.

Also, the stories remained even when the people in them died or rode on or just slept, like Baldesjor. Skord would sit on the chopping block, observing the heap of flea-ridden skins which rose and fell, and ponder the intricate loops and roundabout ways in which that body had moved across the Earth. He would try to think of Flanders, although he did not know what it looked like, and of Visby, said to be a town on a flowering island in the middle of the sea. Then there were Paris, Lyon and Lübeck, where Baldesjor once unpacked his clothes from herring baskets and started wanderings which would as like as not end here in Skule forest.

The young Baldesjor, walking northwards from Paris, met Änglak Ingilsson in Flanders. He was a cloth merchant, and had come to trade in Bruges. He had a lively admiration for France and all matters French, just as had been the fashion in Sweden during the reign of King Magnus. He often said that was when he really should have been alive, or maybe even longer ago. When he had dealt with his business in Bruges he wanted at long last to see France. He picked Baldesjor to help him on his travels with language and writing.

Master Änglak was astonished by everything, and struck with admiration for most things. He was skilful and shrewd in his business deals, but when it came to the French everything delighted him, no matter what. He met the Count de Froissier, whom he found immensely admirable. At night he wept in his bedchamber, moved by the Count's having condescended to speak to him. He believed the Count to be like the nobles at the time of Guillem de Poitier: full of knightly virtues, courteous and given to versifying. The Count de Froissier, in spite of his patched clothes and the stockings sagging on his thin legs, could do nothing to disabuse him of this idea.

Now, it so happened that the Count was in fact one of the people rooting about in France after the great war, like worms in an apple, gnawing and grabbing and leaving trails of muck. Baldesjor had heard of this robber count, who travelled the country with a band of like-minded folk. They plundered honest citizens and raped the women. They made holes in sacks of flour, cut the heads off cockerels and stole sheep. But their manner of speech was refined and noble; at least, this was the case when the Count de Froissier addressed the cloth merchant. Master Änglak went all the way to the Count's cold and empty castle. The horses were brought in across the drawbridge and stabled on the ground floor, where they munched their hay in the handsome drawing rooms. Mould traced whole maps on the stone walls. And still, the cloth merchant saw only what he wanted to see: vestiges of grandeur from an era long gone.

Back home in distant Gotland, Master Änglak had furnished his home with French tapestries and a red carpet from Turkestan. The hangings round his four-poster bed could be pulled on gilt rings using silken ropes, and the bedcover was decorated with fringes and fur trims. Now he slept in the house of the Count de Froissier, with rats rustling in the floor straw and bats whirring about on silent wings. However, he seemed to notice no discomfort.

The Count would say he loved the sound of horses' hooves and frisky snorting, the clatter of arrows against leather shields, the clanging of swords and much more in this vein. The cloth merchant listened, and the more he heard, the more awed he became. But the era he revered was in truth long gone, and his knight in armour was making a living as a highwayman. He had recruited a following of creatures as knightly as he was, who hid after their forays in the stone fortress on the River Vie.

On the banks of the river, in the shade of sycamore and chestnut trees, Master Änglak met Anne de Froissier, the Count's daughter. And so did Baldesjor.

She lived in a thatched cottage belonging to the castle bailiff and his wife. After the plague and the looting, managing the estate involved little more than peasant labour. The bailiff himself had to walk behind the oxen. But he was able to feed himself and his family well enough, and the Count's daughter did not suffer. She slept on straw and coarse linen sheets, and ate turnips, linseed porridge and fresh eggs. She flourished, and might have come to look like a country maid, had she not inherited her father's lanky height. In her, this had become a delicate and fragile build. She was pale and looked well-bred, even in a plain linen skirt. The cloth merchant fell in love with her at first sight, and so did his companion, the scribe.

The Count was convinced that he did not have long to live, even if he escaped being murdered or taking a tumble with his horse on some dark night. He suffered from an ache in his insides, a very French kind of sickness, it seemed to Baldesjor. He was anxious to have his daughter provided for, but did not want her to marry in France, where a divorce could be had for a fur-lined coat, nor did he care to have her marry into his own circle of the nobility. Like his peers, he had good manners, combed his hair flat and used a small piece of fabric to clean his nose. But he had aged a great deal, and the internal ache had worn him thin, so that the stockings sagged on his long legs.

So the Count wanted to provide for his daughter, and the cloth merchant for himself by satisfying his long-standing, burning adoration of aristocracy and Frenchness. No doubt he also wanted to look after his investments in France. Property prices were low during these troubled times, and Master Änglak bought in order to sell again when things became calmer and people's hunger for land returned. He planned for his future, keeping in mind both his wealth and his desires. And at the same time, the future of his scribe was settled.

Skord had heard Baldesjor tell the story of his life many times. It had often occurred to him that people stayed whole only because they span these endless tales about themselves and their lives. For many there seemed to be one particular time during which they had truly lived. In Baldesjor's case, this time lasted between the day he arrived in Visby with Master Änglak Ingilsson and the day his clothes were packed into two herring baskets on board a ship, and he left the island in the sea.

Skord could imagine that time almost as if he had been there himself, because Baldesjor had spoken about it so often. But he preferred to hear the outlaw tell the story again, because it turned his only winter companion into somebody else – it explained and transformed him.

That was why Skord was keener than he might have been to snare birds and bring down hares with his arrows. He longed for the moment when the outlaw was sated and awake. Then the firelight cast by the sparkling, crackling fir branches caused his face to glow. The light fell on the opening in his beard, and out of this evil-smelling hole came the story of the true life of Baldesjor.

'Can you imagine how we felt, Skord?' he would ask. 'Everything was good. The rolling waves of the great sea were all around us. It formed a blue ring around our sunny, flowering island. The city on the island was surrounded by a wall, which protected us. We lived in a fine stone house. Inside it was like the innermost butter-filled hollow in warm porridge made from the whitest wheat.

'Master Änglak was wealthy, not in a boundless, ungodly way, but solidly well off. He had arrived from the mainland after Valdemar, the Danish king, had sacked the island. Property prices were low at the time, and Master Änglak had much increased the wealth of his family.

'There were Germans living all around. He traded with Germans, and kept company with them. He spoke German, but his heart and mind stayed with France. He longed to be back in the reign of King Magnus, when educated people had good manners, spoke the French language and wore respectable clothes, which did not reveal the shape of buttocks and private parts.

'Naturally, I had to keep the accounts and do the writing for his business, but his main reason for bringing me home with him was that I knew so many old verses and songs in French.'

And he had also brought with him the daughter of the Count de Froissier and married her.

'Now the beautiful Anne wore the kind of silk called sioluc instead of the coarse linen cloth from her time with the bailiff. She sat on cushions with knitted and embroidered covers, and put her clothes away in chests made of camphor wood. Do you see – we walked about among all these fine things, and we ate wheaten porridge with no licht or chaff. Can you see this in your thoughts, even though you've never been south of Skule forest?'

Norart of the forest might be a stranger place than Baldesjor could imagine, but Skord had not tasted porridge for a long time. When the outlaw spoke of the warm buttery hollow deep inside the porridge, his voice sounded like that of a young man.

'The fire crackled and the dogs snored. The merchant sat smiling with his eyes closed. Sometimes, as I read, his wife Anne's eyes would look straight into mine. We loved each other, the two of us. But our love was modest and courteous. Yes, it was pure and proper in every way. Master Änglak could hear of this love in every line of verse I read aloud, but maybe he didn't know of it or want to know – wisely, for then his own pleasure would have come to an end. Or perhaps he did know and found all as it should be, and as it was during the time he longed for, when a knight and nobleman would have thought it right that a young poet adored his wife.

'I loved her so much I almost fainted when she walked through the room. If her eyes met mine I would lie awake all night until dawn, and the poetry would pour out of me. I composed pastorals and ballads, aubades and serenades. Much was like what I had heard from others, but I always added something of my own, and I slipped in her name and her brown eyes and slender white arms. I meshed in the silken cords she wore round her waist so that she should recognise their colours.

'All this suited Master Änglak exceedingly well. He loved her in precisely this way, he said. Just as the hunter keeps a dog to retrieve the game, so he had taken me on to find and bring back words in her praise. She was a French woman and an aristocratic lady: there was no way her beauty could be expressed in our crude language.

'Then again,' Baldesjor said after a long pause, 'there is one word: gracious. That's right for her. Gracious.

'But she knew that I was no dog fetching other people's spoils. I brought my own love for her.

'That is how we lived. We could have remained in the stone

house, inside the pale-grey city walls, on the flowering island in the blue rolling sea. But my love started to pain me. When I got to hold her hand, while Master Änglak dozed in the warmth of the fire, my whole body glowed.

'The maids comforted me. They were coarse girls with loud voices, chapped skin on hands and arms and huge thighs. They had pale hams and knobbly feet. "He's love-sick," they would say, pursing their lips. They let me have my way with them, and they laughed at me at lot.

'It was true, I was sick with love. It was as if she was taking everything I owned away from me. It was a curious notion, but I felt that the beautiful, calm and quiet Anne de Froissier was like one of the nagging beggars in the square. "Gimme, sir! Gimme!"

'The wind howled. Laden with raw sea mists, it tore the leaves off the mulberry tree in the garden of Master Änglak.

' "Gimme! Gimme, sir!"

'The beggars would pick me clean the same way the wind ripped the leaves off the mulberry tree. Anne de Froissier would take all that was mine. Name, memory and desire – she would take it all. This was how I thought.'

'The good citizens of Visby knew no verses other than drinking songs and malicious ditties. But Master Änglak got them together in a meadow and arranged a poetry competition. He wanted to show how it was done, and I had to read my best sestinas aloud. They understood not a word of the French language. Most of them were red-faced Germans, who glared sourly at me because of my master. They said he had no right to the poetry prize for something that his clerk had pieced together when he should have been working on the accounts. Master Änglak said I was his apprentice, and that I served him in the same way as a skilled craftsman's lad serves his master. Everybody knew that when it came to a cupboard or a clock, a fine instrument cover or an intricate lock, the master would not himself have made every stroke of file or plane. These verses were his. The subjects, images and inventions were all his. But the shaping of the poem was mine. This talk put me under a lot of strain. I was made to read one more set of poems before the company got started on German drinking songs, and Master Änglak went home. We ought to have kept ourselves to ourselves. We were happy, we lived well together. Master Änglak knew just as much as he ever needed to know. It was pride that brought our fall, and the only one of us without guilt was the beautiful Anne.

'Soon afterwards – autumn was drawing in – I too was assailed by the demon Pride. It had hurt me that Master Änglak had called me his apprentice, the lad who just finished off his work.

'I wanted to show the poems to somebody. I also wanted to speak out about my love for the lovely and aristocratic Anne de Froissier. My love beat against my breast and wanted out, like a nestful of young starlings, just ready to fly. It wanted to be free, to chatter and whistle and shriek.

'So, I decided to confide in my friend Anselmus, who lived in the Kalmar House of the Dominicans. With Master Änglak's permission, I had been sending him cheese and wind-cured ham. I had been getting on very well in comparison with that poor bastard. After returning from Paris, he had seen nothing more of the world outside. So I carefully scratched out old columns of figures, wrote my poems on the parchment and sent them to Anselmus. It would have been pointless to send him things written in French, because he had not had time to learn the language during his short stay in Paris. Instead I tried hard to translate the elegant rondels and aubades into our language. It was far from suitable, Lord knows – but what could I do? I struggled with its knotty and crude expressions and attempted to bend and shape it. This was using the plane and the file in a big way!

'Well, I thought, at least Anselmus might understand them now. Maybe he would be given a hint of the great poems which passed by, just throwing their shadows on the rough floorboards of our creaking folk tongue. I dared hope for nothing more. And this way, I could speak to someone else about my great love for the long-limbed mistress, who would sometimes reward me with a glance, her hand to hold or her belt of silken cords. I had written a poem about every pressure of her hand, and versified a sigh about every part of her belt and every piece of silk in her dress. Lord knows it sounded more like burps when rendered into the language which was meant to be my own. But then, I counted on Anselmus to read with the eyes of friendship, and I'm sure he did. But the dear old donkey thought the poems must be very precious and sent them back together with a herbal salve that he wanted me to have as a token of gratitude for a cheese and a leg o' mutton. The parcel never reached me because the messenger was curious about what was going on between Anselmus and myself. He opened it and scuttled off to show my poems to a cloth dyer's apprentice who could read – may he rot in hell! The very same night they were common currency in the town.

'Some of the tradesmen asked me to come along to a beer cellar. When I got there, they crowded me into a corner and insisted jovially that I should read my verses aloud again, now that they had come to understand what they meant. I sat there, crushed and frightened, because behind the jollity they were hard and threatening. Many of the Germans had been building up a hatred of Master Änglak on account of his shipping business. The old families, who had survived in Visby since before the sacking under King Valdemar and the imposition of high feus, harboured a resentment of all outsiders. They especially hated those who had capital enough to buy houses and land at the end of the Danish War, when prices were as low as could be.

'The worst thing of all was that they were convinced that what was between me and Mistress Anne was a simple love affair.

'They tried to make me read out aloud the lovely poem about the rosebud. When I refused, the knowledgeable cloth dyer's apprentice climbed up on a bench and shouted out the lines as if they were nothing more than coarse and mocking ditties. Then I grabbed the sheet and started to read, thinking I would rather read myself than listen to him sullying the poem. I got to a passage which goes:

> Then I reached out towards the rose-laden tree
> to find its loins and to hold it close to me;
> I caressed the soft bud, first closed so tight
> then unfolding its petals to my heavn'ly delight

By then they were roaring with laughter and groaning and heaving and rolling their eyes. They assured me as one man that it was the most remarkably entertaining verse they had ever heard, and I was truly one hell of a lad even though I looked like a pale-faced clerk.

'What would have been the point of trying to explain? How

were they to understand that everything becomes coarser in our language?

> par les rains saisi le rosier
> et quant a deux mains m'i poi joindre...

The French language has the same word for branches and for the loins of a woman.

'"Les rains!" I shouted. "Don't you understand anything? It does not mean what you're hollering about. The poem is about something else, something fine and subtle. It goes on between two people who love one another. They touch each other from a distance, deep inside each other. And it can happen a long time before their bodies even come close!"

'They just kept on laughing, though. They laughed at Master Änglak and called him a cuckold. They said he never guessed that his own clerk had versified his way straight into the butterbox of the lovely lady. Then they got even more pissed and bawled their own songs.

> "We are joyous joyful jolly!
> Rememb'ring a jolly man with drink
> t'saints will bless us all, we think!
> We are joyous joyful jolly!
> Sing to Sir Änglak and drink!"

Soon they stopped singing about saints and forgot about Master Änglak Ingilsson and me and the whole affair. For most of them it was no more than a beer-cellar joke.

'But some were more sober and malicious. They got hold of the parcel with the poems and threw the lot in through Master Änglak's door. They had given me so much wine I could no longer stand straight. They threw me after the parcel, and let people know that I had stood in the beer cellar and read poems aloud about how I had cheated my master and laid his wanton wife.

'So everything came to an end. The butter in the butter-hollow was finished. The porridge grew cold. Outside, the autumn weather had turned dull and raw. Master Änglak went away and wept. Then he told his wife what he had to do, according to the law. He had to lead her to the threshold of his house and pull off her coat. He had to slash the back of the clothes she was wearing and turn her out of her home. Then he went back into his own chambers and wept some more. When he returned, he was very pale.

' "I shall treat you kindly," he said. "You have been very precious to me. Still, you cannot stay here."

'Strangely, neither Anne nor I tried to make him change his mind by telling him that we were free of sin. We stayed quite silent. True, I was so drunk I could hardly speak. But I could still think a little. I thought that it was better to keep my trap shut. I don't know what Anne was thinking. She had turned pale and kept biting her lower lip. All I heard her say was, "May I take some of my clothes?"

'Her husband started crying once more, and said that she could take all that he had given her. Then I too started crying, because I was thinking of how well we had lived together and how it was all ruined now, even if we insisted to Master Änglak that we were innocent. The citizens would laugh even harder at him if he did not send both of us away. Getting rid of me alone would have been the worst thing he could have done. That is why I did not speak. I dare say Anne stayed silent for that same reason.

'But, Skord, she loved me. Can you believe that? Look at me, look at this thick arm and this broken thumbnail! Look at my bloodshot eyes and the coarse, yellowing beard round my mouth! Yes, she loved me. It is true I was someone different at the time. I was young, slim and could write poetry. But deep inside I was the same man, and that she could love me is the greatest miracle of my life – love me so much that she did not swear she was innocent, did not kneel and beg him for her life, beg to stay with him and with her children. She just asked if she could take some clothes.

'We spent the whole night packing. Master Änglak raged and wept in turn. But he brought a bag of coins and quite a few goods: cheese, cured ham and rye bread. And clothes. We were given plenty of good clothes to pack. He still cared very much for both of us, strangely enough. Or perhaps it was not that strange.

'We should have forgone our pride, both of us, and then I could have stayed with him in the butter-hollow till the end of my days. But that did not happen. And besides, I didn't really want to. I was sick with love, Skord. I wanted her to take all I had for love of me. My memories, my good name. I wanted her to take it from me.

'We were given two of Master Änglak's ships to choose between, a bark and a swift sloop, which were to leave the following week. While they were waiting in harbour for the autumn storm to calm, Anne and I lived in a shepherd's stone cottage outside the walls. We had chosen to go to Bruges on the fast sloop. Our baggage was carried on board. The skipper would send a member of the crew to tell us when they were ready to sail.

'The storm lasted for three days and three nights. During that time in the shepherd's cottage, I lost all that was myself and all that was mine. Name. Memory. Sex. Everything.'

The sea voyage to Bruges was hard for Baldesjor and the lovely Anne. They had intended to buy horses with the money from Master Änglak, and travel on to the castle by the River Vie which belonged to the Count de Froissier. But things were going against them already when they started unpacking their clothes. In Visby the skipper had been given orders to store them securely. However, he already knew of the affair between the wife and clerk – or thought he did – and so he stored the costly clothes in herring baskets. Hauled out of the holds, they smelled as could be expected.

They dared not have the clothes washed at a simple inn, especially not Anne's. Anyway, many could not be washed: they were made of velvet, thick scarlet sioluc, embroidered satin, furs and Flemish cloth. They travelled on, taking the clothes and hoping that the stink of herring would disappear in the gentle air of France.

When they arrived at the bend of the River Vie, where Anne had spent her childhood, they found that the castle had been ransacked. The Count was dead and the bailiff gone. The thatch on his house had burned. Inside the stone walls all had turned to charcoal, and nothing but clumps of thistles grew in the fields.

If they were to stay and claim Anne's right of inheritance to the land, they would need enough money to go to court. Then they would have had to start all over again with pickaxe and wooden plough.

They travelled on with Anne's clothes as their only capital. It was very hard to get the right price for these skirts and coats and finely embroidered silk petticoats which stank of fish. They tried to hide the smell with perfume, but it did not help. On their way southwards, a furious brewer caught up with them: his wife, while suffering from a cold in the nose, had bought a skirt from them.

His lads wanted to beat up Baldesjor, and the brewer wanted his money back. He would not believe that the whole sum had been spent, and groped about inside Anne de Froissier's bodice to find out if she had hidden the money in there.

She was no longer seen as the daughter of a count, nor as the wife of a wealthy merchant. The brewer took her for a traveller.

Neither was she Baldesjor's wife. She was his amatrix, his lover.

Their relationship continued. He had little to tell from this time. During that part of his life, he had not really lived. It was a long-drawn-out, painful period during which their lives did not fit the place where they breathed, a time when their true selves were not at home, but drifting anxiously around as their bodies made their way along the country roads of France.

They had to stop in Lyon, because Anne gave birth to a child. It was a little boy who died before he was ready to suckle, a tiny cry-baby whose yellow face she watched with steady concern and tenderness until it grew smooth and rigid.

Baldesjor cut up the clothes and unpicked the seams. He went about selling the pieces to pearl-stitchers, cap-makers, embroiderers and hose-makers. This was the best idea. But one day the clothes were finished and then he had to start singing in the inns even though he took no pleasure in it. His singing improved after many glasses of wine. But after one too many, he would end up among the rubbish under the table and return without earnings the next day.

Anne had always had a beautiful singing voice, and found learning new songs easy. She had helped him with his verses when they lived with Master Änglak in the white house with roses climbing up the walls. At the times of day when they were apart, he at his writing desk and she supervising the maids in the noisy weaving room, she would send a line or two of poetry through the open window:

> Ben volria mon cavalier
> tener un ser e mos bratz nut ...

She knew he was sitting there, writing poetry on parchment sheets kept between pages in the ledgers. He would write down all that was sent to him through the humming of the bumblebees, the twittering of the birds and the wandering wind stirring the leaves in the large mulberry tree. Hers was a delicate singing voice, but he always caught her meaning.

No one had ever imagined that Anne de Froissier would sing for any reason other than her own pleasure. But now it came about that she sang in the bath-house in Lyon. She became a jugleresse. But to be a jugleresse in an elegant bath-house was something quite different from being just a traveller, who would sing and play and lend her body to all sorts. Did Skord see what he meant?

He saw all right.

Even though he had never seen a bath-house?

Well, he had seen bath-huts.

'Michty me!' Baldesjor said. 'Wooden shacks. No better than shepherd's hovels and straw barns. You must understand, the bath-houses in Lyon and other French cities are built like very fine merchant's houses and carpeted throughout. There would be copper tubs, large enough for two people to sit under a tent, which collected the gentle, sweet-smelling and invigorating clouds of steam and sheltered against prying eyes. You were served the most exquisite foods, and could rest on soft beds, listen to music, converse or amuse yourself in some other way. People drank wine and ate crystallised fruits and pistachio nuts.

'Anyway,' Baldesjor said, 'We lived in a quiet, respectable street inhabited by people such as bookbinders and letter-illuminators. As a clerk, I felt at home there.'

This had become his life, he said. This was how it was.

But why did it not stay that way? Sometimes Skord had to keep asking questions to prevent Baldesjor from sleeping and dragging the story back with him into his sleep.

It did not stay that way because Anne died. She died in the bath-house in Lyon. She was buried in a beautiful dress, and the money was just enough to buy Baldesjor a horse.

Skord was baffled by this. What money?

But the outlaw turned his attention inwards, as if the figures in his story moved inside his closed eyelids, and went on to talk about his horse.

One morning, as he was wandering along the streets of Lyon heavy with wine and grief, he noticed a pied horse tied to the rail outside an inn. He walked towards it, but collapsed and fell asleep.

It was before dawn. He realised when he woke that he had thrown up. He could have suffocated on his own vomit. But the horse had saved him by using its hooves and its soft mouth to turn him over, so he ended up on his belly instead of on his back. He was alive when the sun rose, and he looked into the gentle eyes of the horse. So then it came to him.

What had come to him?

That he had to buy it, whatever the price. And he had to call it Belle de Jour.

Why give it the name of a big butterfly?

Because that was what they had called Anne de Froissier when she walked about singing and playing in the bath-houses of Lyon.

So, he had bought the white and grey pied horse, and started travelling northwards with his bundle of clothes, his hand-organ and his flutes.

And had that been a good time for him?

No. No, it had not been a good time.

Skord had many questions stored up. He did not ask them. How had it been for Anne as she played and sang to support them both? Was she still pure then? He asked himself if the beautiful lady had not died from a shameful disease, caught by whoring in these Lyon bath-houses.

But Skord did not ask anything that might seem to question the story as Baldesjor told it. He did not even ask how long ago it was that all this happened. But he looked at the robber's spotted hands and the folds of skin under his chin and realised that his time of being truly alive was long gone.

When Baldesjor slept, Skord longed for him to wake up. If he failed to move one morning, Skord would miss him and not only because it meant he would be alone in the cottage. But who was he really?

Who was Baldesjor without his story? Just a string of belches and grunts? A flea-bitten, bloated body under the coarse covers? A rough voice, a hand that threw spears and stabbed with dirks. A sore ear, someone who pissed regularly, a snake's nest of hungrily rumbling gut. Was there more to him than that? Who could answer?

The snow was starting to melt and water was rushing down from the high hills. The softening ground showed beneath the slush. Skord reckoned that the bridle-paths would soon stop running with water and become firm enough to use. At this time of the year, he would often look down the hillside to spot any riders coming their way. The first one arrived on a day when an insistent, cold March rain was drenching the snow. His name was Ficke and he had not been with them for a long time. He brought a sheep's carcass and a pot of lard. On his arm was a wound oozing pus. It needed attention and seemed to have been caused by the blade of an axe.

Now Baldesjor woke, and was cheered by mutton and fairly fresh lard, salted and mixed with pieces of onion, and by Ficke's stories of how things were down in the villages.

Then Torn arrived, with his companion Dunsen. They were expected. But they had not been able to steal a horse for Baldesjor.

Haquin was the last to come. He brought the keenly awaited horse, a brown mare trotting along after his black gelding.

Haquin was their leader. This was new. Tideke had still been alive in the autumn. But this time he failed to turn up, and nobody mentioned his name. It was understood by all that Haquin would not have liked hearing questions about Tideke.

Once they had finished the mutton, the paths had become good enough for raids on the villages. Haquin decided that they were to ride norart to a distant farm. The people there had moved in only a few summers ago and would not know where the outlaws came from. If they worked craftily, nobody would trace them back to Skule.

They rode out one morning while the ground was still frozen hard. Skord, slim and light, sat in front of Dunsen, who rode without a saddle. It was tiring, and for long periods he slumbered, leaning against the body of the outlaw. He was hungry, but no one spoke of food, because there was none left. There was no talk of stopping to shoot game birds.

They rode all day and tied up the horses only when it had become too dark to see the path. They slept under the firs, cold and restless in their sleep. When dawn broke, they rode on. The horses stepped uneasily with stiff legs, searching for footholds in the soft soil, as their hooves ground the brown birch leaves deep into the mire. It was barely light enough for Skord to pick out the frozen drops of a chilly spring rain hanging from the blueberry twigs.

They reached their goal before smoke had begun to rise from the farm. The grey buildings cowered like animals in the cold. Skord slipped down from the horse and joined Haquin. Crouching, they ran silently towards the main house. Before he broke the silence, he could sense the presence of sleeping people and animals inside the timbered walls. It was in the air, like a scent or a reek. He banged on the door and screamed in a high-pitched female kind of voice, 'Dear kind people, help me! Please, oh please, help me in the name of Christ!'

Then he shrank into a bundle by the door so that the farmer should not be able to see what he really looked like through the peep-hole. He kept moaning and shrieking and crying until he heard the bar across the door being pulled back. Every muscle in his body stiffened. Haquin leaped at the farmer and Skord tried to slip through the door. For a while, the opening was blocked by the two bodies. The others were coming; horses' hooves were thumping on the frosty grass. They dismounted and Ficke ran, small and bent, between the horses to grab hold of the reins. It was his job to keep them together. The farmer was lying across the threshold, dark blood staining his hair. His jaw was broken and hung wide open. The men made their way inside. Screams pierced Skord's ears. Haquin was shouting to urge them on. Sometimes, there were silent moments interrupting the turmoil and all that could be heard was Haquin's breathing. He panted like a fox as he hit and stabbed. Men's heavy bodies fell in the straw. Skord had to hold his hands over his face to protect himself against a swarm of flapping wings. The flock of hens was looking for a way out.

Skord never drew his knife from his belt. He did not hit or stab, for his tasks were different. They depended on speed, sleek muscles and sharp eyesight, but even more on a kind of second sight, an ability to guess people's secrets. He climbed up to shelves and upper floor joists. He probed cracks between planks to find hidden hatches and searched the bed straw and the pillow slips for bags. A suckling pig, which had been careering around screeching loudly, was slaughtered by a kick from a boot and a slash with a knife. It was silent now. There were two children bedded down on a bench right at the back of the house. They were lying quite still, their eyes shut tight. He felt underneath them for hidden objects. They smelled of excrement.

The farmer's wife was lying on the floor in front of the hearth. Haquin searched her body for keys and Skord noticed that she was quite limp. The silence was broken again when the men saw a bed curtain twitch. They pulled out a young woman, a maid maybe or a daughter of the house. Her shirt was made of strong, unbleached linen and would not give when they tried to tear it. So Dunsen pulled out his knife and cut it, from the chin downwards. The fabric fell apart and although he had made a neat cut, a long line of blood formed on the maid's pale yellow skin. They crowded in front of her, unbuttoning their trouser-flaps, and found her mouth and the hole between her legs.

Haquin was panting like a fox again. He struck her in the face impatiently. Perhaps he wanted some kind of response from her, a sign of life, if only loathing or fear. But she had withdrawn too deeply inside herself. They turned her over and took her, one after the other, while the rest were waiting. Haquin made way for Baldesjor with a gesture of his hand. Somebody else had to step aside. It was not clear whether this was meant to be a kind of politeness between equals or a calculated move to get Baldesjor on his side. He was allowed to get to the rigid body of the young woman, and Skord watched the encounter. He stepped forward, one figure made of skin and cloth meeting another shape. He moved about in the mucus and blood inside her. Some force drove them all. Their movements were jerky, and had been since they woke up: jerkily, they had been riding, beating, kicking and stabbing. When it was over, Skord took the pewter dishes off the shelf and put them away in his sack.

Torn was the last one with the woman. He got out his knife when he had finished. Haquin made a sign intended to stop him – she was to be saved and taken along with them, to be used for a few more hours or days. But Torn was fast as always. This time he was done before he saw Haquin's raised hand. The gash in her throat widened and created another pool of blood under her, bigger than the first one.

As they left, they took the farmer's horses from the stable. They tied them to their own animals and mounted. By now Skord had been given a horse of his own to ride. Dawn had ended and the light, without any snow to reflect it, played gently over their tired, hollow faces. They were on their way into the forest when they spotted someone who had got away. He was crawling in the high grass along the edge of a leen. Torn turned his horse at a sign from Haquin, and the others waited just inside the forest while he rode off. Skord wondered what this was for, but said nothing. There was no point, one way or the other. Still, the deed was quickly done. Torn came back and said the other man had a knife, and he had tried to use it and died with a curse on his lips.

Skord thought, Now this man will go to hell because of Torn. He would be stretched on a rack until sinews and vessels broke. He would be burnt and cut for all eternity, although he deserved it as little as the hand that stabbed him deserved its task. Now they were turning into the forest, riding along and jerking up and down like figures made of skin, moved by something or somebody. They rode with their bags and knives, but they were not really there. They were elsewhere, as that young woman had been when they used her.

She was not there. Nor were they. No one was there.

The light rose over the crest of the hill, the frost still lay on the moss and tiny droplets of ice hung like buds in the bright green bilberry plants. There were bodies and clothes and bundles holding stained pewter and salt-encrusted hams; there were knives and straps and clasps, hair, blood, guts and livers – there was no one at all, and no one was riding through the forest.

S pring was early that year. Long before Easter the roads were filling with people. Haquin, who in the winter had travelled the furthest south, had news to tell: a valuable load was on its way from Uppsala. The members of the Cathedral Chapter were accompanying a special consignment, and would rise early to travel as far as possible before the sun reduced the road surface to mire. The group was on its way to the new stone church south of Skule forest, which was to be consecrated at Easter.

By now, they would have got so far north that the cart could not be used. The load, which consisted of the most precious things, would have been put onto packhorses instead. The packs held chalice, monstrance and paten. Embroidered vestments. Crosses and images. All that was necessary to worship Him as He had never been worshipped before in the far north, where His blood had been drunk from pewter tankards, and His body offered up on wooden platters.

Attacking the train to rob the treasure was not to be thought of. It was guarded by soldiers. People surrounded the riderless packhorses, and the monks carried short swords under their habits.

The outlaws spoke about the treasure every night. They found it hard to sleep during these light, busy spring nights. They made Haquin tell them again and again about the silver vessels and the precious stones and the gold thread in the heavy robes for Mass.

They were all damned. They deserved to go to hell seven and seventy times over. Nothing could make their fates any worse, they told themselves with both pride and fear. They were afraid only of themselves. Haquin told them so, and they repeated it. There was nobody else for them to be afraid of. No Other Being.

Still they hesitated.

Haquin said that they could not make things any worse for

themselves even if they took the stones from the eye sockets of Christ, no, not even if they violated the Blessed Lady and stole the Rose from Her lap. Damned is damned.

They would sit round the fire in the twilight of the spring nights, their eyes watering, pondering this. Nothing could make things worse. And yet none of them dared go into the church and break the Rose from Her lap.

But Haquin had another plan. None of them – yet one of them. Not by battering down the barred door, not by wielding swords and knives. Through a window opening. Like a poultry thief. Just one of them. The only one slim enough to squeeze through.

The rest would wait with the horses at the edge of the forest. It would be done during Holy Week, when everything was in place. Then they would ride soudert with the loot. This would be the end of their half-starved distractedness, once and for all.

Skord had a few objections, none to do with hell. He asked what would happen if the cadaverous priests and the monkish rabble turned up earlier than expected in order to start praying and howling. And what if they stayed in the church overnight? Maybe they thought the Rose would open its petals for them if they just carried on yattering. He had understood Holy Week to be a very busy time for the priest-slobs and monk-devils. He spoke at length. In fact, he was gabbling, but instead of hitting him in the mouth, Haquin argued with him and said, 'They'll be asleep. We'll raid the night before Good Friday, which is their great day for fasting. The night before that they get drunk, eat fit to burst and then sleep like the dead. That's when we ride down there. That's my decision, it's final.'

The fleas bit worse than ever during the days when they waited feverishly for Holy Week. Skord and Baldesjor hunted game birds and hares. Once, they reached a small round tarn where the water was so clear that anyone standing on the steepest bank and looking into it could see seven fathoms down. At this time of year, greyish, rotten ice was being sloughed off from the bank by slurping currents of water.

Skord cut down young birch trees, piled them up on the beach and lit a freshwood fire. Then he undressed, and carefully lowered his clothes between the ice floes. Standing next to Baldesjor, he watched them turning dark as they soaked up the cold water.

When Skord stepped into the water, pushing his slim naked body between the edge of the ice and the bank, Baldesjor shivered. It felt like the stabbing pain in his bad teeth. He was convinced that Skord would drop dead on the bank, if he ever got out of the water at all.

The boy got out quickly. His black hair was dripping wet. He ran round the freshwood bonfire with its light, almost invisible flames rising towards the blue sky. He hung his clothes up to dry on rowan saplings which he had cut before getting into the water. The clothes were so close to the fire that the steam started rising at once. He explained to Baldesjor that this would be the end of the flea plague. The fleas would have drowned miserably even if they had escaped being turned to ice by the chill in the water.

At first Baldesjor had not had the slightest wish to get anywhere near the water of the tarn. But watching as Skord was dancing by the roaring freshwood fire, happy and free of lice, made him decide to try the same cure. He started undressing. Layer by layer, he took off his stiff woollen rags and put them in the water. Skord kept leaping about, but helped him to soak the clothes and use a rowan-tree branch to keep them from drifting away.

Finally Baldesjor immersed himself in the water with a great howl. Skord was worried it would be heard south of the forest, maybe as far as the new church. He helped to hang up the bits of clothing to dry, and then they both settled down as close to the fire as they could get without their skin blistering.

While Skord was sitting there by the fire, he tried to recollect how long it had been since he had tried the waters of this tarn for the first time. It had been summertime, and he had seen the image of a buzzard in its depths. Baldesjor had not been born then. Now he was almost an old man, a grey-beard even when it came to the thinning bush below his belly. He seemed frightened and saddened by his own nakedness. His limbs were thin and knobbly, his hands covered with age spots, and there were scars all over his dirty white skin. He stared at Skord's brown and boyishly slender body, free from any sign of injury or wear, except the cloud of bright-red flea bites around the groin, and the cut stump of one little finger.

'You're still young,' he said. 'You're a summer child. Maybe that's how you'll always be. But I have lived.'

His hands stroked his stringy thighs. It was as if he had not looked at his naked body for a long time, perhaps for many years.

'When did you last do this kind of thing?' Skord asked. 'Was it in the bath-houses of Lyon?'

At that, Baldesjor stayed silent for a long time, but then he answered without his eyes leaving the fire, 'Only once did I enter one of those.'

Then he told Skord how it had come about. It was as if he had stepped into another room in the story of his life. A closed door had been opened. Skord would come to wish he had left it shut.

'A lad came running along early one morning and said Anne had died. We were no longer living in the street of bookbinders and text-illuminators. All that was long gone. I don't know how she died, whether for something she'd done, or because of a deed done by somebody else; whether so much as a grain of intent or meaning guided the hand that killed her.

'They wouldn't let me in. They said she was no longer there, she had been carried away and buried. But the lad came back and told me it was not true they had buried her. He was there to clean the tubs and carry the wood for the fires under the water pans, and so he listened everywhere and knew all the whispered secrets of the great house. She had been carried off – but she had not been buried.

'He told me that her body, with a small black mark under its left breast showing where the knife had entered, was now in the house of a learned man with many secrets. The boy said this man would take any unclaimed dead bodies, and paid people handsomely for not alerting the clergy, who were out to get him. This scholarly man had bought corpses from the bath-house before.

'So I went along to the fine street where he lived. I would have been kicked out if it hadn't been for being able to write. I handed a letter to the servant who answered the door, with a message to say it must be delivered to the master of the house. He was an important man and very learned, but still let it be known he would see me in the garden. He asked how much I wanted in exchange for letting him keep Anne's corpse. I told him she was my beloved and I had come to get her body, and now that she had gone, there was not enough money in the world to make up for my grief and mend the tear in my soul. I demanded her. I did not beg. I said to him that if I were not given her body to carry out of his house, I would see to it he got a visit from the Church authorities.

'When he heard that I could express myself well, he became more polite. He asked me to step inside, and I followed him into the basement. He ushered me into a windowless room. There were vessels and instruments arrayed on shelving along the walls, and a tray set out with a variety of small sharp knives. He put a cloth over it straight away. A body covered by a sheet was lying on a table in the middle of the room. I started trembling when I saw it.

' "You want to give her as beautiful a funeral as she deserves," said the learned doctor, and I concurred, torn apart by sobbing.

' "She arrived naked," he said. "What would you dress her in? A fine dress? An embroidered petticoat, and light shoes made of the thinnest skin?"

'Yes! I wanted all that! But then he asked me if I had any money to pay for it.

'What could I say? It was easy enough to see how things stood with me. I wept even more violently thinking of Anne's beautiful body under the sheet, while the man watched in silence, looking thoughtful. Then he offered to give her a dress and shoes and a handsome funeral. The only conditions were that he could keep her until the funeral, and that I kept my mouth shut. I would get some money in order to be able to leave Lyon.

'A strange thought came to me then. I saw a vision of myself riding up to the inns and singing there, as I had done before. The doctor gave me money and a paper to sign. It stated that he had received the corpse of Anne from me. I pointed out that this was untrue. He shrugged, and slightly inclined his head to the side.

'Well, untruths become true often enough,' said Baldesjor. 'I signed the paper and, still weeping, accepted the money. It was like something in a dream. He offered to pull the sheet back to let me see the body, but I couldn't bear the thought. So I just left.'

After saying this, he fell silent. Skord asked no questions. Steam was rising from the dripping clothes, and they had to wait for a long time before they could put them on again. Baldesjor stayed silent, but he did not fall asleep as he usually did when he had nothing better to do.

Later that evening they rode back down the hill, and he did not speak unless spoken to by Skord. His replies were cross.

The days leading up to Holy Week, the week of stillness, were full of planning and preparation for the Skule outlaws. They were making a ramshackle ladder in three sections. This was to be carried down to the village and assembled just in front of the church. They equipped Skord with bags and straps and a long rope, which was to be wound round his back and waist. There was an iron hook at the end of the rope.

Throughout the preparations, Baldesjor was oddly silent. He glanced at Skord from time to time when he thought himself unnoticed, and there was something bitter in his look. The last evening everybody gathered around the boy to test the strength of the straps and the strings, and to see to it there were no holes in the bags, and the small dagger was sharp enough. Baldesjor alone stayed at a distance. Skord thought he saw pure hatred glowing in the eyes of the outlaw. He suspected that he would have been involved in some kind of accident long ago, if he had not been as slim and agile as a stoat and therefore the only one who could get through the loophole in the wall of the church.

At dawn the next day, Ash Wednesday, they started riding down the hill. Skord carefully avoided looking openly at Baldesjor. He had no doubt at all that from the moment he crawled out of the window-slit in the wall of the church with the treasure tied round his waist, he would have only a little time left to live. Baldesjor had opened a door and shown him something he should not have seen.

Two things baffled Skord. One was that the outlaw could still feel ashamed. He had not known one Skule freebooter with a sense of shame. The other cause of amazement was that Baldesjor had finally told the shameful part of his story. It must all have happened a very long time ago. He had been a young man still, known by a name Skord had never heard. The lovely Anne must have whispered that name in the shepherd's cottage and maybe in other places too, until the stink of herring, the wine and the hunger had overpowered them both.

When he rode away from Lyon, he had taken her name. At first, he had named the horse after her. During the time of her degradation, Anne had been called Belle de Jour. Maybe he had used that name when singing about her – using songs and stories to make her pure and noble again. It seemed to have taken a short time to live through, but a lifetime to recount the story.

When the remarkable mild-eyed horse died, the name had become his own. He kept it and carried it with him still, as he would have worn her dirty coat if he had rescued it from Lyon. The name had become distorted, but he no longer answered to any other.

What baffled Skord was that Baldesjor had finally shown the reason for his shame, after so many years of hiding it. He must have lived off the songs and stories of his adoration of the lovely lady. So it was hard to understand just what had stopped him from telling the story of her death, the learned doctor and the money he been given to leave her body behind. Much wine and many tears would have flowed in the inns on account of that story, and the gnomic doctor with his small sharp knives would have added an element of profitable fear.

Now a sour-faced and stiff Baldesjor rode on through the slush towards the villages. He glanced at Skord now and then. He had given away something he would have preferred to keep. There was little doubt he would do his best to make sure no one but himself would know of his shame. It was his most carefully guarded secret, and perhaps his core of truth. After all, he was not one of those who took pleasure in shameful things. He had not even wanted to show off his shame to an audience in order to keep hunger and thirst at bay.

Although Skord realised that his end would be nigh after robbing the church, his respect for Baldesjor had grown greater than it had been before. They did not often look at each other on the way down the hill. When they did, the glances were swift and wary. Both knew that small talk had come to an end between them.

They arrived in the church village late in the afternoon. They heard the bells toll and smelled burning leaves. The farmers were already lighting fires to ward off all the spirits that came to life on these holy and dangerous nights. Because they were farmers and sensible people, they took the opportunity to burn all kinds of old rubbish.

The bandits stopped high up on the wooded hillside above the church. Skord and Ficke were sent on to spy out the land and listen. On their return, they told of monks howling away inside the church. The praying and worshipping had been going on for hours, but by now they had all left the church and locked the gate.

The outlaws rode on a bit further. They halted under the fir trees near the church, and all of them made the sign of the cross over and over again. Very quietly, they unfolded the ladders, which still caused the horses to shy away.

The spring night was getting darker, and in the fields the bonfires were dying down. The farms below the church hill had become silent. At times a dog would start barking and encourage a few more. But the curs became less and less willing to keep guard and bark as the night deepened, full of the smells of smoke from burning leaves and of earth not yet settled after the thaw.

They waited for another hour or so, until there were no sounds other than the calling of night birds in the forest. This was the darkest hour. It was as if the bare-branched birch trees were moving about in the gloaming. Everything looked uncertain. Focused on for long enough, even the grey stone church seemed to float and change shape.

Finally Haquin gave the sign, a long whistling noise like the mewing of an owl. Skord started running down towards the church, together with Ficke and Torn, who were carrying the ladder between them. The night seemed too light. Climbing the wall he would show up like a dazed spider on crisp snow.

When the two outlaws had joined up the parts of the ladder and raised it, the angle looked dangerously steep. Even so, it did not quite reach the loophole. He started climbing slowly to test it. As he got higher up, his speed increased. The rungs creaked and gave under his feet. When he got hold of the rough edge of the opening and started to haul himself upwards, he could hear the ladder slide away. Ficke and Torn had been so quick that for a few moments,

Skord was hanging from the edge of loophole without any support for his feet. He whistled an owl noise as a warning, and when he felt for it, the ladder was back in place. He could gain purchase with his feet and push himself up towards the narrow slit in the stone. At once, the ladder rattled away from under him.

Haquin had decided that it would be put up again only when Skord had finished in there. The night was too light to let the ladder stand. The Uppsala soldiers might be keeping watch.

He hung on like a tree fungus. The opening was not covered by a skin. He began squeezing through, feet first, and noticed the smell inside the church, a heavy odour of candles which had been guttering and gone out.

He had to unwind the long rope and attach the hook while he was still perched there with the upper part of his body outside the loophole. Then he began pushing his way through. For a while he had to contemplate the possible consequences of getting stuck, complete with the bags and the long rope with a hook. But he twisted and turned his body against the rough surface of the wall, and in the end got through and slid downwards, clinging to the rope.

The stagnant smoke from the wax candles had been at its thickest under the ceiling. As he hauled himself down, he entered a chilly darkness composed of a mixture of many smells. He moved cautiously, and stopped to listen now and then. But no breathing could be heard; no one had stayed on his knees, begging the god to show himself in the dark church.

The rope ended well above the floor, and he had to let go of it. The soles of his feet hurt as they hit the stone floor. He hoped the end of the rope would not be out of his reach. It seemed there were one or two things about the outlaws' plans that had not been properly thought out.

He heard rattling and scratching noises. He listened and the darkness echoed in his ears. Were the noises made by rats? Or did their god move about in the church?

They called him God the Father. But then, they gave bears names like Golden Snout and Dear Honey-Paw. Skord hid his face in his sleeve to cleanse his nostrils of any old scents, and then he sniffed the cold air again. Did it smell of wild animals?

For as long as the darkness lasted he could do nothing but curl up around his own warmth and wait. Maybe he slept for a while. When his eyes opened, the church was filled with a grey light and hanging there, high up on the wall, was the huge god, his arms outstretched. Blood was running down his face and his eyes were sharp black and white. Skord screamed; it sounded feeble. The god stayed above him like a buzzard, ready to strike.

As it became lighter, the morning found him sitting still and stiff with fear. Then he saw the god for what it was – just a wooden figure. The image of the god. But deep inside him, in the muddy depths of his mind, the god lived. The god's splayed body was inside him and strove to join the image on the wall. I'll burst, Skord thought. Then he heard a cooing noise, hissing and bubbling like a kettle on the boil. The tune, rising and falling, was one Skord knew and felt at home with. It was the song of the black grouse, reaching him from the edge of a moor or maybe the bank of a tarn, still half covered by ice and snow. It came straight through the loopholes in the wall, down to where he was lying curled up on the floor. Courting black grouse were playing and burbling with lustfulness, dizzy from the blood rushing to their heads, their fluffy feathers padding their cocky bodies. He bit hard into the sleeve of his woollen vest to stop himself from giggling aloud at that familiar sound of an overwhelming excitement.

Then he peeped again at the wooden image, and it was hanging there as before, staring at him.

Come to think about it, who was this poor bastard? He had been tortured and then they made this image of him. They could not just have invented him out of nowhere – hell, no, they were certain to have hung some poor sod first, and then made a likeness.

He blasphemed some more and grimaced towards the figure on the wall before starting to scout around.

He had never before been in a room as large as this. The stone walls were giving off cold. By this time in the morning it smelled more of paint and lime wash than wax candles. The vaults were touching tip to tip like stars, and were edged with spiky leaves, twisting vines and cucumber flowers. People wandered about dressed in bright clothes, painted on the walls as if they had been pressed onto them in the middle of their busy lives.

He could not see any silver chalices or gold-embroidered vestments, but supposed that they must be hidden somewhere behind the chancel screen. Now that he had revived, he felt he knew his way about. After all, he had been inside a church before, though that was long ago and its walls had been made of tar-coated timbers.

Now that he had calmed down, he recognised Jesus Christ. Christ had been nailed to a cross by Jewish people. He was stuck, no getting away from that. His eyes had been painted in, and so had the rest of his body. His eyes were white paint with round black discs in the middle. There were no precious stones set into his eye sockets. There was no gold crown to take off his head. They had wound a branch covered in thorns round the top of his head, and each thorn was like a coarse nail. No such diabolical thorn bush grew in Skule forest.

Next, Skord walked across the bare floor and opened the door to the chancel screen. It was decorated with carved figures and leafy vines. He was struck by a smell of decaying cloth, but did not find any gleaming silver or glittering precious stones. The altar was covered by a stiff linen cloth reaching all the way down to the floor. The candlesticks were wrought iron, rusty and brimming with cold wax.

Their costly things must be locked into chests, he thought. He was sure to be able to deal with the locks. He always carried a bunch of bent and straight picks on his belt. But he saw no chests when he stepped into the small stone-walled chamber next to the chancel. There was a wall cupboard, but it was not locked. Opening it, he found a pewter mug and plate, a bread box and a jug. He tested the contents with his finger and licked it. Wine. Sweet wine. Almost certainly sweetened with honey.

He found another cupboard behind the door. It contained vestments, two of them, made from dyed wool and with large crosses embroidered on the front and back. No gold thread had been used. Skord had come across Lapps with tunics more handsomely embroidered. There was nothing else in the room, apart from a broom and a rough comb in a pewter handbasin.

He thought of the men who waited for him outside, frozen and damned. Had they really believed their own stories, when they raved about the treasures hidden inside the new stone church? Or had they known in their heart of hearts that no cartloads of silver were likely to reach the border of the forest?

But he realised that there was something they were wanting from in here, something so precious that they risked their lives to get it. Maybe they did not even know what it was. And if he came back empty-handed, what would they do to him?

They were rapists and killers, but still they believed in mercy, or perhaps miracles. Standing there freezing at the edge of the forest, they believed the way children believe in the wet-nurse's teat. Perhaps it would come in the shape of a silver chalice in a sack. Our Good Father with the Honey-Paws would give them something at last.

They would not cease believing if he came out and told them of the empty eye-sockets of the wild beast who was kept in here. They would just wring the neck of the bearer of bad news.

Skord wandered about in the nave but found nothing to appease them with. By now it was light under the star-shaped vaults, and he still walked about as if in a dream, getting later and later. He felt bound by a spell – even though he might not have long to live once he got out of this large stone coffin. And he needed a piss. Standing in the darkest corner and shaking off the last drops, he heard people talking outside the church door. He leaped for the rope, barely grabbed hold of it and caused it to swing away from the wall in an arch. After a few pulls, the hook worked itself loose and fell to the floor with a rattle. As he picked up the coiled rope in his arms and stumbled away, he could hear the key turn in the lock.

He ran towards the vestry but realised that when they came in, he would be stuck in there like a fox in a trap. Just as he heard the creaking noise of the door swinging open, he lifted a corner of the altar cloth. Underneath was a shelf mortared into the wall. He crawled in under it, and tried to straighten the stiff linen cloth to make the front look untouched.

Listening, he could not work out how many people had come in. They were clomping about on thick wooden soles. Footsteps and voices were echoing and bouncing up under the vaults, and one quarrelsome voice could be heard above the rest. Brooms whooshed over the floor, buckets rattled. Now a broom got so close that the altar cloth moved.

In that moment he felt in his whole body that someone was

travelling through the clear spring morning air outside. It had to be a raven. It soared in the air currents.

He took on the shape of a raven.

He could do nothing else.

High up there the wind from the hillside forests was moving swiftly. Its flow was cool, and beneath him sounded the deep notes of the firs. The wind sifted through their branches, and they waved like huge gills and sang in the sea of cold air. He could no longer smell the smoke from burning leaves, the soil, the cow dung or the light-brown water which was rushing from the thawing snow into the ditches. He was high above everything that reeked, everything that itched and burned and stung.

He was the raven.

Nobody saw the dark firs. Nobody watched the raven soar. Nobody heard the rustling of his wings. The forest stayed silent, for hundreds of mornings or maybe thousands, always hidden by dense raw mists.

He could fly until his wings tore. He could soar so high that feathers and flesh and bones fell away. He could travel naked high up under the blue skies.

He was no one, seen by no one.

When he came back down, he was as badly off as before. This was a distressing state to be in, silly and annoying. He was overcome by a sudden hatred of the stone coffin that imprisoned his body. Muttering between his strong, sharp teeth, he spoke curses to make it fall down. He cursed 'Ax, kax and red ants', but it stayed in one piece. He said spells to bring fire and thunderstorms and snakes rotting in holes under the stone foundations, and rats in the woodwork and among the bits of cloth. The church did not even creak.

Voices were still rising towards the stone vaults, but now they were singing. The smell of incense and wax candles reached him. They had started praying to the god who wore branches of a thorny shrub on his head. The one thing comforting Skord in his shame and anger was that there was no response to their spells either. The god did not answer. Skord was prepared to bet his life the god was just hanging there under the ceiling, as before. Soon they would be in the same hungover frame of mind as he had been in after his raven flight, and so be especially unpleasant when they found him.

But as they carried on speaking and singing in the sacred language, his anger and fear faded. The language came back to him, and his lips started forming the words. Rising among the living voices he heard the voice of Magister Ragvaldus Ovidi and somehow he seemed to glimpse the Magister's face behind all the faces he had seen, coarse and heavy, sharp and worn. But that face was blurred, as if lit by a flickering light. This pained him. Usually he ran away from painful things as fast as he could. This time, though, he was stuck under the stone shelf. The sacred language filled him with delight and tormented him at the same time.

'Salve caput cruentatum,' they sang.

Then one of the voices read a long story. One he had never heard before. Or had he? Maybe during the time when he spoke Latin as a starling does, thoughtlessly and unknowingly?

They were saying that some men had been strung up to die. They had tied them to wooden crosses.

They knew a thing or two about lures and gins, these people who could speak the sacred language; they knew about breaking bodies on wheels, gallows, snares, traps and crosses. They sounded like angels now. But the things they knew about breaking bones, cracking skulls and knocking teeth from jaws, about flayed bodies, crushed paws, chopped-off tails and wounds brimming with blood.

Two of the strung-up men were outlaws. The third was someone who had done nothing wrong. He hung on the cross anyway. They would say it was just a mistake. But what kind of mistake was it when the wrong one is trapped? They must have known well enough whom they wanted when they set up the trap.

One of the outlaws used strong language. He sounded like Haquin. His position was not very good. One might say, this was the end of him. But even here, out on the town dump, he found someone who was beneath him, some poor bastard.

He could not reach him with his hard fists because they were nailed down. But he kept talking away, tough, wild talk. He was saying that since the third one was meant to know strong spells, this was the time for him to practise his art and get off the executioner's cross.

But the third one said nothing at all.

Then there was the other bad man, also strung up and nailed down. He was like most outlaws, chatty and jovial. He must have murdered and tortured too, but surely more from absentminded-ness or by accident. Probably he would have felt self-disgust at times. He said that nothing could be gained by harassing the third one. That one was suffering unjustly, and so would feel worse about the pain. It was quite different for the pair of them, hanging there on either side. When their bones creaked, there was a meaning in it, and when a tendon tore, this was how a book stated it should be. But the third one, the soothsayer, had no such support and enlightenment.

Skord began to feel quite sick. The third one, he now heard, was promising the chatterer a stay in paradise.

Maybe there had better be another raven flight.

By now he would just as soon go tumbling into the piled-up ice of hell if it meant getting out of this place. He would have flown into the eye of a firestorm if only he could take off, away from all this. If only he had been able to think, speak, remember another language than this, be it sacred or secular, squeak or howl, if only he could detach himself from this and shut off his ears as the shutters are pulled on cattle sheds at night, and put out his mind as the fire on the hearth is doused when the day comes to an end. But he was stuck.

They started singing again.

'Rosa rorans bonitatem,' they sang. Grinding his teeth, he sang along from his place under the altar. He could do nothing else.

He woke up at the very first light. The air inside the church was chilly again and heavy with the odour of candles and incense. Rats looking for crumbs were climbing up the stiff linen folds of the altar cloth. He could hear the puffs of air through their nostrils.

He was hungry and thirsty. He had been hiding in the church for one night, one day and one more night. By now Haquin must have taken his band of followers back up into Skule. But just as certain was that he would have ordered someone to stay behind to catch Skord if he tried to slip out of his lair. Baldesjor?

He lifted the cloth and sniffed the air in the cold empty church. Next, he crawled out and went into the vestry. He ate of the bread in the cupboard and drank water from the ewer placed on a stool next to a basin.

When he went back, the nave was filled with a light so strong that it seemed to have pushed its way in between the stones. It was the sun, lifting the church out of dust and earth. He could hear the gurgling of the black grouse far away, and a chorus of voices from the sky over the forest. He realised that the songbirds had returned from the bottom of the sea and the islands of paradise. Their song was rippling like water in a stream. He could not stay silent, but had to join in by mimicking. He whistled like a starling and chattered like a chaffinch. The delicate twittering and trilling of the grey wagtail came out from between his teeth, and then he chirruped like redwing.

The blood went to his head and roared in his ears. He gave way to an impulse to sing even more loudly, and sang in the sacred language about the rose dripping with goodness.

He heard people coming in, and when he had crawled back in under the altar cloth he had to bite on the coils of rope under his head. Otherwise songs and speech and whistles would have got out. He wanted to boom with the church bells and read the Mass with the priest. He wanted to mumble and pray and sing praises and be full of holiness – there was nothing else for it! There was no reason for his being in this world except to join in with speech and songs. He would have mimicked a creaking door or a farting horse just to be allowed to make a noise. If only he were allowed to praise this creation, now glowing red from the heat of the sun.

In the end, a great tiredness descended on him. He fell asleep on his coil of rope. When he woke he was alone again and his plight was very clear to him. The outlaws would break his neck when he came out empty-handed. They would leave the job to the mean and bad-tempered Baldesjor, who would complete his handiwork with a certain glee. Should the priests find him, the soldiers would get him, rope, hook, lock-picks and all.

Curled up under the altar and listening to their steps and voices, he had felt a strong desire to get a haircut, speak the sacred language and use a hand towel to dry himself. It came to his mind that there were ways of opening a door which did not involve kicking it.

If only he knew what his fate would be, whether the wretched priests would let the soldiers take him away, or whether he was to fall into the hands of the outlaws, then he could have tried to make the best of it. But he did not know. The stone walls remained silent about his future. There was not even a night bird foretelling with its cries what would be. All was silent.

And then he remembered that there was a way of finding out, and that he had it with him. He had been warned not to use it too often and so far he had not tried it at all. But now he felt his way around the vestry looking for a piece of candle. He lit it from a few embers glowing in a dish they had left behind. Then he sat down on the floor and pulled out from under his clothes the small parcel he had been carrying next to his skin, tightly wrapped in a silk cloth.

He unravelled the thin material and took out the cards he had been given by La Guapa before she died. First he looked for his own card. It was the Fool. He put it on the stone floor in front of him and, with closed eyes, shuffled the rest of the cards. Above the Fool he put down the cards representing his Now. Sure enough, there was the Tower, a building made from heavy blocks of stone. It cheered him a little to think that it was to fall down, but the cards told him nothing about when it was to happen. He carried on, putting down the cards for What Has Been and What Will Be and the Nearest Future. Blindly he put down three cards, each one below the previous one. These would define the whole set and end his speculations.

Just then the candle guttered and died in a small pool of tallow. He could not remember where he had put the dish of embers and had to crawl around on the floor, feeling with his hands. In the end, he got the candle lit again. But something had moved the cards about. The Fool with the barking dog at his heels was no longer in the centre. The Chariot was the central card now.

He felt his heart beating strongly. Whose finger had touched the cards in the darkness? Who was standing there among the shadows intervening in his game?

The young man was sitting in the Chariot without reins and though he did not urge the horses on, it went like the wind!

He realised he was that young man, and things were going to start moving. There would be thundering wheels and hammering hooves and capes flapping and dust whirling and hens scattering all around and gaping mouths and barking dogs and mud splattering high up in the air! Half choked with fear and joy he turned over the blind cards and found Emperor and Pope, saw the Wheel of Fortune and the grinning monkeys which made the wheel turn. Quickly he put them down again, because he did not want to know all of it. This was enough. He was on his way. A bit closer to all that was powerful and radiant, noisy and large. Closer to the world, straight into it!

Now he put out the candle and gathered the cards into a tight, silent bundle. He tied them up and put them close to his brown skin.

When the first light pierced the narrow slits in the stone walls, he walked round the great nave and looked for cracks in which he could hide the lock-picks and the hook.

Helped by soldiers from Uppsala, at Easter-time the farmers trapped a band of outlaws to the south of the forest. Two were taken alive, and locked into a stone-lined cellar to bide the time until their executions on the next great holy day.

An old woman, used to helping with this and that, gave them water and things to eat so that they would survive until their day arrived. She never touched the bars across the cellar door and gave them what they needed through a hatch. Every time she opened it, abuse came pouring out. It was the one called Haquin who gave vent to these foul blasts. Not even the knowledge of what awaited him stopped his cursing. The other one was quiet most of the time, but would ask questions when Haquin's breath failed him. His name was Baldesjor; at least, that was what they called him. He had lost his name once in a stone shepherd's hut on a flowering island far away in the sea. Now he owned only his life, and he wanted to know when he was to lose it and how it was to be done.

For the two men in the darkness of the cellar, the voice of the old woman was like having a bucketful of slops thrown through the hatch as it opened each morning. Soon they knew all there was to know about this village by the sea, visited by people riding along the coast or coming in boats to load up with skins and salted fish. She told them that the priests and monks from Uppsala had found a boy looking for asylum in the church at Easter-time. This was the boy who had got away from the band of outlaws, she said. On hearing that, Haquin swore and tried to spit upwards through the hatch. Baldesjor asked if the runaway had been hanged or beheaded.

But the woman said they had given him a haircut and new clothes to wear and food to eat. Although he was starving, he had only eaten of the white porridge, which showed how refined he was. But then he would be, as the son of a Stockholm merchant and used to living as a gentleman's son before he was taken. He had described how the outlaws had brought him all the way to Skule and amused themselves by such things as chopping off his little finger.

At that, Haquin said the boy was a thieving wretch and the worst crook of them all. 'Is that so?' said the woman. 'Then how come the boy knew how to speak Latin and an even more outlandish language called Italian, and could also read from a book like an angel of God? And besides he was ever so dainty and good-looking and cheerful.' She had herself chucked him under the chin when they brought him to the bath-house to be scrubbed and washed.

Haquin kept cursing and the woman kept talking. But Baldesjor was quiet.

He was thinking about dying. He also recalled everything that he had told the boy. It was such a lot and so childish and shaming that he could not work out what it meant to him. During the days that remained for them, he grew more and more silent. He did not feel any great terror, and his sense of shame too seemed to dissolve and vanish towards the end. He started forgetting. All that had burned and stung, as well as all that had soothed and healed, disappeared, as did the spots of light he had seen at first in the darkness of the cellar. He reflected on the fact that someone out there knew what his life had been like. There was someone he had told. Then he heard a saw cutting into new wood, and blows of a hammer and the creaking of tackles and pulleys. Skilfully, people out there were constructing the apparatus for breaking his neck. He was finished.

So it was, like a bird, a leaf, a flute and a stream which calls, trembles, lights, plays and flows one day, but by the next day has its neck wrung, has faded, gone out, been broken and dried out, so was it with him who had once lived.

The Live Gold

Nicolaus Bosonius had an oven in a room right at the back of his house. A smoke-hole was open to the sky. But people said there was another hole, dug out under the oven and reaching straight into the nether world. Blasts from down there made the contents of his cauldrons glow with white heat. Bosonius was making gold.

A young man called Kopp, the gold-maker's apprentice, had recruited Skord. They had met earlier without speaking to each other, although Kopp had been stealing looks at the stump on Skord's left hand. Skord was often hanging about the taverns near the Cathedral steps which smelled of dried fish and sour ale and of dog piss which had soaked into the door frames.

Kopp had wanted him to get jackdaws' eggs and metal from church bells. Or he wanted hair from a particular cadaver, or blood from somebody with red hair. He handed over glass bottles to be filled with worms or creatures called basilisks. But Skord refused when it came to toad stones. To kill toads and scratch their brains out in order to find a stone as rare as a pearl in a river mussel – this was too much, and he refused.

He had observed a groom called Johannes, who was working for Bosonius, come carrying sacks full of wriggling things. He had often stood on the other side of the street watching the gateway leading into the house of the wizard. Kopp had been boasting about his master, and about how well he himself got on in the house, how trusted he was and how indispensable.

But that was then. By now it was hard to say which of the two was more familiar with the household. Skord lay in the warmth radiating from the oven in the innermost part of the house, the part he had so desperately wanted to see. And there was no doubt about it, this was no ordinary baker's oven; it was Athanor that warmed his backside.

He could hear hooves and carriage wheels rumbling past outside. The whole house was a hive of activity, and Skord would try to get away if there was a risk of getting caught up in it. The cabbage patch was on the slope down towards the river. On the bank they had built a wash-house where Bosonius's wife kept two maids busy boiling clothes in ash-leach and then slapping them clean in the river water, which was very fast-moving so close to the weir. The wife was called Mareta Fontelia. She was the daughter of a priest from the archbishop's diocese and had grown up far away on the flat fields round the city. As part of her dowry, she had a piece of farmland near Vaksala, which Johannes would plough with the help of an old brown gelding. The courtyard of the house was guarded by a sleepy but short-tempered dog called Peliel.

Most people spoke of Bosonius as Old Bos or Bosen. He was built like an ox, heavy but good-natured. The household was made up of the Old Ox himself, his wife Mareta, their only child at home, who was a daughter called Aurelia, Kopp, Johannes, the maids Kisten and Lissa, Peliel, the gelding Troy, two ewes and their lambs, hens, a couple of pigs and assorted cats, one of which had been given to Aurelia when she was little and named Felicula by Bosonius. Recently they had been joined by a young man called Skord.

There was one place in the house where noise was forbidden. That was the innermost room, which at first Skord had mistakenly thought of as the Labororatorium. It was in this large room that Bosonius worked and prayed. He was no wizard. That was just common gossip. He was a scholar and worked in the science called Chymistry. It was not even true that he was looking for gold, or at least not the ordinary shiny substance – aurum vulgi. He was looking for lapis invisibilitatis.

At first Skord thought this must be a stone that could be put in a pocket or shoe and make you invisible. He soon learned differently.

The laboratory was a large room stretching through two floors in the centre of the house. A gallery, reached by a rickety staircase, ran the length of one of the long walls. Bosonius kept his books up there and liked studying in the warmth close to the ceiling.

Kopp, the apprentice, was actually called Lasse Johansson, but had taken his new name because it sounded like that of the doctor who took care of the King's father. For a short time he had been in service in the house of Dr Theophrastus – or so he said. He dreamed of becoming a famous medical man himself.

Skord found Bosen's work – that is, to prepare live gold – pleasing but soporific. One's life progressed in a solemn circular path, ruled by thought and speculation. Somehow, the profundities of the eternal enigmas seemed endlessly comforting, especially in the winter. They lived in a closed and sealed vessel, carrying out their appointed tasks. Kopp pounded, blended, pulverised and kept the fire stoked. Bosonius did the thinking. Kopp also roasted, ground or dried herbs, activities which Bosonius found pointless. However, Mareta Fontelia encouraged these because she could sell the powders and distilled essences as medicine.

The planetary spirits were also supposed to assist Bosonius, but Aratron, Bethor, Phaleg, Och, Hagith, Ophiel and Phul seemed to be as lazy and absent-minded as Skord. He spent most of the time lying on his back in front of the oven. Only Kopp was dutiful and keen. He was preparing for the Great Work, but also for the day when he would become a famous doctor and nobody would notice his knobbly knees and protruding ears.

Uppsala was large and many people lived there. It provided homes for mice and squirrels, hares in the cabbage patches, cows, horses, troublesome goats, sheep, hens, barking dogs, cats, sparrows, hedgehogs under the sheds, bears in their pit next to the castle, pretty caged birds, a hairless dog from China, and a donkey, doves and ordinary pigeons, fat rats with long tails which preferred the mill down by the river, pigs rooting in the muck of the streets with powerful snouts, jackdaws in the Cathedral tower, crows, finches, tits, passerines and people, people, people.

The city was a dense mass of people and animals, stone and timber. Water voles, rats and mice lived in the lowermost regions. They slipped between the riverbank stones round the bases of the bridgeheads, and found nesting places in the hollows round the poles supporting the houses. When the fires were damped down on the hearths, they found their way up into the houses, looking for crumbs and rinds. But their true home was in the darkness between stones. There they felt their way about with trembling whiskers, and sensed from the smell of bloodstains where they should not go. They turned the darkness to tepid warmth, like milk from worn teats, and slept their light, twitching sleep curled up close to each other. To them, the city was well arranged. Showers of crumbs rained down from above into their rustling darkness.

The cats slept one layer up. Many of them were so fat and lazy they could not be bothered to open their eyes when they heard the scraping of rat claws. If they were suitably privileged, their share of the great cake meant warm hearths, bolsters in beds and sunny window seats. Others of their kind sneaked about the sheds and had to look after themselves as best they could. Hunger made them brave enough to bite through the necks of the biggest voles.

Of the people in the Bosonius household, Skord liked speaking to Aurelia, the daughter of the house, best of all. She was five years old when he joined them. Her father took careful note of the birthdays of his daughters and worked out a new prognostication for each year. When he realised how conversant Skord was with Latin, he put a copy of Fibel's Latin textbook in his hand and gave him the task of teaching the girl. She found learning easy and did not have to be made to study. Often they went down to the cabbage patch or the riverbank to read, but they also took pleasure in working without a book. The bumblebees hummed in the mat of clover and the swallows dived, piping and whistling.

When Aurelia heard the lamb answer to the bleating of the tethered ewe, she would call out, 'Agnus balat!' And when the cloud of jackdaws swarmed over the Cathedral tower in the evening, back from the fields round the city, she would point at them and say, 'Cornix cornicatur.'

She liked listening to his stories of the animals living in Uppsala. She felt tenderness, amazement, admiration, even respect for them, and told him so. He described the subterranean city of the rats. He told her of the reindeer with patchy worn pelts and bad coughs which had been brought from some distant and terrible place in the north for the King's coronation, of a donkey which had also died of a cough, and of the badgers and otters which lived by the river and could be heard chattering near the rapids in winter. It was a delight to her, even once she had become an adult, to hear of the hare with silken fur kept for the Polish Queen to stroke, for the sake of her freezing hands.

Aurelia saw nothing odd in the fact that Skord would take on the shape of a bird or a dog, and was not afraid to find his lifeless body in the bed when he had entered under the fur of the guard dog. Peliel was a tough, shaggy dog, who slept most of the time, and whose task consisted of barking every time somebody came through the archway into the courtyard. Aurelia saw with her own eyes how he reacted when Skord's soul flitted into his mind. He threw off his dull guard-dog existence. His neck stiffened, his fur grew glossy, his eyes gleamed and his lips drew back to reveal yellow rows of teeth.

Aurelia would crouch on the flagstones in the yard and slowly stroke his back. He licked her hand, but carelessly, leaving a long dribble of saliva, because he was in a hurry. He rose and walked on stiffening legs and with lowered head out of the Bosonius yard.

Skord could tell her what he had been up to when he returned, tired out and splattered with mud well above his belly. But he did not tell the whole story. There was something about Peliel that Skord could not control, a restless lust when the scent of a bitch in heat drifted past. Then Skord's chosen body jumped and mated with curved back. It annoyed him that he could not rule the body of the dog at these times, and he did not care to tell Aurelia of his weakness.

At times he considered the risks he took by allowing a child, who might be thoughtless and even cruel, to know that he could take on the shape of Peliel. But he felt that he was not in any real danger. And if the girl told of his ability to change shape, the adults would say it was childish play. All fantasy.

They knew that a single suckerfish stuck to the bottom of a great ship could bring it to a halt in mid-ocean, but they did not know that his thoughts could possess Peliel, burning like a flame behind the dull pane of a horn lamp. But the thoughts had to be pure. His soul must not enclose other things when he used it, and so he had to abandon his own dormant body when he entered the body of the dog. After Peliel had run out of the courtyard Aurelia had gone to pat Skord's hand, but it had been cold and lifeless. Sometimes he was fearful that the dog would hurt or violate the girl. He aroused in Peliel something that did not exist in the lazy guard dog, or in himself, the intruder inside the body of the dog. Somehow, it had to do with the essence of a nameless dog, something burning and impossible to extinguish or to explain. It could lead to something they would kill him for, like a bite or an attack.

But Aurelia remained trusting and unthinking. It was Skord who had to bear the pain of knowing this dangerous possibility. This awareness finally made him say that Peliel was too tired to run about, however fiery the soul that drove him. Besides, the years had gone by. The guard dog had lost his teeth and slept so heavily that a servant offered to get rid of him. He was saved for Aurelias's sake, but they got a new guard dog at the gate, an easily excited young hound, which the soul of Skord would have nothing to do with.

Athanor was not like ordinary ovens. When it was not alight, the house of Bosonius was gripped by a sense of desolation and waiting. As it slowly warmed up, the heart of the house started beating. The oven was shaped like an egg and very ingeniously constructed, with many hatches and flues built into the wall to get rid of smoke and fumes. The body of the oven was shaped like a small domed tower.

Few had been allowed to see it. It was not made to heat cauldrons. Skord was pleased that early on, he had not told Kopp of how he imagined gold was made.

The lower part of Athanor was a covered hearth with a hollow shaped to fit a large fireproof vessel. The vessel had feet which fitted into three sockets in the walls of the tower. It was this vessel that formed the dome of the oven – the top of the egg. It had a cover pierced by a hole. You could lift it and look down into the vessel. A fire could be lit inside it as well, with a tripod placed over the flames. When the Great Work was to begin, a pan full of water and containing the sealed glass flask would be put on the tripod. The water would be brought to boil, the neck of the flask and its sealed-in top protruding through the hole in the lid.

Athanor was the heart of the house. They all came alive in its glow. The sound of the roaring fire inside it made them dizzy and fearful, expecting great events. The maids were forbidden to enter the laboratory, and had been heard many a time to declare that they dared not and never would, if their lives depended on it. Even so, when Athanor was lit, their voices too grew louder and their footsteps more lively. Their beaters whirled against the wet linen, and they grew stronger than they had been during the waiting and desolation of the winter days.

The sun and Athanor were of a kind. The heart of the heavens also glowed with internal fire. The world of the stars revolved round the Earth in the same way as the outermost wheels in the great cathedral clock. But the mechanism inside the clock depended on clicking cogwheels and turning screws. This was just a stiff and jerky imitation of the fire-powered heavenly machinery.

Skord knew what the insides of the clock looked like, because he had run errands for the men building the great clock. He had watched a learned monk bent over his drawings, silently handing him food and drink in covered vessels from the booths at the foot of the cathedral steps. Bosonius knew something of this, worse luck. One day he had asked, 'Skord, it must have been your grandfather who worked for Master Peter from Vadstena when the clock was built, wasn't it?'

'My grandfather . . . '

Skord played for time while he calculated. The clock had an inner wheel to measure the breathlessly brief moments between sunset and sunrise, between the lighting and dousing of fires, and an outer one, with Earth at its hub, for the slow revolutions of the stars. In the same way, Skord had to calculate with short and long units of time whenever he was forced to give an account of his life. This was something he always tried to avoid.

'My grandfather – yes,' he said. 'Though he was very old.'

Bosen's pale watery eyes blinked as he looked at Skord. 'No, he was a young man.'

'Oh, yes, when he worked for Master Peder Astronomicus! But he got to be very old. My father did, too.'

Bosen shook his head, his eyes were rheumy.

'Before I was born!' Skord's heart was thumping.

'Well, there you are,' Bosonius said. 'Perhaps it was somebody else. It was recorded that his baptismal name was Christian, and Skord his second name, and that he drowned below the first weir one Christmas Night, two years before the clock was completed.'

It was recorded . . . where? Who had scribbled his name, who had taken the trouble to scratch signs with ink that would capture him in men's minds? Was it Master Peder himself? What was it for, all this writing and shuffling of papers people got up to nowadays?

'I have no idea,' Skord said. 'It's so easy to get things wrong in writing. Especially if you're talking at the same time.'

He bent closer to his own writing materials and mumbled as he wrote, 'Sixteen ounces vitriol, eight ounces nitrium purum to be pounded to pieces in a mortar . . . mixed . . . purified by fire within an iron . . . vessel . . . the remainder to be dissolved in sixty-four ounces warm spring water . . . to inter . . . act . . . for ten days. To be filtered . . . and sixteen ounces of powdered raw tartar added.'

The learned man seemed enthralled by the prescription. Perhaps it held pleasant memories for him.

'A fine arcanum!' he sighed. 'Liquor addicus. What do you call it?'

'Tartaric water,' Skord said, and carried on printing the letters. He tried hard to look busy and a little daft. He was far from stupid, but could be thoughtless. He had not thought much of the world of the stars as he had once seen it portrayed in the great clock. The images had been moved by cogs, pinions, wheels and gudgeons. He had never let his mind dwell on the sun and its unborn infant, the live gold in the interior of the Earth. But it was impossible to be with Dr Bosonius and not learn. Every day, he heard talk of the names and positions of the configurations of the stars, the sparkling houses of the zodiac, and the entrances and exits of each planet. In his turn, Skord instructed Aurelia, and would at times even start by using a gruff voice, sounding just like the Doctor. But it never took long before the words flew easily between them.

Down by the river, he showed her the great water-wheel and told her how the world of the stars turned in the same way, though driven by fire. The movement of the stars was in one direction only, from east to west. And was that not a miracle in its own right? The stars might have tumbled like sparks above a bonfire. But they did not. Nor did they rest, ever. They did not sleep or eat – they were nourished by fire. And they never wobbled in their course. The fiery bodies of the heavens wandered within the nine spheres. The highest sphere was crystalline. Furthest down, closest to the dark Earth, the paths of the planets mimicked the circuits of the stars.

Moreover, there were one thousand four hundred and twenty fixed stars. This is a very great number. If Aurelia looked under a fir tree in the forest she would see lots of little 'ones' underneath it.

Each 'one' is a needle, and the number of dropped needles under a large fir tree is very great, almost impossible to think of.

The signs of the zodiac were clearly drawn in the sky. A huge lion gaped to swallow the sun. But there was no danger: she was quite safe resting there. There was also a ram, a powerful ox, and the crab which had befriended the moon.

Indeed, the stars formed vast signs up there. They had been put into place by a giant hand. There were many ways to read the sky signs. The names of the angels, repeated above in Hebrew characters, were also written in the stars. It was thanks to this holy, almost indecipherable text and to the great learning of Dr Bosonius, who knew the Cabbala, Gematria and Notaricon, that Skord had been allowed to stay in the house. There were in fact secrets linked to his name. Whispering, he spoke to Aurelia of the gifts and insights that had been passed on to her father. These came from the Angel Raziel, and from Yetzirah, Zohar and other learned men of very long ago. The heads of these scholars were as full of Hebrew characters, magic squares and numbers as a simple man's head is full of nits and bugs. Aurelia had poked her finger up her nose but then it stopped moving, because she had become so absorbed by what he was saying.

'You have a good head for learning,' Skord said and tapped her round forehead. 'Every time your father has drawn up your prognostication he has discovered that you will be just as learned as Hypatia of Alexandria. I'll tell you about her some other time, and how they came to burn down the Temple and the great building which held all the books of Egypt and the rest of the world. Look at this, I'm going to write my name the way it is written in the sky.'

They had curled up on the edge of the river. He patted the bluish clay flat and with a stick wrote the Hebrew letters *Seen*, *Koof*, *Raish* and *Daleth*, which had caused Bosonius much deep thought.

'These are dangerous matters,' he said, looking fierce.

There was so much he wanted to tell Aurelia about. Crowding his mind, like a litter of baby toads in a pond, were all the things he was learning about while eating his porridge in the house of the Doctor. The ideas wanted to crawl out and leap about. One warm evening in August, he and Aurelia stepped out onto the gallery under the eaves into the humming, twittering, croaking dark lit by high stars. Could she sense their glow? Could they not be felt, like breaths or pulsations of the blood?

Human beings are made of the same stuff as the stars. Everything in the whole world has been created from the elements in the stars. Call it clay, call it iron or glass, blood or flesh. Liquid or vapour, moist or hard and sealed, or heavy like a sleeping stone.

Yes, the stones were asleep but would wake up one day. Blood was moist but would congeal. His blood, breath and warm persuasive voice, his kisses and chitchat with Felicula and Aurelia would turn to mineral crystals. And the branching crystals would form soil for flowers to grow in – sometime, a long time afterwards. Then his voice would be sensed again, but this time as a smell or a light dusting of pollen, as leaves playing in the wind and the light.

Mankind must open up to the light of the stars. But people stayed as heavy and closed as the sleeping cabbages in the household vegetable patch. They snuffled like the pigs in the barn. 'Covered in rind too tough for anything to get through,' Skord added, and Aurelia carried on lightly, as if passing a shuttlecock back to him, 'They are as blind as the fleas in Peliel's fur!'

'As deaf as the herrings in the barrel!'

'Slow-moving as weevils!'

'As idle as . . .'

'. . . as Skord, the dreaded Nail-Trimmer!'

'. . . as Aurelia, the Nose-Poker!'

Human beings were heads of cabbage, swine, fleas, herrings, arse-scratchers and lice-killers, but above them the stars breathed radiance and reached out to transform them. The stars desired to make people glow with light, become perfect and flourish like suns.

He had wanted to explain it all to Aurelia when they were standing there together in the dense, warm darkness. He wanted her to feel she had reached the axis around which the world spun; that she had come home to herself. Everything existing up there had its equivalent down here. Nothing was alien. There was no chill that could not be warmed by the returning sun, no filth that could not be incinerated in the sealed flask of the world, no disorder.

But he could not give her answers to her all questions. Why was the heart of the skies so full of fire? This he did not understand. Whence came the dizzy need to keep the spheres spinning, this desire for transformation?

All the equipment needed for the Great Work was set out on the shelves in the laboratory. There were glass vessels called helmets and others called violins. There were pelicans and egg-shaped flasks which could be sealed, mortars, alembics and retorts. There were bottles and jars arranged on the shelves and their labels might read crocus veneris, sweet earth vitriol, crystals of iron, balsamus spiritus nitri and sugar of alum. A dark-green bottle contained oil made from human bones.

Bosonius often sighed as he looked at the crowded shelves. In a laboratory the substances should be arranged in proper order. But as time had passed, things had piled up, and several labels had come off or become smudged by acid-stained thumbs and illegible.

The components needed for the creation of the world were also kept here. Using them, everything could be created anew, although higher and cleaner, more like the ideals in the stars. Water and fire. The active and essential Salt. Dangerous and unpredictable Mercury. Bosonius said these were the necessary things. Nothing else. He wanted to pull everything off the shelves and begin from the beginning, using the most elementary components. But Mareta Fontelia protected the bottles.

'We must live,' she said, and managed to sell whatever Kopp produced in the line of tinctures, powders and mixtures. After the death of the King, there was nobody willing to pay for the lengthy laboratory labours of Dr Bosonius.

In fact, everything was simple and most excellent. The sun, the live gold, wandered above. So did the moon, the silver of the skies. Following their own circuits and paths, there went their subordinates: Mercury with glittering and treacherous quicksilver, medium of transformation; Venus with red, warming copper; Saturn with melancholy lead; Jupiter with precious and powerful tin; Mars with sharp-edged iron. Aurum, argentum, cuprum, plumbum, stannum and ferrum – all consisted of unequal parts of sulphur and mercurium vivum.

'Gold,' Kopp told Skord in the beginning, while he was still the more knowledgeable of the two, 'consists of a lot of mercury and a small quantity of sulphur. Very small.'

But how small? This was the crucial question. And how make them act against each other? In the beginning, Kopp had whispered his secrets in confidence to Skord. His ears stuck out, and he pursed his lips so they looked like chanterelles. He insisted that one ounce of the Materia Prima or Stone of the Philosophers could bring about the combination of sulphur and mercury to form gold. He knew where the Materia Prima could be found, though he did not know enough to go straight to wherever it was. It was mined with great care from the rocks, a process known only to a very few. But there are mines, Kopp whispered.

The Philosophers' Stone was a different matter.

Were they not the same?

No, this one was different and acted like a creator or the agent of the Creator. It could not be mined. It was the ultimate goal of the work going on in the sealed vessel, in Athanor, in the house of Dr Bosonius.

This was how Skord learned that in the Doctor's laboratory, no one was trying to make gold. The quest was for the Philosophers' Stone.

Kopp had shown him the twice sealed box containing the Stone that was the Materia Prima. Later, when they had come to trust each other more, the seals were picked apart by Skord's nine nimble fingers. Khalid the Arab had said that the Stone glowed with all the colours the human eye could perceive. Reading the Doctor's books, Skord had learned that the great Raymond Lully had described it as red, like a carbuncle. According to the equally notable Helvetius, it was brilliant yellow. But then, Kopp knew that Dr Theophrastus had said that whatever glow had been evoked from the Stone by Lullian or Helvetian arts, it was in fact red. Dark red.

They poked and picked at the seals of the innermost box. But when they unfolded the cloth wrapped round the most secret of minerals, all Skord could see was a small pile of greyish-brown powdered stone. Maybe there was a shade of green. Was the Stone green? Did it come from the sea? Did it shine like the stones from the eyes of Hermes, the thrice great one?

They resealed the whole package and returned the box to the cupboard. It had made them feel as worn out as if they had stayed up all night and seen in the dull light of early morning. In fact, it was almost midday and the house was filling with the smell of boiled salt herring.

There were many descriptions of the secret life of the Stone on the bookshelves. They filled the long days of winter with calculations, new discoveries and dreams. The thoughts swarmed like jovial worker bees inside Kopp's head. He wanted to find out how to get to the secret mines and how to enter the passages into the mountain and how to extract the ore. He knew that the Stone was like an egg, cherished by the still warm veins inside the body of the Earth. Everything was alive in there. Gold was not a dead metal. The Stone was not grey and brown dust, not simple gravel. So far, greed had not picked the seams bare. The veins were still shot through with light, and in pulsating connection with the sun.

Slumbering during the long winter evenings, he dreamed of excavation machinery and transportation. The winter fantasies centred on an image of the mountain, criss-crossed by passages like holes in a large cheese. Blocks and pulleys groaned, ladders reached upwards to the heights and wooden buckets clattered against the walls.

Skord found his daydreams too were occupied by all that he learned and read in the house of Dr Bosonius. Indeed, such things even found their way into his sleep, which took up more than twelve hours each day during the darkest time of the year. There was no snow ground to dirty yellow slush under carriage wheels and horses' hooves in these dreams. Instead, he walked through grass scattered with dewdrops. Springs leaped from the foothills of the mountains, glittering in the light. He would fill his hand with water, and pat it on his face. Then he fell asleep within his sleep and slept differently and more deeply. During this, he experienced things which old Bosen would call *somnia a Deo missa*.

In his dream he woke and saw a dwarf sitting close to the spring. The dwarf's name was Peliel, and he carried a message from

Aurelia, the Queen of the Mountain. The message was that he should hurry to attend to her.

Peliel, the doorkeeper, led him into high-ceilinged halls where the water running down over the walls had hardened to sheets of rock crystal. There she was. But she was not lively, free and proud as he had expected. She seemed heavy, sitting there with parted legs and lowered eyes. He realised that she was pregnant. Her story of force and foulness reached him wordlessly, in the form of images. They stepped out of the rock face, and joined with her and with each other. The bent man with hard hands, Vulcan, was her father. He stood behind her all the time, coaxing and wheedling. He had made her take the bitter Aquarius, and her life became corroded by the infant she would give birth to and name Vitriola. He watched as Pyrander, aflame with passion, coupled with Castanea, her sister, who was almost as beautiful and serious as Aurelia. The children who emerged from the flames began dancing themselves to death. There was Rubicundus, red-hot roses on his cheeks, and Fugitiva, who ran from his embrace but could not escape. They disappeared together. He who had been conducted into the mountain in order to reach enlightenment, found wisdom and confidence in all the bitterness – how come, he did not know – and whispered to Aurelia that all would be well. Out of this confusion, this restlessly shifting enactment of scenes by creatures of fire and smokelike spectres, from all that was puzzling and corrosive in her life, would come perfection. She would have to endure an alien process, and only after encountering the unknown and deeply frightening would she become the person she was meant to be. Only then would she become Aurelia Aurea, the live, perfect gold.

The dreams brought melancholy and disquiet into the quiet scholarly comfort. The roof guttering began to overflow and frothy brown slush from the streets ran into the river. The river ran high and the strong current broke up the ice along the banks. At this time their calculations took on a new eagerness, and there was much anxious pacing up and down. Tension spread from the laboratory to other parts of the house. The maids became sharp-voiced and quarrelsome. There was a lot of rattling in the kitchen.

When the blanket of snow had disappeared from the meadows

up by Föret and the grass was growing taller, the sadness became mixed with delirium. Kopp and Skord ran there each morning to see how much taller the grass had grown, and whether there was dew on it.

The Great Work could not be started at any time except in the spring under the signs of Aries, Taurus and Gemini. Sometimes the favourable constellation occurred so early that there was no time to collect dew. Instead they had to use the dew kept in bottles from past years.

Kopp and Skord flipped the celestial water from the grass and collected it in a flat brass dish with a spout. When there was enough for it to flow, they fitted the spout into the neck of a bottle. Filling it was slow work. Toads burbled and croaked, blackbirds sang jubilantly as the boys ran barefoot in the grass, wet from morning dew.

The Work must not fail because the dew was not clean enough. It had to be distilled. The unearthly droplets fell into a bowl from the end of the bulbous part of the glass retort, which looked like a bird's head with a beak. Bosonius himself added Ignis Innaturalis, the active salt. But before starting, he sent his assistants out of the room. They were not allowed to see what went on inside the glass vessel. But Kopp knew enough to tell Skord that in there, the creation of the world was re-enacted. It was like a repetition of the miraculous six days. First there was mist and thick darkness above the surface of the water. This was when the first drop was falling. By the time the second drop hit the water, the flask would be lit by a sudden light. Later, as drop followed drop, all the events took place the way it had been at the beginning of Creation many thousand years ago.

Skord asked how he had come to know all this, and Kopp had to admit that he had read about it in one of the Master's books.

'But,' he said, 'people can't just think of something and then write it down, unless it has happened, or is happening or is going to happen.'

Skord pondered this for a while.

'I suppose you're right,' he said. 'But on the other hand, many things will happen, are happening or have happened which nobody has ever thought of or written about.'

They both thought about this, for so long that the ink dried in their pens. Kopp's mouth gaped; he looked like a perch. Then, just as he was getting ready to respond as if at a disputation among scholars, Mareta Fontelia entered, grabbed them by their ears and led them off to work the mortars.

Thoughts usually progressed in solemn circular paths inside their heads when they tried to work out what was going on in the Doctor's back room. In order to produce, or attempt to produce, the Philosophers' Stone, which would help in making the world a higher, purer place, more like a star – or, as Kopp said, to make gold – it was necessary to use the Materia Prima. A mortar made of agate and wrapped in a linen cloth stood on a shelf. At this stage, it was taken down and an ounce of the Materia Prima was pounded by Kopp in the most elaborate manner. He was watched by Bosonius, the Adeptus himself, and his famulus secundus who might by now have become the first, the primus. Kopp made short swift jabs with the pestle and then went on rubbing it against the agate base with a rolling movement. The Stone turned to powder.

Skord had no apparent task. He knew he had to be present because his name was written in the stars with sacred letters following the lines that join the stars to each other. When the learned Doctor had worked out the numerical values of the letters and carried out certain further calculations, he had been able to derive the numbers denoting the letters in the name of he who is thrice greatest. This was why Bosonius regarded the presence of Skord as likely to be propitious.

He took over the manipulation of the material in the mortar, and in measured and regular movements mixed it after the previous addition of Ignis Innaturalis with the distilled dew.

Bosen's white hand trembled a little as he poured the thick fluid into the special glass vessel. It was a bottle with a round base, not capable of free standing. It looked like an egg, but ended with a neck which could be fitted by a glass stopper. The Master next sealed the bottle, using a whitish molten substance poured from a crucible which Kopp had been heating in the fireplace. It filled the cleft between the stopper and the neck of the bottle, and hardened at once.

Kopp now produced a box full of hot ashes which he had been keeping warm next to the fireplace. Skord was allowed to hold the bottle while Bosen tested whether the ashes were at the right temperature. He decided that they were too hot, and stirred them with his white hands, rapidly turning them dark grey. Ash whirled through the air. When he thought the level of warmth was right he signed to Skord, who put the bottle in place with as much care as one would a prematurely born baby in a basket with a hot-water bottle. Kopp fitted the lid on the box without using nail or screw – it slid into place along slots in the box – and saw to it that the seal was tight. Bosonius quickly wiped his hands on a towel held out for him by Skord, before taking the box in his arms and carrying it over to a wooden container. This gave off a rich odour which filled the room.

Because everything that happened in the house of Bosonius ultimately had a bearing on one single process, the pious ewes grazing down by the river had also contributed to the Work. Inside the container was a bed of manure, in an advanced state of decay and glowing quietly. The Work was put to rest in this low steady warmth. It was cosseted like a bird's egg by strong but gentle forces.

From now on it was forbidden to chop wood, mince meat, pound in the mortars and beat the linen during washing. Doors must not be slammed and everyone spoke in a low voice. Bosonius himself sat calculating the rotations of the spheres in the warm room, which stank of sheep dung. When the astral conditions were suitable, the vessel was to be taken out of the container and moved to a higher heat. Meanwhile, they got the fire going in Athanor. The cold brick became as warm as the body of a lively child.

When it was time, thick curtains were pulled across the windows. This stirred up dust, and Skord sneezed so hard he almost ruined all the preparations.

It was night, and all the lights in the city had been put out. Warning bells had rung, and no fires were allowed in hearths or ovens. The fire that warmed Athanor was a secret. It was red now, with blue- and yellow-tipped flames, but it was going to get hotter, like the white-hot heat in the interior of the world. Skord and Kopp lifted the hood off the oven and placed the water-filled outer vessel on the tripod. When it had reached the heat of smoking manure, Kopp flitted across the room, in such a hurry he almost stumbled on the toecaps of his ill-fitting shoes. He opened the sheep-dung container and then the box, to let his Master bend down and lift the flask out at the same time as he wrapped it in a woollen cloth. Kopp hobbled after him to the oven. When the bottle had been lowered into the warm water and the two young men had put the hood back in place, Bosonius went down on his knees. His face was white and he was mumbling.

Skord wanted to say something stronger than prayers. But Bosonius would have none of this sorcery. He was so pious it seemed to have turned him white: white of skin and hair and long beard. His eyes seemed to water more than usual. It looked as if he was weeping. Kopp was sniffling, seemingly wanting to declare his loyalty and deeply felt support in all things. But his eyes were moving, alert and observant, between the fire valve and the smoke outlet, and his fingers kept testing the sealed neck of the flask which protruded through the hood of the oven.

Next, Athanor was to be fired to provide the heat needed for the Unification. Sleep was unthinkable and talking was no longer permitted. But at the moment Bosonius fell to his knees, Kopp's bony hand had suddenly squeezed Skord's. Once he might have been proud to be the only one allowed to be present when Bosen began the Great Work, but now he seemed ecstatic at the chance to share this event. Skord was sitting next to Athanor, hands and feet close together like a cat. The fire burned evenly, without sparks.

Inside, the Unification was taking place. The hot sulphur at the core of the world met the cold, elusive mercury. Joining, they bit like wild beasts. They were bleeding. They fought each other, then merged as they melted in the same death.

Afterwards the decay would begin, the Corruption of the dead body, which had formed as they joined. It would turn into the deepest black of blacks, and Bosen whispered that this was *nigredo*, the darkest of deaths. Now they would lift the lid to find out how the first Work had ended.

The contents of the vessel had become still again. The surface seemed to be glinting with starlight.

'Only once before was the constellation of the stars as it is now,' Bosen whispered. They realised he meant the constellation over Bethlehem.

Kopp raised the heat by adding more short logs cut from leaf-bearing trees. The fluid in the vessel had changed into a moist, bubbling mass.

If the first stage had been stillness and waiting, calm movements and quiet voices, this next one created febrile activity around Athanor. They got the fire under the tripod going. Kopp fell over his own shanks. They found Felicula, who had been sleeping on a shelf close to the oven. She jumped down and wanted to get out, but Bosonius would not allow the door to be opened. The cat was meowing, padding up and down on impatient paws. The tension in the room was such that Skord started yawning and scratching his neck. It was infernally itchy. He could think of nothing else.

They had no idea how many hours passed or how deep was the night by the time the moist mixture in the flask had dried. Now colours blossomed inside it. Deepest blue. Seawater green. Gold, purple and shimmering violet.

'This is the Peacock's Tail,' Bosen said. Soon they were to see the appearance of whiteness, *albedo*. This was the end of the second Work.

And while Kopp restrained the screaming cat, the mass turned white.

Now there was only the third Work to wait for – the Royal Wedding when the red sulphur thrusts its spear into the mercury. From this union the Philosophers' Stone would be born. The Wedding must take place at the highest heat they could create. Already, Athanor was singing. Kopp handed the cat to Skord but she drove her claws into his chest and wrenched herself free. The fur on her back was standing on end. She rushed up to one of the windows, overturning bowls and writing implements, then turned and, meowing, threw herself at the door.

Bosen made a sign to Kopp, who opened the door just a fraction to let her out. The three of them came together as one in front of Athanor. Then the vessel cracked.

Bosonius collapsed and lay on the floor for a long time, his back bent. When he finally got up, he hid his face behind the long sleeve of his coat. He walked over to his box-bed in the far corner of the room and pulled back the dusty velvet hangings.

Kopp picked the pieces of glass out of the oven with a pair of fire tongs. Sticking to the glass were lumps of a white material, brownish inside like bird shit.

Skord pulled the curtain back from the windows and a shabby grey light made the flames look faded. He put the fire out but it kept smoking for a while. The dull morning light fell on mortars and retorts. Soon afterwards they began hearing the noise of wheels over street cobbles and the sharp voices of women from the kitchen. A little while later they were all seated round their porridge in the kitchen and nobody asked them anything.

Time passed. The spheres rotated as ever and the huge wheel of the stars turned. Skord spread out his cards to find out why their experiment had been ill-favoured by the Great Ones. They went through their moves as usual, with solemn faces and shining weapons, but did not answer. He felt they cared little for the creatures living like rats under their floorboards. Sometimes they would scatter crumbs carelessly, and at other times send their wild animals on extermination raids. So, Skord thought, perhaps we should get away from their residences. Maybe all of us would be better off in the forest.

It was said that it was gentler to carry out the Work according to the wet method. Compared with the dry one, the forces released were less dangerous. Huddling in front of Athanor they had not been risking their lives. But the very act of creation was vulnerable to mocking and perverse spirits, and the wet method was alleged to be more likely to release them.

Bosonius stayed behind the closed bed curtains for longer and longer periods. He had his books and papers with him in there. Kopp and Skord lived in a state of hopelessness. They could not be bothered to remove the sheep-dung container. It stood there, glowing quietly as the manure turned to brown humus.

Skord did not even have Aurelia to talk to. She had forgotten him for a younger playmate. The father was one of the Cathedral clergy and the boy wore a black slashed velvet suit, which made him look like a little gentleman, even though he was younger than Kopp. But when he was tumbling about like a puppy with Aurelia, he forgot soon enough about the velvet. They would hide together under the gooseberry bushes, which by now had finished flowering and grown small, green, wartlike fruit.

The clergyman and all his youngsters came visiting. They were treated to sweet drinks and home-baked cakes. He was a widower and looked like a black stork. Skord found the thought of married priests repulsive. Once they got started they set to producing offspring at a faster rate than anybody else. Mareta Fontelia had managed to get her eldest daughter married off to a servant of the Church. Castanea had taken to learning almost as readily as Aurelia, and her prognostication too had foretold scholarship and fame. Instead she gave birth for the priest, as regularly and unavoidably as milk curdles when rennet is added. Her step had grown heavy and her face thin.

Skord felt distaste at seeing the priest-spawn play with Bosen's daughter. Still, the clergy always kept very accurate records of when their children were born, so it was easy to work out that the velvet boy was two years younger than Aurelia Bosonia. He could not really be used as breeding stock for another couple of years.

Mareta Fontelia wanted to console Skord, who seemed so miserable and out of sorts. She tried the old ways, like letting him hold the skeins as she wound yarn into balls. Panting from the heat and her stoutness, she pulled him close, made him put vinegar-soaked pads on her forehead against her headaches, cuddled him and spoke to him in baby talk.

But he had become a young man. Her petting made a bulge appear on the front of his trousers. This made her sweet-talk him all the more, teasing him for what he could not control. More and more often she toppled on her back in the bed, complaining about the burning heat of the summer. He had to prepare compresses, to rub and massage.

His eyes turned black and he became as restless as Peliel in his youth. He was frightened by the sight of the toothless dog, which looked like a leather sack and could be taken for dead as he slept in a square of sunlight in the yard. He wanted to get away, but the cards did not tell him where to go. And there was butter on the porridge.

That summer many of the people in Uppsala fell ill. They had a high fever, and blood and excrement poured from their bowels. After a time they came to understand that God was lashing them using his worst scourge. He had let loose the evil from Mars, the planet of pestilence. The arrows had pierced the inner firmament of the sick. Wretchedness and malice flowed as a bloody sludge. Some got back on their feet, and may have been purged. Most needed no help other than shovel and spade.

For eight weeks the distant stars continued to hammer mankind's evil on their anvils of iron. Lime burned in plague pits and sewage drains. People hurried along, covering the lower part of their faces with cloths. All who could left the city. But Bosonius would not stir from his study and Mareta Fontelia did not want to take the servants away and leave him on his own.

There were many about who were quick to earn money from the pestilence. Foremost were those who fetched and carried and dug. Others claimed to have been in the service of knowledgeable foreign doctors. These were mostly useless folk, itinerant tooth-pullers, runaway barber's apprentices, bath-house women no better than old whores, witches who might have been up to the same thing, and crooks of all kinds. They cheated the sick and fed off the terror of the relatives.

It got to the point where the advancing army of villains upset Mareta Fontelia enough to alert Kopp and Skord. They were driven out of the apathy which had enveloped them since the night the vessel cracked and started running around the houses again with remedies, pills, panaceas and theriacs, offered for sale at only slightly increased prices. They were cheered by the smell of pepper and cloves and by handling the coins. When the summer dew lay heavy and cold on the grass and the stars burned against the dark night sky, they were going full tilt at all their usual tasks. They became fed up with the stench of partly burnt dung and, with the help of Johannes, hauled the container out in the yard. Bosen pulled back the bed curtains and started doing his computations at the big table. Soon Kopp was back tending dripping and hissing pelicans.

No spiritual arcanum was produced. Kopp roasted herbs, clotted toads' blood and concocted huge mixtures of things that scorched and stank and corroded in ways that inspired confidence in their efficacy. Bosonius – and Kopp as well, by his own say-so – was an adherent of the spagyric arts. The learned doctor no longer believed that cures could be derived from plants or living animals. Instead they had to be distilled from incomplete earthly elements.

The bodies of minerals were incinerated until all that remained were the astral essences which constituted their souls.

Bosonius walked through the laboratory, gesturing towards the shelves. Lead, mercury, antimony, rubies and other precious stones – now he intended to drive the soul out of them all in order to prepare glorious, everlasting and spiritual arcana. But he no longer cared for collecting eggshells, blood, toads, leeches and beetles.

'Woe the day he got so involved with the Cabbala,' Mareta Fontelia said. 'But we shall just have to manage as best we can.'

And she did know how to manage in hard times. Bosen had come to believe one year that he had found quinta essentia, only to be deeply disappointed. She took the failed elixir from its dusty shelf and sold it as a cure for burping and heartburn.

Bosen knew less and less about what those around him were up to. He was as pious and slow as an ox tethered to a fig tree. In one of his sacred books, Skord had read that beef gets tenderised when cooked with fig leaves, due to mutual and inexplicable attractions. He told Mareta all these things while she absently let him massage her. She cared little for the wise symbolical meaning, and instead sent the boys out looking for something similar to fig leaves on the stony, juniper-clad slopes west of the city. They brought home whatever they found. An ear-shaped fungus would be dried and ground to a powder to treat earache.

The weeks passed. There was no need for Kopp and Skord to keep running around the houses with medicaments against the pestilence. Instead they were called when there had been a fight; they tended the ill, bandaged and bled them. The weeks passed, maybe years too. Time flowed as sluggishly as water in the river.

Then came a day when everything began to change, at first imperceptibly but as crucially as if, above their heads, the revolving spheres had lurched.

It was a Saturday morning late one autumn. A carriage stopped outside the house, and a man stepped out and hammered on the door in the arched gateway. He announced that he was bringing a gift for Dr Bosonius. Johannes offered to take it but the man said that his orders were to place it in the hands of the celebrated Doctor personally. That was how he put it. But his manner of speaking suggested that the words had been put into his mouth.

He wore a jacket with embossed silver buttons, but was no nobleman. He might have been the servant of someone in a high position. Later on, they were unsure what the carriage had looked like. It all happened so quickly. But the messenger had been mud-splattered, as if he had been riding on the back of an open trap.

The Doctor slowly came out of his study, solid and heavy. Mareta Fontelia said afterwards it was a crying shame he was so slow. Now they would never know who sent that gift. However, there was Bosen holding something heavy wrapped in many layers of material. The messenger had already left.

Bosonius unwrapped the gift in the presence of Skord, Kopp and Mareta, his wife. He put it on the laboratory table and peeled off one layer of cloth after another, as if they were cabbage leaves. Inside was a large slab looking like very old, brownish-black cheese. It was porous and cracked, pitted by craters, fault lines and irregular hollows, which Bosen investigated with his index finger. It was a stone.

It was obvious to them straightaway that it was the Stone. But where did it come from? Only princes and leading bankers could afford to pay the price for even the smallest pile of gravel from the mines where the mysterious mineral was extracted. All this was a gift. From whom?

Usually, a meagre, crumbling portion of Lapis Philosophorum

was kept in a box with a document confirming its authenticity. Not even a brief note accompanied this Stone. Still, it was surrounded by its own dense atmosphere. It radiated the presence of something (Someone?) in a way that drove them wild with the urge to create. Sometimes the presence made itself felt ominously and dreadfully, especially early in the morning, and made them squeal inside, like tormented kittens.

The days passed while they were waiting. It was Kopp who was struck by the notion that they would become rich as well.

Mistress Mareta told him off, and ordered him to get on with washing the helmets. He clattered with the vessels in the copper basin and could not keep his mouth shut. He was babbling. Such a large Stone! They could use all the bits they needed, cut up the rest and sell the pieces abroad.

Bosen shook his head. But Kopp's chattering added weight to a thought he had been pondering for a long time: the Stone should be divided. Its surface had been deadened by handling. It had been subject to so much dealing, cheating and speculation. People had plucked at it greedily and fingered it to death. But if it was truly the Stone, it should be alive inside. It was necessary to cut it open.

This was done late one night, using mason's tools borrowed from a local carver of gravestones. Bosonius had carefully measured the orientation of the cracks and fault lines. The incision was made, and afterwards the cut surfaces gleamed like red winter apples. Nobody must touch the never before exposed membranes, shot through with live and deeply gleaming mineral veins. Theophrastus had been right, they whispered to one another. It was red, richly red as was once the mouth of Kore after having bitten into the Hades fruit, the bloody apple of the underworld.

They fitted the cut surfaces together again and folded the cloths round the wounded Stone. But what were they to do with it? It was lying there, curled up like the Ouroboros under his sloughed-off skins. How could they dare call forth the Snake?

Winter came, time of deep thought and learned computations. They did not touch the Stone. One afternoon in January Mareta Fontelia and her daughter went out to buy fish. It was snowing a little. Mother and daughter were wearing the same kind of clothes.

Veils fell from the brims of their flat black velvet hats down over their coats. Dry powdery snow collected on the cloth and in the folds of their linen collars, shaped with fluting irons. Mareta often took Aurelia with her into town now, so that she would get used to the proper behaviour and dignified walk of a grown woman. Their full skirts swung out around them like bells.

The keeper of one of the fish stalls down by the river turned the cold, scaly bodies over for them and they finally decided to buy a pike-perch. At that moment Aurelia noticed that a covered carriage had drawn up in front of their house. They could only catch glimpses of it through the thickening snow. Somebody stepped out, a vigorous swift-moving figure. They saw the sweep of a black cloak and the glint of a short sword. It must be a person of high rank. Aurelia was keen to get back home, but her mother preferred to linger, giving the guest time to get into the house and be received by Bosonius. She did not want to be seen returning without a maidservant in tow and carrying a basket on her arm. The stiffly frozen pike-perch poking out of her basket made her cross. It had been cheap, though.

Shaking the snow from their coats after getting back indoors, they heard laughter and lively talk from the laboratory. Somebody was in there, whose presence had livened up even the practically comatose Peliel. A large shaggy deer-hound was lying on the threshold to Bosen's study, growling throatily each time the old guard dog came close. The Ulmer dog had been chained up by Johannes and could be heard howling with rage in the yard.

Every country has its history and its great men. Propriety must be the first consideration when describing the lives of people who have served the country in important positions. It is of no concern to posterity that their hose may have been baggy round the knees. This is why no name will be given for the man who had come to visit Bosonius, his old friend from student days. Instead, this man will be known by the title used by his friend to greet him as he came through the door into the laboratory.

'Illustrissime!'

We shall call him Illuster. The nature of his high position shall not be revealed. He had been given the most gracious possible signs of his king's regard. Large resources and important posts depended on his management. Enough said. As it happens, his hose fitted him perfectly, and joined breeches slashed to show the voluminous silk lining.

Now this busy and important man was sitting there joking with his old friend, whom he straightaway called Bosen. They chatted together about their studies all those decades ago. Illuster had travelled south to learn Greek, and he spoke of this time of wandering and adventure. Skord was hiding in the dark corner near the bed-curtains, listening, limbs folded tightly together like a cat. Gaping with excitement, Kopp was sheltering underneath a shelf holding dusty glassware. Outside the snow was whirling in a strong playful wind. It was a new and dangerous wind, a gust of air from the fields which lifted the covering of chilly mist and stillness that had settled over the house.

He told stories. He had arrived in Paris young and penniless, the well-born son of a noble old family which, however, counted for nothing in France. The teaching was so elementary he had had to move on, in boots with worn soles and large holes in his stocking heels exposing the smarting pink skin. And then he arrived in Italy. In Tuscany! Now the names of the cities dropped one by one like the peas of St John: Pisa, Siena, Arezzo! Kopp's eyeballs were bulging out of their sockets. Lucca and Pistoya and Prato! Fancy that! All these names spoken in the gentle, moody language which had once given up to him sweet smells and clatter – they signified streets and houses and rushing fountains, and crowds of people, living, riding, shouting. Fiesole! San Gimigniano and Florence. Oh yes, she had been the flower among the sweet buds – Firenze!

But was Greek to be learned in small provincial towns like San Gimigniano and Fiesole? Skord and Kopp did not dare ask but drank in what they heard the way sphagnum moss soaks up water. The student had drifted around Tuscany, keeping hunger at bay by playing the fool and singing witty songs. He retold old jests about farmers' wives and lecherous monks and stories of ruffians, read out backward rhymes and verses about passionate love. Illuster had done the singing, and his mate had played the flute and beaten a tambourine strapped to his thigh. Now and then he would join in the refrains. Skord and Kopp listened and squeezed themselves deeper into their shelters.

The stranger's body was vigorous. His hair was cut short, grey and thinning at the temples, but had once been dark, thick and curly. Bosen, on the other hand, had always been the same, heavy and white. His back was like a mighty slope, and his wispy hair spread over it like an undulating avalanche over a steep hillside. Surely he had not danced once, like a big bear? Surely he had not sung in his rumbling voice?

But he had certainly known Greek, long before Illuster met him in Florence and became his pupil. Since then they had gone their separate ways. Bosen found masters to listen to among the great Jewish scholars. He learned Hebrew and became one of the viri obscuri, while his pupil joined the viri clari et illustres. Many years after Bosen's own return to his native land, Illuster also returned as someone fully trained in the medical sciences. But he had never got round to practising as a physician and investigator of the secret relationship between people and the stars. He was taken into the service of the Duke, who had been holed up in Åbo waiting for the day when he would be king, replacing his badly afflicted brother.

When speaking of royalty, they lowered their voices. Skord believed he had once seen the new King. Or rather, he had seen a crowd of nobility riding up towards the Castle wearing mud-spattered but costly clothes. Their faces looked tense. The King may have been one of them, and maybe Illuster had been part of the retinue that surrounded him like one body, composed of black broadcloth and the warm flanks of horses.

By now the brother of the King had died in shame. Nobody cared any more for Bosonius's computations, nor for his plans to purify the violated body of the world with live gold. However, every king needs his vis claris et illustris. Bosen's lively student had begun an active and happy period of his life.

'Did you get my gift?' the guest asked suddenly. Bosen rose painfully, went down on his knees and kissed the generous hand. 'Illustrissime!'

Their important guest dismissed this humility with a gentle, almost teasing gesture. As they got to know him better, they often saw the signs: he despised celebration and adoration. But when he did not get these things, his mouth set in a sharp, irritated expression. They understood this was due not to vanity, but to suspicion. Why did someone's back fail to bow as deeply as it should? His grey eyes would stay fixed on this misguided person. His eyes were light, with a contrasting black ring round the irises.

Bosen called on Kopp and Skord to come forward now and be introduced to the guest. Afterwards they would display the Stone in its freshly cut state. Kopp tripped over the toecaps of his shoes and bowed deeply, his fringe falling across his face. Illuster's gaze rested on Skord for a long time. He continued to observe him even as the cloths were unfolded to reveal the Stone. Then he touched the exposed surfaces of the Stone and pronounced it good. He sounded matter-of-fact, as if speaking of ham or boots.

As they came to know him better, they often heard him use coarse and jocular language. He could make a jest out of everything, they realised that. When he stayed indoors with them he would dress carelessly, pile nuts and fig chunks into his tumbler of wine and read books which made him laugh and shout. For instance, he had been reading a book about the Incarnation, the holiest of all miracles. In the book, the question was posed whether the Father, who had recreated himself as the Son inside the womb of a woman, could instead have assumed another shape, maybe a woman or a donkey or a cucumber.

Cucumber, now! Did the book really say Cucumis?

He insisted that it was so, and went on, 'And if He had been incarnated as a cucumber, would He have been crucified?'

This set his laughter rumbling along under the ceiling – there was a big laugh inside that neatly built body. Bosen coughed, blew his nose and avoided his eyes. Kopp stopped stirring the contents of his mortar and looked shyly at Illuster.

But the same man who could be rumbustious and full of jokes, who walked swiftly, probing everything, even piles of rubbish, with the tip of his sword, also had days when he was irritable and inaccessible. These were days when he dealt with his tasks in Council, and two lines would run down his face from the root of his nose to his chin.

Usually he worked in the presence of his King. But at this time, as it happened, there were important matters for him to deal with in Uppsala Castle: extensive revisions due to the changes made after the end of the rule of the previous king. This enabled him to spend more time with them, and he suggested they should start on the Work now that he was there.

They understood they were faced with decisive action. The atmosphere was laden with anxiety, with a tension and power which was no longer inspired by the Stone, but by this swift-moving, fast-talking figure.

Illuster liked speaking in Latin, but Skord avoided answering in that language. His own usage was flexible and expressive, but in comparison with Illuster's it seemed comically barbaric. Illuster spoke like Cicero, in accordance with strict and clear lines of thought. Skord could argue and quarrel, gossip and swear, in a Latin that seemed to rise from some verbal cesspool inside him. While he was still learning the beautifully measured and unambiguous way of using it, he preferred to stick to his native tongue. He did not want to be taken for a prattling fool. Although he was not proud or vain about other things, he was sensitive about language.

When Illuster had finished his Council tasks, he would come to the house to spend evenings and nights in the laboratory. He worked on the calculations together with his old friend, and Kopp had to weigh, pound and measure with great precision. In preparation for the Work, a great many experiments were carried out. Bosen had always preferred computations on paper or in his head as the basis for his conclusions, but Illuster wanted to test them in retorts and crucibles.

In their company, he would wear the strangest clothes: a pair of brown velvet trousers, an unbuttoned linen shirt flapping open and showing part of his chest, which was covered with grey fur like a wolf's. He put on a sheepskin waistcoat, fleecy side inwards, over his shirt, and on his feet he wore sandals kept on by a leather thong between his toes. His black cloak, his sword and its finely wrought, glittering sheath were kept in a chest behind the laboratory curtains. In it were also his black silk hose, boots made of soft leather and a tall hat, its cap ringed by the skin of a brown marten. When the groom brought his horse in the morning, he stepped out into the chill of early dawn wearing these fine clothes. He was never seen dressed carelessly outside Bosonius's laboratory.

During the spring Kopp and Skord were made to prepare for the Work without fully understanding what they were doing. Although they listened as sensitively as hares, the plans and the formula did not make much sense to them. One thing was clear: this time the Work would be carried out according to the 'dry' rather the 'wet' method, though this was both a more dangerous and less certain way to go about it.

They realised that Illuster kept making suggestions which scared his old friend. The house was full of anxiety. Aurelia and her pretty boy in his velvet suit were playing games behind the curtains and on the stairs. Skord followed them whenever he could. He disliked hearing Aurelia's voice rising in breathless giggles when she played with the little priestly smoothie-chops. In the laboratory, jokes had replaced the worshipful silence which in the past had been the rule, even though not always kept. Now and then, Illuster put forward postulates which baffled Bosen and could even make him seem angry. But was Bosen really capable of anger? Heavily, he paced the floor. He seemed to be turning the new ideas over and over as if they were dough.

'All things can be revealed by observing their likenesses,' he said. This was part of his credo. It gave rise to his argument proving the significance of Skord's name, which meant that Skord was allowed to stay in the house, in spite of his laziness. From it, Bosen also derived his belief in the Work. He often mumbled these words. But Illuster would turn round and say in his light, mocking voice, 'But Truth has no analogue or likeness!'

Bosen muttered that those who had a penetrating wit could uncover many delusions – from within themselves.

The two young men were able to grasp the sense of these exchanges. But exactly what was being calculated, weighed and measured was by now beyond them.

One morning Skord woke to find Illuster bent over a small dissected body on the table. He was looking at it through glass lenses, prodding the exposed membranes, and using a knife to cut through bundles of pale red muscle fibres. The laboratory was silent. Bosen had left to go and sleep with his wife. The dawn light overwhelmed the flame round the wick in the bowl. Skord woke the way a fox does. Immobile, he watched the man bent over the body. What was it? A rabbit? He could not see it well enough. But if it was just a skinned pet hare, why did the man wrap it in a cloth and take the small parcel with him when he left the house? As usual, he put his sheepskin waistcoat, his old sandals and his brown trousers into the chest. He locked it carefully, as if he thought the old clothes very precious.

A thanor was being demolished. They watched fearfully but silently as it was destroyed. A new oven was built into the wall. It consisted of two joined units. One was tall and straight-sided and the other divided into several dome-shaped compartments which were connected with each other as well as with the tower unit.

They needed new vessels as well. The old ones did not fit into the sockets in the new oven. Bosen said nothing when Kopp took away the discarded glassware and used the flasks as containers for useful substances. They could see the hurt in his face, though. In one of these alembics he had expected to see the white flame spreading like the arms of the Blessed One.

Christ was not mentioned any more. As soon as the oven was ready they built up the fire and tested many compounds. The laboratory smelled like a smithy. Illuster ordered new glass flasks and helmets, which were delivered, packed in straw, to the Council Rooms at the Castle. Skord had to come along to take them in a cart to the house down by the river. Illuster accompanied the transport on horseback, riding next to Skord, and a groom walked along on the other side. They started out before dawn to avoid meeting other carts which might bump into their precious cargo. Illuster caught sight of a man disappearing through the door of a cattle shed, and told Skord to let go of the handles of the cart.

'Get in there and collect some more straw,' he said. 'Somebody is up and about.'

Skord went over to the shed. He had to bend over to get through the doorway. Inside, there was a thick stench of dung and cow piss, but like the darkness of a spring night, it seemed to grow lighter or less dense as he stood there.

And then he saw the man with the night-time errand to the

cattle shed. He had not come to mind the beasts. He was standing behind a young, pale-grey heifer, raping her. He was panting heavily, and each gasp was proof of how drunk he was. He staggered when he pulled out of the animal. The heifer tossed her head back and forth, and rolled her eyes back to show the whites. He screamed at her and, when she would not calm down, kicked her udders and flanks. In the end he fell over in the muck. He was still panting in his sleep.

The heifer had thrown her head from side to side when she felt the heavy thrusts, and tried to pull free from her fetters. She was calmer now. She moved her hooves about cautiously, so as not to hurt the sleeping man.

Skord did not get any straw. He hurried back out into the lane. He had to stop himself from being sick, and leaned against the warm side of Illuster's horse. He breathed deeply, inhaling the smell from the short dense coat, steaming in the cool of the morning.

'What have you seen?' asked Illuster.

Briefly, Skord told him. 'Sir,' he said, 'this man must be punished.'

'You could kill him,' Illuster answered after a moment of silence. 'Surely that's want you want?'

Skord carried a sidearm, a long dagger, almost like a small sword. He imagined the man in his drunken stupor, lying in the dung-filled gutter.

'Back in you go.'

'No.'

Illuster laughed under his breath. 'Don't you want to?'

'If I had been meant to, I would have known,' Skord said. 'But I did not know what to do.'

'You don't want to,' Illuster said in a dry and almost surly voice. He nodded, and the groom quickly went in through the low doorway. When he returned with an armful of straw, Skord spotted through the doorway the man lying there as before. His snoring could be heard in the lane.

Illuster seemed to be holding back a laugh. But it did not seem to be scornful laughter. Never before had Skord asked himself whether people could choose to act otherwise than they did. He had not considered the possibility that he himself had a choice.

You slashed and pierced, violated and kicked, punished and killed. He had never really believed these actions were necessary. They just happened. They were disgusting and evil. That was how it was and would ever be.

Illuster observed him while the groom packed straw round the glass vessels. His slender fingers toyed with the hilt of his sword. He half smiled.

'But Skord, you must see that my hand can draw this sword any time?' he said. 'If I want to.'

'Yes.'

'But then it may not. If I want to, it will stay.'

Skord was not wholly convinced, but felt he could not argue. The waves of nausea and the sour taste in his mouth were dispersing. Distaste and inner turmoil remained. But he knew these too would fade if he bent down and grabbed hold of the handles of the cart. Silently he did so and, pulling the load, walked on.

They were fired by Illuster's boldness and vigour. Kopp was stirring and grinding as never before. For some time even Skord had been dashing about, ingratiating and eager. Something was going to happen. The moment was close.

But the closer it got, the more stolid and gloomy their master became. Bosonius found one reason after another for postponing the Work. Illuster laughed at him, but not scornfully. He put his arm round the bulky back in its dusty brown coat. Kopp told Skord he could sense his master's fear, and that he too felt afraid at times. If they failed they would have reached a point of no return. The rest of their lives would be like a chilly, dull, grey morn.

'For ever,' Kopp said. 'Do you get that?'

And everything they ate would taste of death.

'Don't people always have the taste of death in their mouths?' Skord asked, his head turned away.

'You've started saying the oddest things lately,' Kopp said. 'Are you scared?'

'No, I'm just bored,' he answered.

A cold, strange tedium came over him more and more often. It would stick to everything he touched. He felt as if no one and nothing ever spoke to him. Yet the rustling waters of the river rushed over the weir as always. Voices chattered and croaked.

He did not want to talk about this weariness. Kopp would not understand anyway. But Illuster sensed it. He might be feverishly excited, but he knew nonetheless. There was no mistaking it. Skord noticed the signs in the same way those masters of covert hints, the learned viri obscuri, would detect the meanings of the cryptic similes they exchanged. They had insight. Those in the grip of melancholia also had insight.

But what was the matter? What had he seen? Kopp would ask.

The answer was: nothing and nobody.

The day finally arrived when Illuster would no longer tolerate any more delays in completing the Work. Bosen asked that Aurelia be allowed to be present while they carried it out.

'We are not pure,' he said. 'But the purity of the child may see us through.'

He also insisted that they all dressed in white. Illuster agreed – or maybe he just did not listen. He was preoccupied with supervising Kopp, who was weighing small metal disks, each bearing the imprint of the planetary sign for that metal. Then, finally, he was told to weigh out one quarter of an ounce of mercury, as exactly as possibly.

That evening Skord was told to ensure that all the windows were closed. In the square in front of the house the fishmongers slammed closed the shutters in front of their stalls, and their carts clattered away along the cobbled streets, carrying the remains of a long day of trading. Flying in from the fields outside the town, dense flocks of jackdaws screeched anxiously until each one had found the right perch in the towers and trees. The sounds dampened as Skord pulled the velvet curtains. It was getting dark, the bells were ringing out, and a chill rose from the rustling waters of the river. The voices of the birds fell silent.

Kopp and Skord were dressed in white cloaks. These consisted of two pieces of bleached linen, stitched together at the shoulders. Bosen wore a white caftan so old its seams were yellowing. Illuster moved about in his shirt and brown velvet trousers. He had put away his sheepskin waistcoat and pulled white stockings all the way up to his thighs, since Bosen took what they were wearing so seriously. When he gave a sign that all the preparations were complete, Kopp went to fetch Aurelia. The girl was also dressed in white. Her mother had seen to it that her gown was properly buttoned all the way up.

They all kneeled. Bosen signalled to Aurelia, but she seemed to have forgotten what to do. Her eyes had become alarmingly blank, and Skord did not dare look at her for any length of time.

'Ora, puellula,' Illuster whispered. She remembered then and started the prayer Oratio Dominica in her light quick voice.

When she had finished, Illuster and Bosen together carried the vessel to the oven, which was by now very hot. Aurelia was kneeling so close to it that her face turned red with heat.

Skord rose. He felt as if a large heavy fish had flipped over inside his chest. He took Aurelia's hand, pulled her closer and led her over to the door. Illuster looked up, and Bosen seemed to be about to stop them, but Skord mumbled a line which he had heard the learned Bosonius use more than once: 'Nonulli perierunt i opere nostro.' Then he opened the door just enough to let himself and Aurelia slip through. He took her to her mother, and ran back up the stairs. They had locked the door by the time he got there.

He spent that night lying outside the laboratory, sharing the space with Illuster's deer-hound. Only once did light show through the cracks round the doorway, and it was as white as a flash of lightning, but lasted longer and faded more slowly until the chilly dark closed in again. Neither whispers nor footsteps could be heard from the room.

At dawn when the door opened, both he and the dog leaped up. The laboratory was filled with a sharp metallic odour, so heavy it could be sensed like a taste on the tongue.

Bosen, hunched up, was sitting at the large table. Skord thought it had all failed once more, but Kopp stepped forward, red-eyed, overtired and agitated. He led Skord up to the oven, where Illuster was standing looking into a crucible containing a hardened pool of molten metal. It could not be gold. It was much whiter. Nor was it silver. It was so hard it showed no marks at all from the etching tool with which Illuster was trying to score the surface.

'We have made it!' Kopp whispered, in his excitement and delight including Skord, who had been sleeping outside the door when it all happened.

Bosonius seemed to have been so strongly affected by this success that he had lost his ability to speak. Seeing him there at the table, sagging and staring with rheumy pale-blue eyes into empty space, one might have thought him afflicted by some dreadful disaster. Illuster, on the other hand, had become unlike his usual self in a way Skord had never before observed. The great man was asking eager questions in a fierce attempt to shift Bosen out of his torpor. Did he not understand what they had created?

He was demonstrating the metal, which he called the 'White One', and took Bosen's hand in his own to make the feeble fingers touch the surface of the compound. It could be neither scratched nor corroded. It had a mysterious power which affected other objects. Ecstatic, Illuster whispered, 'Do you see what this means? Who knows what the White One can do? In a weapon, say. Who could resist its cutting edge?'

How delicately, with what strength and persistence would it not vibrate in the inner workings of instruments? Inside clocks. In the keels of ships. Who could foretell its future? Nobody had ever seen the White One before. Not any human being anywhere. It lay there the way a moist chestnut lies inside its thorny shell when it is slit open.

'We cannot predict what will happen. We are advancing onwards!'

At last Bosen spoke, but he could only utter one single word and it was garbled: 'Humm ... manii ...'

Reverently, attentively and just a little impatiently, they waited for him to complete the sentence. He was very pale and one eyelid drooped down over the eyeball.

'Humm ... manity,' he said.

It looked as if Illuster had not understood. Or at least, he wanted them to think that he had not understood. Skord, who had been cleaning his nails, suddenly felt like saying out loud the thoughts inside the head of his Master Bosonius. He knew of the thoughts because he could hear them.

'Human beings,' he said, 'will garrotte each other using the White One to make the strangling rack. They will slit open the wombs of mothers to get the foetuses out. They will rape and then punish those they have violated. And because they have the White One, it will be done all the better.'

Illuster stared at him. There was sense in what Skord was saying, but his voice sounded like a parrot's. However, the great man answered him as if he had been speaking to a thinking human being, 'The White One is in good hands.'

Skord looked at Illuster's hands. They were small, with short fingers. Still, they did look strong. He thought to himself that it was hard to tell whether a pair of hands were good or evil. It was hard, even if you knew the whole person.

Illuster stopped spending his nights working with them. He would visit, always in a hurry. Eyes shut, the marten stayed curled round the cap of his black hat. Over and over again they stamped the signs of the planets into the metal disks they had first cut and weighed. The die clattered. Illuster demanded a repetition of the miracle. The White One was to be called forth again and again. Surely, Skord thought, people would have got fed up if the reawakened Lazarus had fallen ill again, been put into his grave and started to smell, only to be made to step forward once more to stand there with hanging bandages, and then maybe for a third and fourth time.

When he whined, Kopp reminded him of the great Raymond Lully who had turned many thousands of tons of lead into gold for the King of England. This had surely not been done all at once, without steady effort.

Bosonius was deeply engrossed in the Cabbala. On behalf of Aurelia, he received the proposal Mareta Fontelia had been expecting for so long. The velvet-suited lad, whose name Skord refused to remember, arrived at the Bosonius home accompanied by the rest of the family. The two fathers locked themselves away, the children were given biscuits by Mistress Mareta, and Aurelia wandered off with her admirer down to the river.

Finally, the old man emerged dressed in his by now habitual white cloak. One leg dragged a little as he walked. The boy's father was at his side. To mark the occasion, he wore breeches so wide and puffed up that his legs looked like black wires. Skord thought it peculiar that a priest should want trousers like that, even if they were hidden by his coat when he went outdoors. It was even odder that someone with such miserable legs should have picked these trousers. But nobody else seemed to mind, and everyone was in complete agreement about the marriage. Skord fled.

He began to hang out in the taverns again. He discovered that the serving girls had a folded, wet and hairy slit which could be got at if you made them spread their legs. He pushed his cock into as many slits as he could. Occasionally this gave him an itch and a tiresome dripping condition, and the excited voices of the girls did not hold any joy. They sounded as if tickled to the point of pain. Sometimes they fought, scratching each other's faces, and he came to like watching this. He would annoy them and fan the flames of bitter quarrels in the inns. He flashed his dagger, but slipped away when they started to carve each other up and fall bleeding into the straw on the floor. He had become a scordalus and a scortator, and took his pleasure in the excited shrieks and in the presence of pain, in the degenerate and bitter-sweet, in the fluid dripping from some cluster of petals close to decay.

He knew he would change soon. Usually, the change took place quickly, and then he had to leave. He had remained a slim youngster for a long time now. He looked just as he did when he and Kopp met for the first time, arguing about the prices of bird's eggs and basilisks. But Kopp had grown into a man.

One night Skord was in bed with a girl, and it was so late that the moon had vanished and not a single cat was still sneaking about in the lanes. Like an eager, lusting dog he was using his tongue to find her slits and hairy parts, her hollows and slopes. She was tired after having been much handled and turned over and tickled and pushed into. She would fall asleep on and off and, like a child, sob a little in her sleep. Sometimes she hiccoughed, her breath smelling of wine. There was a draught from the window, and her behind was as cold as ice when he pulled her round to do to her what the dog does to the bitch. He must have gone to sleep too, though he had no memory of it. He woke frozen, knowing that Aurelia was trapped inside and there was a smell of smoke.

He pulled on his trousers, his jacket and boots. The rest he left with the exhausted girl, whose face was pale and grey as she slept. He ran along the lanes to the Bosonius house. The gate was locked, and he had to clamber over the fence round the cabbage plot and find his way down to the river in order to get in. He hushed the dog and went straight to Aurelia's bedchamber. She was frightened when he woke her, but soon calmed down. It was hard for her to understand that there was no time to dress, only to wrap herself in the coverlet and run along in her nightdress.

He took her to the neighbours' house, and they let her in after he had hammered on the door. Then he ran back to knock on the main door of the Bosonius house. He had not dared to earlier because he was afraid that they would forget Aurelia in the turmoil, and then not let him into her room while she was still undressed. At that point they would not have been able to smell the smoke. But now it poured out, thick and greyish yellow.

The Bosonius house burned down that night, in a violent fire which started in the laboratory, and which not even the dogs had noticed before Skord came to alert them.

He had believed the fire would wipe the slate clean and allow their lives to start again, but in stillness and expectation as before – lives full of learned computations, playfulness and dignity. But Kopp and Skord were told to rake over the ash-laden muck round the stone foundations, which jutted forth like rotten teeth, and salvage what they could of the tools and molten lumps of metal. The whole thing started up again with the same urgency. The household moved into another house on the river, belonging to an elderly widow. Even the pigs and sheep had survived the fire, although the matted fleeces of the ewes stank of smoke. Masons built a new oven in the widow's house. Soon the banging of the die stamp was heard again, and the smithy smell filled the room. New batches of the White One emerged molten from the heat. Illuster sent messengers to collect them. Now and then he would turn up himself, but he was impatient and easily angered.

Bosonius had gone into retreat. His study was no longer part of the large room they used as a laboratory. They did not know what he was doing in there on his own, and he never talked to them. They could hear absentminded mumbling when the maids or Aurelia brought him his food.

One day he summoned them all and spoke to them, although it cost him a great effort. It happened on an occasion when Illuster was visiting. Curiously, they all had to crowd into his study. This included the great man, who had so little space that his sword got caught in the bundles of papers on the shelf behind him.

Every day since the fire Bosonius, who had lost his books, had filled several sheets of paper with computations and descriptions. Because they had gathered round his desk, he had turned the papers upside down to prevent them from being read. Presumably he meant to talk to them all since he had asked them in, although he directed his words to Illuster alone.

'You know of my fundamental belief,' he said, 'that all things can be revealed by observing their likenesses?'

Illuster nodded. He was wearing his tall black velvet hat and the eye stones of the marten gleamed.

'You are aware of my gratitude to the Creator for having allowed me access to this world of similes and promises, for having let me live, observe and remember.'

Illuster shut his eyes, as if in confirmation of all this. Skord was being tormented by a fly which had been buzzing against the window and was now crawling on his nose. He worried about having to make some sudden indecorous movement. Kopp's mouth gaped open, as it had in the early days of his youth when he was listening to the Master. If the fly moved again, Kopp might well happen to swallow it.

'In my opinion ignorance is due to forgetting,' Bosonius continued. 'To gain knowledge is to learn to recall the truth which was known once. But then, you do not agree with me.'

Illuster confirmed the correctness of this with a minute change of expression in his eyes and lips.

'Tactfully, you have never told me directly of what must be your perception of me: that I live enclosed by my own wishful thinking, which causes chimeras in my mind and mocking signs to appear on my inner firmament, and that I see these erroneous patterns reflected on the great Gestirn which surrounds and encloses us.'

Skord was baffled to see patches of red spreading over Illuster's cheeks and then down over his neck, and his eyes turning shiny as if brimming with tears.

Bosen went on: 'Actually, you even think that we are neither surrounded nor enclosed in any sense other than by what we observe from our own particular point of view.'

He suddenly sagged slightly. The huge back became more humped and his fingers picked at the papers on the table. When he spoke, he sounded absentminded, as if talking to himself: 'Well, one expects many aberrations from a penetrating wit, to be sure. I have often wondered at your view of the world you live in – what is it like? Around you, all is mockery, apishness and delusory phantasms. That is how you see the world, is it not? What cunning and sly mechanic has set this in motion, if it is not the Creator? And this Somebody, what pleasure can He take in all these distorted images and all the mockery which form part of the Creation? Who is the Illusionist? And why does he wish to mislead you?'

For a while he sat in silence while the fly buzzed about, trying out noses and the backs of hands. The room became very hot. A strong odour emanated from the armpits of Mareta Fontelia, who was standing close to Skord. When Bosen spoke again, his voice had become powerful.

'You have been reminding me,' he said, looking straight at Illuster, 'that Truth is true unto itself and can therefore have no analogue or likeness.'

Illuster nodded.

'And yet out of the flames that consume it the White One gives birth to its true self. And this happens over and over again. Do I have to ask you: have we found the Truth?'

They were all waiting for Illuster's answer, but he took his time. Finally he said in rather a quiet voice, 'We have found an excellent thing.'

'I know you understand that I can no longer be part of the work you are engaged in,' Bosonius said. 'I do not know whether it is good and wholesome, or bad and boding worse. I must abide by the images I have been born to. None other tempt me. In our different ways, you and I have both told ourselves that on the morning of Judgement Day we will wake and be compelled, there and then, to recognise how everything, all the knowledge we believed ourselves to have gained or remembered, has been no more than assumptions and suppositions. In this we are alike, you and I. But in all other matters we must now go our separate ways.'

He went on to explain that this did not mean having to move the production of the White One out of the house. Illuster could still have the use of the oven and the servants. 'I no longer have any use for these things myself,' he said.

He put his hands on those who had gathered in the crowded

room, patted their shoulders and the tops of their heads, and kissed Aurelia's round white forehead. In addition to his benevolence and love they also sensed a hint of impatience in his manner; gently, he pushed them towards the door. They slipped out from his study, scrambled down the stairs and allowed him to close the door after them.

From that day on they saw him only rarely. His skin became paler, almost transparent. The blue eyes which so easily brimmed over no longer sought contact with others.

It was as if Bosonius had ceased to be or had passed on to another place. Mistress Mareta ran the house her own way without asking leave of anybody. However, on the day of Aurelia's wedding, she went in to see him and let him know what was taking place. He nodded agreeably, and then bent over his writing again.

Aurelia was sitting waiting in her bedchamber, dressed up, hair plaited and curled. She was weeping. Her sobs could be heard through the window by Skord and Kopp, who were washing at the well.

'She ought to be pleased now that she can have her fancy man,' Skord said. 'Still, girls blubber over the oddest things.'

Only then did he learn that Aurelia was not to marry her velvet boy.

'It was the father who proposed,' Kopp said. 'Didn't you know that?'

And so they married. There was nothing Skord could do about it. She was joined in matrimony to a pair of scrawny legs, a puckered mouth, a pointed chin with a dangling handful of flab underneath, and two red-rimmed eyes. She curtseyed to him, her cheeks reddening. Everybody present was treated to fine fare, but Skord could eat nothing. He drank wine, though, and in the evening he went out to meet girls who never cried when anyone was watching.

'You've got to comfort me now,' he said. 'A girl I cared for just a little got married today. Straightaway she gave birth to eight children. There will probably be more if she stays fertile and prospers. Be nice to me. No, kiss me prettily the way she would. Don't bite.'

'What was wrong with you, you layabout, were you too poor?'

'No, just too long-lived. Come on, kiss me properly, nicely.'

But he soon became impatient. He started chasing about, and for a long time he did not return to Kopp and the oven. The last girl he visited thought he was asleep in her bed. His heart beat faintly, but he could not be roused. His cheeks were cold.

Just at that time one of the ladies at the Court fell passionately and unhappily in love. She did not love any of the sons of the counts, nor any of the pale Catholic priests who had reappeared among the courtiers now. She kept running down to the stables. At first they thought she had fallen for the Gentleman of the Equerry, then for one of the grooms. But neither was the case.

Her beloved's back was as mobile as a weasel's, and his eyes were fiery and wild and easily showed their whites. The whites of his eyes formed thin crescent moons at the edge of his blue-black gaze, when it was flickering from fear or lust.

Yes, it was true: she loved a horse.

The ladies-in-waiting giggled when they told each other of her adventure, and their cheeks grew hot and their voices thick. Speculation surrounded the woman who had been made a fool for love. When they were all due to travel back to Stockholm, the stable grooms received two contrary orders. She demanded that the brown horse with the slender back be tied to her carriage, to accompany the court on its journey to Stockholm. But the grooms did not obey her. They did as they were told by her husband.

Going along to the stables, they agreed it was a fine animal, and a shame to do what they had to. But that morning the horse just stood there with his muzzle stuck into the manger, and showed none of his old vigour. The butcher they had brought along said he looked like any common run-down beast, and besides his back was too weak for riding. And he went to work with his club and his knife.

It was a bright morning, close to noon, when Skord woke. The girl whose bed he had borrowed for so long was climbing in to lie next to him. Her service had been tiring, and she yawned enough to make her jaws click. Still, she was glad to see that he had come back to life, and kissed his cheek before falling asleep.

He did not want to get up. Outside nigredo ruled. The March slush was forming dirty streams. Summer, long buried, was being resurrected in a state of decomposition, grinning out of the mire. The sparrows were fighting so wildly the horseshit flew in all directions. No, he did not want to get out of bed and start dashing about.

He could think of many things to do out there. Pull back the catch on the door and get inside the steaming cow shed to stand there, waiting meekly. The fiery, easily aroused soul of a young man inside a heifer's warm body. Mild eyes, sharply pointed horns and hard hooves. A stall which was no longer bolted to hold back the large lowered head when the violator arrived. He wanted to do this, but did not. He knew already how it would end. Club and knife. An innocent body in the mire and blood.

The girl had pulled the curtains shut to stop the morning light from annoying her smarting eyes as she slept. But he could make out the chest and the chair. On the lid of the chest her dress was spread out like a ghostly shape. Such clothes they were wearing now! Down at the bottom of the street was the workshop of Master Hans, who could cut after the latest fashion. A waistcoat covered with pearls, trimmings and silk ribbons, slit to let through the puffs of linen undershirt. Before going on duty she would set her hair in crisp curls. She was like the bud on a poppy, but still wanted a little prettifying. How well she knew to hold herself, chin up, a proud Spanish carriage with her small body straight. Under the bed he could see her shoes. The toes were capped in silver. He pushed the shoes forward and tried them on. She was not that dainty, although she had a narrow waist.

When she woke there was another girl poised on top of the chest, just as slim as she, with a slender back and brown hands.

'Sweet Lissla, I've borrowed your outfit.'

'I can see that. You cheat, have you shaved as well?'

'Yes I have, even my legs.' He pulled back the skirt with its slits and ribbons and the stiff petticoat, to let the girl in the bed inspect his calves. 'Please let me try it out. You'll get everything I earn.'

'I know you can spin a yarn better than most, but you need a little pussy under that skirt, and telling fibs won't get you one. You'll be thrashed, and that'll be the end of that.'

But she agreed to let him go, because she needed the sleep. Earnings were down anyway, now that the Court had left. She

decided to dress in an ordinary peasant girl's clothes and travel to
Bälinge to pay her wet-nurse.

'Good luck,' she said. 'And get that dress off before they give
you a hiding.'

He learned how hard it was to keep the hem of a fine dress clean
and off the floors of taverns. Curls straightened, silk ribbons
creased. Sweaty hands left stains on the bodice when they clasped
the slender back. Fluttering, giggling. The sweet smell of hot
spiced wine from the mouths seeking his. 'Rosebud! Sugarplum!
Let me feel, is the bud about to flower? Wet weather coming? You
will oblige me, won't you? I'll die without a bit of your loving,
that's for sure. Now, let's get down to brass tacks. I have another
kind of leathery purse you'd like to touch, isn't that right? I'll
open this one later, fair's fair.'

He did not get thrashed. He was too quick for that. But he did
get slapped because he giggled too much. They wanted him to gasp
and pant and talk sweetly of love.

One night a gentleman stepped inside the tavern door and stood
looking at Skord, who was prancing about in Lissla's silk dress and
speaking in a light voice. It was clear for all to see that this was a
very fine gentleman, a real toff, and the cellar room became quiet
when he entered it. Skord's cheeks reddened, but he pretended not
to recognise the illustrious personage. The gentleman desired to
have him – or the girl wearing Lissla's dress. Anyway, there was
no telling what he demanded and what he recognised.

He did not sweet-talk, nor did he rattle his moneybags. But he
seemed quite certain that he wanted the two of them left alone
together. The landlord found a room for them and Skord went
along, although he knew he should keep clear of men as hot as this.
They toasted each other and drank together in the light of the open
fire.

'Please speak to me nicely,' asked Illuster – for it was he and
none other. 'Later we'll sleep together, you and I.'

At that moment, Skord knew he was in the clutches of an
unsuitable and unruly love. Its stirrings had been felt inside him
for some time, though he had been unable to name it. By now he
himself no longer knew who was underneath the dress.

'You are very beautiful,' the gentleman said. 'Slits and ribbons.
Curls and finery. But what's inside? I want to get at you.'

So far he had not put his arm round the slender back, not even brushed the skin with the tips of his fingers.

'I'm not paying a penny for your beauty. But I want to reach your self. When I look into your eyes and sense who you are, it is as if I were looking at my own soul.'

'My love for you has not flared up because you wear a black velvet hat with the skin of a marten curled round its cap. Or a pair of shoes with slits on the toecaps. No, not even because of your short, broad hands. I can see you inside your eyes.'

'So what shall we do now, you and I? Go to bed together?'

'I could undress in front of you. Perhaps that would be the best idea. Because the last thing I want is for you have reason to say I lied to you.'

'You've lied before,' said the gentleman. 'The flecks in your irises prove it. Are you sure you're not lying just now?'

There was a rustling outside the window.

'There's a starling inside the shutters,' Skord said. 'What if I went away from you, leaving only my dress and my body behind? What would you do then? I don't think you would rape or flog the body.'

'No,' the fine gentleman said. 'I lust for you but my hands are controlled by my tenderness towards you.'

And so they began undressing each other eagerly, as if they wanted to get beneath each other's skin.

In the morning, Lissla found her dress on the chest. It smelled of the kind of perfume fine gentlemen put on. Skord had rolled himself up in the curtain which used to hang in front of the door. He was sleeping with his back to the room and woke unwillingly, not wanting her to touch him. When she asked how it had been, he said he had not earned any money that night. When he had woken up properly, he showed his teeth and insisted he had resisted with great modesty and fought as if confronting evil personified. By now virtue bored him, and he wanted to hand back the fancy dress.

That year, spring was grey and slushy. Skord had gone back to Bosonius. He was sitting at the die-stamping machine, impressing planetary signs into small pieces of metal. Kopp and Mistress

Mareta had taken over all business matters. They spoke together behind locked doors, kept accounts and would leave the audit office with grave faces. The tedium was killing Skord.

Through the window he could see the clergyman's young wife, Aurelia Bosonia, as she went to buy fish in the market. She wore a wide-brimmed black hat with a veil to keep off the sleet, and walked with great dignity between the fishmongers' stalls. She was trailed by her four daughters, the oldest of whom was thicker round the waist than her stepmother. The son, the darling boy, was last in the string. He carried her little bitch called Hypatia.

This was jaw-breakingly dull. He could not even be bothered to have a look and see whether the Mistress's belly had begun to pout a little. She did look content, though.

Could girls learn to put up with anything? Did they just sob for a while, and then turn jolly again?

Although her prognostication said so, she did not become a scholar. She never got to marry her velvet darling, and instead she got the care of children while still a child herself. It looked as if she was playing with oversized dolls. And who knew what was growing inside her belly? It could be Death himself, hidden in a body no larger than a fist.

Then a flurry of snow swept the small troupe out of his sight. Skord bent over the stamp.

Illuster was always accompanied by his dog. It slept on a rug next to his bed in the Castle. When his master and Skord were sharing Lissla's bed, a sheepskin was spread on the floor underneath it for the dog. It wore a heavy leather collar with silver studs and a disc with an engraved message:

> I am Illuster's dog.
> Whose dog are you?

It was a deer-hound, a male with a strong and wiry build and a high-arched belly. Its short, furry coat was grey. Its back formed a long curve and its head was small and smooth. It looked built to run very fast. Indeed, the body seemed drawn in a single fluid stroke, to accomplish one thing only: running.

Skord wondered whether this was a stupid dog. Its eyes were expressionless. Quietly, the dog stayed close to its master at all times. If they lost sight of each other it would without more ado leap over any obstacle that separated them – be it a peasant's cart or a bench with several people sitting on it. It seemed quite an old dog, although its tough, wiry body had kept its agility. The grey fur had turned white round its nose and its eyes were very pale. Illuster often rested his beringed hand on the dog's back, his fingers playing with the row of vertebrae which were prominent under its pelt. One day he spoke to Skord about the dog. They were alone at the time.

'He's getting old,' he said, letting his fingers run through the fur. 'His temper is getting worse. It seems he's got bad teeth, and maybe painful joints as well.'

He grabbed hold of a hind leg and waggled it back and forth at the fetlock joint. The dog quickly pulled the leg close to its body, but Skord could see that it was knobbly and stiff. It occurred to him that Illuster might want the animal dead, and planned to ask Skord to carry out the deed. There was no question about it, he would never undertake such a task. He opened his mouth to make this point. But Illuster carried on: 'Maybe he'll live for one more year. Maybe not. We'll see. But when he's dead, I would like you to do me a great favour.'

'Bury him?'

'That's right.'

His fingers were still plucking at the short fur. The dog was at his feet with its flank resting against the soft leather boots, and its blank and possibly stupid eyes closed.

'Some time after he gives up the ghost,' Illuster continued, 'well, just a few days afterwards, you will get a message from the Castle to say that I've died too.'

No! Skord would not believe that. Under no circumstances would he believe that. Whoever had predicted this – using cards or lead or entrails or any such ungodly rubbish – had to be wrong!

'I know this, you see,' Illuster said. 'That is how it's going to be. You will get a message.'

Then Skord recalled that the last king's father had dismissed the stargazers from his sickbed, telling them that the twisting loops and paths of the planets were well known to him: he could feel them in his own body and so knew what his fate was likely to be. He stared at Illuster, whose fine-boned body held some similarity to that of the old dog.

'Then, and not before, you will bury the dog for me. This is how it should be done. Take the cadaver to the charnel-house next to the Cathedral. This must be done at night, but as soon as possible after you receive the message. Remember that. Then find the coffin bearing my coat of arms. Open it and put the dog's body into the coffin. Screw the lid on tight again so that nobody notices what has happened. That's all.'

Skord felt so distressed he could think of nothing to say. The agreement was sealed. There was no talk of any money changing hands. The whole bargain was struck without Skord uttering a single word. They shook hands; Illuster kissed him and left the room. He could be heard roaring with laughter in an exchange with someone outside the door, as if he had received no dire premonitions from the stars or from his own body.

Skord spread out his cards as soon as he got a chance. They did not reveal any death. He laid them out again and again, but the true face of Death, the Destroyer, never appeared. When Illuster was visiting next time, he asked him to choose his own card and then cut the deck. He did so, smiling, and said in a low voice, 'Skord, you don't trust me.'

When he had left, Skord laid out the cards and knew that they must reveal the truth unless they were no more than coarse and skewed images on bits of paper. Illuster had picked the Magician as his card, and Skord thought that very fitting. But of the three blind cards, the Fool came up first. After him came the Hanged Man. Again and again he put the cards down with the Magician in the middle. But the Fool kept turning up.

Who was the Fool? He was worse than a dog. Someone upside down – like the Hanged Man – standing on his head and crowing. Someone who wandered away, his dog at his heels, in torn trousers and with stick and bundle over his shoulder. A buffoon and a trickster. Why should he keep appearing? How dared he show his twisted, grinning snout, his pouch full of stones, his pointing stick?

Time passed and nothing special happened either to Illuster or to his dog. Skord's memory started to slip. Maybe there was nothing out of the ordinary about the great man's request. It was well known that people wanted all manner of things in their coffins. He had heard of parrots, prayer books, locks of hair, even boots. But why did the great man want to keep the arrangement so very secret?

Time passed, and the dog with the silver-studded collar still leaped over greengrocer's carts, though, in all honesty, only over the smaller ones.

Well, of course I'll see to it that he gets his mangy cur in his coffin, Skord thought to himself. We have shaken on it. That handshake was as powerful as the slap I got from a man no less bright than this one, although the other lived very long ago. It's likely Illuster will die some time after his dog. How long it will take is another matter.

He set about making preparations, and got a jar ready containing strong oils and resins and added a quantity of poison.

This was his embalming fluid for the dog. This meant that a long time could pass – indeed, however many years it would take between the deaths of the dog and his master. When necessary, Skord would be able to carry out his promise without too much trouble.

Sometimes the veil of the present would tear slightly and he would think of other times. Or maybe he was seeing, rather than thinking. Images flew in through the tears. The time in which he was living, with its troubles and cares, its running and walking, sleeping and eating, frayed and thinned until transparent. Master Peder Astronomicus had constructed the huge clock in Uppsala Cathedral and Skord had been one of his workers. They had built time into its rings and cogwheels. The mechanism moved quickly at its innermost centre, near the hub. There it kept the time for walking and running, and the short hauls between breakfast and evening meal. The time of the stars was measured by the movements of the distant outermost rings.

He was different from the people he lived with, in that his time was measured by a different ring. It turned more slowly. Those whom he learned to be fond of changed so quickly: the skin on their cheeks turned as dry as paper and the backs of their hands became spotted with grave-rust. It pained him. He knew that soon they would be no more; their time wheel turned swiftly and before long would cast them down into a world that did not revolve around him. He knew by now that he had to leave before the pain got to him. But when was the right time?

The cards made slapping noises against the table. When his companions had fallen asleep under the table in the tavern or had ambled home through the wynds, he sorted out Sceptres and Swords, Coins and Chalices, until he held in his hand the small packet of twenty-two powerful and silent images. But whichever way he laid them out, they never answered anything other than: Wait. The monkeys on the wheel mockingly predicted great changes for him. The tower collapsed with much black smoke under a warm shower of gold. But nothing happened. The chariot driver's hands did not reach for the reins. The angel with the star poured the clear water back and forth. It looked like a shining plait, caught in the movement between the two beakers.

When?

The bridge of Illuster's nose seemed thinner, and his eyes had become a colourless grey. On his cheeks two sharp folds cut through the pale skin straight down to his chin. His scant hair was silvery.

When?

Not today. Nor tomorrow. The blood warmed his skin. His movements were quick, if a little stiff.

Not yet. Not today and not tomorrow. He was still strong and vigorous and full of lust.

From sitting indoors amid the acrid fumes from helmet flasks and retorts, Kopp's skin had become greyer and his limbs scraggier. He was carrying heavy responsibilities now, a man in the prime of his life, who already had long bald inlets into the hairline at the temples. On the other hand, Skord looked the same as when they first met, apart from the stubble which shadowed his cheeks in the evening and grew sharp and black by the end of the night. Mareta was an old woman now. Her tread on the stair was heavy, and she had to lean on Kopp. Bosen had become almost transparent from all the time that had flowed through him. But Aurelia was beautiful. No longer like a child. But beautiful, beautiful, beautiful.

He did not want her to shrivel like an apple. Every year she was with child. Some died and some lived. They stretched her life to the utmost. But she was still beautiful.

Once, not early on but after her third child had been born, he went to the house where she lived to see her alone. His mouth was dry and his heart beating hard. He meant to tell her that he wanted to leave. His intention was to ask her to come with him.

He sneaked in without being noticed by the servants working outside the house, and stood on the steep, narrow stairs to the first floor, listening to the sounds from inside. The grinding of a mortar came from the kitchen. He could hear the sharp voice of one of the maids, but neither crying children nor barking dogs. Recognising the peal of low laughter coming from the first floor, he tiptoed on.

He thought of how he would put his mouth to her ear and whisper, 'Aurelia, you're so beautiful! You are so terribly beautiful. You are not to go about your life like this, you must not catch spots of grave-rust from the man who forces himself on you every night. Don't let your life collapse and time tumble you down among mud and stones. You shall come with me, and together we will step lightly on the earth. I shall become a gambler. Slapping the cards down will make the coins roll into my pockets; my fingers are nimble and we shan't want for anything. It would be a jolly life and an easy one too. Come with me, Aurelia! Neither of us has become wise and scholarly as we once planned. But we can be cunning and cheerful instead. We shall dupe Him. We shall dupe Death, the Destroyer.'

Again, he could hear her laughing. But it sounded muffled, as if she were laughing into a pillow. He had reached the first floor, and stopped in front of the closed door of a bedroom. She was speaking in a low voice in there, but he could not hear what she said because her giggling masked the words. Did she have somebody with her? Or was she talking to herself? He could see nothing when he bent to look through the keyhole. She had plugged it with something. He removed the plug with the point of his knife and looked again.

He saw a bed. It must be Aurelia's. For sure, she was lying in it. What he saw most clearly was a pair of buttocks. They were young ones, round and in vigorous motion. Whoever owned that bum, there was black hair in the crack. And the velvet pants were off. They were lying on the floor.

It felt as if the knife had come through from the other side of the door, straight into his staring eye. Aurelia giggled again, a hot, strangled sound. He did not want to see any more. There was nothing more for him in the silent house. Aurelia had everything that she could wish. She was already cheerful and cunning. He realised that for her to run away with someone like himself had been a impossibility from the start. What would have become of her? A card-sharper's sidekick. A thief's wench. Someone who walked the roads. Here she lived in her own home, a respected wife and loving mother. Oh yes, so very loving he wanted to drive his knife into her darling velvet boy, who had got older and grown black hair in the cleft between his pink, mobile buttocks.

Skord slipped down the stairs and got out of the house without being seen. He must get away alone. But when? And where to? When the cards failed to answer, he didn't know what to do. He had to stay for a little longer and try to look older by affecting a dignified way of walking and a serious face, like Kopp's. But after his visit to Aurelia's house his heart was a tarn full of blood, whipped into choppy, violent waves.

Although the cosiness and drowsy daily pattern in the house by the river soothed his anxiety for a while, it awakened again when there was a royal funeral in the Cathedral. Many noblemen were worried. The Duke arranged a big gathering in Uppsala of the clergy on his side. He called up his soldiers. These were not good times for those who had supported the dead King. Illuster was nowhere to be seen.

One afternoon a carriage stopped outside the widow's house, and someone hammered on the door. When Johannes opened it, a strange manservant was standing there. He carried a large object sewn into sailcloth, which he was to hand over only to Christian Skord. Johannes, who had aged and had stiff knees, clumped upstairs in his clogs to get hold of the overgrown apprentice. Skord came down and received the burden into his arms. He had no time to ask any questions before the carriage rattled off, taking the messenger with it.

He needed only to feel the knobbly row of vertebrae under the sailcloth to understand the nature of the gift. He carried it into the laboratory and cut open the seams. There was the body of the large deer-hound. Its coat was stained with clotted blood, and when Skord probed with his fingers, he found a hole at the back where the skull joined the neck.

Over the winter, he had left the embalming fluid in a shed cold enough to cause the jar to crack. He had forgotten; he had not wanted to remember his promise. Even now, he did not want to think about it. Because it was chilly outside, he could leave the corpse in the woodshed until he had thought of what to do.

But he could not think. Inside his head was nothing but loss and emptiness. He knew he would soon feel grief biting his heart like a wolf. But he did not want this knowledge. His heart was beating and his head was whirling, empty of thought. He curled up and slept a lot.

Four days passed like this. Johannes nagged him about the burial of the dog. The weather had turned, and it was now too mild for it to stay in the woodshed for much longer.

231

'Put coarse salt inside the sailcloth with the dog and sew the whole thing up,' Skord said.

Then Mareta Fontelia received another message, to say that the illustrious one had died in Stockholm Castle from an illness. There had been a wake, and his corpse had been seen by, among others, men sent to report back to the Duke whose brother he had served. These men, who were heavily armed and in a great hurry, had not troubled themselves to show more than token distress in the presence of the majesty of death. It was hard to guess what their real reason was for coming. Now the coffin was on its way to Uppsala, where it would stay until the funeral procession was ready to depart for the castle and church belonging to Illuster's family.

Skord lay on a bench, covered by an old sheepskin. He wanted to be totally empty, but the turmoil inside his head troubled him more than thoughts. When it was night-time and all was still, he got up and went to the woodshed. The dog cadaver looked like a human body inside its shroud of stitched sailcloth. Carrying it in his arms, he waited for a long time in the gateway before crossing the street. He did not dare cross the square to the Cathedral but kept close to the houses, and stopped now and then to listen for footfalls.

In order to pick the lock of the charnel house, he had to put his burden down. The sailcloth shone brightly white, he thought, in the gloom of the spring night. Presumably they would call it desecration of graves. He wondered what the penalty was. Illuster had surely considered the risks. But he had never offered him money. Which was why he carried out the strange task he had agreed to do.

A wolf sinks his teeth into the heart. The tarn that has held the sky's clear reflection becomes filled with blood. High up in the fir trees there is a discordant howling sound.

Plod onwards. Plod onwards. Keep away from the wolf who wants to tear at the chambers of your heart. Quick, hurry to get there so you can fulfil your promise. And then never care any more. All faces stiffen. They become blotched and dissolve. It does not matter what you have found behind the faces. It is gone. Quickly now! Quick . . .

He had brought a stump of a candle, and lit it to find the right coffin. The mountings gleamed, skulls and crosses in silver. Illuster's sword had been tied to the lid of the coffin with a piece of rope. Skord recognised the weapon. He started unscrewing the lid. When the lid came off, there was no bad smell. He pulled it away cautiously, fearful in case it hit the floor and made a noise.

Then Illuster rose from his coffin. Although he must have been rather stiff, he stepped swiftly down to the floor and immediately started cursing.

'Do you have any idea how long I've been waiting? Didn't I tell you to get on with it? To hell with everything. The devil take this damned finery! Help me off with it now.'

Taffeta ribbons and black veils and a waistcoat stiff with pearl embroideries fell to the floor. Skord just stood there, his arms hanging at his sides.

'Why, I do believe you're speechless for once,' Illuster said. 'Have a look under the cover. I put my boots and trousers in there. I ran out of water, but I could breathe air coming in through these holes. How long did you think I could live on air?'

Now that he had put on his trousers, they pushed the shroud into the coffin and laid the dead dog on top. Finally Illuster pulled the cover over the body.

'It's still too light. Is there anything else to put in?'

Skord found a spade.

'Let's screw it down.'

Finally, he walked about checking that they had not dropped a ribbon or maybe a stocking on the floor. He blew out the candle, and whispered to Skord to push the door open. As soon as they had left the Cathedral precinct behind, Illuster put his arm round Skord's waist, and they started staggering along as if they had been spending too much time in the taverns.

'You've got to find me somewhere to stay. It must be with someone who asks no questions.'

Skord took him to a girl called Lisabeta.

When she came home in the morning, she found them sleeping with their heads resting on the same pillow. In a basket under the bed were the remains of a meal. She was fearful Skord might have disappeared, leaving his body behind in the bed like a discarded suit of clothes. And the other one looked pale as death. But when she touched Skord's wrist, he was wide awake in a flash.

'Sweetest Lisabet, I've borrowed your bed,' he said. And then they struck a deal with her to take over the bed and the privy for a couple of days. They gave her money so she could go home and pay her wet-nurse, as well as give her mother some money for sustenance. Illuster told Skord that he would soon be on his way.

'What, to walk the roads?'

'To begin with. Do you want to come?'

He asked. He did not order.

'Yes,' Skord said.

His heart beat in his chest like the wings of a powerful bird. Illuster said that his shabby clothes – the brown velvet trousers, the sheepskin waistcoat and the sandals – had burned when the fire ravaged the home of Bosonius. Since then he had been afflicted by great worry and tedium.

'My trajectoria have got tangled,' he said. 'Every day I trundle along the same paths, and I come across my own tracks too often. I never feel really hungry or thirsty. Tedium stares me in the face.'

'And what of the Duke's men?'

'Oh, well, they gawk. Their faces look like the rump of your trousers.'

He gave Skord's behind a friendly slap which made a resounding noise on the leather patch. He had once been trained in the medical sciences, he said. Now he intended to practise these again. But not before they had reached the German states. First of all, however, he wanted to spend a few days in Uppsala, in the greatest secrecy.

'I want to find out how my funeral is conducted,' he said, 'and I want to hear what they say in the speeches over my dead body.'

He wanted Skord to join the funeral procession. He was to listen and memorise all readings, in order to be able repeat to him what was said in the Address of the Cadaver Cypresses, the Speeches of Comfort, the Honourable Memorials and the Candid Tears of Grief at the grave of the well-born and illustrious one.

On the morning when Illuster's coffin was carried out of Uppsala, a heavy spring rain fell straight from the skies into the bare soil of the fields. The coffin was wrapped in black velvet edged with silk fringes, the catafalque was upholstered in black broadcloth, and the horses pulling the hearse were draped in black. But Skord could not but observe the black stuff getting splattered and the horses raising their tails under the silver-trimmed velvet. He felt sure the material was already stinking of stable and dung.

He could no longer muster any amusement at the idea of this solemn and noble funeral procession being on its way to bury a dog. Rather, he thought it looked the part only too well. He was half asleep on the horse's back. When he looked up, he could watch the water trickle off Bosen's black hat as it jogged up and down in front of him. It seemed to him that the most remarkable thing about the funeral procession was that his old Master had silently emerged from his study to follow the friend of his youth to his grave.

The whole procession came to halt at an inn some eight miles out of town. The courtiers climbed down stiffly from their carriages and, making sour faces, wandered into the taproom. The Duke was represented by dignitaries who regarded themselves as too important to travel along muddy roads to a rustic parish church among the fields.

The inn served them hot meat broth and warmed-up pasties. It had all been brought from Uppsala. The mourners were followed by a team of cooks, as if they had been on their way to another battle of Läby Ford. Skord was leaning against the taproom wall and sipping the hot broth when his eyes fell on a knot-hole in a wooden board. He felt as if this hole and his eye were meeting each other's stare and attracting each other. The hole was the stronger: it drew Skord back into his past. He felt smaller, thinner, happier and more excited. His body itched as if it were crawling with fleas. He could not stand still. The straw rustled as he moved. He heard snoring, and knew monks and soldiers were in there. He wondered if he could sneak away like a weasel in a hen-coop without waking them. And he stared at the knot-hole for as long as he could see it in the flickering light of the embers. When all was dark he slid down from the creaking, straw-filled bunk and, with his shoes tucked under his arm, got to the door and opened it as quietly as possible. But it creaked anyway, and they shifted in their sleep, all the monks and soldiers who had believed his story about being a wealthy merchant's son fallen into the hands of highwaymen.

The night was bright with stars but he knew no more about stars than a jay. He walked and walked in the starlight until he found a barn. Afterwards he managed by lying and begging, begging and lying, and once in a while mabbe, deil kens, trying his hand at chopping logs or, anyhow, kindling sticks. Finally he reckoned the monks and soldiers would have left on their travels, and he dared enter Uppsala. And what joy he felt when he was finally inside the city, which was stuffed like a bird's crop, and sitting in front of a baker's stall at the Cathedral steps with a full belly! There were more stalls to steal from than he could count. The city was one great squirrel's nest, and nobody knew Skord. He was free. He was nobody. Nobody could know nobody.

Finding the knot-hole had revived him. There he was, slurping on his funeral broth, and this other Skord seen through the knot-hole had existed long ago, so long ago that Bosen would not even have been a babe in arms. He grew quite tearful at the thought of old Bosen once being a fat yellow infant, waving his rattle and dribbling. His hand shook and spilled some of the broth. The old, transparent Bosen looked at and through him with almost colourless eyes.

After the break at the inn they travelled on, now on small roads dissolving in the rain. Twice the cart carrying the coffin got struck in ruts as deep as ditches and they had to borrow farm horses to pull it out. Now and then the faces of the courtiers, maddened with boredom, could be glimpsed through the carriage windows.

Late in the afternoon, they arrived at Illuster's place of birth, and if it had not been for the long spring twilight, the burial would have been carried out in the dark. The castle was tall but without towers, a stone barn whose walls were streaked with damp. First they went to the church, a much smaller building. The family vault had been opened and the coffin with the dead dog was placed inside. It was covered in wreaths and draped, the great man's sword lying on top of the velvet cloth. Skord listened to what was said at the graveside, preparing to give an account of every word. At first, pewits could be heard calling from the fields until darkness closed in and the noise of bare branches crashing against each other in the wind was the only sound heard over the voices of clergymen, versifiers and orators.

He could not make up his mind what to tell Illuster: the truth or a more agreeable picture of his funeral. Playfulness seemed impossible in Death's territory. He was the ruler. It was He who pulled the strings, who dirtied the black cloth, threw gravel and mud, broke the windowpanes and the stems of the lilies. Skord sensed His presence out there among the shadows, somewhere close by. It was as if He were lurking there, grinning at them, a bedizened gentleman with stained clothes.

When Skord returned to Uppsala he had forgotten almost all of what had been uttered at the graveside. This frightened him. Usually everything he heard said in verse and pretty language stuck in his mind as sand sticks to a damp foot. What caused this forgetfulness? He remembered nothing more than the very last words uttered into the dark and rain-laden air.

'Now sleep sweetly with divine parole,
small Body! and live on, great Soul!'

It was an early morning full of birdsong when he and Illuster set out on their travels. By the evening they settled down at the edge of a forest, lit a fire and roasted turnips in the embers. Skord had stolen them from a storage pit. They did not dare show their faces anywhere, nor ask to pay for food or order relay horses. They were too close to Uppsala, and Illuster was famous enough to be recognised.

Skord thought he could still hear the hum of the city behind the birdsong. He closed his eyes. The big bell in the Cathedral struck and the little one rang out in support. The air carried the sound of the bells out over the flat land.

Then Illuster touched his arm and told him to wake up and eat. It was not bells he had heard. It was the calls of wild geese. Now they themselves would be like birds, sleeping in the open countryside. They would have to huddle together for warmth. Kalmar was far away, and they must get there in two weeks. That was how long they had to catch the ship which was to take them to the German lands.

But when they were on the verge of sleep, Skord thought he could still hear the hum and prattle of the city. He could hear the sigh of the air leaving the slit throat of the clubbed horse. The rustling of the water in the river. The fire singing under pots and pans. Rats' feet pattering through the straw, and then from somewhere upstairs the muffled laughter of a girl. And the bells of the city rang on and on in the chilly air.

The Lost Ranks

Hier liegt

der Hoch-edle und Wohlgeborene

am Himmel gelendete

IGNATIUS TUGENDREICH

doctor illustrissimus
et celebrissimus
auch einmal Ihre Königliche

MAJESTÄT
zu
Schweden

Rath und Chantzellér
aber das weisst niemand mehr
als ich

dessen Wahlspruch war:

PER LUSUM ET LASCIVIAM

but only for three and twenty days

He betrayed me with his words
his lovely and lively words

Fliesset herbe Tränen-Quellen
mit betrübten Perle-Wellen!
Come busy Earthworms, here end your fasting,
feast to celebrate the only lasting
Truth in this world:

ALL SOON WILL PASS
and sweet words pass first of all

No dog lies buried here
but a man

handsome, lively, lustful.
He lived one life in his Body.
It sleeps here.
His other life was in his Words
and these are silent now.

When he was young
he went on
pilgrimages
and learnt
many arts and outlandish languages.
He wandered far
all the way to
ITALY
and saw foreign places
and peoples.

O wanderer
the past will always catch you up.
A scraggy old man will tap you
on your shoulder.

He found also
The Well-Regarded
and Artful One
who escaped

PER LUSUM ET LASCIVIAM

He slept under cold skies

THE ILLUSTRIOUS ONE
with his warm body
close to his beloved's
in whose glowing ear he whispered sweet words

For three weeks and two days his jest lasted. Then
seriousness returned. He found a new Prince.
He found new power and concerns and tasks. He
even found himself a new dog, which he named

He wanted me to wear a coat with gleaming buttons, engraved so
that all who asked

WHOSE DOG ARE YOU?

could find their answer. But I left. And I wept.

Fliesset, fliesset Tränen-Quellen
mit betrübten Perle-Wellen!
Winzelt, lächzet, ächzet, klaget
unter Nächten eh' es taget.
Bleiche Lippen flüstern niemals mehr.

Sleep Sweet Body!
What a thousand words had built
Cruel Death destroyed.

❧

They were standing in the pouring rain which trickled off hat
brims and shoulders. Mütz snivelled. He had caught a cold, and
was probably frightened as well. But he did not dare pull at his
master's coat while he was still reading. The boy had not learned
his letters, but thought to himself that the inscription on the
tombstone was oddly long. Qinnamon's hooves trampled up and
down as if she too were impatient and worried about them being
left behind.

The slow snake of marching foot soldiers crawled past outside
the cemetery wall. Skord took the reins handed to him by the boy,
and they started walking along the path to the gate.

So long ago! So many years, so many changes, movements,
faces. So much shouting. So much rain.

Time flows. It drags you along. But in the end it will always
flow past you. Then there is stillness. The dead rest in the still
waters.

Fliesset, fliesset herbe Quellen
jaget, jaget Zeiten-Wellen

'The wagons are out of sight now,' Mütz said in a voice thick with cold. He could not breathe through his nose.

'We'll soon catch up with them.'

Skord helped the boy up to sit behind him. The large calm mare moved out onto the road. The crawling mass of people pressed into her, pushing her up against the wall.

One should have an officer's belt, Skord thought to himself. They would make room for us then. A belt, and a coat that was not full of holes. He was wet to the skin. The damp shirt felt cold over his shoulders. People swore at him and pushed at his horse.

'Maledicti saxones!' he swore back at them, cautiously avoiding German.

Only the Elector's companies remained. The wagon-train had gone. Not a soul from the Emperor's ranks could be seen in the rain-laden fog. The air smelled of wet soil and rotten straw.

Pissing rain. Well, now, the boy could be right. They might be far behind. He tried to take Qinnamon along the ditch at the edge of the road to get past the marching men, but the verge collapsed. It had been trodden to pieces and dissolved by the rain. They had to work their way along through the slow-moving horde until they reached open fields. Only weeds grew there now, yellowing stalks and sodden lumps of leaves rotting in the autumn rain. Clumps of thistles. Drifts of nettles where men and horses had pissed during their weeks in camp. The army was like a large, voracious swarm of insects moving onwards, a mass of worms feeding off the German provinces.

He was still thinking of the grave, and wished he could have stayed on in the village where the cemetery was. He wanted to know how Illuster had spent his last two decades, to ask around to find out how he died – if there was still someone who knew. Had there been somebody with him, and what had they said over his coffin at the end? It was a long time since the great man concluded his activities on this Earth and went to a place where he could no longer hear the booming of the cannons. But he had not died poor. His tombstone was proof of that. No question, his passing had come at the right time. Nobody believed any more that the White

One would bring about miracles inside the hot iron barrels of the cannons. Accompanied by Skord, he had settled in the Electorate and acquired a new name as easily and carefully as growing and trimming a new goatee beard. He had brought many hopes – plures spes – and most had surely been fulfilled. But since then new doctores of the chymical and metallurgical sciences had turned up. And the cannons were still booming.

Mütz was hungry. However, there was no way they could stop now. If they were to catch up with the wagon-train, they had to use the open fields and every gap there was to get ahead. Besides, there was no food to be bought. High command had decided that whores and traders were to be left behind. Hatzfeldt had ordered a forced march. Once, Skord had seen him at a general's march-past, a small count wearing a highly polished cuirass sitting on his horse on the top of a hill. Now, his orders demanding speed travelled back through the ranks, driven by non-commissioned officers who roared and splattered mud everywhere. Their horses trampled people.

That was something Qinnamon never did. She cared for people and showed respect for them. She needed to stand under a tree to shelter from the rain, she needed water to drink and oats to eat. But they had to get on and her fodder-bags were in the wagon carrying the army chests.

Mütz asked where they were going, and Skord said he did not know. There were so many rumours.

'We are retreating,' he said. 'You should be pleased about that.'

Still, Mütz opined they should never have left Perleberg.

'They are all joining the chase now,' Skord said. 'They have picked up troops from Westphalia and Pomerania. Starved wolves. You should be pleased Hatzfeldt wants us out of all this. He could have pushed you right into the maws of the King's hordes or Leslie's.'

'But where are we going?'

'Some of them think Mecklenburg. The Lüneburgers are supposed to be there.'

But that afternoon the rumours travelling back along the lines said they were to take up positions, and defences were already being dug on the hillsides. They could hear the cannons once more. They did not know whether the sounds came from the town. Skord and Mütz asked those riding back along the lines about the wagon-train, and were told they had to cross the river. It looked like a dirty stream, but was so bottomlessly muddy they could not ford it. Somewhere, this swamp-water stream joined a bigger river, which then flowed into the Elbe. And the Elbe flowed into the sea. Though where, they were not sure. More and more often, Skord thought about the sea and swift ships. About going back home. What Mütz was thinking about he did not know.

They arrived at a bridge which could not be crossed. There was a tangle of carriages, caught in the mud and in each other, among them a large travelling coach drawn by six horses. Lots of people and horses were pulling, and officers with red belts were everywhere. They could hear a furious voice from inside the big carriage, which had a coat of arms on its doors and got away before anyone thought of requisitioning large, calm Qinnamon to join in the pulling.

They did not get across until the afternoon. They rode on through swamps and morasses. Skord said it was one fucking awful place to stop and fight – if that was the plan. Mütz said he wanted something to eat.

Riding through a forest, they came across someone lying on the ground, one from their side. Skord examined him. He was still warm, but nothing could be done for him. Mütz kept away and his teeth were chattering.

'Knifed,' Skord said. 'They're beginning to catch up with us.'

They mounted and rode on. As the twilight fell, the rain started up again. They got out into open ground and heard howls and loud voices from a clump of trees. Once more, it was their own side.

'We're getting close now,' Skord said. 'Soon we'll be there. We'll find the wagons and you can have a chunk of bread and something to drink. Gee-up, gee-up! Qinnamon knows we're close.'

Rangers had caught a Swedish marauder in the wood. Perhaps the very one who had used his knife an hour or so ago. They were amusing themselves by filling him up with water. He had stopped howling because his jaws were propped open with a piece of wood and the water was going down his gullet, inflating him and stretching the skin over his trunk. When the water overflowed, they put him on the ground and started trampling on his belly.

They let Skord and Mütz join them as they rode on, but did not say whether they had made the Swede talk. Maybe that was not the point anyway and they had just wanted to let him taste the Swedish drink. Banér had caught up with them and they were going to fight him. They pointed to a hill and said it was called Schreckenberg. This made Mütz start shaking again. The wagon-train was up there. The wagons had been used to create a fortress, leaving gaps for the artillery.

'Bald geht es los,' they said, nudging Mütz pleasantly. 'Morgen früh. Wird spass – ne'?'

In the open field the ground was sometimes sandy and sometimes soft under the hooves. Sometimes it was marshy, with narrow paths leading through woodland. Now and then people rode or ran straight through the big formations of marching foot soldiers, the swarm of insects progressing through the rain without knowing where it was going.

When they reached the crest of the hill and found their company, the corporal of the rangers made his report in a way that had unfortunate consequences for them. 'We found these two,' he said. Then they rode on. Two non-commissioned officers started roaring.

'We weren't trying to get away,' Skord said, but was suddenly hit from behind and above by the flat of a broadsword. He held on to his hat as protection and crouched down as the blows rained down and the horses' hooves crowded in close.

'You two will get punished later, after the battle,' he heard. Then the officer, whom he had not had a chance to see, rode away between the wagons.

'Los! Los!' shouted the sergeants and pushed them towards the field-surgeon's wagon. They crawled inside and pulled the canvas to.

'Battle fever is gripping these shits,' Skord said. 'That imperial fucking turd was so keen to get stuck in, he couldn't wait. I hope he craps his pants full before the end of tomorrow. Heigh-ho, young Mütz, it's time to start working.'

Inside the wagon, the driver was asleep flat on his back. Nothing had been unpacked, but then, nothing had been touched either.

Skord checked the locks on both chests, the little one and the big one. Mütz started getting the stretcher poles ready. He had got hold of the bread he had hidden behind the chests, and chewed as he heaved with his good arm and his stump. They tried and failed to wake the driver when it was time to pitch the hospital tents. He smelled of drink. It was dark by the time they finished and crawled back into the wagon. The rain had stopped.

That night many came along to buy powders and lucky charms. Business was good, but Skord needed to sleep. He turned away those who wanted their fortunes told, because he felt uneasy about what the cards might foretell for the next day. Also, he thought it prudent. The officers punished soothsayers these days, if they discouraged the men. Outside Magdeburg, they had hung a sibyl of great repute. She dangled from a tree in a line with seventeen men who had been caught looting. A strange sight. Everybody agreed on that. Her full skirt had been swinging like a bell.

They did not get much sleep, even during the early morning hours when people had stopped banging on the wagon door. All through the night they heard officers hollering and cart-wheels creaking. When dawn broke they were lying there waiting for the sound of shooting. Still nothing. But the crows had arrived. They were signalling to each other between the trees, short croaking calls in the darkness.

When it grew lighter they went out to forage. The driver had woken up by now, and was in the queue outside the baker's wagon. He had heard someone say the enemy had moved from Fretzdorf to Dossov during the night. This no longer sounded like mere rumour.

Mütz always thought the waiting was the worst part but Skord preferred the quiet. They tore strips of cloth for bandaging and rolled them up. The boy held the cloth clamped under his stump and the strip between his teeth, using his left hand to do the tearing.

He had started out as a drummer-boy but one of his hands had been wounded by grapeshot from a shell. It had hit so badly that his hand was torn to pieces. Nördlingen had been a fine victory. The Swedes lost twelve thousand men, and those left had to limp off. But it had not been such a success for Mütz, whose arm turned black and stank. When he heard that not one of the Swedes' own regiments had been among the twelve thousand casualties, he turned to the barber-surgeon Kristiern Scordius to find out whom they were really fighting and why. The surgeon was amused by the thoughtful drummer-boy from Hinter-Pommern who claimed to be eighteen years old, and might reach that age in a few years, if he was lucky. At this point he was lying in a barn in a village called Hirnheim. For every day spent in the damp, foul air, the wound smelled worse. In the end the whole lot, well beyond the elbow, had become so black and pasty that Skord had to amputate. When the stump healed, Mütz became his helper. The driver was a drunkard, and Skord needed more support in the sick-wagons. They both felt this arrangement improved their standing. Just as the army apothecary had a provisor, so the army surgeon now had his own one-armed famulus. Another lucky outcome of Nördlingen was that Skord had got hold of Qinnamon during the plunder and managed to keep her.

First he thought he would name her Keziah – it was said there were no women in the land of Palestine more beautiful than the daughters of Job. But her skin reminded him more of the sacred cassia. So he called her Qinnamon, after the scented, dusky brown bark of the cinnamon tree.

This was what the shambles at Nördlingen had brought them, both good luck and bad. Mainly good luck, it must be said, or at least advantage, depending on how you looked at it. But Skord knew full well it was pretentious to think that they had bettered themselves. He was still second to last in the order of the ranks, lower than the army lawyer and just above the drummer-boys. Even the whoremongers in the trading wagons could argue the toss with him. During this morning of waiting, his neck and back still hurt from the beating with the sword, and he could not help worrying about the punishment the officer had ordered. It was unlikely to be forgotten. He had never heard of anything being forgotten in the army.

By noon, the turmoil of riding and running men behind the wagons was bad enough for Skord to tell Mütz to stay in the tent to keep guard so nothing got stolen. When the cannon crew between the two neighbouring wagons shouted that they could see the Swedes, he ran out to look. It looked as if the distant marshland itself was moving. Half an hour later the snake had crawled closer. He saw it splitting into two.

By noon, the cannons started roaring but there was no break in the forward march across the marsh.

'It's Banér!' Mütz looked jittery, and was making little leaps as he ran.

'It's all crap, don't take any notice,' Skord said. 'Stay in that tent until I say.'

Any fool, even the regimental baker, knew something was up by now. Mütz might be right. Maybe the Beast himself had arrived. His men marched in battle order. The left wing wound its way westwards, below the hill they called Schreckenberg and down towards the moor, where it seemed to disappear. The right wing could be seen marching towards the sandy ridge called Scharfenberg. At the foot of the hill he observed several skirmishes already, between both foot soldiers and cavalry. He did not want to count. The squares moved. There was agitation down there but order too, a harsh, sharp-edged order. Skord felt mildly nauseous and reminded himself it was time to eat something.

Around two o'clock it erupted. Right from the start they had a lot to do. Mütz made himself very useful in spite of being crippled. He was not afraid any more or, at least, did not have time to feel fear. He ran with the cauterising irons so that Skord could stop the bleeding. He bandaged, pulling at the ends with his teeth to tighten the knots. This was marshland, and the air was murky and damp. Skord suspected the wound tissue would rot.

The tent was humming with rumours. The Wild Boar himself was supposed to have led his cavalry to the top of the ridge in order to advance towards the imperial lines. Later it was said he had got there; that he was coming at them now. Who could tell what was what inside a stuffy tent? All that afternoon Skord saw nothing of what was happening. He just saw what had happened. What had happened to groins and abdomens, what had filled chest cavities with blood and torn the bones in hands, which looked like delicate basketwork. Most things were too fragile for what had happened to them.

For a couple of hours or so the mood was one of triumph. It had taken hold as suddenly as the sense of panic. They were running! The Wild Boar himself was lumbering away now. He'd got his tusks into more than he could chew! (Some men could keep talking even though their livers were shot through.)

The cannons thundered ceaselessly and their ears were deafened every time the nearest one was fired. They were trying to bandage a severed shoulder joint when the heavy canvas was ripped apart and fell on top of them. The voices and screams told them that victory was not on their side. Skord got hold of Mütz's leg and together they crept slowly towards the wagon. When they peered out they saw a big man slashing the arms off the last of the cannon crew. It was not quite as quick as slicing the shaw off a turnip, but quick enough because the gunner had been shot in the belly and could not run. They hid under the canvas, and Skord put his hand over Mütz's mouth to stop his whimpering.

For a while it seemed they were in the eye of the storm because it was almost silent around them. Some of the mutilated creatures lying around on the ground were still screaming.

They lay still until the musket fire started up again. Skord raised himself to look out, and saw a thinned-out row of musketeers step back to load. One of them was shot down where he stood, puffing at the matchcord. The other side had light muskets which did not need a forked stand, and could shoot again and again while their own men were pouring powder into the firing-pans and packing it down with ramrods. When the cavalry set upon them, Skord was really frightened. He thought maybe the Beast himself was among the riders. He pulled Mütz along to hide behind a wagon and then, crouching, they started running down the hillside. Near the bottom they slid in the sand. They tried to stick to the steepest parts, because they reckoned the cavalry could not chase them there and risk the horses breaking their legs.

Then they rolled in under some shrubs, and stayed still again. After a while, they ventured out and ran down the hillside towards the marsh. Once they were very close to a troop of men on horseback. But they pressed themselves down under the cover of low alders, and the horses passed close by, splashing through the black mud.

Bit by bit, they worked their way towards a wooded ridge, and by the time the evening light failed they had reached the first scrubby outcrops and dry ground. Somewhere among the stunted trees a blackbird sang, weakly and listlessly, as if the gathering darkness was taking its pleasure away. But still it sang on in the shadows of the trees.

They did not frighten it as they crawled along the sloping woodland floor which smelled dankly of rotting leaves. Close to the many stems of a large hazel bush they found a place to lie, and hidden by its leaves they felt safe for a while. The blackbird continued its autumnal song in shadows.

They heard horses scream and men moan. Silence never came. It grew dark, but out there they still went on butchering and mutilating. There was laughter too. Now they were looting. The bird had stopped singing. The darkness thickened and filled with the fumes rising from the marsh.

Towards dawn the rain started up again. Mütz was thirsty and wept. During the night he had thrown up several times, and his face looked pinched and drawn. When he moved he smelled very bad. He wept and wanted to get on. But Skord whispered warnings to him.

'They'll never take you prisoner with that stump of an arm. They'll run you through. Go to sleep. It's the best thing you can do.'

'I'm cold,' the boy whispered.

'Go to sleep now.'

A crow had settled in an oak split by lightning. They glimpsed it through the leaves of the hazel bush and it was as if it had noticed them. Again he ordered the boy to sleep. He commanded, looking deep into the boy's eyes.

The corpses did not belong to the ground they were resting on. The iron shrapnel did not belong to the cannons. There was no eyeball to fill the empty socket. There was no arm to match the mutilated trunk. The blood had nothing to do with the muddy marshland water. The leaves had been scorched and did not belong to the trees. Hunger had gone. Pain was not expressed by the open crater of a mouth. The screams had died away. Understanding mattered not at all.

All was nothing but what the eyes could see.

A body lay in the wet grass under a hazel bush, but it was not resting. It was vacant. The soul that had left it did not ride the body of the bird, nor did it root around inside it like a maggot. There was no divide between the soul and the bird-body, between man and animal. Just wings lifting a weight and watchful eyes.

M ütz woke stiff and frozen. Skord looked as if he were asleep but did not wake when the boy nudged him. Mütz whimpered with terror when he realised that Skord's hand was limp and lifeless, and that his head could be turned from side to side without the eyelids moving.

It was silent around them, so silent he could hear snapping and scratching noises from underneath the leaves. Then he caught sight of the crow. She had come closer and sat there, looking at him, on one of the lowermost branches in the oak tree. Without opening her beak she said, 'Sleep, Mütz.'

How could she speak inside Mütz's head using Skord's voice? He did not understand and it frightened him so much he felt sick again. But he did go to sleep.

When he woke much of the day had passed, and Skord had recovered his senses. He said the imperial army was retreating, and the Swedish cavalry had started pursuing them. Thousands of men were left behind in the marsh and on the sandy ridges. Saxons mostly. All of them were dead. Mütz asked whom he had spoken to. Skord answered that he had not met anyone at all. He had kept far away from people and just tried to get a bird's-eye view of what had happened. It had been dreadful, but it was over now. They had better get going. But the boy was worried that they would not be able to find their regiment. And he was thirsty; he wanted water. Skord had to hold him back from running off to drink from the marshy pools.

'You'll get cadaveric poisoning,' he said. 'Let's follow the edge of the forest until we find fresh water.'

But they found no running water. All the pools were black and reflected the autumnal sky, with its armies of clouds moving in formation from west to east.

Mütz stuck to the idea that they had to go back to Schreckenberg to try and find their wagon and the two field-chests. He did
not believe the Swedes would cut them down. Surely they too
could use a barber-surgeon and his apprentice.

Now the boy was leading the way, but Skord could not work
out why he himself was following. There was nothing for them on
the hill where the wagons were standing, their canvas hoods ripped
to pieces by the guns. Some of them had caught fire. They could
see trees with torn fire-blackened branches up there. Nobody
screamed any more. Only the crows made a racket, sounding
unashamed and sure of themselves. They were the masters now.

Yes, they were the masters of thousands of corpses, maybe
seven thousand of them. Seven thousand, with such delicacies as
eyes still in place. Skord thought about the rumours of peace and
suddenly believed in them. There would be peace in the Germanic
world. When another hundred thousand or so had died, then peace
would indeed be unavoidable. And then they would celebrate
peace with rockets and fireworks, and shoot down any remaining
leaves playing in the branches of the trees. They would feast
together at tables spread with the most exquisite spicy delicacies,
and as they became brothers and Busenfreunde, the racket would
get noiser at the groaning boards. The noblemen, the field
marshals, the Elector himself, the Chancellor of Sweden, the King
of Hungary and the Hohheiten and Durchlauten, the representative of the Cardinal and the most elevated leader of the Spaniards,
all the generals who were princes and counts and earls – all would
screech and shout like food-crazed crows.

He walked with the boy over sandy ground which was
beginning to slope upwards. The corpses kept drier here. All were
looted and stripped naked. They walked over grassland with rabbit
holes and molehills and tough yellowing grass. There was plenty
of activity, both above and below the grass. Soon the dead would
be plundered of everything but their bones. The rain started falling
on the faces and into the open mouths of the corpses.

So this was as far as they got, he thought. They had enlisted for
many reasons. The most common was starvation. Or badly
wanting something other than a dour, enslaved life. If they were
young noblemen and the hope of old families, they would have

aspired to glory. Or loot. Some, quite a few, came because they wanted to be valued as human beings.

But when all was said and done, nobody had come for any reason but hunger. There were no other reasons in the regions through which the armies had marched. Only hunger.

Hunger kept them going. Hunger and lies. If they had not been told lies, none of them would have marched anywhere. Now they were lying there staring up into the sky with the rain dripping into their gobs, whatever reasons had made them come or whatever had forced them. He wondered if any of the stiff, gaping rain-butts down there in the mud had ever cared whether they were ruled by a king or a pope. Or minded whose horses trampled their fields to mud – whether they belonged to the Elector, the Emperor, the King of Sweden or of Hungary.

Now they did not worry any more. They only gaped, and he thought some of them looked surprised. Stunned. As if they had realised they had been lied to at the very moment the skull was hacked open or the belly ruptured. Or as if they knew they had been mouthing lies themselves, in order to keep the fire going in their hollow chests and to fill the enemies' body cavities with terror.

When Skord and Mütz reached the top of Schreckenberg, they found their wagon among the lumber. The body of a young lieutenant, a former patient of Skord's, was lying across the remains of a broken drinking-water butt. His belly was open and his private parts cut off. His grey face was still recognisable. It looked stern and withdrawn. Looters had pulled his boots off and Skord was able to examine one of his less successful efforts, a heel with a gun wound which had never healed back to flesh. Irredeemably, it had turned black and now the bone protruded, looking like a spur. The lieutenant had come from a recently knighted family in need of merit in the field, so he had packed his boots with rags and hauled himself up on a horse to go into battle.

Skord looked for Qinnamon. Of course they had taken her. What would they call her? He tried to remember Swedish names for mares. Dolly. Maybe Happy or Slut. Not Snowshoes because there was not a trace of white in her fetlocks. There was no place on her coat which was not dusky brown and as smooth as silk.

Mütz had found a flask of water, and now he spoke only of how hungry he was. It would have been better if he had found a pair of trousers, because he was unbearably smelly. But none of the corpses had any clothes left on their bodies, other than torn vests and scraps of shirts, soaked in dark blood.

The field-surgeon's chests were both gone. It was of course quite obvious that they would have been taken. But it was only at this stage that Mütz seemed to understand how badly off they were. Skord thought he must have harboured some kind of hope himself because he had followed the boy up the hill. He needed a rest, though they ought to be quick and get away before any marauders came by, on foot or on horseback. He felt dizzy with hunger and tiredness, and wanted to crawl inside the wagon. But the canvas had been torn to shreds. Not a single bag of powder or lucky charm remained from his stores.

He sat leaning against a wagon-wheel, thinking about his instruments and medicaments, and the years it had taken him to earn the money to buy them. In the lid of the large chest, he had an array of knives, saws and cauterising irons. There were slots for the very fine artery forceps and the trepanning drills, and spaces for the medical scales and the safety pins. He could have listed each item, had anyone bothered to ask. Everything meant to have an edge was stored carefully and kept finely ground and sharp. The silver cannulas were straight. Now they would be able to reset Swedish dislocations and use his excellent Zugwerk to align Swedish stumps. The barber-surgeon or Chirurgeon who unpacked the chests would find the thread tidily wound and not a single brass roller missing. There were almost a hundred glass bottles containing tinctures. Elixir salutis. Pillulae Scordii, Oleum microcosmi. Compresses. Bandages. The brass mortar and pestle. Scoops and pans for plaster-making. Weg! Kaputtgemacht. They would have made off with the whole damned thing, no fear. Whoever had got it would be wealthy. Almost wealthy. But Kristiern Scordius was poor now. He was everyman, just one of the hungry stomachs, an imperial swine on the wrong side of the front line – wherever it might be. And if he and the boy found it and were allowed across with their heads, arms, legs and private dangling parts intact, then the punishment for running away would still await them.

'But we didn't run away,' his famulus said between sobs.

'You could always try to tell dear God in heaven of your opinion,' Skord said. 'Come to think of it, He had a great day yesterday. Let's go down now. We've got to get out of this war.'

But Mütz wanted to go back, home to the regiment. He believed in bread and meat and beer, not in punishment.

'There's not likely to be much left of the regiment in the first place – just look around you,' Skord said, 'and besides, for as long as there's just one demon around with a fucking officer's belt on, he'll remember our punishment well enough.'

On their way down the slope they found Qinnamon.

Not that she was dead. No, not yet. When he pressed gently on the wound in her belly, it filled with a thick green ooze mixed with blood. She was lying on the ground. Someone had taken her bit and bridle, but not given himself time to finish her off. She neither screamed or neighed when Skord went down on his knees next to her. Her breaths came in gusts, and her hot nostrils were full of mucus.

He felt hatred. Without opening his mouth, he spoke to her. He told her things which were untrue then, but would become true in time.

They are dead, he said. They are finished. The grass is trampled and burnt. But new grass will grow. Grow through the floor-boards. Prise apart the tiled floors of the cathedrals. Wood will rot and mortar dissolve in the rain. The crosses will fall, and so will the gallows, the racks, the wheels. They will all rot.

The horses will roam the sea of grass, and it will be quiet. You will hear only the voices of the birds and the whirling of their wings, the rustling of the brooks and the sounds of the sea as it beats against the patient beach. Cinnamon flower, once more beautiful than the daughters of Job. More beautiful than Keziah. More beautiful even than his third daughter, Keren-Happuch, the splendid one. Oh, you most beautiful creature!

You will stand there during the long, cool evenings the way you once did when I found you, Qinnamon, as twilight was falling over the field. The corpses around you will cease fouling the air with their stench. They will sink into the grass and roots will fill the silent cavities of their mouths. You will stand again as you once did, glossy and brown, in peace and quiet with the three other horses, cheeks lightly touching their flanks and sides, tail sweeping, its shining black strands flicking round the eyes and muzzles of those standing there with you, Qinnamon, your clear eyes under long straight lashes, your light, restless hooves in the grass, your body filled with vigour and peaceful strength. This is how it will be when everything around you has become quiet.

His left hand rested on the hot, glossy skin of her cheek. It moved gently down under her jaw, searching among the bundles of muscle. When it found the right place, the hand holding the knife came and set her free.

In the evening, they were out of the marshland, but had still found nothing to eat. Then they came across a jumble of wagons which had got stuck and overturned in the mud. All had been thoroughly looted. Skord noticed a pair of feet and legs under a wagon. The boots had been pulled off, but the trousers were left.

'Give us a hand, Mütz,' he said.

But they could not raise the capsized wagon without a lever. When they returned with a strong elder trunk Skord felt sure that the long yellowish feet had moved. He walked round to the other side and looked under the wagon for the face. It too was yellow and pale and stiff. He took a hen's feather from his pocket for his usual diagnostic test. When he touched the skin of the eyelid with the feather, the whole face twitched. The man's chin was beardless, but he had a thick fox-red moustache. Skord felt under the chin and placed the point of his knife under the edge of the Adam's apple. Then the half-dead – or possibly half-alive – man opened his eyes, which were blue, and started cursing.

'Bloody pile of shite,' he said. 'Fucking screwcunt.'

He went on for a while, using a wealth of expressions. Skord waggled the point of the knife and replied, 'May the deil tak ye, ye're that foul-mouthed. Y'orra bummie.'

When the man heard Skord speak in Ångermanland dialect, he thought at first he had been found by one of his own. He said his name was Torben Pärsson, and that he hailed from the village of Markom, south of the forest of Skule. He had travelled across to Germany with the Hälsinge regiment, but a gunshot wound in his right leg had healed so badly he ended up with a limp. This was how he became a wagon driver and got to serve under Captain Mathias Franck in the company of mercenary dragoons led by Alexander Gordon. Later on, he said – Skord took it he had been on the run now and then – he had arrived here under Colonel Berghoff, who had been standing with Vitzthum's reserve troops at Fretzdorf. When the General had refused to move, the Colonel was enraged and marched away with his troops. And now Torben was lying here and did not know whether the rest of the reserve had got there in time.

'Everybody has got to where they were meant to be,' Skord said. 'That was the marsh for most of them, though some have got dry ground to lie on. As for us, we're on our way out of all this, and I had the idea we would go through Finland back home to Skule.'

But Mütz, who seemed able to guess what they were talking about, said he wanted to get back to their regiment. Skord interrupted him, because he thought it unnecessary to say too much about where they had served and come to lose one arm and two field-chests.

'You'll never belong to any regiment or any company other than die verlorene Haufen, whichever side you enrol with. So you'd be wise to follow me. First of all, go down to the river and wash your trousers.'

They hauled out the lad from Markom with the foxy moustache, and found the buried parts of his body in as good a shape as could be expected. The pain caused by hasty movements affecting his broken ribs seemed an advantage to Skord until they had worked out whether they could trust each other. Still, they had become stronger than before. Now they were more likely to find food, if there was anything left to eat on their side of the Elbe.

One evening they set up camp in a small clump of trees, almost an island of woodland with ash and beech. For the last few miles they had been walking across sandy moors covered in rough heather without seeing any living things other than crows. At the edge of the marshes they had picked up a thing or two. Skord had kept his tow jacket but thrown away his pack-sheet trousers and put on new ones made of good broadcloth. Both he and Mütz found themselves strong spears. Skord acquired a helmet, which he adorned with a hare's tail and two hoopoe feathers. It was too heavy to wear on his head when he walked.

Torben had kept his fine leather trousers but found red

stockings, a red jacket and a leather waistcoat with elegant slits which allowed the squirrel-fur lining to show. The scooplike helmet was his own, dating from the time he was a private in the cavalry. In addition to his long knife, he carried an officer's sword which he reckoned he could sell when they got away from the ravaged countryside into areas where people still had cereals, cattle and coins. They had got hold of a bandoleer as well. Its eleven powder measures were used up, but the tinder box and powder-bag were untouched. They had not found any boots. Even though those ahead of them had been in a hurry, they had given themselves time to pull off the boots. All the corpses were barefoot.

Mütz had kitted himself out in a jacket with padded ridges on the shoulders and embroidered sleeves, and trousers which still had the remains of their linen lining. On his head he wore a tight-fitting cap of felted wool. It was meant to go underneath a helmet, but he had not found one. He had cut two holes in the front and carried his knife there. Secretly he felt he looked very frightening, and no longer talked about trying to find their regiment.

They were less poor than they had been when they set out, but still there was nothing but horse meat to eat. By now, after three days and nights, they had to scrape a greyish membrane from the meat before frying it. Torben, who had been on his own before, taught them to use gunpowder as a spice. Still, all three of them longed for salt. Salt and beer. Torben also longed for women, and spoke at length about the randy Polish women who travelled with the traders. He said they used to stand next to their wagons with just a cloth or a blanket on, and when the soldiers were walking down the camp lanes at sunset, they would open up the blankets and show what they had got.

Skord, who had walked down the lanes of the imperial camp in the same sunsets, had a good idea of what they had shown. Most of the time it was pretty scrawny and floppy. The women used to come to him for cures for the pox. They caught dysentery, just like their customers. He said they too were soldiers, in their way. Torben found this so funny he laughed out loud with his mouth full of partly-chewed horse meat.

Skord found little to make him laugh. Cold tedium ruled him since he lost Qinnamon. He felt like one of the living dead. They walked through countryside which all the birds had fled, except the crows. The branches of the trees were shot to pieces. He remembered the blackbird singing in the shadows when the cannons had fallen silent. When they had finished eating, he lay down on the ground to listen. But there were no birds in this wood.

'People coming!' Torben shouted. 'Put out the fire!'

Mütz peed on it, and stamped on the embers. Far away on the moor something really did move. In the haze of the sunset, it was hard to distinguish how many were in the group, two or more. But they were not on horseback. They came closer, as slowly as lice.

There were two of them, and they were carrying bundles. Inside the wood, Mütz and Torben whispered about what the bundles might contain. Silver cutlery and tableware, if these were wealthy people on the run. Salt pork. Lard with pieces of apple and onion. Or maybe just rags and worn shoes. Even when they were poor devils, refugees would bundle up whatever they had. They were getting closer, and the wood was lifeless and silent. There was no smoke. Only eyes behind the leaves.

'It's a woman! One of them is a woman!'

By now they were close enough for the white of kerchief and headscarf to show. The face of the man looked like a pale grey stain. It seemed he was clean-shaven. So, not a farmer.

'Maybe a Jew! Wealthy!'

'Maybe the bundle the woman is carrying is a child,' Skord said.

He had taken off his helmet. When the man and the woman arrived under the first trees, they stopped and put down their burdens. There was no child in the bundle of blankets. Just the two of them, with their pale faces and unseeing eyes. They forgot to look around, maybe because they were so tired.

Then the three rushed at them, shouting. Skord and Torben dealt with the man, Mütz with the woman. He used the blunt end of the spear, and he kicked. The man went down on his knees at once, his hand clasped together. He was no Jew, nor a poor devil. He was nothing.

He was nobody and became nothing. When they had opened the bundles, Mütz said, 'This is working out really well.'

No, Mütz no longer spoke of the regiment. He was pleased enough to belong with them. He said 'we' and 'us'. 'It's working out well for us.' He enjoyed belonging. His forgetful, affectionate, easily led soul was like soft ground yielding to the impressions and tracks left by others. Other people's voices and eyes drifted like spots of light across the bottom of his memory. If nobody heard him or nobody saw him, he would become lost in darkness.

The lad from Markom was of a different kind; he was someone who could have wandered on his own. Like many lone wolves, he praised himself too highly and despised others. He softened when Skord talked about his home on the southern side of the forest. How long this effect would last was unpredictable.

They stayed together. They stuck to each other except when things turned out badly. Mostly it went well enough for them and time passed. Fragments of time, the splinters, strips and rags of the streaming days that formed the years were good or, at least, good in part. A fine broadcloth waistcoat lined with lambswool. A plump Polish girl who laughed when she was tickled. A physic for the squitters.

Once they came across a cherry tree, flowering on its own in a burnt-out valley. They spoke about Markom then, and also about the other villages on that side of the forest. Further to the north cherry trees would not come into flower.

The Swedes took them just outside Stettin. Mütz disappeared and nobody knew if he had been enrolled, or if he was reckoned to be an imperial spy and taken to the gallows, arm stump and all. The other two were interrogated. They stated they had been prisoners of the imperial army, but had recently managed to escape to rejoin the defenders of the true faith.

Nobody believed them, but they were moved on to an inquiry presided over by an officer who ought to recognise them if any part of their story contained a grain of truth. His name was Mathias Franck, one-time captain in the Gordon regiment of dragoons, where Torben Pärsson claimed to have served as a wagon-driver.

Torben was recognised. Skord was trickier. He did speak an extraordinarily incomprehensible Ångermanland dialect, and did not understand a single German phrase. Generally, he said very little. But he observed.

The Captain was a heavily built man with black hair who roared and shouted as his countrymen would, convinced as they were of their descent from Magog, son of Jafet. Even those Swedes who had never heard of Isidor of Seville and his eleventh and fifteenth volumes would shout in a manly, Gothic manner.

Still, Franck was apparently no ignoramus. Skord's eyes flitted like swallows around the room with the stone walls. He noted a leather chest with its lid open. It was full of books and manuscripts. The Captain's large hairy hand was resting on top of a pile of papers, and when he had moved it a little, Skord was able to read upside down one word: PHILOSOPHISCHE. Another word became visible when Franck moved and banged the tabletop with the palm of his hand to add emphasis to some Swedish and indisputable opinion: FABRIFACTION. Eventually, when he rose and began walking between the door and the window with vigorous steps and creaking boot leather, it was possible for Skord to read easily:

DIE PHILOSOPHISCHE FABRIFACTION
DER METALLEN VON DEROSELBEN
EIGENSCHAFT, ZUSAMMENSETZUNG
UND TRANSMUTATION

The hand was wilful and energetic; plenty of blobs and scatterings of ink.

When he was taken in to see the Captain, the door had been locked from the outside. The windows were barred. He had realised that for some reason they were both in the same predicament. Later it became clear that Franck was, if anything, worse off. His death sentence had been signed. Now he was waiting, but not patiently. He raged and cursed at the Commandant in Wismar, a member of the Ulfsparre family. Ulfsparre seemed to be the origin of Franck's misfortunes, and was given many colourful names. He also swore about the shaving water, the bed clothes and the terrible food, and about Kristiern Scordius, who spoke so that no one could understand and had black hair, yet said he was Swedish and a good Lutheran.

The Captain raged on. Skord's bent head signalled submission, but his eyes wandered where they could. Now and then he would stroke the long, soft tuft of beard growing from the tip of his chin. As if absentmindedly, he started drawing a figure in the greasy dust on the table. He made a dot and surrounded it by a large circle. The Captain's black eyes gazed briefly at the sign, but he carried on ranting. Then Skord created a square which enclosed the circle and, after a moment of thought, a triangle enclosing the circle. Now there was a silence in the room.

Skord made a new and larger circle touching the three points of the triangle. He went on to add a second triangle inside the outermost circle, this time placed so that it became interlocked with the first one, to form the star-shape they call the Seal of Solomon.

The outer parts of the figure got a little blurred because the Captain had spilled beer on the tabletop. But he put his head on one side and seemed to be taking in what he saw, because he remained silent. He was not an old man. His dark eyes were lively but the whites had a yellow tinge and were criss-crossed by red veins, as if sheer biliousness had caused them to burst. The look in his eyes grew gentler as he gazed at the sign. The dot in the middle seemed to attract him. He sank into a deep well of reverie. The room became so silent they could hear the sparrows fight over the horse dung outside the window.

When the Captain looked up from his profound contemplation, Skord was sitting there smiling at him, a strand of his beard wound round his index finger. If there was something he respected, it was deep thought. But the respect was leavened by joy. This was not a matter of jesting, but of a curious, tingling excitement. Suddenly the stuffy air and the chattering of the sparrows became mixed with a sense of rich promise. He had spent three days and three nights in a stone dungeon. The gallows could be glimpsed through the window-slits. Nigredo filled the cavernous cellar. He had heard the screams of those being questioned and knew what was awaiting him. Pain and fear. Disjecta membra.

Madness ruled. Wounds stank. Flesh putrefied and turned black. Shadows and melancholia still enveloped him, but soon he would be sacrificed and the pain would become real.

But now there was instead bright daylight. Captain Franck's prison quarters looked out over the town. The sparrows fought in the sunshine on the cobbled yard. He could see a swan in the moat. It floated like a bubble of air and feathers on the sluggish green water. Now it was albedo, a time of promise and hope.

They began speaking together in good German, keeping their voices very low.

The conversations continued. The inquiry into Skord's past ceased, and he no longer had to return to the dungeon. Franck stated that he recognised him as a barber-surgeon's apprentice from the regiment of Åke Oxenstierna. This was as far back in time as the siege of Riga, and it would take months, if not years, for the records to be produced. Meanwhile, Skord was allowed to act as batman and house servant in the quarters of Captain Franck.

They spoke together about Chymical Science. Skord was not able to show what he could do with his hands, because there was not even an oven in the room, nor were they allowed to requisition anything. But words knew of no barriers or restrictions. They moved under the wide mantle of time belonging to the goat-hoofed and winged Cosmos, touched the crystalline sphere of the fixed stars, and burrowed beyond the rotting ulcers on the crust of the Earth down to the live, unborn flesh.

Humbly, the Captain admitted he was not even sure he was an adeptus. But he was full of desire. It was in fact the only thing that buoyed him up. Fundamentally, he said, he was a profound and thoughtful person who turned inwards to the secret, star-studded Gestirn which existed inside human beings but of which so few knew.

Skord said he was just the same. He would like to work towards achieving rubedo and fulfilment together with someone who had the same contemplative turn of mind as he had, and who searched for the Red Rose for its own sake, for spiritual reasons.

Still, there were several practical considerations. A pardon had to be obtained. For this, money was necessary. A lot of money. Fast ships had to be found for the homeward journey. Furthermore, Skord thought that if he got a certificate of service as a barber-surgeon in the army of the true faith, signed by Captain Franck for instance, then he could sit his chirurgical examinations in his home country. He gathered it was necessary for the candidate to cure two incurably ill hospital patients, but saw no problem with this. It should be possible for him to become a city physician within the year or sooner.

Living on a quiet street. The Captain as a neighbour. Practise arts and manual dexterity in great seclusion. A small city, like Stockholm. A cobbled yard, a tall fence along the street, and a flowering cherry tree in the yard. Porridge made from barley flour, and blueberries with milk. An attic study. If the heat under the roof beams became to much in the summer, he could move down into the yard with his books, to sit under the cherry tree. A quiet life.

Captain Franck confessed to the same deep desire: a life of profound and quiet study. He would be ready, if he could first just rip the guts out of Ulfsparre's belly. Money was on its way. Documents had been composed.

Yes, things looked quite bright. Their talks about the Cosmos continued while they were waiting. But the Captain roared when he found maggots in the salt pork, and when the responses to his documents arrived. Sometimes he descended into a state of discouragement, and then he neither cursed nor brooded. He just got drunk, and wanted company. But Skord was unwilling to drink the heavy German beer.

When Mathias Franck began drinking heavily, his talk became quite different. He would mark the tabletop by banging it with the beer mug, and say he would soon be gone. He also said that when a man dies he stays dead, and the dogs crap on his grave. No more, no less. God does not exist, and hell is no hotter than warm piss.

Skord took care not to contradict. But he did try to get Mathias to lower his voice. Too much free speech was not advisable in their situation.

'Why do I bother with you, you cunning horsefly?' Franck said. 'What are you – Polish? A Gypsy? How many lies have you spun? And how much wickedness? You're sticking to me, that's it. Shoo! You're like one of those flat flies on a cow's rump. Only way to kill you is with one's nails.'

He was jocular and splashed dark-brown, bitter beer in Skord's face. But when he had slept it off, they would talk again about the Rose and the Cosmos.

Nobody could tell what would happen to them. The documents

went to and fro, and the weeks became months. They could be sure of only one thing: they would not be forgotten.

No, the army was not going to lose Captain Franck. He was suddenly set free, told of a decision to pardon him, and forgot all the quiet things in life so completely that he did not say goodbye to the batman, who was down in the prison kitchen washing his linen. He left three good shirts behind.

Skord met up with Torben again in the stone dungeon, and for some time it seemed that the army had, if not forgotten, at least suspended its judgement of them.

One day in January they were woken, taken to court, sentenced for the crime they had been discovered committing, that is, of being in possession of a mail bag and a saddle with the three Swedish crowns stamped into the leather and only incompletely filed off. After three weeks, they were taken in a transport of foot soldiers and goods to the fort at the River Kajana in Finland. This brought them many miles closer to Markom and Skule. But Torben Pärsson never reached his home. His fox-red moustache grew paler and joined up with the long beard on his chin to form a greyish-yellow wad, like the rear of a horse. Some years later it grew thinner and white. He lost his teeth and got chilblains on his heels and toes, which turned black. When he died he weighed little more than a bundle of sticks. But he was not forgotten. The Commandant of Fort Kajana recorded his death as 'unexpected'.

These were the underground years. Skord did not count them. Here time did not loop in erratic trajectories. Time was a room. No one travelled anywhere since there were no roads to travel.

At first, the room was a stone basement in the fort. It was the filth which flowed over the floor and belonged to the underworld. It was the stench, as solid as the walls around them, and it was the screams. Sticks and stones were used to hammer home the truth that they were evildoers, villains, murderers, thieves, malcontents, deserters, rogues and outlaws. They knew these things without needing to be told, but the soldiers and guards, stuck in the same place, had to inscribe it on their backs in order to maintain the difference between themselves and their prisoners. They were all caught in the same underground world.

Later, the room became a small island in the torrent below the fort building but inside the perimeter wall. They were made to move into a timber hut, put up there quite some time ago. This was carved into the lintel above the door opening:

PHS NPS HAF PITTIN IT UP
GOD KENS WHA WILL TAK IT DOON
22 MAI
1622

But PHS and NPS, whoever they were – or, more likely, had been – had been forced to work at speed. The hut had been built from unseasoned timbers, which had dried out as time passed; now there were wide gaps between each one. They tried to stop up the gaps, but all the moss on the island had been used up long ago. Only stunted elder and willow grew down by the water's edge. They lived surrounded by the raw mists and noise of the torrent, summer and winter. Usually, there was nothing to feed a fire. The Royal Crown Estates would distribute firewood, bones for soup, turnips and flour, but, as Skord had said, quite erratically. He was hit over the mouth for that, to teach him not to use such fancy words. What was fancy or practicable was decided, like everything else on the island, by Piru-Erkki.

There was an order enforced at the upper level of the underworld, which ultimately derived from the promulgation at Mount Sinai. The higher authority in the tower and the fort did not carry sticks, muskets, knives and clubs in vain. Among them, the Commandant was highest and therefore closest to the Lord Lieutenant of the County, the Queen and God. Next came the guards in descending order of rank all the way down to the old private soldiers serving as prison guards. Everyone below this should, in the view of the upper echelons, be regarded as common filth, in which one pile of shit was to reach no higher than any other. But a hierarchy existed even there.

Piru-Erkki had the highest standing. You belonged either to his circle of almost-equals or to their lackeys. Some could go right down to the bottom layer and become the slaves of lackeys. Slaves and lackeys were used for sport, as well as for labouring and running errands. It was a kind of sport Skord found hard to take. It did not involve kind words or play. Only heavy breathing, ruptures and pain. He would moan that he was suffering from the French pox but still he did not escape. His wizardry should have been useful. But here it often failed him. In the cold and filth of the underground he could not find the spirit and ferment needed for good magic. Everything went at half cock, and was barely enough to save him from the worst kind of maltreatment. His dexterity and talent for barter and trade did nothing for him, because here people took what they wanted. Nor was there much worth stealing. He had to control his tongue. All artful talk annoyed Piru-Erkki. In the beginning Skord had let himself run on, but few listened to his flow of chatter and no one was amused. They seemed as indifferent to a nice turn of phrase as to all attempts to kill the lice by freezing or heave the worst muck out of the hut.

Nor did Piru-Erkki care much for medical skills and advice. He treated wounds the hard way, and was not interested in being soft on others. He claimed to have killed somebody who disturbed his sleep at night, and warned them all against excessive coughing. So Skord had no use for his ability to heal either. All he could do was to keep his back pliable and bent over, and watch his tongue. He did not end up on the lowest rungs of the underworld. He was one of the lackeys and, after two years of deaths among them, the only one left.

When the insects started swarming over the water round the island, Skord twisted a fishing line together and bent and filed his first barbed hook. First he used leaf-caterpillars as bait, and later flies tied from bird's down and pretty feathers. He also started a worm-pit by making a pile of leaves and rubbish.

The torrent boiled and glittered with fish. The salmon trout had light, almost silvery sides with red spots glowing the colour of blood. There was plenty of whitefish, and there were grayling, shy and hard to catch. Piru-Erkki permitted fishing. Neither he nor any of the others liked the bland taste of fish which had not been well cured in brine. Still, hunger made them put up with it. But only Skord could eat raw fish. This was how he managed to hide some away down at the water's edge, and by high summer he was already more agile and less scurvy and haggard. His thoughts moved more easily and stopped circling endlessly around how he was to get something into his belly. He also felt words being born of his thoughts and came up with one or two really nice turns of phrase. But he had nobody to talk to. The torrent rumbled, gurgled, roared, tinkled, boomed. It did not listen.

One light night he was sitting on his haunches at the edge of a small pool of still, deep water. He often crept down to cast a line there whenever he was able to stay up at night. There was a rustling noise in the bushes on the bank and he saw a black pig making its way down to the water. It poked about with its snout in the mud between the stones. He stayed with his rod and thought about how unreachable the Commandant's pigs were. They were on the wrong side of the stream and never got into the water.

Some time passed. The fly floated on the still black water and was slowly pulled towards a small whirlpool. He pulled back and was just going to cast again when he thought he heard a dog's bark over the roar of the fall. He was used to the mocking noises and false voices created by the water as it leaped over the stones, so he did not look up until the excited barking had steadied. Then he noticed a black dog standing at the parapet of the fortress just above the island, where the soldiers used to stand when they amused themselves by throwing stones at the prisoners. The dog barked for a while longer, then jumped down and disappeared.

It was at this point Skord realised that something was happening to him. He forgot rod and fly, and became indifferent to the stinging midges which crawled into his eyes and nostrils. There was a saying that whoever went down to a stream at midnight and saw a black pig and then a black dog, to him the Horse of the Burn would show himself. He sat very still, hunched up, scanning the opposite bank. He was not sure he wanted to see the Water-Kelpie in a horse's body. There was no knowing who he was, except that he belonged to the usually invisible creatures from the other side. They said he was wicked or maybe seemed wicked, although really innocent and unknowing, but born out of mist and fog, out of soil and silt and bottomless mud.

There was a flash of white close by him. The outline of an agile back, no thicker than his forearm, slipped out of sight between the stones. He did not get to see any more than that. But something was happening to him. During the nights to come, he saw more glimpses of that swift-moving back in the half-light.

'What do you want with me?' he asked without moving his lips. 'Ill or well? Where do you come from and who has sent you?'

It was not by chance that the small light-coloured creature had let himself be seen. It would have been easy for him to avoid being spotted in the twilight. But powerful portents had foretold his coming. What was he? Not a stoat or a weasel. Maybe an otter. But it was uncommon to find such animals in places as far north as this. And what caused his whiteness, which made him so shining and visible?

Skord called him with tight lips.

White worm, creeper and twister! Come closer, you small bundle hiding under stones and among roots. Do you hail from the other side? Come whoever you are, you arch-backed, looping creature! Whom do you serve? Is it honey on your tongue, or venom? Earth is your father, and your mother too; you are dust and so am I. We have lived on the same earth, and drunk the same water. I am condemned to this underworld and have to eat bitter roots. But we are of the same kind, you and I. Come closer! Do not leave your brother in the night and mist. The torrent is roaring, it is terrible here among the stones. Speak or stay silent, but do not slither away, you silken back, you little silver paw, you golden snout among the sharp-jawed! Come closer, show yourself to your brother! We were born of the same earth!

When he still did not show himself, Skord looked in the scattered heaps of stones and under the willows and often found scraps: eggshells carrying the marks of sharp incisors, bones of frogs and heads of toads, bitten off just behind the poison glands.

One evening the twisting creature came along and perched on a stone for a long time. His fur shone white without any darker shades but along his back were stiff hairs which gleamed like pure gold in the low late sunlight. He held his small head with the round, alert ears upright as he watched Skord. He did not stare steadily and challengingly the way people do, but politely in that he mostly looked elsewhere, and now and again showed he was noticing and interested by quickly glancing back. His red eyes looked like small, brightly lit gems. Skord sat still, his heart hammering. He did not dare say anything, not even behind closed lips. When the agile animal vanished with a soft, fluid movement, his tail repeating the arching line of his back, Skord felt joy in his stomach and chest, yes, even high up at the base of his throat. This was something he had not felt for a very long time. It was summer. He was stuck in prison, but even here it was truly summer and nights were light. The black waters formed little loops of silver at his feet. Moths and feather midges and mayflies were dancing. They had been prisoners during a hard winter. Now gentle summer had freed them. They were saved and refreshed. Dear Lord! Summer had come to this place too and until now, he had failed to greet and enjoy it. The cold, heavy winter fog had been driven away, and so had the snow and the coughing, the damp chills and dank air. Earth had dressed up: she was looking lovely in a green dress and had prettified herself with flowers. She offered sweet perfumes and loveliness in return for having been released from winter's cold prison. The great stream danced in jolly currents. Springs and streams gurgled and rustled. The waters were freed from ice and let everyone know by their rippling melodies and hearty laughter.

The birds were singing though it was night-time. It was still light and all the branches were bursting with greenery: sticky, tightly folded leaves which would be smoothed by the next morning's sun.

They were free and had not been destroyed.

When he sneaked back into the hut to join the hard-knuckled and sharp-jawed men, they were asleep in their own evil gusts of air, and he was able to put down the branch with the fish and curl up without being spoken to.

Now he began leaving fish for the small arch-backed animal, which he thought might be an otter. But when he came down in the morning, the trout fry were untouched, dried out and stiff. Skord had wanted to reach him in this way and did not like giving up the idea. Maybe leaving fish looked like a cunning trick. Skord gave assurances, many times, that all he wanted was an agreement between the two of them. By now he was convinced there was a good spirit alive inside the white fur.

One night he was sitting a little way off, licking his paws in order to prepare them for polishing his whiskers, and Skord told him that they had set up a trap for him over by the hen-house.

'I don't know where it's placed or what it looks like, because we only hear bits and pieces of what is said among those up there on the wall. Just look out for anything that stinks of people, because they know you're the egg thief.'

The small animal arched his neck gracefully before slipping away and vanishing into the glowing grey light. When they met the following night he sat much closer to Skord than he used to and uttered something sounding like a hiss.

'Who are you?' Skord asked.

'Frret,' the animal said. When Skord leaned closer he heard it again: 'Frret! Ferret!'

It sounded as if he was trying to speak in a hoarse, unpractised voice. Later, it got better and better. He used words with care, once he had got voicebox and tongue under control, and soon one would not have known it was the first time he tried speech.

He said he really was a ferret, and told of how, once, he too had been living as a prisoner. It had been an agreeable and rather lazy existence in a Ukrainian village. He had been born to be tame, and his task was chasing rabbits out of their sandy burrows when his master felt like hunting. Mostly, he remembered soft pillows and bedlinen, a large, slow river rich in fish, the warmth from a big fire on the hearth and, especially, the smell of burning poplar wood. His master had been good and had never forgotten to feed him for as long as he himself had food.

Skord explained that, although he was a prisoner now, things had been different for him. The ferret's ears twitched and he placed his front paws close together, showing clearly how eager he was to hear of Skord's past. But his interest faded when Skord said he had been a barber-surgeon and owned two great chests full of medical and surgical equipment. Skord could still list everything in the chests and did so, though he realised that he was speaking to the rustling river water and to the alders, dipping their long-fingered branches into the water as it rushed past. The ferret had disappeared.

He came back a little later, when Skord had finished his list, and, sitting between two stones, said he had been wondering what Skord had been before he acquired possessions.

'That's harder to tell,' Skord said.

The ferret inclined his head, as if he understood. 'How come you started to take an interest in collecting more than you could eat?' he asked.

He admitted there was a certain sense in hiding things and keeping stores. He himself might bury an egg under the moss and sometimes find it when he was hungry. But to the best of his knowledge no living being ever left anything behind that did not decay and disappear. Could Skord please explain why his human companions were so keen on collecting and storing things? His master had not behaved that way, but generally people often died without eating what they had amassed.

Skord explained that they did not know when they were likely to pass away, and they all hoped they would live for longer than anyone before them. This was the reason why they filled up these great stores.

'Besides, among people, those who own nothing are worth less than bedbugs. They squash such creatures with their nails. Or lock them up in stone cellars.'

Then the ferret thanked him for answering, and said good night with the expectation – or was it a wish? – that they would meet again.

That they did. It was not worth Skord's while to think of taking over the ferret's body to get away from the island and his own powerlessness. The ferret resisted, without either of them saying a word about the matter. In spite of having been tame and enjoyed the good things in life – eggs and house rats, sometimes cream and as much fish he could eat – he had a profound distrust of people. He preferred to stay out of sight and have nothing to do with them, even those who kept hens. Indeed, Skord thought he observed resentment and even disgust at all things human. But the ferret was too polite to enlarge on this, because outwardly Skord looked like a human.

That said, he seemed to feel less adverse to prisoners, who did not wear caps and collars made from animals like minks or stoats. Once he had spotted Count Brahe himself visiting the fort, a poisonous toad of great girth. He was sitting on his horse wearing a sable-lined cloak. The ferret noted his great lump of a belly hanging down in front of him and assumed it must be yellow lard the Count had collected to last many days to come.

But the ferret accepted thin people who moved quietly among the stones on the riverbank. At least, Skord liked to think so, and they kept talking together. As Skord saw it, their conversations were exchanges between two free beings, carried on over many nights in the grey light amid the roaring of the torrent. The ferret explained he did not want to be anybody's servant any more. Whatever he might be offered by way of eggs, cream and fish, he preferred his freedom. Skord agreed that he too wanted to stop being a lackey, but had to choose slavery so as not to get killed. He also said that at times he had seen little point in freedom when it meant marshes and moors where he would be picked up before long, and once more enrolled or put into prison.

'Yes, you do speak like a human,' the ferret said. 'Just for a moment I thought you were something else.'

This hurt Skord. The ferret's words cut him, causing a sharp pain where no one for a long time – maybe ever – had managed to get at him.

'Who are you?' he said. 'And what have I got to do with you?'

'Nobody and nothing,' was the answer of the ferret. And he disappeared between two stones.

But they met again a couple of nights later and got talking. After a rather pointless and polite exchange about fishing and weather, Skord said a little sharply that the ferret must find humans attractive in some ways, since he wanted to continue their conversations.

'I don't mind a sensible talk between equals,' the small, light creature said, 'but I do not want any agreements or contracts between us.'

'Nor do I have anything against passing the odd night-time hour or two in conversation,' Skord said. 'But I am not keen to hear any sneers or meanness about humans.'

The ferret was sitting very straight on his stone, his front paws close together. When he heard Skord's answer, a small twitching movement ran the length of his body, from the stiff, shining whiskers to the tip of his tail and out into the sharp-clawed paws. But he answered politely that in so far as they had time to spare from feeding, before the club struck or the trap slammed shut for either of them or both, they should of course spend it as pleasantly as they could and in mutual respect.

There was one human being the ferret liked speaking about, and that was his master. He had not been like the others, but turned inwards towards the night. In the end he had left farm and family, and set out wandering. The ferret had followed him, although the companionship brought him no visible advantages. He had fished on his own, stolen eggs and caught toads in the marsh pools. His master had walked barefoot, mumbling long strings of words which were hard to catch. The words might have been calls or greetings aimed at the person he was searching for, as he drifted from one village to the next. In the end there was no need for him to keep saying the words. He had said it was as if the words had moved into his heart, where an inner tongue kept repeating them. From then on their partnership worked well again. They talked agreeably. When things were terrible the master encouraged him with a phrase he used so often that it stuck in the ferret's mind. He had kept saying, 'Thus I believe the travails we endure will be as nothing to the glory revealed to us in time.'

Finally they had travelled so far west that the Swedes picked up his withdrawn master with the mumbling heart, and held him on suspicion of spying. He was tortured, without giving anything away about his inner voice, and then taken to the fort on the River Kajana, where he had been left to rot. He had never complained or despaired. The ferret had often visited him in prison and stayed on after his master's death because the riverbank was rich in frogs and good hiding places. He admitted to staying for reasons really to do with their friendship. His master was of course dead and had turned into an uninteresting heap of bones with the odd rag and tendon still attached. But the heart of the ferret was still full of affection which he did not know what do with.

He enquired whether Skord knew anything about the glory his master had so often referred to, and whether he might have reached it by means of some part of his being that had not been affected by torture and illness.

With this, their talk took a new turn. They no longer spoke of the day's fishing or possession of this and that. There was no further mention of field-chests.

Skord had to admit that he could not answer the question about glory. But a few nights later he himself had a question to raise, which had preoccupied him for some time. 'Your master would appear to have turned towards the night. When he taught his heart to speak on its own, perhaps he called out to the night. There are strong and unfathomable forces about at night-time. We try to name them and make them work in our favour. But I have found no way to make them obey.

'Nor do I know,' Skord said, 'whether they make sport with us and if so, what their purpose might be. Many people claim to have good relationships with the forces of the night. When I am high-spirited enough, I humbly try to practise some magic skills. But, to be frank, I'm not familiar with the Ones Who Cannot Be Understood – with those Beings, who might be called Someone or possibly Not-Someone.

'It seems to me,' he went on, 'as if He or They leave us to act in a room which confines far too closely the powers we draw from night and darkness.

'Ferret, there is something I must ask you. You have lived both the human way and the animal one and, in your being, you may have some connection with this darkness of which I know nothing more than to respect it. Have you found any will or purpose or even – dare I ask? – any benevolence out there in the night?'

The ferret answered that such deep thought did not come naturally to him, but he was profoundly impressed by those who were gifted in research and speculation. His dead master had often spoken of unverifiable matters. He had believed that the forces did not spring from darkness but were of the light.

'Of the light, truly?' Skord asked.

'Yes,' answered the ferret. 'At least, that's how he put it. But the light is not yet created, as it were.'

'Can all things take their origin from a state not yet created? Besides, we have light around us, surely, at least during the day and in summer also during the night?'

'Most of the light – at least in the opinion of my dead master – is not yet created,' the ferret said. 'But I must admit our conversation, agreeable as it is, is now taking a course beyond my understanding.'

The water was gurgling between the rocks. Feather midges and night mosquitoes danced above the deep pools. If their rapture took them too close to the surface they were caught in the black water. To their fragile wings it seemed as tough as tar. Skord felt cold. The ferret was sitting on a stone in the torrent, cleaning his whiskers and nose with his front paws. It was still light, and they could hear a flight of woodcocks. It sounded as if tiny sheep-bells were tinkling eagerly inside their throats and long ribbons of ringing calls were woven above the marshland, which had started to give off a strong fragrance mingling with the smoky night-time mist. After a while Skord wished the ferret good hunting. As for himself, he returned to the human stench, with some ordinary-sized trout threaded on a branch.

The white ferret and Skord would never meet again, though they did not know this when they said good night.

Mathias Franck came travelling from Uleåborg. By now, he was a lieutenant colonel and responsible for recruitment to the army fighting the Russians, a brand-new war in which he was to do well. Skord recognised him at once. His hair, now streaked with silver, was still worn almost shoulder-length. His trousers and jacket were made from broadcloth of the colour called sang de boeuf. He had a wide linen collar and his boots were made from new, pale-yellow ox leather. Skord was among those prisoners who were freed and then enlisted. Franck fancied himself as his saviour, and gave Skord a comradely slap on his bony back.

After living as best he could on the island surrounded by raw mists and rushing water, Skord was pleased to be given clothes and fed cured pork with peas. But after a week on soldier's rations he nearly shat his guts out. The Lieutenant Colonel led his squadron across Torne River and down to Nordmaling, and then further south. When Kristiern Skord saw the first field of flax in flower, near the first village south of the forest, he deserted.

South of the forest, life was good and solid. It was like the damask made in Ångermanland, strong and glossy and resistant to dirt.

Just below Skule Mountain, the first field of flowering flax belonged to the Pastor, the Reverend Menandrius. The Pastor's daughters were put in front of the loom as soon as they were able to reach the pedals. It was the Pastor himself who worked out how the linen thread should be tied so that the pattern showed, dark against light and light against dark. The house maids, who had been told how to make simpler cloth, marvelled at the way the patterns took shape and said it must be magic or second sight. None but the daughters could interpret the Pastor's heddle-notes and as grown women they never used anything less than twelve shafts. They knew the secret or at least could guess at how, by setting the threads at right angles to each other, their father created patterns of glossy sheen and plain weave in reversed mirror images on the two surfaces of the cloth.

Menandrius sowed his flax in deep, rich soil and took pride in his fields being almost free from weeds. The flax was beautiful when the plants were in flower and again when they were resurrected from death and decay. The fine cloth was first wound tightly round the beam, but when spread out, it reflected the purposeful, incisive mind and good intentions of Pastor Menandrius. How deep was the glow of the final cloth, guided in its making by the sharp eyes and sensitive fingers of the daughters! And look at the selvage, said the maids, letting the cloth run between thumb and index finger. It was then folded and packed. The traders going south put the bundles into their sledges, together with such wares as cloudberry jam, mese cheese, dried fish, frozen birds and skins. The Stockholm merchants would pay as much for this linen cloth as they would for the finest table damask from Haarlem in Holland.

Even while he was writing his sermons, Pastor Menandrius could not stop thinking about the preparation of flax and the weaving of linen. These tasks supplied him with metaphors, not so much in the strict and profound sense of Aristotle, but simple similes for the relationship between God and Man. Surely it was worth while to ponder on how God sowed the souls of human beings on Earth and let them grow, in order to prepare them for a new and eternal life. But all that grows in a field of flax cannot end up glowing and white. Some lives are so knotted from the start, and their thread of life so marred with tufts, that they could not possibly be meant to become white cloth. What should be done with them?

Pastor Menandrius had to deal with just such a life in his own flock. It was a slattern of a girl, a skinny slut, made plain by ringworm and bruises. Her name was Lena, and later on she was called Rick-Yard Lena and later still just Rick-Lena. The father was a norwoodsman. The mother had died and in the winter the children were often seen begging. Then the father finished up dead after a forest accident, and the children were left in the care of the parish. The eldest boy went on living in the cottage. He kept his father's saw and axe, and now he was the one who cut timber for the farmers. Lena, the girl, stayed to cook for him and milk the goat.

There had been ugly talk about them when the father was alive and now it got worse. Finally the Pastor and the farmers in the parish decided that the brother-and-sister household had to be dissolved. The girl went to the manse.

She was born in perdition. Still, the Pastor did not always have it in him to be as strict with her as he ought to. He grew weak and hard at the same time. For she was like wild valerian, which glows in the night and has a sweet but sometimes sickening smell. Her corruption was stamped deeply into her, like a hoofmark in black mire. Someone – maybe many – had trampled on yielding ground.

Some time later, the girl grew fat-bellied and had to be got rid of. That summer she lived in a brew-house. After she gave birth in September, she was allowed to move into a run-down empty cottage. It was called Paith because the cattle track started there.

Without letting on to anyone, a couple of farmers' sons came along and mended the chimney breast so that she could light fires. She lived as well as she could up there at the forest's edge, and it was during this time that her nickname stuck. She used to meet those who had been good to her in an old rick-yard and tried to clear her debts to them there. The Pastor died, at the age of fifty-eight, without having been able to do anything about the ruin she was born to.

She bore three children. Though the thread of her life was rough, she seemed to have found a way to live and was counted as a member of this solid village south of the forest. She and her bairns rarely had to go hungry, and when the spring iced up, she fetched her water from the well. She would walk down the cattle track too early for anyone else to be about, with her eyes downcast.

One morning when she reached the well, a man was standing in front of it. She had thought no one would be up so early and made to turn back when she caught sight of him. But she needed the water. Quietly she walked to the well and started hauling. The man, who was young and pale, was standing silently a bit away from her. When she got the yoke up on her shoulders and hooked on the pails, he asked her for a drink of water. This troubled her. 'I have no scoop,' she said.

'I could drink from your hand,' he replied.

She had never seen him before and did not know what he wanted, but put her pails down again.

'No,' he said. 'Do not offer me water to drink from your hand, because I cannot touch it. Do you not realise how soiled you are?'

This frightened her because she could see from his clothes and his white hands that he must be someone in authority, young as he was.

'Do you not understand how sorely you have sinned?' he asked. 'You cannot take your water here.'

She was frightened, but asked, 'How can we live without water?'

He said she had better find it somewhere else.

'Where? This is July, when the heat of summer is stronger than any other time.'

But he said she had to leave the village. 'Do you not know who I am?'

She did not know and stayed silent. He said he was the new pastor.

'You can no longer share the body and precious blood of the Saviour.'

'I want water,' she said. 'My little ones are thirsty.'

'I am being more merciful than you deserve,' he said. Then he told her that it had been decided she should be tried for having led a whore's life and borne three children in secrecy. He had risen early that morning to warn her.

'On your way,' he said. 'Go before they come to get you.'

She lifted her pails again and started walking. But she had not taken many steps before she stopped as if she were waiting for him.

'Go!' he said. 'You think I have done this because of your face or the white skin on your neck. Do you not understand that you are a corpse, still whole on the outside but rotten within?'

She left after that.

The young pastor returned home. Rick-Lena was a little older than he was and he had been scared thinking about her. Seeing her had not made it any better. There was something stern and dark running through the corrupt loveliness he had heard spoken of. His hands had been shaking when he set out to tell her that she had no right to the body and blood of the Saviour. But he had not planned to warn her of her banishment. Now he felt confused and did not know what he was to say to his wife, the old pastor's widow, who was a most proper and strict lady and thirty years older than her new husband. So far he had acted in parish matters as she advised. She knew the conditions. It was she who had enlightened him about evil being rampant and looking after its own in darkest secrecy inside the cottage at Paith. Up there it was like an earwig's nest, she said. We must be rid of this vermin. Now he was unsure why he had warned Rick-Lena and thought he had better keep quiet about the encounter at the well.

Rick-Lena took to the forest. Her escape became known the same day. It would have been right and proper to go out and get her back. What with the children and her bundles, it would have been easy to catch up with her on horseback. But they let her run.

'Do you not understand how badly you have sinned?' the young priest had asked her.

Only when she reached the forest did she begin to understand. The children were hungry and afraid of the forest. But she felt very repentant and did not mind hunger and thirst. The whole night she lay benumbed in her shame, neither asleep nor awake. She was stiff in the morning and found it hard to get up. The rain had stopped but the trees were still dripping. The wet leaves and ferns were rustling. The two older children had crawled in under a fir tree and were still asleep, close together, when she touched them. The little one, wrapped in his swaddling, was lying where she had left him on a bed of moss. She did not know if she had heard him cry but a sound like the babbling of a brook had haunted her in her dwalm. It had stopped now. She could hear only the brook itself, gurgling and rattling over the stones. The little one was swollen and hot. The midges had left bites on his face, neck and hands. His lips had cracked and the thin skin was flaking. Upset, she tried to give him water from the hollow of her hand, but he would not take it.

They could not live on their own nor survive on berries and water. She walked with her children to Skule and met those who lived there, the outcasts. She offered them her body in exchange for food, but they took her daughter's as well. The youngest child did not live long. She was never able to wake him from his feverish stupor. The water and milk she tried to give him just poured out of his mouth.

She saw everything that happened to the girl. It took place in front of her eyes. The older boy grew up in the forest. He became quick and obedient. Soon he would be a robber, an equal among the freebooters. As for herself, she had hardened long ago. A cold surface had settled over her penitence, her shame and life of sin. She was exactly what the pastor had said. She remembered his words and asked herself every day: why does a corpse try to live? Why does it stump around, eating what it can find, sometimes tidying its hair?

Once she approached the village. Eight years had passed by then, but she knew they would recognise her. Still, she came out of the forest and went down past the cottage and the rick-yard, and continued down the cattle track. It was early dawn on a chilly day in May. None of the people would be about so early in the morning. She wanted to drink and then return to the forest without being seen. She hauled up a pailful of water without letting it hit the wall of the well, and drank. All was done soundlessly in the cold of the morning. She was just about to steal away when she saw she was not alone. A man was sitting by the well. He asked her for a drink of water.

'If you knew who I am, you would not take a drink from me,' she said.

He said he knew who she was. He still wanted a drink of water because he was thirsty. She burst into violent weeping.

Can a corpse weep?

They were sitting by the well when the first of the women came to get their water. They did not seem to recognise her. Perhaps I am dead, she thought. She could tell who they were, although they had grown older. She recognised the men as well, as they came clattering past with their horses and tools. Some of them had once been at work between her legs. She thought of how they had been kneeling on the flagstone floor of the church while she had been sitting by the brook in the forest. They had sucked sweet wine from the wounds of the Saviour. They had been stuck to his body like horse leeches.

'First my father sinned against me,' she said. 'Then my brother did, and then the Pastor. All said the sin was mine.'

She waited for him to say something, but he did not. So she went on, 'They sinned against an innocent. They cast their uncleanness into the cup of a flower.'

He reached out his hand and she was not sure whether he wanted something of her or was taking his leave.

'Don't go!' she cried.

He did not take away his hand. It rested on the ground, palm upwards. She spat in it then.

'What do you want with me?' she shouted, although he was so close to her he could have heard her whispering. His eyes were closed, and she could see he was in pain.

'It's not as bad as that,' she said. 'Surely you should get up and leave now, if that's what you want.'

But he did not move. She turned away to avoid having to see his face. For a long time she sat curled up against the morning cold, and when she looked again he had not gone away. His pain seemed worse than before.

'You can drink if you're thirsty,' she said. 'If you could come all this way, surely you're able to haul up a pail.'

His lips were swollen and cracked. But he did not suffer from thirst alone. It was as if her uncleanness had been cast on him. She had done it, but could not work out how it had come about. The furious itching which had tormented her little one and the thirst she had let him endure because of her penitence, and the tearing pain driven through the body of her girl, and the beatings which hardened her boy – all these things she had thrown at him, and he had borne the impact. It was as if sin had been a burden she had been carrying for others and could no longer bear, like a sack of stones, a cluster of snakes, a pail full of boiling hot lye or a belly bursting with bad blood.

'But must it be borne by someone?'

He was sitting there with his eyes closed. She did not understand why he had to take on her burdens, nor why her wickedness made her throw them at him.

'Lord, if it is that we can only rid ourselves of pain by making somebody else suffer, and suffer more than we did; Lord, if we must live in degradation before we can rise and begin degrading another; if sin is a burden we must hand on; if you are the one who in the end must take on my uncleanness, if you are the open chalice, then, Lord, I curse you!'

It had been early in the morning when she met him. Everyone had been asleep, and she had walked so quietly her steps had not woken the dogs. She did not know why she had walked to the well.

Now the evening stillness had fallen. They had sat by the well while the women had come and gone with their crocks, and nobody had taken any notice. It was as if both of them had been invisible, or as if he was and had cast a cloak of gentle forgetfulness over her, making people hurry on past without tearing her hair and clothes, spitting in her face or pulling at her limbs. When it started getting dark, they were alone again. His face was in shadow. Soon she would no longer be able to see him. She began talking again.

'It has done me some good to meet You,' she said, wanting to hide that he had hurt her. 'I do not recognise Your face. You hold your head to one side. You are pale and sweating blood. You reject me when I leave my uncleanness in You. I do not want to exist in a world where the violated must violate others in order to become free, and where the guilty cannot rid himself of guilt without passing it on to someone else, as if to make him carry hot lead.

'But meeting you has caused me pain,' she went on. 'I do know Your face. I have seen it before. Its pallor and sweatiness come from holy piety and eagerness to save me. But this salvation offends me, and drives me out among those who have taken to the forest, God's own children.'

'You pull me towards You,' she said.

Then she saw: his face was not a face and the skin stretching over it was not skin. It was dark night. Still they did not separate. He stayed awake all night, and she slept at times and felt cold.

It was early morning now, before the dogs of the village had woken, and before the women had started rattling their crocks. The cows had not yet come down from the forest to have the milk pulled out of them, and their lowing had not yet roused a soul. Then he indicated to her that she should go.

'You pull me towards You,' she said, 'and now You make me leave You.'

'You walk away alive,' he said.

Then she rose and pulled her skirts together, and walked through the wet grass towards the forest. She did not turn round because she knew she would no longer see him next to the well.

Late one summer a squadron of cavalry rode through Skule forest led by an officer who urged the soldiers to make great haste. Rick-Lena saw them. She did not know why they were in such a hurry, nor where they had to get to. She had lived for so long among the outlaws that she knew nothing of other people's wars.

At a rest break in the forest one man ran away, and they had to go after him. A few hours later they gathered again, and two of them had the runaway tied to a horse led between them. But when they had got him down, the horse veered off and disappeared into the forest. The officer, whose name was Drakenstierna, but was known as Black Franckie, roared that it was one goddamned thing after another. They knew that all the horses ridden by the escaped man tended to become difficult and keen to set off into the forest. Now they would have to delay further in order to look for the horse and catch it. They strung up the runaway.

Those living on the hillside had listened in the forest and watched the riders from high up in the cave. Rick-Lena went along to see if they had left something behind. She followed the smell of smoke along to their camp site. When she arrived in the clearing the fire had burned out. Coming out from her hiding place behind the firs to root among the rubbish round the fire pit, she caught sight of the runaway. They had strung him up from a sturdy pine. But he was dangling from one foot. Maybe the officer wanted to spare him. His face was turning blue and his long hair, which was black and soft, was hanging straight down. She took out the knife she always kept in the waistband of her skirt, walked up to him and cut him down.

Drakenstierna's Treasure

It is night and he is sitting at the table writing. His pen scrapes like the claw of a bird. Sometimes it twitches and splutters as if the bird is trying to take off. But it is only chaff that has interrupted the flow of the writing. The candles in their holders are dripping. He is sitting still and the linen of his shirt is tinged green by the reflection of the coat hanging on the wall. He writes on, forgetting to feel cold.

The door is open and lets in warmth and the sound of the old woman's breathing. She is dying, but her lungs still demand air. He hears her and he does not hear her, just as he feels cold and does not feel cold. His foot in a dull yellow sock pushes against the floor. Pieces of chopped juniper have stuck in the wool. He dips his pen in the ink-well and stares without seeing at the tabletop beyond the paper. He has been chewing on the quill, and the tip tends to split when he shapes the powerful stems of the letters.

'Forgot, with no Hope for Life,' he writes. Then the pen stops, though there is no unevenness in the paper. Something has occurred to him. The candles flutter in the draught from the window. He looks up. The small panes between the cames reflect the candle flames, which are moving like water plants in a current. Then he hears the groaning sounds. He also realises that the young woman is standing in the doorway. He has heard and not heard her skirt and socks swish across the floor. She says to his back, 'She moans so.'

'She's insensate,' he answers, and puts pen-nib to paper. He hears the sounds of skirt and socks as she leaves. He does not write, but instead tries to stare through the darkness in one of the small window-panes. But all he can distinguish is the star-shaped, fragile ice crystals and the mirror images of the fluttering candles.

It is Christmas night. Now and then the timber walls creak. He grasps the sandbox and holds it for a long time. He wants to go on writing, but listens instead. The dying woman gasps for air; it makes a rasping noise in her windpipe. He thinks about how only the three of them are at home. The others are well on their way to church. Heavy horses in the snow, lumps of snow in the fetlocks, sliding runners and clouds of icy steam from mouths and nostrils.

Now the ink on the nib has dried. He dips it, but does not write. Something has taken over. He is no longer engaged in the writing. His gaze wanders from the paper to the boxes. Inside are dead insects: weevils, dung-beetles, spinner moths and saw-flies. He observes the bottled frogs. The herbaria are full of plants. Straw, he says to himself. Straw.

Rattling and gurgling noises come from the old woman's airways. It sounds as if the air is tearing the tissues in windpipe and lungs. He can hear the girl sobbing. He puts the pen down, rises and walks over to the chest by the door. He opens the lid and rummages among clothes and papers until he finds a small package wrapped in a frail piece of silk. Cautiously he carries it over to the table.

It is Kristian Skord, and he has not changed apart from losing his long soft goatee. It has been replaced by a pair of butterfly wings above his mouth. He is almost a doctor now. For a long time he has been studying the contents of chamberpots with great interest, even getting up very early in the morning to examine what has been expelled from the rear ends of unwell ladies. Most of his consultations have been with women, but he is an eminent stone-excisor and has had male clients. He is skilled at mixing the ingredients for pill-balls and rolling them in lycopodium powder, and preparing poultices and applying them to tumours and to abdomens with aching ovaries. He has cut up cadavers and poked about in them to learn more about how things are arranged. He very nearly became Doctor of Medicine at Leyden in the Netherlands.

He has ended up in this village below the forest of Skule after having been all set to travel as the assistant and guide to a learned professor of medicine and botany on a journey to Lapland. However, in his eagerness to demonstrate the wonders of Skule forest, Skord ran about so hard that he had a bad fall in the

Slåttsdal ravine. He was taken by stretcher to the village and, since his leg was broken, left behind in bed while the Professor rode on accompanied by two young counts and an illustrator called Holzborn.

It was annoying but he did not despair. Once he was able to get around with the help of a stick, he began collecting insects, birds' eggs, rare plants and reptiles. He put them into boxes and composed labels, he pressed, dried, drew likenesses and preserved in spirits, which he heated in a copper pan with a spout. This kept him busy all summer long, and by the autumn he had started writing.

He is planning to sit the examinations to become a medical doctor. This is a firm intention of his. But sometimes his intentions are shifted by something, some invisible, almost imperceptible obstacle – just as an irregularity in the paper prevents writing from flowing evenly from the nib of a pen. He becomes irresolute. Now this has occurred so many times he has decided to use the cards. Christmas Eve – or the morning of Christmas Day – has some time to go before dawn, and this is a good moment to ask questions about what will be. During all the time he has been writing, which has been his occupation for most of the autumn and winter before Christmas, he has been speculating about his own fate. He realises his fate seems curious, or rather downright peculiar, but it is similar to the movements of the pen across the paper. He sees his complicated curriculum vitae and itinerarium as a running text. But there are interruptions. It is as if small pieces of chaff sent by Satan are stopping it from following the direction he believed in and planned.

Now he wants to know. He is holding the bundle with both hands and is just about to unfold the frayed old silk when he feels frightened. At that moment, the girl comes back, this time pleading and sobbing: 'She moans so, and she hurts!'

'I'm coming,' he says.

And so he puts the bundle back and feels greatly relieved. Quickly he opens the cupboard and takes out a bottle and a small bowl. Using enough coarse powder from the bottle to cover the tip of a knife, he dissolves it in a quantum from another bottle. This he does not measure, but pours with care, not roughly. It is obvious that he has got a good eye. The girl sighs, a long shivering outgoing breath. Skord smiles a little because she reminds him of the bitch he uses for rabbit chases. She sighs like that when she wants something – a chunk of meat, a pat on the head or a hunting trip.

They approach the old woman, who is propped up in bed supported by a huge pile of pillows. Her wrinkled yellow face is immobile. Skord tries to get her to swallow the mixture, but the girl takes the horn spoon away from him and shows him how to get it in between the parched lips. The tongue is glued to the palate. Nothing happens. The liquid pours from the spoon over the cheeks and chin of the old woman.

The girl, whose name is Anna-Märta, starts weeping. Skord feels truly upset about her, and about how badly her father and mother and brothers have treated her by going off to the Christmas morning service, leaving her in charge of her sick great-grand-mother, for whom she can do nothing. He pats Anna-Märta's bent back and goes to fetch a basin, cupping-horn and lancets. He lines the knives up inside the box while she is out of the room so she will not have to see them, and asks her to heat the horn. She warms it so carefully that he has had time to lance the blood vessel by the time she comes back. He places the cupping-horn over the cut, and then they both sit waiting by the bed. The air rattles and pipes inside the old woman's chest as before. Anna-Märta weeps on, quietly and without bothering to wipe her tears on her apron.

In the end all becomes silent. The sharp rasping stops. When he takes the horn away, the wound seems almost still. He puts a towel over the basin and carries it away himself. When he comes back, Anna-Märta is leaning her forehead against the old woman's soiled arm.

'Come away,' he says. 'She's asleep.'

He half supports, half carries her into the bedchamber and shuts the door. He has never touched this girl before. She is pretty, with pink cheeks and round arms, and at times he may well have thought of it fleetingly. But her father and brothers have promised her to a young man she admires very much, the eldest son at the nearby farm. Now something is happening between her and Skord, regardless of plans and intentions. It seems to him that it is happening outside time.

He wants to comfort her because she is so terrified, and this gives him comfort too. She smells sweetly under her skirts, in her mouth and her hair. Under her chemise, her back is smooth and her breasts even smoother. The hair on the small mound under her belly is pale red and soft, like a little cap with a tassel. She is no innocent but neither is she experienced. She is weeping herself warm, she weeps and weeps and he gives up trying to stop her. He does not want to risk her coming to her senses. She is kissing very eagerly with lips swollen from weeping, and the tip of her tongue is full of curiosity. She gives his bottom a big noisy slap and then she laughs between the sobs.

'What are you doing?' he says, baffled.

He is inside her in a place that is very soft and wet, and is trying to stay there for as long as possible because he feels – he knows – that this first time will also be the last. She seems to know this too, because she is very eager to touch him everywhere with her hands and lips and tongue. She moans like a puppy dog when he rummages inside her. He is worried that she might be hurting, but when he asks she says no, she is not.

'How brown you are,' she says over and over again. There is a huge, almost ludicrous difference between her white skin and his dark-brown one. They compare arms and stomachs, and she wants to look at the part he pushed inside her and seems amazed that it too is brown. Soon afterwards they complete what they should not have begun, although he does not want it to stop, and nor does she.

They dress hurriedly because through the chamber window a strip of cold green dawn can be seen over the forest. The Christmas Mass travellers will be back soon. The old woman is lying there as before and Skord moves the candle to and fro in front of her open eyes and puts a feather against her lips. But nothing moves.

What happened between Anna-Märta and Kristian Skord during Christmas Eve was of no concern to anyone, especially since there was no repetition. It certainly seemed to matter little to the girl herself, because she never gave him as much as a stolen glance, let alone any squeezes of the hand or little pushes with her leg under the supper table.

She grew round-bellied, and this might have scared him or at least caused him embarrassment. But because it was far too early to have anything to do with what happened during Christmas Eve, there was no need for him to worry. It must have been during the autumn that she set about getting the swelling, which was growing inexorably under her apron.

There followed, of course, outrage and tears of shame. The betrothed who had been too forward hung his head in front of the father and the brothers. The wedding which had been planned for the summer, now had to be got under way in time for Lady Day. That day the moon was a thin sliver of silver, like the rocker of a cradle against the light skies of the spring evenings.

'If there be a cradle for Lady Day it means many bairns in the house,' said the maids. Anna-Märta moved to the farm of her parents-in-law after the ceremony and started preparing baby clothes. The eldest son made a fine cradle with carved rockers and painted it with lilies, cucumbers, the date and other marvels.

Skord was long gone by then, having left before the March sun had begun to corrode the layer of good sledding snow. He packed his collection of natural objects among the bundles of linen cloth, crocks of cloudberry jam and frozen bodies of birds. In his overnight bag he kept the draft of his application to the Royal College of Physicians to be allowed to practise the art of Medicine. He was going to add to it a careful and authenticated account of his practice to date. He had cured a county official of severe stone pains and got a certificate to prove it. He had got some life back into the widow of a captain at the garrison; she had had a stroke and had been deemed a hopeless case. He had also soothed the pains of the army fiscal officer Strolert and the goldsmith Jesper Bäck, both of whom were suffering from kidney disease. In the latter instance, he had brought about a cure using several medicaments of a chymical nature. Now he was going to apply to practise Medicine and to sell chymical preparations and elixirs. He had received two warnings for practising quackery and trading in medicines, but now there was an end in sight to persecution from the learned establishment. He had got himself a powerful patron, the great professor who had journeyed to Lapland and who was now waiting for his collection of curious natural objects. He knew Kristian Skord to be as nimble with his Latin as any doctor of medicine or philosophy, and would put in words in his favour when he finally was called to viva voce and written examinations.

'Indeed, Skord,' the Professor had said, 'there is no question, you speak Latin as well as anyone. Nonetheless, I advise you to curb your tongue somewhat when they examine you in that language.'

It would all go well. The future looked bright. He would get a place in the world, in the very world. The pressure would lift.

And what could stop him from going on to a doctoral disputation? With more free time and peace of mind, he intended to develop his learning in Latin texts. To keep the money coming in, he would have to practise his profession when he arrived in Uppsala. During the winter he had been peddling cures to get enough to live on. It was now likely that he would be allowed to peer into the chamberpots of the nobility, and he feared that these more demanding patients would drag him away from learned studies and solemn application. While he was thinking about all this, he pulled at his left earlobe with the thumb and index finger of his right hand. It was already rather stretched because he had been wearing a ring in it. But he had removed the ring and was hoping that the hole would close up and disappear.

If once in a while he thought of white-stomached Anna-Märta, he pictured her with her foot on the rocker of the cradle, full of delighted tenderness for a small red-haired beastie with strong fists and blue eyes. He was right as far as it went: Anna-Märta had given birth to a son who looked very much like his father and his family. But she had produced something else as well.

With the afterbirth, which was expelled only after many hours of agony and bleeding, came also a small bundle or foetus the like of which the midwife had never seen. She was not even sure it was meant to have become a child. It was lumpy and covered in dark, wrinkled skin. It had teeth and hair but no eyes, arms or legs. She put it in a basin and covered it with a towel. But because it was so strange, she could not but show it to the maids. Just a couple of days later the whole household knew that Anna-Märta had given birth to something disgusting, which had been buried in the ground straight away. One of the maids said she had seen the midwife pull out a long tail of hair from the monster, and averred the hair had been black. The proper child had a wound in the small of his back which was healing slowly. It was obvious the troll spawn had been stuck on there, trying to suck life out of the true child.

Anna-Märta suckled the red-haired bairn and rocked the cradle with her foot, but she was not happy. Sometimes she woke at night sweating, and sometimes she screamed in her sleep. People spoke ill of her after the birth. She was aware of this and it frightened her.

By now it was many decades since seventy women had been strangled or beheaded and then burned on a hill in Torsåker because they had had carnal knowledge of the Wicked One. No one wanted to smell the stench of burning flesh again. People remembered well enough that many of the accusers had ended up among the condemned. So nobody raised a finger to point at Anna-Märta. But people whispered.

Then she started screaming. It happened first one night when she woke up from a bad dream. Later, she just carried on. They had to take her back to her parents because she scared her child, and nobody seemed able to stop the night-time screaming.

Back home, her mother took her in hand. The screaming ceased, and Anna-Märta confessed what she had been up to on that Christmas Eve. People began to recall a thing or two about the prattling rogue who had stayed in the house over the winter and called himself a learned doctor. Nobody really believed he was the Foul One, dressed up in elkskin trousers and velvet waistcoat. It seemed incredible, given how kind he had been and how many times he had made them laugh. Still, there had been something bad and weird about him. His left hand had only four fingers, his hair was black even in the secret places, he could speak lines of abracadabra and had studied books which had to be read from back to front.

Anna-Märta was shamed in front of everyone now and realised she might never be allowed to see her child again. So she said he had grown claws when he put his hands on her breasts to violate her. She also said he had made her meek and shaky on her legs by giving her a magic potion which he mixed from a powder and fed her with a spoon made of horn.

Her father and brothers were not particularly taken by all this heathenish talk of magic and said there had been enough talking and screaming now. They settled with the parents-in-law, making some use at the time of the story about the powder, the tincture and the horn spoon. She was allowed back to her child and husband. The brothers promised to deal with the rogue and quack, should they ever clap eyes on him again. Once they had done with him, he would be able neither to walk nor practise his lewdness again.

As far as the brothers were concerned, it was over and done with. But then something happened, something so strange and extraordinary they would never have believed it, had it been reported by anybody else. When the first amazement, doubt and fear had died down, it made them take certain unusual steps, which were not without danger. It also made them write a letter, taking advice from their father, who was better at the art of writing.

S kord was called to the presence of his patron, the Professor, at the beginning of the summer. When he rode out to the Professor's mansion house outside Uppsala, he felt happy and convinced the meeting would go well. The birds were singing away, and in the Professor's garden moss-roses and monkshoods were in full flower. It was very agreeable to converse with this learned and highly placed personage. Skord was given cold punch to drink and almond cream to eat, sitting with the daughters who were stitching and embroidering, and the two lapdogs which kept bringing him leather balls to throw. He threw the balls onto the lawn, they fetched them and he threw again.

After a while, the Professor asked him about his time in the village below the forest of Skule, and about the farm where he had been staying, dwelling especially on the two brothers and their father. Were they sensible and reliable people? Skord could confirm that. Indeed, yes, it was his considered opinion. He was straining not only to be indefatigably charming – for instance in his treatment of the young ladies' bow-wows – but also to give an impression of sound judgement and trustworthiness. Much was at stake for him.

He did not know how much, though. A goldfinch sang in a cage, in competition with a male chaffinch sitting in a plum tree covered with green fruit. A small stream tinkled into an artificial pond, and the little dogs ran for their balls in pretended or real fury.

'Anyway,' said the Professor, 'reliable or not, they're likely to be grasping and enterprising, like most farmers. They have written a letter to me, stating that they have found something most remarkable.'

Skord nodded. He was well aware that the Professor's journey north to collect natural curiosities had led to many offers. The transports from the north had brought both dried and frozen finds.

'These people have written to say they have caught two giants,' the Professor said.

The two daughters giggled at that over their embroidery. Skord's eyes were half closed. His outward appearance still suggested helpfulness, trustworthiness and discernment. But deep inside him something happened. It was as if he had kept a large flatfish in there lying on its left side. Suddenly, it flipped over.

'They are probably hoping for some extra income,' he said.

'They are quite open about it,' answered the Professor. 'They are saying that the two huge men can be used for labour, will surely interest learned scholars and can also be kept in chains and shown to the public.'

'Chains?'

'Yes, they were caught and are kept captive. Presumably it's a case of two unusually large men, maybe deserters, who had taken to the forest.'

'Indeed,' Skord said.

He realised he had been invited because the Professor wanted to be reassured that the letter concerned large men. So he needed confirmation. Skord looked under half-closed eyelids at the company which embroidered and conversed in the strong evening sunlight. He no longer noticed the two lapdogs yelping at his feet.

'There is a tendency to exaggerate the natural in the direction of the supernatural,' he said. 'It is very apparent in these villages near the forest. The brothers are no exception, even though they are otherwise sensible. They have had their problems with trolls and suchlike up there.'

The Professor made a face which indicated that he could recall a particular stench of burning.

Then Skord rose and took his leave. Arguably, it was a little rude to go before having been dismissed by the learned and influential host. When he left the garden the lapdogs pursued him, yelping excitedly. Sheltered by a flowering mock-orange, he aimed a kick and got one of them, so putting an end to the pursuit.

The following day Skord returned to Skule, riding a small, shaggy brown mare. He did not need ponder what to do when he arrived.

As soon as he got north of Oringen, people were speaking about the giants. But nobody had seen them. He stopped on the slope leading down to the last village and looked out over the area. Next to the road stood a ramshackle cottage, and on the grass in front of it an old woman was stirring a cauldron. She fed the fire with fir kindling, and the smell coming from her pot was not entirely pleasing. There was no mistaking that mese cheese was stewing in there.

The old woman's name was Tässa. She not only knew about the giants, but also about Anna-Märta's giving birth to a monster, and about the man who had passed himself off as a learned doctor and would be cropped in front by the brothers to stop any more carry-on of that sort. She talked on like a rushing stream, which did not stop her observing the stranger, who listened attentively enough but was otherwise so distracted that he forgot to eat what he had paid for: goat's milk, a chunk of ripe cheese and a piece of bread. Before riding on, he stood there for a long time with the reins gathered in his right hand. With his left hand he pulled awkwardly at his right earlobe. Tässa observed him closely, and after he had left, went straight to the chest to change her headscarf and take out her shawl.

Skord rode on, but slowly. After a while he veered off into the forest, letting go of the reins and allowing the mare to follow branching paths up into the thicket on the hillside. The paths had been made by the old woman's goats, which now advanced to watch the stranger as he got off the horse to let it graze.

They were spotted animals with large, dangling skinfolds under their cheeks. They were curious, and some of them rubbed their horns against his saddle-bag and chewed the material. When he was not watching, they got hold of his leather cap which was lying on the ground and pulled it away. It was wet and torn when he retrieved it. By now the big billy goat was so irritated that Skord had to leap on the mare's back. It took him some time to lose this motley crew, and wind his way up the hill. From the crest of a ridge he spotted Tässa, the old woman, skirts tucked up, hurrying towards the village. He was not surprised, but decided to stay on the ridge and await further events.

He brooded on the infant troll which the old woman had called a monster. It caused him pain. He could not remember pain like this since the night after cutting off his finger.

Both from curiosity and a desire to cure, he had carved and poked about inside both corpses and diseased bodies. But he knew nothing that could help him to understand the birth of the monster. As far as he could see, some of those conceived, hatched and born were intended to become neither men nor animals. But what were they intended to be?

He lay for a while in the short, smooth grass with his coat under his head, watching through the quivering canopy of the aspens as rags of cloud careered across the sky. Then he rose and looked down on the village from the edge of the slope.

This was the last village before the forest – or the first after the forest, if the traveller came from the north. Over it brooded the mountain, blue and covered with a fur of trees. The sea, reflecting the cold colour of the sky, slipped inlets up into its leens and fields. It was a flourishing village, and its fields of corn were shifting from blue to a dominant green, which in places was lightening to yellow. The houses were silver-grey and carefully jointed at the corners. The stakes for the haydrying racks were stacked on the leens, lads and lasses separate in neat piles. Most things down there were past flowering, about to ripen and ready for harvesting. The sheds, rick-yards, stone cellars and barns would be filled. Down there people strove, envied and desired. Few starved. The sea held back, only licking the shores.

He spat in the general direction of the village, but the glob, heavy with mucus and road-dust, did not reach any further than the shrub aspens on the slope. Then two riding figures left the farm belonging to Anna-Märta's father. They were her brothers. Good hunting, he thought. You will not find me where you plan to go looking. The gentleman has taken to the forest. When he returned to the place where he had been resting, the goats had caught up with him. His coat was useless when he had extracted it from under their hooves. It smelled of goat's piss and was badly torn. Still, he felt he had better keep it because he knew he had to sleep rough now the brothers were after him.

It took a long time to lose the goats. The herd followed him, noisy with its bleating and its rattling bells. The goats' creaking voices and staring eyes with slit horizontal pupils expressed nothing. The folds of skin under their cheeks dangled; their hooves tapped and clicked on the ground. If he had had his handgun and dared make a noise, he would have shot in the air above their heads. But both his saddlebag and his gun had been left behind at the first resting place. I'll find them again, I'll find them, he told himself as he rode on. Now, his task was to get to the farm swiftly and without being seen, while the brothers were away.

He left the mare at the foot of the hill, and made his way across a sedge meadow to the farm buildings. Hidden in a ditch behind meadow-sweet which had grown almost to man's height, he watched a girl walk towards the byre carrying two pails of water on a yoke. She was accompanied by a groom, carrying a heavy stick in his hand and a small gun held by a strap over his shoulder. He waited until they had left the byre before going closer, keeping out of sight behind the dungheap. By now he had been standing for so long in the black mire of the ditch that the damp had got through his boot-leather.

He could not go through the byre door or enter through the hatch in the upper part of the barn without being seen from the house. He had to use the trap-door over the dungheap.

As soon as he crawled into the summer-empty byre, he could see them. They were lying on either side of the food-trough, chained to wooden uprights and without so much as a bundle of straw beneath them. Their hands were tied together at the wrists so they could hardly move them to pick up a crust of bread or a turnip from the bucket of food. On leaving Uppsala, he had said to himself that if they were really giants and not just large men, he would ask them where they came from and what their names were. But now there was no need. Instead he asked if they recognised him. At first they said nothing, and he could see that they were afraid.

They were surrounded by the sour smell of dung and summer flies were crawling languidly over their faces. Finally Granarv, who had always been best at remembering, said, 'Did we not owe you a pancake once?'

'That debt was paid,' Skord said with a smile. 'Now you've got to get out of here. You're too large for the dung-hatch, so we shall have to wait until it's dark.'

He began to undo their fetters, taking care not to rattle the chains.

'At this time of day no one is likely to come by, but if they do, you've got to lie stock still until they're within reach. They can't use their guns at close quarters. But clout them quickly because they're cunning and fast.'

They had noticed, Groning said. They had been captured by men carrying guns, and been sprayed with grapeshot and bullets which had stung like fire.

They were both very sad and discouraged, and did not yet dare take comfort from his help. As darkness fell and the byre filled with shadows which grew dense and black in the corners, they stayed lying on the floor, speaking together in low voices. They were too large to stand upright indoors. They did not have enough room under the ceiling even when they were sitting down. Skord asked them how they had fared since the last time they met, and Granarv said they had been living as best they could. But since the old crone, their mother, went and died up there in Oringen, times had mostly been bad. Skord thought it was their present captivity and humiliation which made them take such a black view of their past. Remembering things was not their strongest point, he knew that.

They asked how he had been and what he had been doing with himself since they left the forest hut in Oringen. He told them it had been quite a time. Adventures of all kinds, but so far he had escaped in one piece – unless you counted the little finger he had lost early on from sheer stupidity. They stared at him with blinking and runny eyes, and somehow did not seem to believe that matters had turned out as well as that for him. That might have had something to do with his crawling in through the dung-hatch, smelling of goat's piss, wearing a torn coat and with his black hair tangled and full of chaff and straw.

There were, he told them, two kinds of adventure in this world, and one sort might well seem tamer because it took place in the thought and the spirit. He could see the two mightily strong and very decent giant brothers did not have much of an idea what he was talking about, but he carried on speaking of spiritual and thought-provoking subjects. It was so long since he had spoken to anyone without having to dissemble or be on his guard. Rounding off, he said of course he had unfortunately had many adventures of the other, less spiritually inspiring kind, especially of late. These had involved much riding and running and fencing, and more than once he had saved himself by being fast on his feet. He had also once been hung upside down from one foot, a predicament which he could assure them was harder to get out of than their present one.

By then it was pitch dark outside and he went up to the window to sneak a look at the house. They dared not risk leaving until all the lights were off. By now the light up there was faint and flickering. He guessed it must come from the damped-down fire on the hearth, before they put the embers in the fire-pan and covered them up. Doors slammed, and someone rattled household pots in the dense, strongly scented darkness of late summer. He saw a couple of men come out to piss, but when they had closed the door behind them, all was silent.

They began to try to extricate themselves. Granarv was first to slide along, and even when the whole upper part of his body had emerged from the barn door, his legs were still in the dung-gutter of the byre. At the door, milk churns and crocks were stacked on shelves and bridles, tools and timber-chains hung on the wall. Skord whispered to them to go quietly for god's sake, so nothing would fall and make a noise.

When Granarv pushed at the barn door, his huge hand almost covered the doorway. Groning crawled after him, and when they were both outside they followed Skord's directions, took off down to the dank leen behind the barn and crawled into the high stands of meadow-sweet, with its white clusters of flowers glowing and filling the night with their fragrance. It looked as if a pair of large sledges had made their way through.

The cur had started barking as soon as the barn door creaked open. Now the bark sounded close, and Skord realised she was free. He turned and ran towards her to hold her back with potent words. He succeeded, but could not quieten her. It was a greyhound bitch with a curled loop of a tail and pointed, cupped ears. She barked so hard she was bouncing where she stood, her whole body shaking. As soon as Skord turned and started running, she was after him and he had not got far before she was hanging on to the seat of his trousers. Behind him he heard doors slamming and voices shouting. People started running, and someone had lit a horn lamp with a flickering yellow light which swung from side to side.

At the bang of the first shot the cur loosened her grip, and when she attacked again he managed a kick which sent her rolling over and howling. A swarm of pellets crackled past his ears. He changed direction as he ran so as not to lead them towards Garnarv and Groning, who had slipped away into the darkness. The forest had swallowed their big bodies, and he could hear no sound from them when he hid for a few moments behind a block of stone.

He began running again, veering between tree trunks and rocks. He could hear the men swearing behind him. They shot at random a few more times and then gave up. Their eyesight was poor in the dark, much worse than his. He knew they would get more people and horses and better dogs together as soon as it became light. That was why he had to get as far into Skule forest as he could before dawn.

No woodland is as wild as the forest of Skule. It lies between the coast and the high hills, starting in the arid, alien landscape below the treeline. Nowhere else is the Baltic Sea so deep, nor do the islands have such precipitous peaks. The sea is a cold autumnal blue and the red granite glows unquenchably beneath the attacks of the waves against the rocky precipices. The forest grows on hillsides and on the steep sides of the dark river ravines. The slopes are covered with moorland and the streams leap from waterfall to waterfall. There are fields of scree and stones everywhere, deep clefts and heavy, sharp-edged rocks. Only the still, clear-water lochs are smooth-surfaced, but their depths chill the eye.

Strands of time run through the forest. The high fields of scree are solidified waves of stone, long swells of unmoving time. Tall trees, once whispering in the wind, have sunk into the peat bogs, where time ferments in the marshy pools. Here and there, flowering woodland penetrates the darkness of the firs and the sea of stones, forming wedges of broad-leaved trees, fragrant night-flowering plants and humming frail-winged insects. There, the noble trees sing. The leaves of linden and hazel dance in a gentler wind and their roots send tendrils into a richer soil than the meagre ground under the firs. It is forgotten woodland, flowering in borrowed time.

A large crack has opened up in one of the rock faces. The stone has fallen down or eroded away, leaving behind a cleft with perpendicular edges. It is no wider than the gap between two people talking. Deep inside it the dark is lifeless; there are only stones and shadows. A mountainside with such a deep crack, visible from far away and unchanged within human memory, must be a mark or a sign. And if it is not a sign, if it means nothing, is that not even more thought-provoking? In any case, it is a fact that the cleft in the mountain, so straight and bottomlessly deep, existed long before any brain able to formulate thoughts and images. Nobody knows whether the immense crack found a purpose for the thoughts, as they began to swarm around the mountain. Thoughts flutter like feathered moths inside people's heads, but the crack stays where it is, cutting a gash through time.

People have always tried to slash and burn their way into the forest. And when it proved resilient, when even the goats failed to tear the bark off the trees, they tried to control it by naming. They found everything malevolent in the forest: stinkweed and wormwood, devil's nettle, dead-men's bells and poison parsley. They named the plants which neither stank nor stung nor killed according to who fed on them: hawkweed, bear's foot, cowgrass, swine's snout and chickweed, hare's thistle, bee's nest and cuckoo's meat. For some, playfulness, for others, plain practicality.

The rest became known as grass to most people, but there were also those who named the useless but lovely plants with such names as sweetfern and rose-bay willow-herb, forget-me-not, sweet cicely, water nymph, angel's eye and herb of grace.

But the forest just grew and flowered. It flowered with senseless frenzy, remote from the names. Some wanderers went all the way down into the deepest hollows under the stones and the darkness of marshland pools, and on to the steep silent braes of the lochs. They named the curious plants growing in these places, calling them bog onion and brittle bladder fern, ghost orchid and pinesap. Still, the forest flowered on heedlessly, long after the namers had been silenced, roots twisting through their gaping mouths; it flowered, known and named only by those who hummed and clicked and twittered, by the rustle of wings and rattle of claws and thud of antlers against tree trunks.

Kristian Skord arrived in the forest of Skule a night in late summer when the darkness was dense and gentle. He might have heard claws and padding paws and rustling wings, had he not been racing. He stumbled and ran in bursts until he staggered to a halt from tiredness, next to a small stream. He could not see it. It was just a singing, tinkling noise in the darkness. The leaves enfolded him and the stone grew smooth and offered up its stored warmth, and he fell asleep.

He was stiff when he woke. The trees were dripping in the grey dawn, and he thought he should make haste and get on before they came, the people and their dogs. He drank some water and ripped off a handful of dewy-blue whortleberries before setting out. His boots were soaking and heavy to drag along. When he sat down to rest, he could feel the moss on the tree stump against his bare skin. The cur had torn the seat of his trousers.

Suddenly he felt exhausted. It struck him how long he had lived. Here he was, bare-bottomed in a coat smelling of goat's piss. His hair was tangled. A blue-black shadow of bristle was growing on his cheeks. In his mouth, a couple of cracked molars were aching. A finger was missing.

What was the point of trying?

Recently, he had felt his aspirations to be reasonable. He would have been satisfied to practise his skills as a surgeon, physician and adept of the spagyric arts with the blessing of the Royal College of Physicians. He asked for nothing better than his own corner in the world and a useful, quiet existence. Bitterness welled up inside him when he remembered how Anna-Märta had given birth to a troll foetus. What ugly names they gave things they could not understand.

What have I to do with you?

He started walking. The further into the forest he went, the fewer became the scars from paring hoes, saws, broad-axes and fire. Then they ceased altogether, and he entered a forest which aged as slowly as he did. The moss took its time. The lichen waited patiently for the rain. Long loops of black lichen, branching and swelling in the damp air of late summer, were hanging from the branches of the firs. Ancient trees, mouldering from internal rot, stood there waiting for the storm when a gust would send them crashing to the stony forest floor. But the wait might be long, and only the creak of wood when the wind swept through the forest canopy told of what would happen once the waiting had come to an end. Trees that had fallen over a very long time ago could still be distinguished under their covering of moss and grass. On their straight bodies the beaker lichen stayed open to sky and rain, the cranberry branches gleamed and the ferns climbed. All happened very silently and so very gradually that it seemed to take place in another time, with a slower rhythm.

Here and there the rock face lay bare. The lichen formed a rough, knotty membrane over the motionless foreheads, skulls and backs of the sleeping stones. Out on the scree slopes and near the rock-falls their sleep was so deep it resembled death. Neither lichen nor moss could get a hold there. The interior of stones might seem still and cold, but even these stone eggs were being hatched in gentle warmth. Waves and surf had moved them. They had breathed and were breathing still; they were waiting but not a sound nor an undulation in the sea of stone gave them away.

Creatures who lived quickly, with heartbeats like flapping wings and fast, faint breaths, moved between boulders and tree trunks, among leaves and branches and grass. Flutter and fly, he thought. Soon you will starve to death. The sweet, moist things will become dry; the juicy ones will wither and turn brown. Dance anxiously for a few hours or days. Your wings will lose their powdery glow. Swaying and whirling, you will fall towards the bottom. But there is no bottom, you swarmers and flutter-wings, silver moths and forest butterflies. Below you there is only a rotting soup formed from creatures which were once sweet and juicy, had beating wings and thin, easily flowing blood.

The marsh boils its brew. Steam wells out, mist and troll-smoke. You must know, little ones, that this cauldron is bottomless. Your fall is endless. Wings dry and crumble and decay and dissolve. The bottom is never reached. Because, flutter-wings, there is no bottom; there is no end.

He kept walking steadily upwards across steep slopes. There was talking inside him, and there was talking also under the soil and between the stones. Sometimes he was aware it was the waters of the streams. But oblivion like banks of raw fog drifted through his body, and through the forest too. Sometimes he would emerge from such strands of fog and recall that he was alone in the deep forest without knife or tinderbox, and that people were out to get him. He was never sure if what he heard was the distant barking of dogs or water breaking against stones quite close by.

Then came a long period of forgetfulness during which the forest changed shape. He looked at it with different eyes and, through the green jumble of twigs and leaves, saw another forest which was also the same as this. He remembered. He had been here. The forest had enclosed him. It had been nameless. There was nothing else. Nose and ears recognised the forest. Long ribbons of scent floated through the air and spoke to him. He felt his nostrils vibrate and his ears grow sharper.

But the forest shifted again and became a room with pillars. Between the pillars there were directions and paths. Inside his head, words and images rose and sank. Blow a clean sweep, he whispered to a breeze moving through the tops of the fir trees. Clear out the words.

It did not help. Down where he was it was quite still, bathed in a pool of green light. The wet leather made his boots heavy to drag along. He kicked them off and sat for a while with his feet in a chilly stream. Under the water, his skin looked yellowish. His toes moved searchingly between green drakes and water bugs. Common hydras waved. Small suns glittered in the gravel on the bottom, like cold gold.

Afterwards he could not manage to get the boots on again. They chafed. So he let them lie. But his feet were no longer used to sharp stones and piles of broken branches. They were not hard like horn, but tender-skinned and bleeding. And his head was full of laments.

Blow them clean away, blow them away, he whispered.

When his feet started bleeding he wanted his boots back, but could not find them. There was no path for him to follow any more. The forest turned around him like a huge clockwork. The water he had drunk sloshed about in his stomach and everything he put in his mouth tasted watery: whortleberries, crowberries and pieces of yellowing witches'-butter. Wherever he tried to lie down, the forest rejected him. It made itself sharp-edged and damp; it chilled and pierced. The burning in his stomach grew worse. The more he drank, the more his guts ached. In the end he got the squitters. It came spraying out from his bowels.

The churning inside his head continued. It was as if there was a great cupping-horn in his head and the words were seeping into it. If only his thoughts would fall silent! If only he could stop seeing harps and pillars, woven carpets, church windows, lyres and altars in the forest – not to mention bows, fingers, ears, door handles, beakers and cups, clubs and coins, strings of pearls, mirror glass. If only his head would keep quiet and let the dark settle over its images and words.

If moss could be moss without a name. If he could sink into it.

The water spoke, but he did not want to listen. Not everything with a human voice is truly human. But what is it? What is it telling me, all this busy, prattling, rustling, twittering talk going on all around me? What are the shapes emerging only to dissolve into the green tumult?

People have gone ahead of him into the forest and named the inhuman things. Fairy lights have gleamed in front of them. Dwarfs' nets have stuck to their faces and they have made wry faces at trolls' grapes and witches' brooms. They have named the yellow and the white slime on fallen tree trunks. Dizzy with hunger he sticks his fingers in it. He takes trolls'-butter and wolves'-milk and tries to eat. But mockery and fear taint their names. The butter is inedible, the milk is poisonous.

Beings move in the dark shadows. The other ones. He knows they are there; knows and remembers. But they do not want to know him. They do not like coming close.

He tries to remember but it is like trying to mend dwarfs' nets. Starvation he remembers, because it is tearing at his guts. He also remembers fragments of a poor life, mostly lived in a dwalm, as if he had eaten sleep-thorn. The others live somewhere nearby. There are scraping noises in the undergrowth, but rarely is anything seen. They do not build huts for themselves; and they look grey, like stones and lichen.

Still, they live. Mostly they tear at things with their fingers, but sometimes they lay a table on fern leaves. Far away memories glint like fairy lamps: days of warmth and satiety in this hunting, tearing, clawing life.

They do not damage anyone intentionally. They lead a hard life but never plan to cause pain. If they find a lost human child in the forest they walk around it. They ogle it in astonishment, sniff and poke at it. In the end they will prop it up against a stone or the trunk of a tree. Maybe they will spread some fir-tree branches over it against the cold, or an old fur cover. When later on the wolf comes they will lurk among the trees weeping for the sake of the small child; sad it had to get torn to pieces.

They wander in loose groups, observing people, with a mixture of longing and disgust, as they pick up the scents of pancakes and cruelty. Thought and intention. The smell of blood. The taste of iron. The human scent is made up of these things. But the trolls drift along, almost invisible in the strands of mist. Winged night creatures make spots in front of their eyes and holes in the chilly air.

No, they cannot hold on to anything with their minds, or with their fingers, which are like the weaving branches of water thyme. They evade.

Yes, they are here but elusive. Those with whom he belongs are evading him.

He is empty. This bag of skin has shrivelled. It only contains a bunch of bones. Thought and intention have drained away. They are there behind the trees watching, but soon they will forget what they were watching and believe it has always been there. Maybe moss will grow all over it, and fine root-threads through it.

His mouth was filling with milk. It came from a tip with a
hole in it and he was suckling. But it was a hard nipple, a
teat of horn. The milk was warm and fat. He was about
to doze off again, but got a kick in the midriff and heard a voice
say, 'Get up, you cunt!'

Then somebody else sniggered, 'Seems he likes sucking and all.'

His eyelids were swollen and it was hard to open them. He
rubbed his eyes and peered through lashes glued together by pus.
He saw boots, most of them torn, but with handsome spurs and
worn with trousers as tight as the skin on unskinned eels. The man
with the sniggering and fluting voice squatted down on his
haunches, and Skord looked into a swarthy face, grinning at him
with red lips and rotting teeth. A long feather bobbed above the
brim of his hat.

Outlaws, he thought. But why let me suck like an infant? And
why are they speaking in low voices?

He got another kick. 'Up, you cunt!'

Wisest response: don't. He rolled his eyes up until the whites
showed and let the milk dribble from the corner of his mouth. He
could smell a burning wood fire, and when the man who bent over
him became fed up and left, he peeped again. A burning pile of
fresh wood. He was looking through whortleberry branches,
moisture gleaming on the dewy bluish leaves. Very close to the
fire, snakes were hanging, threaded on a branch. They were
smeared with ashes. Then he thought: Those are fish, not snakes.
Lampreys. Somebody had rubbed them with ash to get rid of their
slime. He felt he already knew a lot about these men. The most
important thing was: they were obedient. It followed that there
was someone whom they obeyed.

When he pulled himself up, leaning on his elbow, people came
over to stare at him, mostly nastily. He reckoned it would be a

good idea to greet them but his tongue felt like a lump of wood in his mouth and his lips could not form words.

One of them started frying the lampreys. The fat dripped into the fire and it smelled good. The others pottered about, scratching their groins to relieve the itching from the tight trousers. He had fallen into the hands of outlaws, all right. Then he heard someone whistle like a starling and everybody looked in the same direction. He hauled himself up to rest his aching back against the trunk of a pine and give himself a sightline above the whortleberry plants and the white-moss. First he thought they were carrying somebody who was sitting bolt upright and being bounced up and down. Then he realised it was somebody on horseback, but riding in an oddly distracted way and not using the reins. The shaggy horse came clear of the undergrowth, and Skord saw it was led by a man on foot. The person sitting on the horse and being led along was not a man. It was a little old woman.

The chattering stopped. When the horse stopped in front of Skord, those who were standing closest took a few steps back.

'Get him up,' she said and they darted forward and kicked Skord until he stood upright in front of her, swaying. She looked at him closely and then said his name. He realised immediately there was no point in telling her that his father had called himself Kristernin Skord. She actually recognised him. One eye was coated with a dull bluish-grey membrane, but the other was fixed on him. That eye was brown. She did not make a fuss about her discovery, and he persuaded himself that she might not have much of an idea of how long ago it really was since they met. She must be as old as the hills and so to her, times long past were perhaps covered by mist or twilight.

'Age comes slowly to you,' was all she said. And then, 'This is the second time I've saved you.'

'Servus,' he mumbled between stiff lips and nodded.

The gaze from her bright brown eye travelled quickly round the camp and her rough voice, like a fieldfare's, gave orders. Behind the opaque veil of her other eye, she had withdrawn into herself. He wondered if they still called her Rick-Lena. And how had she come to rule over a band of evildoers? Under her narrow plait of hair, her neck was as thin as a grouse hen's. But her body had swelled.

They helped her down from the horse. He caught a glimpse of a man's boots under the huge skirt, stiff with dried mud round the hem. Under the folds of the skirt, she had been riding astride the horse's back. Nobody jested about this. Her small hands, brown and dry, had not gripped the reins. Now they were toying with a clay pipe hanging from her belt. They supported her over to a tree stump and she sat down. Skord collapsed back into the whortleberries. They were on a lochside, and the ashes and rubbish scattered round the fire told him this was a site they often used. When he turned his aching body he saw reflected in the water the greenish-black shadow of the Slåtterdal mountain with its cleft, and realised he had reached the clear Tärnätt Water. At the edge of the beach opposite stood a small shed. Maybe they had brought old Lena from over there. The banks were steep and rocky, and here at the camp on the north side of the loch only sour-pines grew.

They passed a couple of lampreys his way, and a crust of bread, but on the whole they had stopped bothering about him. He dozed, his head resting against a clump of heather and whortleberries, because he felt the alertness he had mustered was no longer necessary. She had taken him under her wing. They asked no questions and would not torment him. At worst he would have a bit of trouble with whoever had been forced for his sake to do something as unmanly as thieving milk from a goat.

His body was weary, as if after a fever. He assumed he had tumbled over a root or a stone, fallen and been found senseless. On his torn trousers there were damp patches looking like mould. He had no boots and seemed to recall he had walked away from them. But he was baffled by seeing a swollen and flaring red ridge running across his ankle. How had they found him? Had he been hanging from his foot?

He felt more and more strongly that he was the subject of scrutiny. He had been turned upside down and had his pockets emptied. This did not scare him. Rather, he felt his spirits rise, in so far as that was possible with a stiff, aching body, a dry palate and swollen, half glued-up eyes. Someone (or Somebody), who could have let him flutter down towards the bottomless pit, had taken notice. Once more, he seemed to be back in a meaningful world. No, he was not afraid. But he did not understand what he was supposed to learn by being so decisively put back in the same circumstances. He would have to leave speculation until later, though, because now the first task was to get back on his legs and then find himself trousers, boots, a hat, a knife and a horse.

During the first few days, he trailed after them like a pack hound with a bad leg. Once he was up and about, nobody cared any more and there was no more goat's milk forthcoming. They travelled from place to place in the forest. Rick-Lena often rode off with only a couple of men with her, and returned with bundles and crocks. These were put on pack-horses and taken away by new riders. They would come back after a few days, and then there would be much counting of coins and Lapp silver. This surprised him and made him feel a little contemptuous, if a man with no hat and no seat to his breeks can afford to feel contempt for others. So, they had become traders.

In every other way, they looked like outlaws and behaved as would be expected. They wore silver-studded belts, and jay and magpie feathers in their hats. Listening to their stories he realised they were using up their lives as quickly and as carelessly as the outlaws had always done in these hills. They died from unstaunched bleeding or broken necks, or ate themselves to death after long bouts of near starvation. Unlucky birds like ravens and Siberian jays were always following them at a distance. But they worried about sickness and would pay in silver for him to read something strong over them when they felt threatened from inside. Although they were prepared to risk a big haul on a single game of dice, or drunkenly swap horses with some travelling rogue, they were petty and cautious when it came to sharing out plunder.

At the time there was plenty of food about, and soon Skord was reasonably fast on his feet and lively again. He started showing off skills that were quite beyond most of them and intended to increase their respect for him in spite of his being hatless and bootless. He calculated shares of booty on the back of a piece of bark using the rule of tenths, which he let them know was called Computus Decimarum. It made them dizzy to watch him put rings round numbers, which then gave birth to zeros. It made their heads feel as heavy as lumps of pig-iron. But he counted right and proper, and soon he got himself a pair of trousers.

He produced a solar prism and set a beard on fire. This caused an outburst of amazement and extreme jollity. The man who had to put out the flames in his beard with a wet glove grew very angry, but did not dare take revenge on the trickster.

The old woman took no notice of him until he got himself boots and decent trousers. At first he walked about in bark shoes picked up in a shepherd's hut. This was irksome. But a few weeks later four of them raided the farms north of the forest, and then he managed to pull the boots off a terrified farmer. On the same occasion, he came by a broad-backed mare. She was a clever beast, who would turn her head now and then and look at him when he tried to urge her over obstacles in the stone-falls. She must have been almost twenty years old, and had led a hard-working and uneventful life. He called her Inertia. In his heart he felt it was indecent to give mocking or demeaning names to animals forced into one's service. As soon as he could, he swapped her for a spirited young black horse, still not gelded. He named it Frenzy.

For a long time he rode fast, as if searching for something. Once he thought he was on the point of finding what he was looking for. The stones rattled downhill under the hooves of his horse and he was thrown forward, ending up in a cutting made by a stream. But he did wake up again. By then they had slaughtered the horse, which had broken both front legs. Skord had not managed to break his neck, but felt as if a rusty herring grid had been shoved down his back. He was ashamed when he saw the dead horse. There was foam round its muzzle, and its eyes showed rigid whites with a blue sheen. He was taken to the old woman, who asked him if he thought himself invulnerable.

'I keep trying to find out,' he said and grinned.

'How many horses will you kill before you know for sure?'

She might have been concerned only for the turnover rate of horses, or she might have wanted to care for him. Then he thought maybe she was making a joke at his expense, and in fact despised him for only half finishing his task. This made him brood. Ought he to go looking more seriously for his death? No. It existed. He did not doubt it was there somewhere and intended just for him. And perhaps it had more to offer than just freedom from this painful, frenzied, disgusting life which seemed to him far too long.

Revulsion grew like wolves'-milk on rotting tree stumps. Horses ridden to breakdown, girls using pretty words to hide their fear.

And the crone, riding from cave to cave, counting her stores, bartering and selling. The outlaws had become tradesmen. They preyed on the people who had to ride through the ravine and made them pay dues, but with forethought. In the future, some of these people would do deals with the outlaws. Others had provided reports or services.

'Bloody hell,' he said the first time that he got to see a hiding place full of barrels and sacks of cereal. Butter, bleached and unbleached linen, herrings in brine, dried pikes, barley, malt, reindeer skins, unsharpened scythes. There were even copper sheets with inscriptions in raised lettering. They had broken up an aristocratic coffin in order to make a spirit still from it, but had been frightened by the letters. They imagined these might spell out strong curses. Now the copper sheets were destined for a brazier in Härnösand. He had traded with them before and belonged to those who were not made to pay any kind of fee if he took a load to the north of the forest.

The rule of an old woman. Aforethought and orderliness. She perched her small barrel-shaped body on the herring-barrel to sit down and count. In her hair, she smeared some kind of salve made from beef marrow, and a strongly smelling tincture which made it separate into shiny strings. The white and grey strands which had once been so black and thick were now plastered against her head on either side of the parting, and tied with a leather strap at the back of her neck.

'Outlaws were free men once,' he said as he was scribbling figures for her. 'Now robbery seems to have become part of the Kingdom of Sweden.'

'Inside it or outside it,' she said, 'we live in the Kingdom. And these days, not every burp of disgust or rebellion is paid for with the lives of horses and men.'

To show his contempt he went off into the forest for a few days. But his stomach grew sloppy and he suffered from the cold. Was it a dream that he used to be indifferent to cold and wet?

He returned and showed up outside the hut where they lived. The forest had begun giving off the smell of autumn. He realised that soon he would have to share with them the stealthy ice-cold drafts, the crust of ice on the water and the flaring and unreliable heat from the hearth. He would have to put his fingers into their bag of salt, inherit a sheepskin-lined blanket from someone who had coughed for the last time, endure their fleas and their troubles, and their longing for spring and big plunder.

'You're a rogue,' Rick-Lena said. 'You could turn tar into milk just by using that runaway tongue of yours. Your sleight of hand is such there's no need for you to hold a knife to the throat of whoever you want to steal from. Why do you stay on here?'

She spoke in a voice too low for anybody else to hear. Often, her toothless mouth would repeat the question, 'What's here for you? Why do you stay?'

He could have answered that his reason was tedium. To avoid argy-bargy with the Royal College of Physicians. Or he could have answered it was grief. Grief over your black tresses, which now are the colour of fatty ash. Do you remember I bedded you once? Inside that butter-crock body of yours, is there still a small tongue of flame left of the fire which licked me a long time ago?

Lena, Lena.

He hung his head, and she glared with her brown and bright eye. Hissing noises came from inside the bowl of her pipe. She could not know what it was like for him, this never-ending and tiresome living. Still, he would tell her odds and ends about it.

'Once I visited a Professor,' he said. 'He had shown me good will. You might say I had been – and was – a kind of studiosus perpetuus. He had made his servant drag me out of a canal in Leyden, and brought me back home to Sweden. The events I'm telling you about took place one Midsummer's Eve on his farm near Uppsala. Everyone who lived on the farm had gathered on the lawn in front of the house and were holding hands. There was another ward of the Professor's who could play the viol da gamba, and one of the maids sang like an angel, and an old woman could click her tongue against her palate on the beat and knew the same dances as the gamba player. One imagines she picked up the tunes when there was music-making in the master's house, and all the windows were open and lights glowed from candlesticks and chandeliers.

'So, they played and sang and clicked the tempo, and the rest of us moved in a circle holding hands. There were the Professor and his lady wife, and five or was it six of the children, and another student and I, and the maids and the Professor's servants and

323

drivers and the old hag and the gamba-player. I remember how the dance came to an end. We all bowed to one another. By then it was chilly outside and almost dark. Honeysuckle glowed white in the shadows, and we could hear the corncrakes. We bowed to one another and left.

'That summer I rode off and stayed away for a long time. When I returned to Uppsala, I rode out to the Professor's farm. It was silent. The grass in front of the house had been freshly cut as if the ground was prepared for the dancers. It smelled strongly. It was as if, just a short time ago, we had been standing in a circle, bowing to each other. But they were all dead.'

'Dead?'

'Yes, they were dead. Afterwards I asked around. But I knew it already, standing there in the twilight and beginning to feel cold. I realised that even the littlest one had departed for ever. She was so small that she had to reach straight up in the air to put her hand in her father's. This tired her arm after a while, and instead she grabbed hold of the tails of his justaucorps. I remembered that. But she was gone too.

'I hurried back into town again, to my sleeping quarters. I was gripped by a cold ague. I fell asleep, but woke again in the middle of the night thinking hell had opened up with all its tortures, and I could look straight down into it. It was cold. My spirit was exhausted. For long periods I dared not move a finger for fear my heart would burst.

'In the morning the landlady's maidservant came to empty the pot and bring my shaving water. She had red hands and round bare arms. She took pity on me and held me in her arms as if I were a small child, and wept when she understood how racked with pain I was. When she cradled me, I had to keep my eyes closed to stop myself from screaming. I saw her round arms turn brown, saw how they mouldered and dried; her white forehead seemed to grow spots and the warm parted lips to shrivel and fall away from the teeth. I felt she grinned at me, and pressed me to a ribcage full of dust and worms' nests.

'But the sight faded, and I grew warmer and more at peace in her arms. Never again have I been as fearful and faint as that night. But it often happens that I get a vision of people I have known and lived with, quarrelled with and perhaps laughed at a little or fooled once or twice: I see them forming a circle. Holding hands, they step in delicate turns. But now they bow to each other and let go of each others' hands. All walk away. They disappear into the dark, and I will never see them again. They too will never see each other again, nor feel a warm hand in their own.

'Afterwards it may be that I set about riding or drinking or shouting hard, the way you know well.'

'Fancy all of them being dead when you returned,' Rick-Lena said. 'That's strange.'

'Yes, it is strange, sure enough,' said Skord. 'Strange and terrible.'

Sometimes he felt he knew that she too had a secret. But she did not tell. She oversaw transports of stolen goods, and planned the arming of men and horse-thieving with the same care as if in charge of setting up the warp on a loom or filling a large stone-built cellar with salted meat and fish. He would never find out whether greed or caution guided her small brown hands. Had she settled here to gain things that would end up as piles of shit and dust, when all was said and done, or had she been directed to act as keeper of the lives of people and horses?

One or two things took place without Rick-Lena's knowledge. Often it had to do with girls living in the cowherds' huts over the summer, far away from the village.

Skord used to listen to them when they called to the cows. They would create a mesh of sweet words. Surely the cows would have come anyway because they needed milking, but the girls would not stop using tender calls. 'Coo-rose!' they cried. 'Come, come, coo-bairns, come, little wee coo-bairns!' They gave the cows the nicest names they could think of: Bridelinen and Fineflax, Applerose, Silkydolly, Rosiedove and Happyfind. There was so much play in these girls. But they wasted it on cows.

He watched from under the fir trees on a slope just above a small clearing where the grey timber sheds stood close together. He thought he could smell nice things: fresh cheese and pancakes; a bubbling mese-cheese pot, in which summer was condensed into brown sweetness.

Then the idea came to him that he would play with one of the girls. Like everybody else from the villages, she believed the crows and ravens circling over Skule Mountain were the souls of dead outlaws. So Skord took a baby raven from a nest on the slope and trained it all winter long so that by next summer it would be able to speak. When the small hornless cows came bumping and weaving up the cattle trails, the raven was a grown bird with a shining coat of jet-black feathers. Skord had taught it to say, 'I love you! I love you!' It had taken time, because the bird he got hold of was not the cleverest of ravens. One morning he climbed to the top of the tree-covered slope above the cow sheds, and waited until smoke started rising from the chimney. The black-spotted white cows were standing about on the leen. He kept waiting until the door opened. Then he threw a piece of meat tied to a stone down on the grass, and released the raven. The bird went for the piece of meat, but when the girl came out, did not dare pick it up. It circled above her and cried what it had been taught.

Just imagine how distracted a girl can become when she is overwhelmed by amazement and playfulness and admiration! And fear. She forgot her cows. She forgot them until they started mooing because the milk made their udders so painfully tense. But by then it was too late.

He made her stay in a cave with a fire and a bed of fir branches. She did not dare go out, because outside it was evil-looking and rough and there were wolves and bears. He brought silver ornaments for her to wear, and silken fabrics and ribbons. She was made to taste sweet wines in order to keep warm and stop crying. But she was made ill by the dank cave, where cold crept along the ground. Skord rode off to fetch sheepskin blankets and honey and spirits. When he came back her face was grey and her lips were colourless. She picked at the sheepskin with stubby beringed fingers, her hands still cracked and callused from work.

'Silkydolly, little one,' he said. 'Stay with me.'

Because he wanted to decorate and honour and caress her. But she became greyer and greyer.

Afterwards he never wanted to return to the cave again. He made somebody else take her away and cover up the body. It was not hard to find someone because there were rings to pull off her.

But the raven came back. He circled and circled above the cave mouth. In order to tempt her out he tried the cry he had learned. But by now he had forgotten everything except the beginning. 'Iloo!' he called. 'Iloo! Iloo! Iloo!'

In the middle of a bright, midge-ridden summer, His Majesty the King journeyed north along the coast towards Skule. He travelled fifteen miles per day: on horseback, in a carriage, by rowing boat. Horses' hooves and iron-shod wheels rumbled. Clouds of dust rose and mud splattered in all directions. Bumping about, he carried out the tasks of governance in one carriage, which was followed by another rattling with silver cutlery, condiment sets and gilt-edged china. Then came a carriage packed with officers' uniforms and formal wear, shoes, boots, hats and parade armour. After this there were several carriages full of courtiers, officers, architects, doctors and illustrators. Most of them stared grey-faced with exhaustion through the carriage window-panes. They were suffering from colic and stones. Only His Majesty, a young man, stormed onwards without a thought. He handed out portraits of himself, donated swords and promised church bells, promoted members of the clergy and the officer class, pardoned prisoners, inspected regiments and redoubts. Events were organised in his honour, public whippings and beheadings and displays of curiosities.

He was to inspect the highwaymen's cave in the rock face above the ravine in Skule. They had erected joined-up ladders to take him all the way up. When the king had started climbing, the ladders creaked. He halted, and those standing below holding on to the first rung whispered, 'Would the gentleman be afeared, then?'

Every time the ladders creaked and rocked, he paused for a bit, but finally got there. He poked about with his sword in the gravel on the cave floor, where some unrecognisable rubbish was lying about. This seemed to satisfy him and he climbed down again.

Rick-Lena heard about his journey long before it started. She knew well enough that many folk from the coast were keen on promotion. They would hound the outlaws, regardless of what business deals and agreements they usually observed. They would want some bandits to show off and lead to the scaffold in the presence of His Majesty. So quietly she gave leave of absence to her band. One by one they rode away to hide more safely and survive until the royal progression had turned back and normal business could start up again. When the message came that the hunt was about to begin, only four men were with Rick-Lena up on the mountain. One of them was called Ravel, a man with a cleft lip and a torn ear. He used to be a blacksmith, but got drunk and killed somebody. Another was called Gullik, a small, fat but strong man, who almost always had a grin on his face. He was a thief and had escaped from a quarry. The third man was called Bonny Birger. He was younger than the rest, black-haired and with eyelashes as soft and long as a girl's. He was a troubled soul and a weak, spoilt young man, who had once been in line to inherit a large farm in Jämtland. When he was annoyed, he had a rather frightening ability to shift household goods about without touching anything. Before his eighteenth birthday, both his inheritance and his future had been lost in talk at beer-sodden tables in taverns. He had been arguing that his countrymen worshipped many gods. There were three of them: a father, a son and a dove. He had spoken particularly about the animal god, that is, the dove. People gossiped about the tavern talk, and the clergy summoned Birger for an interrogation. His parents urged him to run away and gave him a large sum of money. They remembered another young man, pale and drunk, who had indulged in actionable talk in village inns. His name was Olof Rahm, and he had been beheaded. Birger was meant to flee abroad from Trondheim, but the money ran out quickly and he ended up in Skule. Now he rode in Rick-Lena's band.

Kristiern Skord was the last one who had stayed. He did not want to go. He was apathetic. But he said he could not ride away and leave the raven, which lived off pieces of his heart.

'Sheeps' hearts,' old Lena corrected him, and he glared at her. 'What's the matter now?' she asked. 'Do your greasy old cards foretell that your fate is to stay in the forest of Skule?'

'There are words that should not pass my lips, like "fate" or even "human life",' he said gloomily.

She smiled at his gift of the gab. 'Come, come,' she said. 'Why offer yourself up to have your teeth knocked out and be made to dangle in front of the King's company?'

'Why should I scamper away because the royal progression is coming? The whole coast is bowing and scraping. Even the herring are obediently bending over. Soon you'll need royal permission to fart in this country. King and Bishop have laid down regulations about worshipping God. The God of the State demands that all souls stand in line and sing his praise with one single gob.'

'But they don't do it,' Rick-Lena said.

'No, they don't. But that's because they're lazy and greedy and just a little cruel. They praise nothing and nobody.'

'Come on, go now,' she pleaded. 'They're on the move.'

'I was a lover once,' he said. 'Did you know that?'

But she did not answer.

'I was a lover, you see. I was courteous and attentive and full of delight and cunning. But I was in love without knowing my beloved. I strove and twisted to get into her, like a small brown trout. To me she was a stream full of secrets, and I wanted to enter her, coming as I did from a cold sea of oblivion. She was fast-moving and capricious and cruel one day, and another day warm and gently flowing like a river in the evening sun. I wanted in. And I wanted to play. I was courting human life itself and the whole world.'

Rick-Lena smiled, showing her pink gums. He felt like saying 'Stop grinning, you old bag,' but remembered that she had had teeth once, and soft breasts where now she had wrinkled frog skin. So he was too courteous to say it – he stopped himself from sheer chivalry.

'Shit,' he said instead. 'Everything is shit. If it isn't shit already, that's what it will become. Do you know, I thought I had been put in the world to find out its secrets and praise them? I thought the beating in my breast and the flaring of the stars and the rustling in the grass were all secrets put there by God. Or by the Four Dogs or a gigantic Gematrion or Somebody Else. Somebody or Several Others. I observed, of course, that the world was full of trickery, artful devices and magician's illusions. It was a riddle or a hoax. I thought if I could only talk to it, there would be answers. I imitated everything I heard. I whistled like a starling and cawed like a raven. I chattered like a parrot, and learned both holy and unholy languages. But I was so busy cawing and chattering and whistling, I did not stop to find out if there were any answers – that's how keen I was!

'You see, I was keen, but not in a hurry. And there was an answer in the end, but it came in an utterly different way from what I had imagined. The answer was whispered to me, sweet words in my hot ear. You see, old thing! In the midst of all this muck, in this old bed straw, in the mire and the shit heap, I had an answer. It was not *the* answer, but still the words were very beautiful and dear and precious.

'I became aware that the heavens did not turn around us like a great clock, but instead Earth revolved with us among fiery spheres. We were sparks thrown out into a vast night, and our souls were eternal and made of fire. But every time we died the souls would change their shells. How many times did I not die then? It was like the many tender little deaths of a woman in love. In that sense, I died and died again under a cold sky, in a huge space.

'This was my answer: the mouth against my ear, and parts other than the tongue speaking eagerly together. Every limb, all the skin and all the clefts and hollows and holes; all of them could talk and answer as if they had tongues to speak. Tongues of fire, you see! Because what Bonny Birger said, and almost lost his head for saying, is not right: the Spirit is not a dove with blinking eyes and red feet. He is fire, but when He is merciful the fire is like a shaft of gentle sunbeams. He reaches everything and everyone. You know, don't you, how the beams of the sun shine on each and every bundle of rags and scurfy misfit in the world. But at the same time as they give to each individual according to his need, they also enter into a general union with soil, water and air. And this is what the Spirit also does.

'You may snort into your pipe and glare at me, but you can't swear yourself free. The Spirit has entered you too and glowed inside you, as embers glow through a pile of ashes. I know, because I was with you more than once when it happened, though it may well be ungallant to remind you. But I don't give a damn now. However, He grows cold and withdraws after a while. He has got so many general tasks, and so many particular ones. Those He has just licked with tongues of fire, He next has got to abandon. Not cruelly, maybe not for ever. Can you hope? Will He come back? Or has He abandoned you?'

'Don't shout,' she said. 'People will come if you keep on ranting. Make yourself ready now. We're going to Jämtland.'

'Fuck Jämtland,' he said. 'Listen. Back then, a very long time ago under the chilly sky of a night in spring, it was said that in each and every person there is an eternal spark, which cannot be put out. Now, is this likely to be the case? Consider Ravel. Consider Gullik. They burp and chew and hit and stab with knives and scratch their arses and maybe do a handful of other things, of which at most one or two make them different from you and me. But they hide their eternal spark very well. It must be a fucking expensive possession, a right treasure, the way they keep it hidden.'

'That reminds me, a treasure!' the old woman said eagerly. 'Bonny Birger knows somebody who saw a mass of silver-worms in a place in Jämtland. The whole thing was out and moving. He thinks there was treasure in the direction it moved. He says he might be able to sense where it is.'

'Crap,' said Skord. 'What a lot of crap. And I mean the treasure especially, and the whole of Jämtland generally.'

'Somebody lived there called Drakenstierna,' Rick-Lena said. 'He was the commandant at the castle, and known as Black Franckie. He was cooking gold in his spare time. Then he buried the lot for his dowter, so she'd have something to fall back on when he was gone.'

'Drakenstierna? Franckie? Did he really make some gold in the end? Well, he owes me. 'Cause if that black bastard made gold, it's thanks to a chymical trick or two he learned from me.'

'You daftie!' Lena said. 'He's long since dead, and so is his dowter.'

'He made gold and buried it, did he?' Skord said. 'He who couldn't tell what was up and down on a glass alembic. If he did, it's mine. I've been to the underworld with him!'

'If you say so,' old Lena said. 'Sure you have, and up in the sky as well with the stars and sparks, no doubt. But now we're travelling to Jämtland.'

'The underworld is full of filth, but of gold too. I was there for years – decades – but I never collected anything except dirt under my nails. Instead I was hung upside down with my pockets turned inside out.'

'I know that,' she said. 'But now you must listen. This man saw the silver-worms, and do you know where they were going?'

'The silver-worms? A crawling mass of worms wriggling along . . . don't you think I've seen the silver-worms? I can see them now, and they have got a king out in front. The thing's wriggling off to hell with all the little grey ones. Crawling to a steep slope, right to the edge of a rock face!'

'Pull yourself together,' Rick-Lena said sternly, because she was angry now. She was thinking of how she had to rule a lot of maniacs, and run a household for them.

He answered her just as sternly that he would shout as and when he thought it proper. He had come to the world to find out its secrets and announce their nature, and such work was not done either with the scythe or the knife. But instead he had the gift of the gab, he insisted, and his mouth was his knife and his scythe, his spade, his church bell, his –

'Try shutting your face now!' the old woman said, almost at boiling point. 'Put an end to that famous gabbing and get up on that horse!'

He did as he was told then. But he was still muttering about the raven, saying he could not leave it.

'But you hate him,' she said. 'If he follows us and screams, I'll ask Ravel to put a bullet through him for you.'

They rode down to the waiting men: Ravel, Gullik and Birger, who was in his own way quite bonny. They had all believed Skord would come along in the end, even though he himself had not. He came because he felt the underworld owed him a great deal.

The raven followed them, calling out his 'Iloo! Iloo! Iloo!', and then he flew back to the cave. Afterwards he returned to circle above them as they rode along. It was as if with his calling, he tried to keep the fourth rider behind and tempt him back to the cave.

He cried and cried. Ravel swore he would shoot him unless he tired and stayed away. They were moving westwards. The old woman rode in the middle of the road when it was wide enough, and wore a birch-bark collar against the rain.

D rakenstierna's gold was meant to have been buried at Kungsnäs farm. That was what some people said. Others were just as certain it was to be found somewhere under the grass at Gallhammar. Yet another party believed it was inside one of the hillocks at the Frösö redoubt and hidden for him by Franckie's master of ordinance, the blasphemer Kempe.

But Pastor Ragundius kept his own counsel and quietly saw to it that the Church bought the Shade, a large wooden mansion house where Drakenstierna's daughter had lived and died. Later he moved in there, leaving the manse to the curate and his large family. But he did not act from kindness. He dug up the garden until it looked as though moles, normally found only in the southern counties, had worked their way under the ground. But even in his old age he never found so much as a single grain of gold.

Late one afternoon two men arrived at the Shade. The dogs barked, and a face could be glimpsed through the bubbly pane. Thus the Pastor knew what the visitors looked like before his housekeeper announced them. As she had said, they were two ne'er-do-wells. When they were shown into his study, bowing all the time in a most refined manner, he noted that one of them was halfway respectable, and the other one a fool. The aspiring gentleman called himself Dr Saintsday. His hair was black and he wore his moustache falling in thin strands round the corners of his mouth. The row of buttons on his justaucorps was a bit sparse. Soiled linen, which had not been treated with starch and iron, showed at the bottom of his sleeves. His woollen leggings also had missing buttons. The gaps had been tied with bits of yarn.

'Does the Very Reverend Gentleman recognise this unfortunate man?' he asked, indicating the fool, who was scruffily dressed and smiled with moist lips. The Pastor did in fact recognise Birger Birgersson, one-time eldest son and heir to one of the large farms on Lake Näckten. The Doctor confirmed that this was indeed the person who had been forced to leave his home as a result of impiety and gross blasphemy. He had returned now, seeking mercy and reconciliation in the lap of Church and family. His wish was to throw himself at the feet of his betters, primo the Pastor, secundo his father.

Pastor Ragundius's red-rimmed eyes blinked. He looked at Birgersson with distaste. Then a brief discourse followed, on the topics of blasphemy in general and past utterances about the Holy Spirit in particular. That is to say, Dr Saintsday discoursed with himself. He stacked up arguments for and arguments against, and created a tall, tottering tower of thought. Birgersson had been living in an abyss of ignorance, he said. Inside this dark crevasse, notions had circled, dived, leaped, jumped and fluttered like demons or bats, or – if it was not too offensive – like a certain dove. On the other hand, the Pastor lived differently, or so Saintsday's argument went, since he had an orderly set of concepts, and order presupposed exclusions, which the ignorant Birger Birgersson was unable to make.

'And, however you select,' the black-suited Doctor said, 'what is selected for removal will – in one way or another – remain.'

Which is why, as he explained, Birger Birgersson could be compared to a hunting dog that would not stop taking hens, although his master had instructed him to deselect hens from his usual orders. Now, if as a punishment, the master had tied the bird to the creature's collar, then the carcass, a hen or, in the other case under debate, a dove, would hang there as a painful reminder of his inability to choose concepts and consequently the proper behaviour.

Ragundius had not had to hold his own in a spiritual debate for decades and inside his head, the hens, doves and bats were swapping places far too fast. But in no way had he lost his grip on reality. This was a matter for the Archdeacon. He looked at Birgersson, and noted that his neck was dirty. This hunting dog had better be kept out of the pack, as it were. In addition to blasphemy and hatred of the divine, he had in all probability other matters on his conscience. Ragundius asked how he had been earning his keep since he fled the parish. Saintsday answered, referring to the fact, surely familiar to the Very Reverend Gentleman, of Birgersson's rather unusual gifts. In the right circumstances, he could guess the thoughts of others, find lost objects and also, it might be said unfortunately, exert special powers over matter. The Pastor was surely aware that plates and other household items took to flying about on their own when the unhappy youth was in a bad temper. The Doctor glanced commandingly at Birgersson, but the Pastor's pipe rack and plate shelf stayed put after all. The black-suited man now offered snuff from a box made of alder-root. Something yellowish brown stuck out of the dark powder and the Pastor's fingers touched it as he took his pinch.

'It's a dead man's tooth,' Birgersson whispered, while the Doctor turned away to place his pinch and at the same time scrutinise a couple of ragged volumes in the Pastor's bookshelf. 'It came from Lasse Färn, who was many times a murderer, and it was rather hard to lever out.'

The Doctor had taken out and opened a book, which gave off a sharp smell of mouldering paper. Suddenly he started reading aloud with a singsong intonation, smiling as he read. But the words were incomprehensible. It sounded like a curious mixture of baby talk and hawking from deep in the throat.

'What is this?' the Pastor said, baffled.

'It is poetry written in the Persian language,' Dr Saintsday answered casually.

The Pastor surmised some trick. Was is not easy enough for anyone to hold forth with a flow of incomprehensible words over a page in a book no one else was able to read?

'What does it mean?' he said.

'Now, let me see ... one of the angels of on high, as he flew through the heavens in holy gliding flight, like a kite ...'

'Kite!'

'Well, that's how it goes, more or less. It refers to a kite, not an eagle,' the Doctor said, going on to extemporise a declamation from the decaying book:

'He heard sighing, weeping, a voice laden with pain
and then the voice of the Lord answering the sufferer,

saying: I am here! And the angel went to the Throne of Heaven
and asked the Highest Being who this was, in a universe
resounding with voices a thousand times singing His praise and
    glory,
that his sighs should be answered by the Lord.
The Lord did not know. I only know, He said,
this voice spoke from a pure heart.
Then the angel turned round and glided on strong wings
towards the shadows of Earth, towards its dark shell.
There he found the one who had sighed.
It was a man, worshipping next to a spring.
A creature without sin, though a heathen,
who in the soulless murmur of water searched
to still his heart's profound thirst . . .'

'Enough!' the Pastor said. 'This is sacrilegious!'
'Indeed it is,' said the Doctor.
'These books are not mine,' the Pastor explained. 'They were
left behind by Commandant Drakenstierna, God rest his soul.
They were war booty.'
'Clearly.'
'And you understand the Persian language?'
'Only very poorly.'
'Where have you educated yourself in such matters?'
Dr Saintsday told of how he had been in the service of Lord
Sparwenfeldt, now Lord Chamberlain, at the time when this
learned man, who was able to speak more than a dozen languages,
had travelled all over North Africa and Europe in order to collect
memorabilia of the ancient Goths. Among other things, he had
been able to serve the great man by visiting libraries such as those
of the Escorial, Ambrosiana and Vaticanum. There he had copied
manuscripts in Turkish, Persian and Arabic and gone on to
prepare excerpts for the large and polyglot dictionary compiled by
the future Lord Chamberlain.
Outside dusk was falling, and dusk was also gathering inside the
head of Pastor Ragundius. However, his wits were still holding
out, and he said he found it incredible that a most highly placed
personage, such as Lord Sparwenfeldt, would have had in his
service someone of the Doctor's appearance.

'I too found it so,' Saintsday answered humbly. 'But there was a small secret linked to this.'

'What secret?'

Well, now, the fact was that the learned courtier suffered from severe constipation.

'And if there is something of which I have a thorough understanding,' Dr Saintsday said with a shy, gentle smile, 'then it is the curing of severe constipation.'

'Is that so?' Pastor Ragundius said, bending forward intently.

Now Dr Saintsday started speaking of certain extracts and residues of distillation which would, after being dissolved in badger fat, move the content of a patient's bowel, were it set like marble, and also, this was his promise, provide an easy, liberating and lasting relief. Would that be of interest?

It was, very much so. The Pastor declared himself not at all lacking in interest and wanted to try the remedy. Birgersson's case should be investigated. It would appear unlikely that thought-reading could have provided him with sufficient income during the time passed since leaving his home.

'Of course not!' Dr Saintsday said. 'Did I not mention it? Birger has been using his gifts in a much more profitable manner.'

'And what would that be?' the Pastor asked.

'Finding treasure.'

In everyone there is a small torch which, when lit, makes the whole edifice go up in flames. Pastor Ragundius was on fire now. He tried to hide it. But in taking farewell of the Doctor, his outstretched hand trembled.

'We've got him now, like a flea in a box,' the man who called himself Dr Saintsday said when they were outside in the yard. They had come to an agreement with the Pastor and were to return the following day with the ingredients of the mixture that would make the Pastor feel his Saviour lived. Bonny Birger would have had a good night's sleep and be in readiness to employ his gifts. They were convinced the treasure was buried at the Shade. A farm labourer had found a gold coin in the mud, but when he had returned to dig deeper, the wolves got him and ripped him apart. No one knew where he had wanted to dig, because the wolves had not left his remains alone and in one piece at the place where they attacked him.

The riders mounted their ill-kept horses. The Doctor slapped his dusty black tricorn hat against his thigh so that the folded-back brim flapped back down. He pushed it well down on his forehead, and the jay feathers fluttered over the top of the hat as they rode off. Standing by the window in his study, the Pastor gazed after them. Darkness was falling quickly now. It scattered like soot on the shoulders of the riders and had soon obliterated both the men and their horses.

They had surprised Pastor Ragundius wearing a dressing gown and a snuff-stained shirt. When they returned the following day he was dressed in his official garb. He had put on a black woollen cap rather than a wig. A starched and reasonably white collar spread like two blank sheets of straw-paper below his bony face. The black broadcloth of his coat was turning brown and grey with age. He wore black woollen stockings with his knee breeches, and shoes with raised wooden soles of the type normally only used outdoors to protect against the mud. He had dismissed his house servants for the day, as agreed. However, he began regretting this as soon as Dr Saintsday and his companions had got inside the door. There were more of them than he had expected. Two men had joined them, one small and fat, the other tall and heavily built. Their eyes shifted about, scanning the household goods and lingering on anything shiny. An ancient but hearty old woman had come too. She waddled off into the kitchen at once, where she started to mix up and heat the remedium which – or so the Doctor insisted – could have caused bowel movements in the body of Michelangelo's Moses.

It was a curious experience, like a dream. Although Pastor Ragundius was no dreamer even at night, he was conducted round his own house as if it was a strange place known to him from a dream. Doors opened to drawing rooms that had never seen a fire lit. They received him with chilly gusts like puffs of breath against his cheeks, their wallpaper buckling from damp. The floorboards creaked before anyone stepped on them.

But none of the things he had hoped for actually happened. The wood of the walls and the banked-up soil under the floors offered up no more secrets than when he himself had tapped, bent and dug. Bonny Birger progressed in a dazed state, lightly led by the thin Doctor's hand. Sometimes he rolled his eyes and spoke as if in a dwalm. But nothing was revealed. Worse, a revolting and penetrating odour was spreading from the kitchen and seeping into all the rooms. Making an effort, the Pastor shook himself out of his dreaminess and demanded to be told: Did Birgersson truly have the extraordinary gift that Saintsday had been alleging?

Yes, indeed! And proof was provided by his current failure. Dr Saintsday explained: a rogue who by some sleight of hand or other tricks deludes his audience, will always be seen to be successful. How could he fail? Such a one would trust to the double bottom in his box, to the card up his sleeve. The tricks always worked. They were in place, waiting securely. But Birgersson – the beautiful young man who relied only on a sensitively adjusted responsiveness to the innermost vibrations in all living things – was often subject to the immediate conditions. Autumnal mists creeping along the ground. A head cold. Bad temper. Rats between the joists.

'Why should a treasure of gold vibrate like a living thing?' the Pastor asked.

'Precisely! Most excellent! What it is to discourse with a man of learning at last! This is the case: gold in itself does not vibrate, any more than a cow bell dug down into a field. But, as has been well demonstrated by the finest scientific scholars in Europe, the innermost essence of all living things is in a tremulous state. Small, very fine oscillations. As the blood is driven round the body by the heart, so the brain drives the lymph which is the basis for our perceptions. By means of this fluidium, all membranes in the body are kept under tension, which in turn makes the oscillations possible. In extreme excitation, this tremor is so intense that it is transmitted to dead matter. The treasure oscillates in response to the alternations in the person who buries it. But the cow bell does not tremble, because the cow that lost it was calm and indifferent.'

The Pastor asked why just this person, Birger Birgersson, should have the ability to perceive the oscillations of matter. Why had he himself not been gifted with this ability, indeed, why had not everyone?

'Once more, your finger is pointing to punctum saliens! In fact we all have this ability. But from habit, indifference or boredom, we have let it go. We never accorded any significance to these very fine tremors, this trembling in the states of our minds. Here again I must refer to the inability to select which characterises this unhappy youth: Birgersson cannot use elimination so as to fit in with the greater Order. He shakes in response to the slightest influences. And, between us, some are less than good.'

Now they went back to the kitchen, where Ragundius was entreated to swallow the drink, thick and bile-green, which the old woman had prepared following Dr Saintsday's instructions. The Pastor explained he would try it when he was alone. But now they had better leave, since he expected an important visitor. He dismissed them with this lie.

When they had disappeared, Ragundius poured a portion of the drink into a bottle and on his wooden soles, tottered off to the sheep-pen. He tested the remedy on a ram by levering its jaws open and tipping the contents of the bottle into the corner of its mouth. When, come the evening, the animal had still not expired, the Pastor drank what remained of the concoction. The following morning he experienced a wonderful release.

Quite frequently, Skord would wake in the morning only to find that he had lost the present. He was unable to get up over the edge of time's abandoned waste-pit. Lying there, he felt that everything had been blended to the point of being indistinguishable. Everything he had ever chewed, carried, caressed and seen was mixed together in a seething mass. All the voices he had heard joined with his own into a babble. He had to haul himself up over the edge to reach the entirely distinct single day ahead. He needed to feel just one wind against his cheek, and hear one voice speaking to him. He wanted to have one horse with its own special name, and follow one road to a determined place. He must get up and force himself to forget that the horse too would fall, and that the road he took would lead irrevocably down into the nonspecific. The quick steps on the stairs, the slopping sound of the hot water and the light voice of the serving girl greeting him mingled with all the other steps, water-filled basins and voices, forming a cacophony of sighing and shrieking, such that he could no longer tell the sounds from living throats and lungs from the laments and rattling of matter.

Even if he succeeded, half-awake as he was, to pull himself out of the non-time into that which was ahead of him, he could not always make out either order or meaning. He seemed to hear disjointed nonsense: jaws grinding, tongues speaking, indifferent eyes scanning and lustful ones crawling. He had a vision of what these eyes watched as the sights rushed past: the sides of meat and pieces of gold, the fur coats and girls' bodies. He wanted to get up out of this valley of rubbish, out of this Gehenna. He wanted Order.

But when he was finally awake, had picked out the steps of the girl on the stairs and recalled her name, and prepared to shed the debris of non-time to step into the new day, it sometimes happened that the cupful of warm shaving water she handed him bore the stigmata of times past. A greasy line of soap and skin-flakes and yesterday's stubble marked the edge of the cup.

'You're to wash the shaving cup every morning. Is that clear, sweet maiden? It helps, see?'

But he did not say what it helped against.

'Well, can't get on in this world if one's half-asleep, yawning and heavy of heart! Nor is it any good sitting on one's bum, wearing it out. Allez!'

The maid scratched her neck where red flea bites signalled the battles of the night, and waited for him to say more nice things. Maybe 'Sweetest heart', or 'Little dove'. But he was pulling on his trousers and stuffing his shirt, still moist from sleep, under the waistband. So she went off downstairs again, slowly and still listening.

One girl. One horse. One single road. And it led to the Shade. Pastor Ragundius believed his house had been invaded by thieves and charlatans. But he was still keen to see if he could use them.

Skord believed in Bonny Birger. His gifts did not depend on trickery. Or, if they did, the illusionist was working at a level higher than human. They had visited the young man's parental home and been received without enthusiasm. Birger had hardly sat down in front of a meal of oatmeal soup before the plate broke. To mollify his mother he had found a lost silver spoon, gone for two years, by sheer power of thought. It caused great excitement when it was retrieved from the corner between the stove and the water-butt. The good atmosphere did not last. Birger's younger brother had some quite annoying things to say about the returning brother. Afterwards, a row of pewter mugs on a shelf shook and two fell off without a human hand touching anything.

Skord and Birger were boarded in the old folks' outbuilding, where the family lived in the summer. Ravel, Gullik and Rick-Lena had never showed their faces. They were allowed to sleep in a brew-house.

Skord was convinced the treasure was hidden at the Shade. It was very likely that Drakenstierna would have wanted to provide for his eldest daughter, who had no right to inherit. It was said she was most unlike his other offspring. He only fathered girls, and

344

those born in Sweden had all been plump as piglets and learned at an early stage to stand up and declaim:

In Skåne land, the fearless hero of whom I sing,
the enemy bravely fought: he is my king!

They had bodies like mangle rollers by the time they were old enough to marry. Soon they had turned into ladies with provincial hairstyles, bolstered by sheep's-wool chignon-pads. They scolded their maids, and sat hemming linen, their feet under sheep-skin covers. All of them looked like their mother, a woman with a receding series of yellow chins.

The eldest one had been dark and thin, people said, and called Julia. Her mother was not the mother of the little plump girls, but a foreigner whom Drakenstierna never married. It was known that the natural daughter had somehow been provided for during her lifetime. He had intimated that she was in possession of a fortune. He also said she cared little for her wealth. Julia is sitting on a fortune and she doesn't give a shit, were his exact words. Franckie never changed from the coarse soldier he was.

Some bungling, guileless artist had painted her portrait, and it still hung in one of the great cold rooms at the Shade. Skord had been there in the twilight of that first evening. He had opened a warped window, letting in the smell of apples and wet, mouldering grass. It was almost as cold in there as outside. Ragundius had not lit any fires. Shadows ruled in the cold.

They had been tramping through the spacious rooms on the wooden floorboards, greyish white with staring knot-marks. Then he caught sight of her. She had been painted on buckling linen canvas. The main colours were shadowy greens and black. The face was skewed and the body like a boy's. Her arms were stiff and her hands hung straight down in front. No, whoever painted this was hardly able to draw people. And yet, it seemed to him as if she was in there, and was looking through the face of the scarecrow made from oil-painted linen, following his movements in the cold rooms. The scrawny body in the portrait was only a screen she hid behind, and the angular face a mask. She was there behind it and spoke to him.

Look at what was mine, she said. What was mine for thirty-eight years to use for smiling, and weeping too, once in a while. You are right. It was not exquisite and perfect. On the contrary, it was twisted and skewed. But I put it on and played my part. The world was an apple orchard. It allowed me in. I felt at home with it and found it answered me in a language I could speak. I kept warm by the small dancing flames in the fireplace. In the autumn twilight I could stand there in the smoke of burning leaves. Here is the apple I bit into, still damp. Its flesh has not yet turned brown round my toothmarks.

Arriving here, I felt at home. But sometimes the body I had slipped on had a hard time. It became feverish and racked with aches and pains. Then the world became a forest littered with dead branches. When I spoke, it answered only with chattering and murmuring, as if from waters for ever running to nowhere.

When she spoke to him in this way, Skord felt a sharp pang. He wished he could have been with her when the rest of the world turned their backs. He wanted to go to her. He would have trod lightly over the groaning floorboards, carrying a cup of hot milk mixed with a generous spoonful of brown honey.

He stopped at a window and looked through the bubbly pane which made the air seem to tremble. There was a movement down there among the trees, a flash, a twitch.

'Did she go riding here?' he asked.

'Yes,' Ragundius answered. 'She kept two horses.'

Skord felt he had heard it all before, even the names: Windswift and Snowy, they must have been called.

'She rode them like a man, astride their backs,' the Pastor said, making a face.

Skord felt an almost painful excitement at the thought of the maiden parting her legs, opening herself for the warm back of the horse.

'Did she hunt?'

'Yes, she did. Her hounds were good for hares.'

Their names were Bell and Ring, Skord thought. But he did not say so.

He felt enclosed by her life as if it had come alive and warm again in the cold rooms. Hounds barking. Wet leaves under the soles of one's boots. Dough being slapped against baking boards. Misted windows. The smell of burning birch bark.

Yes, she had lived here and lit candles to ward off the dark. She had not been dragged down into the lake, nor had she fallen in the forest, thirsty and crazed by insect bites. What a miracle it was that she had made the world answer her. He was profoundly engaged by the life that had been hers. It attracted him. It had been a good life, solitary and thoughtful, without too many things banging about or obscuring the view. In that life, she had not lost sight of that which is beyond time and change. But he understood, of course, that he saw her life reduced to its essentials. It was a clarified distillate, as potent as the smell of shrivelled apples in an attic boxroom. He knew that the length of the days, the tedium of the seasons and the ticking descent of the hours into darkness had all vanished, the way water evaporates from drying apple slices.

'Almost a wild creature,' the Pastor said. 'Brought up playing and free-thinking. The Lieutenant Colonel did not act in this irresponsible manner towards his true daughters. One might ask oneself who the mother was.'

'Did he sometimes come to stay here?'

'No, but he visited frequently. Allowed a table to be laid. They ate and drank, and then she would read aloud to him in front of the fire. The readings were from heathen texts and utter nonsense.'

He is an idiot, Skord thought. Even if Latin flowed out of his ears onto his beard, he would still be an idiot. And he smells. Nastily, like fish that has gone off. And yet it was first and foremost through Ragundius that he could get an idea of how she had lived. Could it be that she had freed herself from the Highest One and his messengers on Earth? Had she slipped away when she caught glimpses of the black broadcloth of their cloaks, and heard their voices grinding like millstones?

There was someone else who knew something about her – the old woman in a corner by the stove, one of those women whose tasks entailed tearing curls of birch bark off the logs, stirring the ashes and checking the warmth of the baking oven. She existed on the verge of dismissal, but still earned her keep. In Julia's time she had been a little scullery maid. She said Julia Franck must have had resources, because she paid her church dues in gold coin.

'Why was she charged?'

'She never went. On Sundays she walked to the spring.'

'The spring?'

Yes, there had been a forest spring which would yield water even when all others had dried up. It burst forth between stones, followed a course towards the north and formed a pool, like a deep black pupil. She had put flowers in it.

'Which kinds of flowers?'

'Black vanilla orchids. Violets. Evening primroses.'

The old woman whispered as best she could. Names she would never have made her dried-up palate form again, if Skord had not come to listen to her. Once a retriever bitch had given birth to five puppies, and Julia called them Ita, Sic, Tot, Similis and Idem. The crone in the corner by the hearth could still repeat the whole string of names.

Skord took a quick look into the profoundly cold library, where the shelves creaked even if no one stepped on the floorboards. Such abundance! Outside, the cold waters of the lake glittered. In a field the furrows after the autumn ploughing had a sheen of violet in the brown. The garden had grown onion and thyme. The forest provided the dark meat of hares and game birds. The old woman had been telling him how Julia herself would skin the hares. Her long brown fingers pulled off the skin like a stocking. She insisted on sharp knives. Then a frying-pan smeared with dripping. Damp but mangled linen on the table. A jug of water from the spring. Never wine, the woman said. There was wine, kept in the cellar room where they stored turnips for the winter. It was in dark glass bottles which had been lying there for so long that they were growing mould. But wine was on the table only when Draken-stierna came to visit.

In the kitchen, they set large fires in the hearth. No need to ration the firewood. When the afternoons were chilly she often came to see them and settled in front of the fire with her book. She ate an apple and put her feet up on the iron fire-guard. Yes, she did wear boots under her skirts.

'Was she good to you?'

Neither bad nor good, that's how she was. Often impatient. Sometimes cheerful, even though she had not met a soul. She did not like thunderstorms. She would stay inside and wanted a bowl of vinegar and water. The old woman looked around carefully to make sure Ragundius was out of earshot, bent forward and whispered, 'Julia Franck liked hearing about t'others. She always

348

listened out for them. Them invisible ones journey where they please. And Julia could see them.'

Yes, she had seen them. She had heard their enticing voices, gently mocking. The Highest One Up There demanded worship and obedience, and wanted to rule over a state where the subjects turned their faces upwards. What had made her turn her gaze downwards to observe the others in the grass, in the depths of the pool and in the damp moss? When He made His thunder boom and His storm roar, she waited in her bedroom behind closed shutters with vinegar compresses on her temples until the stillness returned, and she could hear the voice of a bird and the flapping of its wings.

How had she come to find her way? When did she step aside? What traces had she seen in the wet grass, and whose enticements had made her follow?

The God had sent serious men in heavy broadcloth coats. They carried swords, erected gallows. But the smiling creatures, the enigmatic beings – whose messengers were they? How come there is a giggle from somewhere in Creation, a murmur of voices and muffled, animated singing? That narrow road, that practically invisible path of which the black-coated ones had no idea – that was the one she took.

He was told she had been a lonely little girl. Her father had kept her back when her stepmother and the younger girls travelled southwards. Following his promotion, his wife was to set up a new house. But it was a long time before he joined them down south. The war delayed him; messy and bloody things, frequently stinking awful. In short, grave matters. He lived at Kungsnäs during that time, but often stayed in the Kårböle barracks. The girl was left alone with the servants, and the house grew cold. The maids heated only the kitchen. The window-panes in Julia's bedroom became covered with ice crystals. Two dogs slept in her bed. They were called Troupe and Uncle. They were warm, and when she stroked their backs they would open their eyes and look at her. But they never whispered anything.

Perhaps it all began after that bird had come to the window. She did not know then, but it was a jay. He had far too large a head on him, and his coat looked dusty. But at the edge of his wings his proper colours showed, intensely blue with a black border and a string of white pearls. Did he speak to her?

Skord felt sure she had been free, and that her freedom was made up of cold and damp, trickling water and grass furred by frost. She must have listened. Emptied her head, and listened instead with stomach and kidneys and blood. Maybe she felt then how the water in her mouth tasted of something other than iron. But when did they begin to gather around her? When did they decide to dare whisper to just her?

We are here, they would have whispered. We are powerless and nameless. We are here – surely that means much? Here, they rustled. Here.

Are you, truly? Perhaps we are, perhaps not. We do not know. We are powerless, of course. But it is not power we want. In many ways we have not got our shape yet, but we are not misshapen. Perhaps we are halfway created. We exist only in what you glimpse out of the corner of your eye. You catch sight of us, and we come into being. Care for us with your good eyesight, dearest beloved child, sweet girl . . .

They pleaded on their own behalf. But it did happen that they left behind a drop of blood on a stone, or a rigid eyeball. She was not afraid of them, but did not know them well.

They kept whispering: He alone exists, but He is not with you, not like us. Inside the triangle His eye is blind. Painted. Its pupil is not the tunnel into that which no one has seen. He is not here the way we are. We are near. You hear us sighing in the tops of the fir trees, murmuring among the stones on the shore, and rustling under the swift-flowing water in the streams. In the autumn our hair falls off, like the leaves fall off the trees. It falls into the water of the tarn. No one knows our names because we have none. Ours is not an earnest and purposeful company. All we ask from you is that you are careful.

Be attentive. Be aware of us. Tread lightly. We will reward you. We will let you have the finest reward there is on this green Earth: you will be here. You will sense this without having to say so: I am here, and I am where I belong.

Can you hear the echo of your steps when you are walking in the forest? Or the mountain resounding with your singing? Earth is still so young and unused to the voices and tramping of human beings that she responds in amazement. Tread lightly. Sing gentle songs. Do not drown our voices. All beings are not yet completed. Not even humans are fully shaped. You can hear us, glimpse us out of the corner of your eye. When we are rustling in the grass and moving among the shadows, we ask you this: let us come into being!

The Pastor, accompanied by Birgersson, investigated house, garden, barn and stone cellar. They frightened badgers, bats and voles. But although Bonny Birger shook like calf's-foot jelly, they found no treasure.

Ragundius was irritated with Dr Saintsday, who seemed to have lost interest in the treasure-trove project and become utterly useless. Sighing, he crept about the house and the forest. He read poetry in books he had taken from Julia Franck's book-shelves. He had replaced the jay feathers in his hat with a late harebell and a meadow saxifrage. But both he and Birgersson ate and drank heartily.

After almost two weeks, they had found two copper pennies, not current coinage, and a rusty garden fork. The Pastor wanted to dismiss the whole clan and return to his quiet, lonely, mole-like existence. At last this seemed to alert the Doctor. He put down his book of verses and said they had better do some thinking. Ragundius approved. His confidence in oscillations was diminishing.

One consideration was that during his aimless wandering in the ill-kept garden and around the spring in the forest, Skord had found more than the Pastor and Bonny Birger. He had retrieved a gold chain from the gravel at the bottom of a small stream. It had no lock and had been soldered together. What a slender arm it must have encircled! And how come it slipped off? Did the arm become too thin in the end? Near the spring a gold coin was partly uncovered: he unearthed it with the tip of his boot. It gleamed in a damp place under twisted alder roots. A tortoiseshell comb set with grey pearls turned up underneath the thick star-moss covering a large, flat boulder. Skord had a shrewd idea pearls of this colour were rare and costly. Had she been so well provided for that she had carelessly worn her jewellery in the forest?

He said nothing about his finds. He did not think these things would lead him to the treasure. Instead he asked Ragundius how Franckie himself had described his daughter's patrimony, and the Pastor repeated the words on which was based the chief undertaking of his old age, as well as his prime:

'She's sitting on a fortune and doesn't give a shit.'

'Maybe we should take these words somewhat more literally,' Skord said.

He led them to the privy. Bonny Birger sat on it and started trembling straight away. Skord had never seen Pastor Ragundius so fired up with enthusiasm. Most of the time he was governed by a sense of rank disappointment, which seemed to have left him with only one dour demand: life should have a pay-off. Now he was rapturous and completely taken with the notion that, beneath all he had given so unwillingly, a treasure would be found.

They started digging the very next day. It was early in the morning. The moss glowed, the dead grass glittered. The night-time powdering of frost had begun to melt and the drops of water made the first beams of the sun break up into the colours of the rainbow. The mountain blushed like a girl. Moist strands of mist veiled the bare, worn patches in its old skin of stone. The trees had lost their leaves and their bluish grey and white trunks stood naked against the dark forest. A terrified black grouse cock crashed through the branches for a long time. He flew straight ahead, a heavy body carried by invisibly flapping wings. Frosty fog was still hanging around the tops of the pines, and all the tiny islands on Lake Näckten sailed along in water which was slowly becoming still as thin ice floes formed on its surface.

They dug. It was a stinking job, so Skord moved slightly aside and undertook the task of keeping watch. The Pastor and Bonny Birger attacked the old privy from behind and shovelled out still fresh and later decayed human dung, mixed with white-moss.

If the mind of Pastor Ragundius was dominated by the concept that life should have a pay-off, Skord on the other hand was convinced life should entail learning. As he stood in the wild garden behind the house and let his eyes roam over the forest hidlins, he realised that soon the two digging men would reach the subsoil without having found anything. This enterprise would teach him nothing he did not know before. It also became clear that he had better ride away promptly, out of Gullik's and Ravel's reach. They would not be easy to deal with when it dawned on them that they had spent several weeks hidden in the cold brewhouse, waiting in vain.

While sounds of shovelling and scraping continued, Skord ambled towards the house. He wanted to see Julia one last time. The portrait was off-putting seen in the bright light of day. The light was reflected by the uneven linen canvas, and the face looked more skewed than ever. No, she did not reveal herself here. He walked upstairs to the attic, his footsteps echoing. In the furthest corner of the cold attic was a leather travelling case full of her clothes. He had seen them before, but never touched them. Perhaps they would retain something of what had been truly hers. A smell. A soiled collar or a sleeve shaped by her elbow.

He found skirts and jackets made of thick wool, but also a wrinkled silk skirt with firmly pressed pleats and a matching bodice stiffened by metal strips in the seams. In the deepest layer, he touched something smooth. The cloth seemed to live under his fingers. He pulled up the heavy garment, a sleeveless coat with straight shoulders, shaped by hers. It was made from the finest broadcloth, black and shining like silk, trimmed with braiding and held together with hooks and eyes, neatly hidden under black silk ribbon.

His fingers felt along the fastening. He wanted to get in. Her warmth would have stayed in there. He undid the hooks, one by one. Nobody had opened the coat since her death. Ragundius's bony hands had surely probed every piece of clothing she had left, but only to satisfy himself there were no lumps that might be due to sewn-in gold coins. He had never undone the hooks. The coat would be pristine inside, and Skord longed to get into it.

He opened up the coat, and it received him. It received him, and the inside was alive. Backs, tails, paws – several dozen ermine skins, edge to edge. It was as if they were cowering close to each other in a trap.

There is a skill in killing stoats. One cracks their skulls with a wooden mallet, so that the skins stay unharmed and beautiful. The skin should be pulled off while they are still warm.

Seeing a single stoat with its long, flexible back, is it possible to think of twelve dozen of them? Like lemmings. Or fish. Or infantry.

Yes, stoats too can gather into hordes. But only when they are dead or dying. You have got to be really determined to collect so many. Here, dozens of skins had been stitched tightly together once the blood had dried.

You wore the coat of a queen, Julia. But turned inwards.

First he retched, and then fear gripped him. He had paws. He had fur. He became swiftly streaming blood and sniffing nose turned into the wind. But his body stayed lying on the coat, with his booted legs stretched out on the attic floor.

He had paws. He crawled into fur. He jumped ahead over soil which smelled of blood. It was a speckled hare's skin and a hare's strong hind legs which shot him across the ground in long arching leaps. It was not dogs which drove him. It was his heart; it came from inside him. He had seen her.

Yes, he had really seen her.

Ragundius found him on the floor of the attic room, his hands cold and his face greyish white. The old woman who had come with him was sent for, but she did nothing to wake him from his insensible state. On the contrary, she said he was not to be moved. She sat with him until warmth crept back into him and his eyelids started to twitch. Then she gave him warm milk to drink and stayed, letting his head rest in her lap. A smell like that which rises from the marsh in late autumn came from her clothes or perhaps from between her legs.

'Franckie never made gold,' Skord whispered.

She nodded to show she listened and understood.

'The treasure,' he said. 'It is in the forest. Beneath roots and stones. This is what I have found.'

He searched his pockets and gave her the chain, coin and comb to hold in her hand.

'Julia Franck scattered the treasure, she hid it in many different places so that no one would find more than a small part.'

Rick-Lena fingered the gold and the pearls. 'Do you think she hid these things?' she asked. 'That she buried them? Or do you think she just dropped them?'

'There's more,' he said, 'hidden with care and cunning. No, this comb never slipped from her hair. The hair it once held became matted with blood to a stiff mass. And she knew it.'

'Do you think so?'

'Yes, Franckie's daughter knew very well. The bracelet did not slip off the wrist of a girl who had grown too thin. The hand was chopped off. The faster the better. The chain went into the saddlebag . . . Black Franckie never made gold. His nigredo was in the cities he burned. That's where he picked up the gold.

'She lived her life here, her mobile, thoughtful, searching life. It was not a life of plenty, but it still cost something. And the burnt cities paid that cost for her. They paid in blood and screaming, in gaping wounds, in joints twisted round. In the booty of war.'

'And she knew it?'

'She knew the way it is necessary to know,' Skord said. 'I don't think her fortune sickened her. Rains had washed it, and snow and oblivion cleansed it. And none of it could be handed back. To whom should it belong, if not to her? Who could have gone back to the bad times and found the rightful owners? Once a farm hand found a gold coin in the earth and returned to dig for more. Remember?'

'Yes. The wolves got him.'

'That's what they say. But these were not wolves but dogs. And they were not called Bell and Ring. In her later years I don't think she gave her dogs names.'

They heard Ragundius stumping up the attic stairs in his clogs. The old woman gripped Skord's shoulder and said he must hurry to get away.

'Don't worry about the priest-carrion,' she said. 'He wants nothing better than for everybody to leave so he can carry on digging in the shit on his own. But Gullik and Ravel think you have found the treasure and hidden it in some new place to cheat them of their share. They're very moody.'

He set out early the next morning. When he reached the ridges beyond Näckten he could see Lake Stor, cold and blue in the late autumn air. The Ovik Mountains already had a scattering of snow on their tallest peaks, and on Falconcatcher Mountain, the forest was given a reddish sheen by the just risen sun.

He rode past Kungshammar, where King Magnus and Queen Blanche had come in their flight from the Great Death. They had wanted to follow the paths of patience along the horse trails to Nidaros and the grave of Saint Olof. He did not know whether they ever got there, nor where their bones were, and the pearls in Queen Blanche's hair. This was long ago. But still not so long ago that he had not spoken to someone who had ridden with King Magnus's embassy to Avignon. He would have been able to tell Skord if the falcons gifted to the Pope had been caught round here.

The white falcons had not travelled willingly. Nor had the ermines in the coat of King Magnus – that much Skord had learned, though it had taken him a long time. On Dog's Hill he noticed an area of snow shaped like a bird, maybe a crane. It looked as if it had been skinned and the white shroud of feathers spread out on the slope of the hill; as if it had been forced to offer up its beauty and freedom as a gift.

M aybe there is no occupation on Earth more engrossing than making gold. Sitting in front of Athanor, nothing else matters – not the dank stone wall of the prison, nor the sour bedstraw and the maggoty salted pork. In that oven burns a fire which one day will draw back the veil from profound and terrifying secrets.

Lieutenant General Otto Arnold von Paykull was born in Lithuania and never thought of himself as a Swedish citizen. When he was captured after the battle of Warsaw, he was sentenced for high treason in contumaciam. The King of Sweden regarded him as a subject who had served the enemy. This was bitter, and Paykull's prospects were very dark.

In prison he let it be known that he could make gold if given access to a coal-fired oven and certain ingredients of a chymical nature, as well as mortars, alembics and pelicans. There were learned and influential men who believed him. He got his utensils, but was unsuccessful in the beginning. Strange odours came out of the prison kitchen, yet nothing but black slag could be scraped out of the crucibles.

One afternoon during the last autumn of Paykull's life, a prison guard came to tell him of a man waiting outside, who had been brought from the thieves' dungeon in Smedjegården on the advice of Dr Hjärne and the orders of the King. He claimed to be knowledgeable about a variety of arcana and wondrous mysteries. His services were now offered to Paykull, who was sitting at the coal fire he always kept going, sublimating something smelly. As usual he was deeply engaged in the matter at hand, and looked only absent-mindedly at the dark, thin man who entered. The man bowed so elegantly and aristocratically, it seemed he was unaware that he was dressed in rags and stank of prison dungeon. Paykull refused to speak to him until he had been given clean clothes. But the conversation, which began with the man stating that his name was Kristernin Skord and he was the Lieutenant General's most humble servant, turned out to be both long-lasting and rewarding.

During the whole of that autumn and the dark winter months before Christmas, Paykull and his new batman worked, pulverising in mortars of alabaster the whitest wine-stone and best cream of tartar from Montpellier. They left the mixture to sweat in large stone dishes and dried it over a low coal fire until it turned into a fine powder which they dreamily sifted between their fingers. They prepared sulphuris antimonii and tested several grains of lead to find out if it was good and pure enough to turn into gold under the influence of the tincture. All this they did without haste, indeed holding back as if acting in a dream and wanting to extend these very meaningful hours. Meantime, they conversed about original generation and transformations, about the creation of fleas out of stagnant water, flies out of foul, damp air in bad weather, lice out of the sweat of people and horses, and bedbugs out of white-moss. It seemed to them that the present as well as its origin was being revealed. They felt in their own world, at home with its filth and rough stone, rotting straw and stinking water; but at the same time they were able to step aside and contain its phenomena within the framework of science.

On one of these dark days in winter, one and a half grains of lead finally turned into incontestably pure gold. It happened as if in a dream. The process was calm and peaceful. Without flames or bangs, the metal melted from one state of being into another. The egg opened sweetly as if from a still pool.

It would appear that there is a huge jest built into the very ground plan for the ordering of matter. The consequences of this are many and sometimes very intricate. Inside Kristernin Skord was born a bitterness, which turned the joy rancid. Indeed, in the midst of triumph, he felt and kept secret a certain anger.

So that was how easy it could be. When all went to order. When Somebody permitted. One time would be one big crude joke, crackling farts and sulphurous flames emerging from the egg of life. The next time, it would be pure gold; gold pouring as easily as a gentle smile. Someone smiled. But who?

They had made gold, and Paykull thought himself saved. But, hardly two months later he was decapitated and deposited into a mass grave gouged out of the frozen soil. This was on the orders of a raw young king, who had not even taken the time to read the certificate of purity which accompanied the cargo of gold.

People who do their best are not trusted. But it is well known that rogues are decorated with silver blobs and have pretty ribbons strung across their chests. The King who in his immature and rash hurry signed the execution order for Paykull had been sent one hundred and forty-seven ducats and two bags of gold-dust from the slag, and in addition a signed certificate from the inspectors. He had been promised pure gold to the value of about one million thalers in the coin of the realm, and a written assurance that Paykull would instruct a native-born Swede in the knowledge. But the sentence was carried out, in the month of February at the place of execution by the North Toll Gate. The blood that had nourished an incessantly inventive, acute and imaginative brain poured into the slush for the entertainment of gaping hooligans and boneheads from all walks of life.

Many years later Skord came across a coin struck from von Paykull's gold and held it in his hand, feeling that he held the very hours of still, febrile waiting in the prison by Norrmalm. The reverse side was embossed with these words: HOC AURUM ARTE CHEMICA CONFLAVIT HOLMIA A. 1706 O. A. VON PAYKULL. The front of the coin carried the image of the King, and Skord did not know whether he had changed his mind immediately with regard to Paykull's gold, or whether the coin had been struck long after the blood had stopped leaching from his brain.

In the beginning Skord was forgotten while the scholars carried on debating the proposition that Paykull had been a verus adeptus. He lay on the bunk next to the cold oven, breathing in the smell of rotten straw and coal ashes. During this period the cards always showed him the image of the Star. He could not understand this except as mockery. Where in this icy hole, this sour hell, would she be, the woman who filled her vessels from an abundance of running water and with caring gratitude returned it whence it came? Life had bad breath. The only advantage of his present position was that the lice died in the cold.

In April he was pardoned after submissions by Dr Hjärne, and ordered to work in his laboratory at Norrmalm Square. He could not recollect ever having been so bored. He ground and pulverised, sublimated, distilled, boiled to dryness and collected the remainder, never seeing more than the coat-tails of the exceedingly learned and very busy doctor. He had assumed that Hjärne would ask him questions, but their conversation was forever postponed.

The Doctor had never doubted that the Lieutenant General had been a verus adeptus. He had stated his opinion with conviction, and wielding pen and ink had entered into violent battles on this issue. However, he had not sat down face to face with Kristernin Skord in order that they might investigate the Secret of Secrets together. Instead Skord was left in the large laboratory together with other chymicists with worn seats on their trousers and much-mended stocking heels. They carried out the most simple-minded experiments over and over again in exactly the same way, and then wrote up the results after weighing, measuring and testing. To Skord it seemed Dr Hjärne believed in the Secret only some days. At other times, he seemed driven by a dreary and stubborn determination with an obscure, deeply hidden goal – if such a goal existed – which Skord was incapable of understanding.

But he could grasp the big disappointment, and was gripped by it. He turned cold with astonishment at the thought of the pure and incontestable gold lying in a box in some attic, regarded as a soon-to-be-forgotten oddity. On some days he felt as if the blood had been pouring out of his own brain that day in February at the North Toll Gate.

One day something happened in a draughty corner of the laboratory, which made Dr Hjärne most excited. As far as Skord could understand, the result implied not the slightest joy or usefulness. It also smelled exceptionally badly. But the Doctor kept tiptoeing round the bowl containing the repulsiveness and blew his nose repeatedly in a snuff-kerchief, as if he wanted to hide his tears.

Skord was so upset that he said something he should not have done, the night after this event. It happened in front of an old laboratory servant, with whom he shared a bench and a couple of sheepskins at night. To the old man he said straight out that he had never been particularly for Christ, in whose name altogether too many bones had been broken, joints twisted and eyes put out.

'Just think about it,' he said into the dark, 'If He was truly sent at that time, then surely He must have been sent at other times. And perhaps not always as a human being. In that case, how many times had they murdered Him as a child, thrown Him out with slops into the gutter or forgotten Him among the rubbish in the attic? Any thinking person must ask himself this question in a world where the very acme of education leads a man respectfully and worshipfully to observe formic acid – ants' piss.'

Skord spat into the darkness. But even though the spittle was quite solid, he never heard it land, because suddenly his bedfellow got going. The old man lit a spill. His eyes were running, his mouth working. He was a bald and ancient man, who had been given permission to sleep in the laboratory at night. He kept the ovens going during the winter to prevent the fluids freezing in glass pelicans and demijohns. These days it was tacitly agreed that Skord, who was without family and home, could also sleep there if he chopped and carried in wood from the woodshed in the courtyard to help the old man, whose name was Moshe Feigenbaum.

Skord had never thought much about the old man they all called Moses. From living in the laboratory he had come to smell of strong acid. He moved swiftly in spite of his age and slipped across the floor like a weasel. He was always about the place making himself useful, but did not draw attention to himself. But this night he burst into flower and stayed in bloom for nine nights more.

During the rule of the King's grandfather's cousin, Moshe's father, whose name was Eliezer, had arrived in Norrköping in order to set up a school for the children of his family and friends. He was a scribe, and had been earning a living as a tailor. Moshe grew up in the house of learning, and was a pious little boy. He became a good scribe. From his sixteenth year, he went every morning to the City Hall where he worked as a copyist. By the time he was eighteen, he was asked to accompany a clergyman to the Parliament in Stockholm in order to write his speeches and letters because the reverend gentleman had an abscess on his thumb. Rabbi Eliezer had died, and Moshe ben Eliezer, who now called himself Feigenbaum, hoped to return home with money for his poor mother. Now a widow, she tried to support herself by sweeping and scrubbing the floors in the house of learning, and tending the fire in the schoolroom. But he never did return. The demon that had caused the pus in the thumb of the pastor from Norrköping also separated Moshe for ever from his family.

Moshe was employed as a clerk and copyist in the Crown Estate Office. He wrote out requisitions and inventories. His soul felt as dead as a chair-leg during this period. But the demon inspired him to write sighs and exclamations in the margins of the lists he was working on. They were intended for burial in the Castle archives, and he had no reason to believe they would ever be read.

But the Regent had her moments. Acutely short of cash, she hit on the idea of scrutinising the inventories of royal properties, and so it came to light that Moshe had used the lists to sigh in Latin. His foreman cuffed his ears, but afterwards he was promoted. Later he ended up in the Castle as a learned man's scribe.

At that time, a man lived in Stockholm Castle who thought differently from others. The Castle was later burned down by ignorant demons, blind to the plans of the Almighty. The man, who grew up in a warmer country called France, had not originally been different from others.

Now and then Skord had to keep himself in check so as not to show his irritation at the old man's apparent belief that he and the strange man were the only thoughtful and well-travelled human beings in Europe, possibly the world.

The man had taught himself to think. His thoughts were of two kinds. One of these categories he called the Method. To express these thoughts he used more calculations than words. The Method was not given by the Almighty, nor was it handed down by wise men since time immemorial. He had thought it out himself. The Method did not enable him to make gold, but could help him find it. The strange man insisted that those who understood how to use it would have such power over matter that on command things would rise and fall, dissolve or mix. The Method could make the water flow up the riverbeds.

Moshe Feigenbaum, whose task was to make fair copies of the strange man's notes, never dared ask him about anything. But he claimed that, sooner or later, the answers to all his questions were revealed on the ink-stained sheets of paper, or in the dictation from the man's thin lips.

There was nothing in this way of thinking that actually contradicted the words in the Torah on God, Creation and Man. But when Moshe was allowed to share these thoughts, he felt as if the Talmud had never been written, or even that it would be necessary to write it again. There was a particular essay which the strange man would not have printed (to protect his neck), and which instead the scribe had to copy many times so it could be sent to learned friends all over Europe. It was called 'About the World'. Now, while Moshe had not always understood the Method, he had found it much easier to take to his heart the strange man's other kind of thoughts, as they were explicated in this essay. Soon the words ran with the blood through his veins. For instance, it was said that Earth circled round the sun like a mosquito round a lamp.

Skord did not have the heart to tell the old man that it was no longer necessary to whisper when confiding this observation to someone.

Moshe had learned that, having finished creating, the Almighty had withdrawn and left the world in a cold space which could be traversed only by the Method, not by prayers or appeals. There was little point in quarrelling with God, or inviting him to join in debates on all sorts of questions, as Moshe's father Eliezer had done, sitting on his tailor's table. God did not answer. When old Eliezer had felt himself answered, the words had come from inside his own soul. God had implanted in the soul the knowledge He had reserved for His World. Using the Method, the world would become much more accessible than through prayers and appeals directed up into a distant space.

Man has a Soul, Moshe continued. Man also has a Body. Skord followed these arguments with the greatest attention, but now and then he felt sleepy. If Moshe fancied that the strange man in Stockholm Castle had been the first to hit on the idea of Man's divided nature, then sheer respect must have made the former scribe unquestioningly hang on to other mistaken ideas in the Master's teaching. But what he said next turned out to be of inordinate interest.

The body, Moshe went on to say, moved like all other bodies in the world according to the laws that God had formulated and established. These laws were immutable, but not unfathomable. In the text Moshe had copied, everything was a body, from a grain of dust or a coltsfoot to the biggest mountain or all the water in the oceans. They acted on each other to such a complicated extent that the Method had to be exceptionally refined to reveal the patterns dictating their mutual interactions, and so enable influence to be brought to bear. But those who knew the Method would be able to make rifts in mountains, and will different bodies to move as they wished.

Skord stared at the old man as he was speaking, and suddenly realised he no longer believed in this tale. It was more than likely that there had never been a strange man in the burnt-down Castle, which still seemed to stand there at times, when one tried to stare through the dancing snowflakes over the bridge. Possibly Moshe had thought it all out himself, or maybe caught words floating through the air during all the years he had listened to people talking in the offices of the Castle and in the large laboratory hall full of workbenches.

Never mind, people had the right to tell whatever tales they could. Skord had no objection to believing or pretending to believe there had been a man in Stockholm Castle who had thought differently from all other people before him. But he found it hard to keep listening in good faith to what the old man was saying about mankind. How could he state his objections? There were two good reasons for keeping a straight face: politeness and caution. It would be crude and rash to knock down the old man's stories – like letting a drunken peasant into the theatre. And what would happen if he said to him, 'Listen, Moshe, I'm a most strange creature, not a human being, and therefore able to think differently from you.' Could he rely on the old man not believing him, and seeing instead his narrative as a story intended to provide a framework for his objections? This was a option he had never tried to take. It could mean danger. He did not dare.

'The animals,' Moshe Feigenbaum said, 'go about their lives according to the laws the Highest Being has designed for them. They are tappets, cogs, wheels and joints in His great Machine, and they rotate for ever in the Carousels in which he has placed them. They eat, mate and give birth to offspring which eat and mate.'

At this point Skord objected: 'They also leap for joy. They run about. Flick their tail feathers. Swim with the evening sunshine on their heads. Tumble in the snow, and slide down rock faces. Some sing heartbreakingly, and sometimes their hearts break.'

'No animal sings, runs or leaps for reasons other than to keep alive and reproduce,' Moshe answered.

'But what about the strong male salmon leaping in a waterfall? If you had seen the shining body of the salmon above the sharp rocks and foaming waters, you would have realised he jumps higher and more daringly than he needs just to get on. There is something more. And when bog rosemary traces a pattern of flowers over the moss, and when the water in a stream glows red in the sunlight and finds its way over a bed of gold and gravel, and when a chaffinch in the top of a fir tree sings more strongly than his heart can bear – then there is something more!'

'There's nothing more,' Moshe said. 'Only the human soul adds something more. That is beauty and courage. And longing. All the other bodies in the world just keep rotating in their Carousels.'

A demon lived in the icy wastes of space. He knew about all the bodies and their movements. By calculating their consequences all the way to the end of the world and back, he could tell what had been and what would be. He was also capable of making the careful computations needed to intervene in the relentless machinery of the world, and by manipulating it produce different results. For instance, by starting an abscess in someone's thumb.

The strange man who had visited Stockholm Castle had not known about the demon. Moshe Feigenbaum only heard about it in the decade after the man's death. The stranger died as a result of the raw cold which reached into the Castle from the rushing waterway below its ramparts. Its icy fog could be seen at night whirling in an evil dance above the black water.

Moshe had been told to collect his writing set from the room where he had been working for the man. When Moshe entered, the stiff corpse was lying on a stretcher. Rats had already gnawed holes in the fingertips of his silk gloves.

The icy fog finally took Moshe Feigenbaum as well. The icy fog, and then the rats. Skord was outraged with grief and misery when one morning he found the old man stiff and cold. He despised the demon who had to keep poking about in the machinery of the Carousel, perhaps in order to prove that everything went round and round, and that the rats foraged to mate under the floorboards and then breed, so that the offspring could go looking for more food. That is, as soon as the food had become still enough for them to dare to come out and touch it.

There was much pattering of paws and scraping noises at night, and Skord slept badly. One night he heard the rustling of claws close by. He looked out into the dark of the small hours and distinguished a shadow which might have been old man Feigenbaum if it had not been so small. It was no rat. He stayed very still, staring with aching eyes into the greyness. But he saw no more of the creature that had moved across the floor than a curved and agile back.

Later that morning, he again heard the sound of paws which did not belong to a rat, and when he opened his eyes, still feeling drowsy, he realised it was a small weasel. It had stopped and sat up, holding its head high and its back set into the arching movement about to carry it across the floor. They stared at each other. The weasel's eyes were black and shiny.

'Is that you?' Skord whispered. But there was no answer. The small weasel started moving and ran to the wall, where it disappeared into the shadows. Skord did not know what to believe. He felt as lonely and as deeply bored as ever.

During the days that followed, everything continued as usual in the laboratory. They were made to repeat what they had already done many times, sometimes with small changes which they had to record punctiliously. In June, when the grasses flowered along the Strömmen firth, he ran away.

The Star kept coming up. If it had not been for her, we might have lost him – just as, for long periods of time, he continued to lose himself.

Xenia

The story is coming to an end. The hero is very thin and his shoes are letting in water. He suffers from corns and an acid stomach. Nothing has worked out quite the way he planned. When we find him again with the help of the Star, it is winter and snowing hard in a biting wind. There are blizzard conditions in the villages, and the oil streetlamps, shaking and swinging from their chains, have almost all gone out. He is standing outside a lit shop window in Västerlång Street, counting the coins in his purse. He is on his way into the shop, but not sure he has enough money to pay. However, he does not appear to be one of the wretchedly poor. His ragged and worn black garments have a certain style. The nap on his top hat is raised by the gusts of wind.

A covered sleigh has stopped in the street. An elderly Ambassador is sitting inside it, a survivor from times gone by. He is wearing embroidered tails and silk knee breeches under his coat. But the most important thing about him is his gout. He has asked his valet – a black Negro – to run down the street and buy some confectionery. Once upon a time, His Excellency was admired for having *l'esprit jusqu'au bout des doigts* and his compliments were quoted everywhere. Now he has to bring sweetmeats when invited into company for supper. Aches and pains do not inspire wit. There are lumps on his elbows, one of his knees and his left ear. One big toe has been swollen and bad for decades. Some days his foot refuses to support him. There is acidity inside his old body and acidity in his soul. He is knobbly and aching.

In order to get a better idea of the contents of his purse, our hero walks up to the last lit streetlamp. At that very moment the Ambassador recognises him. This is a man from the old days! The very fellow who years and years ago cured him of paralysing gout pains. With electricity!

The man in the black suit now enters the shop and does not hear the old gentleman hammering on the carriage window with his stick. He is in there for an age, and when he leaves, His Excellency opens the carriage door and calls him. They stare at each other briefly. But our hero does not want to be recognised. He escapes into the whirling snow and gets away, even though the Ambassador tumbles out of the carriage and tries to hook the handle of his stick into his collar. Just then the valet arrives on the scene, and his master shouts, 'Catch that man!'

The Negro throws the parcel from the confectioner's into the sleigh and dashes away after the fleeing man. He is away for such a long time that his master is about to send the coachman after them both. But then he turns up again, his face a jet-black patch in the falling snow.

'I had the door shut in my face, but I know where he lives,' he says.

This is how it came about that the old gentleman, leaning on his stick and the arm of his valet, totters up the stairs in a house on Corpus Christi Wynd. They have to stand in front of a closed door for a long time, hammering on it and shouting, until a crack opens and a woman peeps out, showing half her nose and one eye. She lies, saying there is nobody in there with her. But His Excellency has got his stick into the crack and levers the door open. It is close in there, and smells of frying lard and reheated coffee. They have to advance as far as the kitchen before they find him. He is eating, but rises slowly and watchfully. He has of course taken off his snow-covered coat. Underneath he is also dressed in black and, like the Ambassador, wears knee breeches. He does not wear a wig in the old-fashioned manner, but his black hair is so long that he really does give an impression of being a contemporary of the Ambassador – another survivor. The old gentleman senses something appealing in this man's manners, something which contradicts his crowded and smelly surroundings. The only thing that does not tally is that this man is nowhere near as old as he should be. He insists immediately that he has never had the honour of making His Excellency's acquaintance. Visibly embarrassed by the impoverished table, set with mended chinaware on a bare tabletop, he ushers the visitors into the room next door. It is freezing cold and furnished only by a tidy bed and a box of books.

The assertion that they have never met makes the Ambassador furious, and his valet has to calm him down and get him to see that if the man in black had been there to treat him at the time, he would now be at least as old as His Excellency himself.

'It was more than forty years ago!' he whispers. But the old man does not budge. He claims he can recognise the only one who ever freed him from his gout pains – any contradiction is ridiculous, and besides he is not used to being contradicted by lackeys.

'Tais-toi, blackamoor!'

But it is not his rage which silences the valet. It is something else, something very odd. He keeps staring at the man's left hand. But he says nothing.

Then the man in the black suit says he is beginning to understand. His eyeballs gleam and he waves his hands about in a way reminiscent of birds flying. When he pulls at his earlobe they both stare at him as if he were doing something they would not miss for the world.

'My father!' he says. 'Good Lord, it must have been my father! He had an electricity machine!'

'And is it still about?' asks His Excellency.

'No, no – such a machine would be totally *démodé*.'

But that would not bother His Excellency at all. It had cured him!

'Nowadays,' says the black-suited man conspiratorially, almost in a whisper, 'light massage is done with magnetism.'

D o you feel heavy? Just as well. Sleep now. Your chin is drooping. Your large eyeballs have stopped rolling. Fancy, a Negro becoming so pale.

Well, now, my boy. You've got much to learn. In the first place, I am not who you think I am. How could I be? As you said to your master – It cannot be him! It was forty years ago, of course. And thirty-six since you and I last met. But there you are, you were mistaken! I was not me. I – or he – did have a stump on my left hand where the finger of Mercury should have been. That's true. I pointed at you just now – or he did – sticking out the fingers of Venus, Jupiter and Saturn and reaching out towards your black – now not quite so black – forehead. The finger of Mars was crooked into the palm of my hand. And where the finger of Mercury should have been you saw but a stump. Curious. But I am not him. Nor am I truly me.

I have a certain resemblance to the man you're thinking of. I have a purely accidental likeness to that man, indeed, to many men – even to myself. That is to say, I look more like you than like a swine.

May I ask what makes you so sure that you are a human being – quite apart from this rather superficial resemblance that makes you hang around human beings rather than a herd of pigs? You find swine distasteful. They grunt, they potter about. They guzzle rotten potatoes and bits of dead bodies.

I have seen people do that.

Are people human?

As like each other as leaves are.

Look at the leaves. Can you not in the blink of an eye eliminate their similarities? See the networks of nerves, spreading and curling and twisting. Not a single one has the same pattern as the next. Spots, rust. Dots, warts; jagged edges, shifting colours. Dry rustling. Long, drifting waves. Spreading and shrinking. Leaves.

Are they leaves?

I don't know.

Yes, my dear boy, it has been a long time since we met and you have grown a bit fat. Your skin is not the same glossy black, and your black curls have got grey in them. I suppose you have had a good life. But you have felt the cold. Yes, to be sure, you have been frozen and coughed a great deal since you made that long journey across the seas. I made it twice.

Awake and watching you sleeping, your chin drooping and your eyelids heavy, I imagine I hear the sea beating against the beach. Do you remember the sand? The huts? The pigs? He calls you Gugo, but you were called something else then. Do you remember? Can you recall what your name was, in the huts down there on the filthy sand? Gugo is not your real name. It's a lackey's name. The comical noise a blackamoor page makes when referring to himself. Gugo, you used to be a *pagiazzo*. An amusing little devil.

'Pleeze, milor. You ring?'

He found it entertaining that you learned his language. But not too well, eh? Just like his old lizard brother, the gentleman you now serve. Gugo, you spoke twaddle with your old master. Niggertalk. You did not dare speak to him the way you can with me.

His brother was never a real lord. Not a count or even a baron. You found that out soon enough. Crossing the ocean is not a bad way to change identity – name, even face. A man has problems, maybe his affairs have got tangled – females, politics, money. Goodness, I had one or two little difficulties of my own. Things had got a little bitter and twisted, you know.

Let your eyes stay closed, Gugo, but see me. What did you think I was? A gambler? A *vaurien*, a good-for-nothing drifter? Or even some kind of gypsy with a little more education than usual? I wonder what you did think. You were a small, jet-black, bright-eyed demon. You picked up a great deal. Did you think I belonged among *les couleurs*?

Wrong, Gugo. Nor was I some common or garden horse trader

375

back home. Your self-appointed lord met me just as he had got into very hot water, a most painful predicament – in fact, a totally awful *disgrâce* ... he had been trying to fix things with the representative of the Russian Empress, can you believe it? Unauthorised peace-feelers. High treason, no question about it. You get executed for that. But he was pardoned. Still, he had to go overseas. And I went with him, because, well, I too was in rather a jam.

I was a chymist and mechanicus. Quodlibetarius. A doctor, in a manner of speaking. Personal medicus to His Lordship. My specialities were electricity and galvanism. But I did not manage to take the machine with me. Got a bit rushed in the end. As often happens.

I'm sure you can remember me with phlebotomes and lancets. Towel over my arm, red woollen ribbons round my legs. In short, the complete and proper surgeon. Not a horse dealer. Not a beachcomber or a hobo of mixed blood.

You shan't brood over what happened, Gugo. Don't speculate about me and my share in the unpleasantness. You will forget. You must know and forget.

The sea is hissing. The sand is rustling. Dry palm leaves are crackling in the wind, a heavy and humid wind. It comes from far away out on the Sargasso Sea. The wind of oblivion. What you cannot remember cannot worry you. And there is no need to brood over what you know. Now I'm going to light a small pipe. Sleep, my boy. The wind is caressing your cheek. You are a small, jet-black, bright-eyed demon. You have a good head on your shoulders and you are in luck – silk breeches and a turban. The small pageboy who serves His Lordship his chocolate. You learned to grate it and put it into boiling water. Add creamy milk, whisk a little rice flour into it. You soon picked up little skills like this. Nowadays I suppose you prepare it for his old lizard brother. Does he too want it thick and dark, with a few drops of anise or a splash of strong, sweet rum? The old Ambassador. He wants to be free from his pain. He wants to be young again. We shall rub him gently. If you are good, my lad, nice and forgetful, then I will teach you the magnetic massage in which I am frankly more versed than Cederschjöld himself – in fact, almost as good as the great

Wolfart. It is a little less fashionable these days, but for as long as His Excellency approves, we shall go on rubbing ... you'll learn a useful thing or two, *mon vieux*. So forget the disaster. Besides, it wasn't really that bad. Nothing is, come to think of it. A word. Or two. Nothing really unpleasant, Gugo.

It was April. A damp heat. It started on the veranda. The annoying words were uttered there. Or, at least, that one word too many. His Lordship had received a message to say the ship carrying the newly appointed Chief Attorney was winding its way among the islands. He wanted to arrange a reception for his friend from the old days. *Grande fête.*

But how to arrange a *fête* in a backwater like Gustavia? An island about ten miles lengthways and little more than three across. Your world, Gugo. I wonder how you remember it? Ugly rocks and boulders; treeless and stony and desolate. Seething marshes and stinking swamps. Or was it paradise, as you recall it? Was paradise there, on the sands down by the sighing sea? Do you remember the huts? The dog crap and pig turds and hen shit? Or would you rather remember the pink wooden house with a pillared veranda where you could crouch in the shade?

Paradise, well, now ... such words were used early on, in his very first letters. 'I have arrived in heaven and in hell,' he wrote to his old friend. But I was told to delete 'hell' in the fair copy.

Do you remember how he had me examine you before you were bathed and dressed in a page's outfit? No wounds at the roots of your nails, nothing round your mouth or on your little brown cock. In hell, even a seven-year-old can have the Disease. He had it himself already. But he preferred not to know. Did you catch it?

You are sleeping, Gugo. Sleep and remember. Then you will wake up and forget. Hell is far away. As far as paradise. You will never see it again. Never hear the moist evening wind swooping in and rattling the crowns of the palms.

Maybe the good idea came drifting along on the Sargasso wind. Anyway, it came after a bout of drinking. It was not my idea. It was entirely his, and derived from his own words: Heaven and Hell. He was as delighted by them as by sweet brown rum.

He would welcome the Chief Attorney with a tremendous *fête*.

He was to arrive in Elysium! Step straight from the ship into the Light, the Fields of Happiness, a flowering, fruit-laden, honeyed Bliss! And later, in the soft, chattering darkness, when the hot and humid wind from Sargasso had died down, then Tartarus would be displayed!

A *fête*. A *tableau vivant*! A representation in which everyone would be himself and yet someone else, at the same time actor and *spectateur*.

He was very excited. His lazy melancholy ceased, and his drunkenness became less heavy – these were lively April nights on the veranda.

Surely there would be enough to make a heaven! Plenty of the light elements. Air and water: purple clouds against azure, golden and saffron-coloured skies, wine-red seas, yes, and also waves of heavenly blue, or fringed with gold and silver, swelling and sighing. Aeolian harp strings shivering under the moonbeams along with the blue-black leaves in the trees. Zephyr fingering silver strings. Of course, doves and nightingales were in short supply, and there were rather too many chattering parakeets, not to speak of vultures, scorpions, lizards etcetera, etcetera. Actually, it was easier to create an impression of the Tartarean deserts and chasms – storms, mists, rock-falls, terrifying, bare mountains, plunging comets, marshes, fumes, ignis fatuus, smoke, ashes, bones and so on and so forth.

We pondered heaven a great deal. After all, it was not such a simple thing to represent. Well, what is heaven actually like?

What is your heaven like, Ogdu? Was that not what you were called – or something like that? Is there warm sand in your heaven? Spotted piglets? Hissing and squeaking? Do you tumble with the black-spotted little ones in your heaven, Ogdu?

But it's not a very nice heaven. It smells of rotten fish and dried excrement. And the pigs bite. They are as starved as you are, drum-belly.

Hell has always been easier for people to imagine. The great Swedenborg, who had seen a thing or two in his lifetime, tells us that there are many hells, set up and equipped for private use. They are by no means general institutes for mass correction and punishment. What would be the point? They are in fact rather like heavens, though with small but crucial distinctions. Our private hells do not stink of scorched hair, thickening blood, dung and burnt flesh, but rather, for instance, of bowel gas and unwashed stockings. We will feel more at home in our own hell than in heaven, if the great Doctor is to be believed.

Perhaps you have spent too many decades in the land of long, pale twilights and your notion of paradise is now less fantastical than when you rolled pellets for my pipe. What do you eat in your heaven – gooseberry fool?

A sensible heaven: in the end we too decided in favour of that. The Attorney had after all just sailed from Sweden.

Clean-swept streets, a small tidy veranda, girls dressed in cottonade and nettlecloth. A gingham-checked, flowery paradise, giving off a sweet odour of freshly baked cakes, made from fine flour, anise, fennel, cumin and syrup. Somewhere special, after the months of seasickness and stench from the ship's holds. A highly unexpected paradise, and one in which the endless coffee-drinking would not cause an acid stomach, because I would be there with my powders. That's what I thought.

But His Lordship thought differently. He wanted to send me to the other place. Listen to this. 'Now, Schordenius,' he said, 'you had better play the flute or hang about doing something else with the blacks. We need a watchful eye there.'

Me? Why me? I didn't like carrying arms. I handled lancet and forceps and cared little for whip or pistol. Cared not at all.

'We need you down there, ' he said. 'Besides, you rather belong there.' And gurgled with laughter. Do you remember his laughter? I thought, he's pissed, which was right enough. But he had not changed his mind the next morning. 'The beach,' he said. 'Don't be difficult, Schordenius. Dress up – you can be a medicine man, a *sorcier*, whatever. It'll be fine. I need people I can trust down there.' So was I supposed to belong there?

'I come from a family of Danish clergy.'

'Well, then . . .'

'I am a medicus, a chymist.'

'Still, there's a hint of *couleur*.'

Those were his words. The word. It was not good.

He placed Hell on the beach. The general plan was to have glowing fires, black faces, abysmal howls and thumping drums.

379

Personally I thought the spectacle was overdone, and besides it smelled of shit, as I'm sure you remember, human shit, pig turds and decaying fish. I disliked the whole notion of Hell. It seemed to me clumsy and smacked of the peasant somehow. The effect might be comical, I said, but he laughed it off and was proved right, of course. Towards the end it was far from comical.

But nothing really happened. You must remember that. And then forget. I told him it would be safer to create Hell with words, and maybe Paradise as well, and offered to help. A Prologue, an Ode, a Play for voices and music. Words are unshakeable. They remain stable. But churches of marble will tumble down in the end, as certainly as paper palaces and mud huts with straw roofs. Actually, it is often a word that does the damage.

But His Lordship would not put his trust in words; he had to build it all in cardboard and wood. He was rather primitive, a soul with *couleur* in a whitish, flaking and reddened body.

So they built away. I took no part. The time became taken up with preparations. Sewing and hammering. At first the Negroes stood about looking cross, but they eventually came to life, prattling and shouting. Somewhat worryingly so, in my opinion. Prattling on a loud, tense note. I worried, you see, that they would get to the idea of unsettling the whole edifice. Setting fire to it. Goodness knows what conclusions they drew from all these splendid constructions. Did they really understand that it was all an act, a representation of something else? That it must not go too far? And did they realise who was playing this game?

I felt tense myself. And ill at ease. That word ... it was corrosive. It lay there, nagging, like a stone in a bladder. Made itself felt. Yes, I felt it very much and it would not go away. Might say it got worse.

It became so bad that I kept brooding over what exactly he might have had in mind. Was I supposed to be descended from a Negress, or to have a Mulatto in the family? Was I a Cabre or a Sambo, Mestizo, Quarteron, Greif or Mamblou? In his most valuable opinion? Or had he been contemplating something more of a gypsy nature – a Zincalo, descended from wandering Hindus?

You are black, my dear chap. Once as black as a pair of polished patent leather boots, now more greyish brown with a hint of blue. But undoubtedly and indisputably a Negro. Even nowadays your face can frighten the maids. But you have never had to worry about where you belong. And you have had a decent life, a bearable life, haven't you? He could have sold you for hard currency, maybe twenty piastres or even twenty-five, if you had had more muscle than the lackey job gave you. Healthy body, quick and obedient.

So you've been lucky after all, Gugo. And you've been allowed to keep the skin on your back. You know what happened in the end to some of the Tartarean demons from the Hell down on the beach. Though do forget it. It is not an agreeable memory. Don't go on worrying about it or about my part in the festivities. It was, I assure you, of little consequence. A minimal contribution. But possibly not completely without effect. One or two words.

An index finger. Nail and all.

Well, Jesus Christ Almighty! Everything went well until Miss Euphrastenius vomited. People's hands supported her white forehead, she shook and turned herself practically inside out. The question of what had made her so ill was raised, and everybody pretended not to realise that the silly goose had drunk herself sick.

Anyway, many felt unwell, especially those who had been travelling with the Chief Attorney. Residual seasickness, plain tiredness and exhaustion. But nobody asked me to help. That night, I was anything but a medicus. I don't know what the new arrivals made of me – if they took any notice at all. With travelling pistols in my belt, I must have looked just like the slave driver His Lordship had fashioned me to be. I had refused to carry a whip, and the hunting knife he had made me take I put under my bed before coming out. Perhaps the general nausea was due to the air. It still stank a bit. We had put strongly aromatic bark and leaves on the fires, but the smell penetrated. The table servants, who dished up from the cooking pots, were in full costume. Everything looked wild and Tartarean, more or less according to plan. But he had not planned for sickness and speculations about poisoned food.

Someone tried to be entertaining and told a story about a medicine man who had been found on one of the neighbouring islands. He had poisoned one hundred and fifty slaves belonging to a French baron. Ouuuuiiiiii . . . how the little miss screamed. Fainting and cramps.

Then I uttered my little witticism. I was standing next to the Governor's niece. Miss Euphrastenius's mother had also eaten from the pot on the fire. Indeed, she was still gnawing away on a small bone when her daughter started throwing up. 'Oh, deaah, whaat can it be?' she said. 'What's in this aaawful food?'

Then I said it.

She was still holding the bone – supposedly from a chicken – delicately in her fingers. 'What do you mean?' she screeched. 'Would His Lordship really have allowed them . . .'

'Of course not,' I said. 'Not at all. But they may have taken matters too far on their own.'

She started screaming. And the Governor's niece bent forward and was sick right over my patent leather shoes, which were thankfully more or less hidden under the sand I was standing in.

Afterwards there was an outbreak of great confusion in the humid darkness, and several more guests puked and had convulsions. Nobody was any longer quite clear which of the ladies had been told first, and who had actually said it. So it became distorted, and they believed she had noticed herself what she had been putting into her mouth – with a nail still on it, and all. Pots were overturned on the fires, two huts were burned down. Shots were fired and, what with one thing and another, I beat a retreat. After all, I carried arms only with great reluctance and had not the slightest wish to contribute to the turmoil.

That was it, *mon vieux*. Don't think about it any more. Don't ever think about it again. It was a stupid joke. It sprang from a resentful mind, from sheer irritation actually. I knew perfectly well that even in Africa Ibos do not do such things, and I said as much to His Lordship. But the locals were not given to making jokes either, at least not in their current circumstances. I must emphasise that.

The following day. A grey day. A dirty, bleached sky, a black sun. A terrible forenoon, a long afternoon and evening of punishments which were initially light or only moderately hard, and intended to extract information. So much talking. Interrogations and inquiries. His Lordship was as sober as a judge, and assisted the Chief Attorney. I have been around and cannot claim that they were more awkward or less inventive and persistent than the French or the English when it came to establishing the truth. The truth they uncovered was immaculate, and provided a conclusion to this lamentable business – this not entirely successful party. As His Lordship put it: cards on the table. Nothing must be concealed. Had something taken place – criminal or just distasteful – then the guilty would be punished.

Some cheered. The ladies had stayed indoors, but there were lots of people about. I'm sure you will understand that this was not a good atmosphere in which to speak openly about the joke. And especially not for someone presumed to be of *couleur*. Christ Almighty, I had no intention other than to cause a bit of an upset: running around, overturned pots, fires going out and His Lordship roaring.

The rest was deeply regrettable.

But we will forget it. Besides, it was bad luck.

Gugo, you've had an exceptionally bad attack of toothache. But nothing very much else to worry about. Soon you will wake and the tooth will continue to sleep. Like your memory. All is well now. You will eat gooseberry fool in paradise.

Goodness, what a strange existence it is that allows us to be born again and again – as innocents. And that again and again it gives us responsibilities – responsibilities we are unable to bear.

Wake up now, my dear chap. Look at me. Do you recognise me?

The stale cooking smells and the cold were driven out of the two rooms in Corpus Christi Wynd. Kristiern Schordenius cured fevers, diseased lungs, hernias, gout, palsy, cramps, grand mal, convulsions, dropsy, bellyache, jointache, headache and toothache, and this he did almost exclusively for patients from the upper classes. It was no longer a matter of reading cards or invoking spirits. Every intervention was based on modern scientific theory, as he often emphasised. Late at night it happened that he laid out a star of cards for himself, and the numinous assurance of the Wheel of Fortune coming up time and time again made him shiver. Whoever turned the handle of that winding-engine was out of sight. One individual was on his way up, while another was enthroned on top, with crown and wings. But a third one was always and inexorably on the way down.

A wine-red settee had been carried up the stairs and helped give the front room the air of a salon. It reminded him of the yellow velvet-covered fauteuil where his assistant had reclined, as with closed eyes and in deep magnetic sleep she read books placed on her stomach. This was more than fifteen years ago. There was not a soul interested in her stomach-sight any more. Now she stood at the cooker in the kitchen, while his patients – mostly women – shook with cramps and tremors on the sofa. She may have been discontented, but she never said anything. She had a velvet settee and a chandelier, and took pleasure in Schordenius's new trousers – the cloth was of the thirteen shilling variety – and his piqué waistcoat and his stick with a bone handle and a silk cord. He had bought himself a new coat as well. The old patched tail coat had been sold. She roasted real coffee beans and spread butter on the bread instead of dripping. They had come into better times, indeed, better than ever before, and it had all started with the thirty-eight magnetic treatments of His Excellency. Yet she did not look really happy.

Surely she no longer dreamed he would marry her, as she once had when she was young and much courted. Although she had seen him in his *caleçon*, and knew he got constipated from eating beans stewed in syrup, after eighteen years together she still found him the most extraordinary man she had ever met. He seemed foreign, and his eyes looked as if they were burning, she said. He no longer liked hearing this. She also said she could predict that one day she would gladly give away both the velvet settee and the chandelier if only he would stay. He did not understand why she spoke like that, in the middle of their happy rise in the world. But it made him shiver, because Anna Lena indisputably had the true gift of seeing into that which is hidden.

When the day finally arrived she recognised it, though he himself did not. She knew as soon as she saw him with the girl. That evening she told him about it. She sat on the edge of the bed with her back turned to him, rolling down her stockings. He could see her vertebrae under the chemise. She had become sharp and a little worn out, but her stomach protruded.

It was autumn. It had been raining all day. The girl was the last patient, and had been supported up the stairs by her two brothers. Her father had walked in front, a dry little old man who could have been her grandfather. Water dripped from hat brims and coat collars as they stood outside the door. The girl was pale and seemed indifferent to where they were taking her. That alone was unusual, since most people were very edgy by the time they arrived. She allowed Anna Lena to take her coat and stood still with her arms held straight out. Her body was scrawny. How old could she be? When she was standing there in the hall with the wet black strands of hair glued to her forehead, and her eyes half shut in her almost white face, it was impossible to tell. She looked like a child, so maltreated that its face had become furrowed and marked. The wide-brimmed bonnet on her head had slipped sideways. She had one of the bonnet ties in her mouth and was chewing on it. Anna Lena had to coax it out of her mouth.

Was she a somnambulist? No, not really. She looked at Schordenius. And he looked at her. Yes, the day had come. When

Kristiern Schordenius closed the door to the drawing room in Anna Lena's face, she put both hands on her stomach, just as she had used to do in the days when with closed eyes she had been able to look right into him. This time, it seemed that what she saw caused her pain.

There was something about that girl. As if a special light had entered from somewhere. From where? And a smell, dense and unmistakable. Not bad, not even stale. If he had dared describe it he would have said almonds, perhaps. Sweetness with a hint of bitterness. Moss. Common fern. The fur of a cat that has been sleeping in the sun. But when he passed the settee, where she sat withdrawn into herself, she seemed as odourless as water. When he moved about near her he noticed that she was sniffing the air. The wings of her nostrils twitched. What kind of person was she? A child?

'How old is she?' he asked.

'She will be twenty-four soon,' her father said. 'But, as you can see, she's immature. And she does not speak.'

'Dumb?'

'No, sometimes she says things.'

She had rested her head against the tall back of the settee and was looking out through the window. Her eyes seemed to follow nothing except the raindrops. These hit the pane and became shivering streams which joined and flowed down towards the windowsill. She observed this attentively. But when Skord approached her and bowed, her eyelids closed.

'Miss!'

Her eyes did not respond. But she had looked at him when she entered. They had looked into each other.

'What's her name?' he asked in a low voice.

'Xenia.'

Skord whispered her name. The girl did not move. She was sitting with her hands crossed in her lap. Childish hands, reddened and scuffed over the knuckles. The cambric blouse showing under her dress was stained and flat. She seemed to have no bosom. Her collarbones were sharp under the white chilly skin. She had made an abrupt curtsey but only after her father had prompted her with a hand movement he had had to repeat.

'Is she really twenty-four years old?'

The father nodded. His name was Linderskjöld and he owned an estate somewhere in the distant north. He had taken a seat as far back in the room as he could get, with one son sitting on either side. It looked as if they expected a miracle to take place any minute. When Skord had been looking at the girl in silence for a long time, the younger one seemed to become anxious. He shuffled his feet and his hands clutched the handle of his stick. Finally, as Skord remained silent and kept pulling at his earlobe, the worried son cleared his throat and said, 'Is it not impossible to observe this poor dear child without feeling greatly moved and filled with compassion?'

Her feet in dirty brown boots showed below the hem of her skirt, spattered with muck from the streets. They did not reach down to the floor. No, what Skord was feeling was hardly compassion. Alertness, rather. And a strong movement somewhere in his midriff, but not of the kind her brother suggested. It was as if he had sensed danger.

'I know so very little about your sister. Has she had fainting fits?'

The father nodded.

'Cramps?'

'No, long periods of insensibility. She may lie there for twenty-fours hours or longer. She is pale then, there is occasionally a little cold sweat on her forehead, but she is otherwise unafflicted.'

'And when she wakes up?'

'She is very thirsty. That's all.'

'Not hungry?'

'Nauseous. But it gradually passes.'

'Over how long a period have these fainting fits occurred?'

Linderskjöld did not answer and instead exchanged glances with his sons. It looked as if the old man had become confused and needed their support. In the end the older one answered: 'A very long time, really. No doctor seems able to deal with this condition.'

There was something not right. The large, blond heir was being evasive.

'Please help her,' the younger one said. He had come up to Skord and grabbed his hand in both of his. 'I know you can.'

'My dear sir! You will not go without due reward,' the old man said and red spots flared on his sunken cheeks. 'You will get a good ... well, in short, please help her!'

'Her features are quite beautiful,' the younger brother said, the eager one. 'But as you can see there is no ... you know, no animation, no emotion ... nothing. She will remain lonely. Closed in on herself. She has no education. You must wake this child! We have heard so much about you!'

'When did it start?'

'Five months ago.'

'That's not a very long time.'

'No.'

'You just said her condition had lasted a long time.'

'I don't know,' Linderskjöld said and looked at his sons for support. His grey hair was powdered. There was a kind of rustic and slightly old-fashioned distinction about him. He was wearing a coat with large pockets and embroidery around the buttons and button-holes.

'She has not been at home.'

'Where has she been?'

'We don't know!' he said, with a glance at his eldest son. When he saw his son's disapproval, he raised his voice: 'Can you doubt that this child's soul has true nobility? Look into her eyes!'

'So far I have not doubted anything you have told me,' Skord answered.

They got no further that afternoon, and the girl Xenia seemed as uninterested when she left as when she arrived. When Anna Lena pulled the coat sleeves up her stiff doll's arms, she just stood there staring at the wall in the hall with her mouth hanging half-open. Was she perhaps retarded?

He sent Anna Lena to Linderskjöld's quarters. He had taken rooms near Norrmalm with the widow of a Gewaltige at the prison. The county squire had also brought a coachman from the estate, and this man had the gift of the gab. They lived at Sånga, he said.

When Skord heard the name, he felt another movement in the pit of his stomach, this time almost painful. Sånga on the river's edge. Sånga below the forest. Was there a Sånga still, and how much water had flowed past the high banks of the river since he last saw it?

'And the girl?' he asked.

Now, that was quite a story. She had been taken.

'By whom?'

Well, now, no one knew. But he said it was thought to be spirits.

'Not one, but many. What else did he say then? Anything that made sense?'

No, Anna Lena had to admit there was little sense in an otherwise thought-provoking narrative, which was worth listening to. Did he want to hear it?

No, he didn't fancy listening to superstitious nonsense. He turned his back to her and sat looking out through the window, his pipe growing cold in his mouth.

'Go back,' Skord said. 'You have to find out where she's been.'

But Anna Lena could not get anything different out of the coachman. It was as he had said from the start. She had been taken. Held captive. For twelve long years.

'Sublime nonsense,' Skord said. 'Such things are an offence against common sense. We shall have to ask her father again.'

He would have preferred to see him on his own. Possibly in the company of the younger son, a small, plump and lively man in his thirties, whose name was Abraham. It was he who was to take over the estate by the river, or in practice had probably done so already. The elder son, called Niklas, had left his home in Sånga a long time ago. He was trained in law and worked directly under the Secretary of State for Trade and Investment. He was a very busy man. Yet he saw to it that he was present at every visit to Corpus Christi Wynd. If he could not find the time, the others also stayed away. It was he who answered the questions concerning the childhood and upbringing of the girl Xenia.

'She has not been at home,' he said. 'That is correct. And we don't know where she's been. Since her return, some five months ago, she has experienced these fainting fits. Mental absences and other peculiarities of behaviour, as you can personally easily establish, and for which we seek your medical help.'

'How long was she away?'

'For twelve years.'

Silence fell in the room with the settee. The girl was sitting curled up, looking out through the window. It was impossible to determine whether she understood what they were talking about. He was not even sure she heard them.

'Hardly a negligible period of time,' Skord said.

'Indeed not,' Niklas Linderskjöld answered. 'But she is back now. We have sought your professional help in order to lift from her the effects of her experiences. We have no knowledge of their nature. She cannot remember where she has been. She sometimes speaks of the time before her disappearance and seems to retain certain memories.'

'How did you know it was she? Twelve years is a long time.'

'She is the living image of her mother. And her dress and little shoes worn at the time of her disappearance were there next to her. They were worn and dirty.'

'What did she answer when you asked her about what had happened?'

'Nothing. She turned her head away.'

So the story was told. He met the Linderskjöld brothers and their father twice more before he made any attempt to magnetise the girl.

'This is a casus of exceptional importance,' he said to Anna Lena. 'We will progress with forethought. There are cases of this kind which have meant good fortune and fame for magnetists. And immense wealth. Repute in scientific circles. Everything.'

Anna Lena pointed out that he had already done very well since the encounter with His Excellency. How could things get any better? A person can only eat so much, and surely no one could wear more than one suit of clothes at a time? In her eyes, Schordenius could already pass for a gentleman. He smiled a little at this, and whispered, 'Europe is waiting for us. The world!'

But she thought, 'He doesn't mean us. He means it's waiting for him.'

Skord himself did not know what was waiting. But he intended to hang on to the notion that it was fame. At last.

Although old Linderskjöld had been so keen to have the girl magnetised, he later became very anxious, and asked repeatedly if it could hurt her. In the end he seemed to be vacillating and this infected the younger son. Skord was in the odd situation of having to join with the elder and seemingly more sceptical of the sons in attempts to persuade the others, who at the outset had been desperately pleading with him to carry out the treatment. He explained that it would under no circumstances entail more than simple manipulation. There would be no reliance on magnetised objects or sparking electricity machines. In order to help calm them down, he offered to demonstrate a magnetising session, and told Anna Lena to sit on the settee.

Although it was a long time since she had shown off her receptivity and unusual gifts, she immediately went into a state of inertia which Skord, in his exposition, called the first stage. He lifted an arm and let it drop. He shook her lightly, and her head flopped on her neck and her eyes rolled up. He demonstrated the second stage – Anna Lena's eyelids closed. It looked as if she was asleep.

'Slight cramplike movements may occur at this stage,' he said. 'Some sweating, possibly a minor increase in temperature. But nothing dangerous and all completely transient.'

Anna Lena sank deeper into her magnetised sleep, trembling a little, but showing no responses to pain when Skord pricked the back of her hand with a small sharp phlebotomy knife. He explained how in the fourth or uncomplicated somnambulistic stage, she would appear to be awake. But her eyes were still closed as she answered his questions. Apparently she could perceive visual and other sensations, even though her sense organs had shut down. Skord stated that all perception now took place via the pit of her stomach. He put a playing card with its back facing them on Anna Lena's stomach, which looked rather lumpy under her apron, and asked her which card it was. She answered in a weak voice, 'Seven of clubs.'

It turned out to be the right answer. Still old man Linderskjöld looked neither elated or impressed. Rather, he seemed somewhat ill at ease. Skord decided to cut the experiment short, and briefly described the fifth and sixth stages of self-examination and general clarity. He stressed that it was a matter of spiritual insight, a totally disembodied connection to nature and the universe, and also to the past, as well as the absent present and the future. During these stages, these levels of clairvoyance and general insight, Xenia herself would prescribe the means and methods by which her rehabilitation could be accomplished. And, last but not least, she would become able to tell of her mysterious disappearance and absence.

'No need for that,' Niklas Linderskjöld said. 'We have come here to get a cure for her, that is, to bring about her arousal from this mental absence – from this strange and inexplicable alienation.'

'And these fainting fits! Above all, the fainting,' his brother exclaimed. Skord made Anna Lena carry out a little more reading using her stomach-sight, and then answer some questions about what he was tasting while he put in turn salt, vinegar, syrup and ground chalk on his tongue. Finally, old Linderskjöld was asked to choose a substance, and reluctantly picked an astringent stone from among the shaving things in Skord's travelling bag of toiletries. Anna Lena's face contracted into a faint but quite visible grimace when Skord licked the stone. 'Alum,' she said in a toneless voice.

The whole thing had gone very smoothly, and yet failed somehow. Skord could not work out what was wrong. He slowly pulled Anna Lena back to consciousness and let her explain that she remembered nothing. After that, he briskly decided to start the magnetising of Xenia the following day.

'At a quarter to eight,' he said efficiently, wanting to give as little time as possible for old Linderskjöld to consider the matter. The old man was obviously uncomfortable. What was the cause?

Still, they did come. The daughter was wearing her coat, which she let Anna Lena remove, and the kapok bonnet with the chewed ribbons. She was not so absent that she could not walk straight into the salon and sit down on the settee. This made Skord feel strangely touched. Her consciousness seemed limited and perhaps she was already in a somnambulistic state. But she did know where she was, and that her place was on the settee. She reminded him of a small dog. During the last few visits she had not seemed completely indifferent, but had walked about in the rooms and into the kitchen where Anna Lena was, showing a kind of cautious curiosity which seemed to him like that of a dog. Or rather a fox.

He had asked to be left alone with her for the first couple of minutes. As soon as they had shut the door behind them, he pulled up a chair and sat down immediately in front of her. He had planned to deliver a high-flown introductory speech, but realised it would be a waste of time as soon as he uttered the opening words (which referred to clarity and insight and the flight of the present). She was not listening. The thought that it was just as well went through his head. In fact, it struck him that he had spent most of the time talking pure rubbish. Be that as it may, she seemed not to be listening, and he had to content himself with trying to focus on her, sharply and steadily. But it was impossible to hold her eyes. They would rest on his for a moment and then flicker away. For quite a while she observed Anna Lena's cat, which was lying on the rug in front of the wood-burning stove. It was a fat old male with dirty white fur. He was uninterested in what was going on in the room and ogled his own, slightly deformed image reflected in the curved brass doors of the stove. Sometimes the image vanished as his eyelids closed and he seemed about to fall asleep. Skord was not sure, but it occurred to him that for a few moments the girl was imitating the cat. Or was the cat imitating her? He dismissed this fancy, which momentarily confused him. The girl was now looking out through the window again, but unseeingly, as if she had adjusted her vision to the far distance and was looking past the black roofs with their creaking and swinging weather vanes.

He had to start the manipulation without having caught her gaze. This will go to hell and back, he thought. In the absence of responsive eye contact, he had to stare straight into her right eye. Without losing contact with the eye, he put his thumbs in the middle of the girl's forehead and the other fingers, slightly bent, along the line of her eyebrows towards her ears. A while later he swiftly moved his thumbs to her eyelids. She blinked and he touched them lightly. Earlier he had felt his force weakening and been close to despair. Instead of a strong flow of pure willpower, he had been taken over by half-crazed notions and hazy thoughts. Now it seemed to be going the right way after all. He moved his bent fingers over her body, so close that his fingertips came into contact with her neck and shoulders, with her bony arms and not quite clean hands. He suddenly felt a wave of tenderness for this

393

frail body, for its skin and the smell of isolation that surrounded her. It made him almost dizzy. He knew he had to control himself. The process would fail if he was conscious of anything other than force. Pure force.

He pulled his hands well back from her body and placed his thumbs in the pit of her stomach. But he was trembling. Then he brushed past her thighs, legs and ankles. She was not a child. She was thin and fragile, true enough. But not a child. The whole manipulation induced a sense of vertigo and tremulousness, as if he himself had been magnetised. A wave of heat swept through him. I'm feverish, he thought. Everything is going to hell.

Then finally her eyelids closed.

'Do you feel heavy?' he asked.

She did not answer and he continued. His fingertips wandered, brushing past cheeks, shoulders, the almost invisible mounds of her breasts and the lean thighs. After a long while, maybe ten minutes or more, he asked her again, 'How are you feeling? Heavy?'

But she seemed to be asleep. Her eyes were closed and her mouth half open. A narrow string of saliva hung over her chin. He rose quietly, opened the door and called her father and brothers.

Usually people expressed wonderment, even amazement and fear. It was quite a miracle, after all. But the three men looked straight ahead, composed and almost disappointed. Then Skord saw that her eyes had opened again. In fact, she seemed more alert than he had ever seen her before.

He made a few more attempts during the days that followed. They were all very tense, he himself, the father, the brothers and Anna Lena too. She followed the magnetising sessions through a crack in the door. But it did not work. The girl looked around her impassively, fingered the stuffed armrest of the settee and dangled her feet. For a grown woman she had remarkably short legs. Overall, she was small-boned and slight, and gave an impression of frailty. But Skord was no longer convinced that her mind was as diffuse and her mental capacity as feeble as her father and brothers wanted to believe. He gave up after the fifth attempt to magnetise her, and this was followed by long hours of discussion. Their voices murmured soothingly in the room with the red settee. The pipe smoke formed whitish blue veils, which Xenia tracked with her eyes.

Suddenly they saw that she was unconscious. None of them had noticed her fainting. She was lying on the settee with her head over the edge, drooping on the thin stalk of her neck. Her face was pale and grey, her mouth half open.

Anna Lena went to fetch a cordial, while Abraham helped Skord to move the insensible woman to the bed. They rubbed her wrists. The cordial just spilled in a trickle from the corner of her mouth. They tried smelling salts and vinegar compresses for her temples, but she stayed lying there. That was usual, her father said. No movement. Regular but very faint heartbeats. Almost imperceptible breathing. Cold hands and feet. Skord noted that even the tip of her nose felt cold.

They had opened a window to let in the chilly air of the October evening to revive her. Suddenly, the cat leaped out through it. Anna Lena screamed. It was a bold leap, and they saw the cat's body land on one of the lower roofs. It disappeared out of sight, balancing along the roof-tree into the gathering darkness.

Anna Lena wept, and called for him through the window. He was a very lazy old tomcat who liked best to lie close to the warmth of the stove, and nowadays never went out at night. His behaviour was peculiar, and Anna Lena moaned and said that he had been frightened and that they had to stop the magnetising sessions and leave the girl alone.

'Stop it! Leave her be! Let her sleep till she wakes up herself!' she shouted. 'Something evil is going on! The cat felt it! Now we've lost him. He's killed himself.'

Skord told her sharply not to be so silly. Other things mattered more than the life of a cat. Sobbing and oddly furious, Anna Lena withdrew to the kitchen. Skord thought she was embarrassing. But as likely as not old man Linderskjöld and his sons were too worried about the girl to notice his domestic problems.

When the window had been shut properly, Skord fell into deep thought. For a while he seemed almost as absent as Xenia, but his eyes were open and stared straight into the wallpaper. Niklas Linderskjöld spoke to him more than once, rather sharply, but without getting an answer, and finally went to the door to order a carriage. Skord snapped back to life then.

'I advise against moving her,' he said. 'Has she ever been moved before during her fainting fits?'

'Not at home,' the father answered. 'But she is in a strange place now.'

'I repeat, it is ill advised.'

He also said a window had to be left open. Not necessarily in Xenia's room. But open.

So started their vigil, as they waited for her to recover consciousness. The brothers and the father took turns. They spoke with Skord about her case, more or less as they had before. But into the second day, there seemed little left to say, and Skord was aware that without deliberate concealment, there were matters they avoided speaking about. He asked the lively and open Abraham straight out if there was anything else which might cast further light on this curious casus.

'One of the most curious in my entire practice,' he said. 'Do you know where she was for those twelve years? What you know – or even surmise – you can tell me about without fear. You must have complete confidence in my discretion, and also realise that every stage in the progress of this condition is of the greatest importance.'

'I do not know where,' Linderskjöld said with such simple candour that Skord believed him. 'I have not the faintest idea where she might have been. And she still disappears.'

'In this way?' Skord asked, indicating the slack, lifeless body on the settee.

'Yes, but also literally. Out of the house. Occasionally she's missing for a couple of days or longer.'

'Many times?'

'Three.'

'And how does she return?'

'She's just there. Once she was naked. But her clothes were next to her. She had put her boots on.'

'Only these?'

'Yes, she was sitting there with only her boots on. As if she had forgotten how to dress.' He bent forward with his face hidden in his hands and groaned, 'We can't lock her up! Or should we?'

'Probably not,' Skord said.

By chance, when Xenia came back to consciousness, Anna Lena was alone at home. She was in the kitchen thinking about what to cook for the girl if she woke up. Abraham and Skord had been attending her during the last few hours. Both men were pale and tired out, and neither had had much to eat during the last forty-eight hours. Linderskjöld had just left to hand over a couple of tickets for the Dramatic Spectacle to an acquaintance, so that somebody would enjoy them. Skord had slipped off down the street to buy tobacco. Anna Lena had some lean braised veal on stand-by, and thought she might prepare it. But she forgot her concerns about food when she heard a determined mewing outside the door. The tomcat was back. A miracle! He was his old self and quite unharmed. She offered him some cream, which he turned down. However, he approved of some veal served on a saucer, and Anna Lena sobbed a little for sheer delight.

Then, all of a sudden, the girl came in. She made her jump. Anna Lena thought she had been snooping. The girl was still pale, but did not look ill. She looked around in the kitchen as if searching for something. When she spotted the copper pan with the water, she went over and picked up the scoop. She drank like a calf and then disappeared back into the salon again. After a while Anna Lena came after her with a dish containing a couple of slices of wheaten bread soaked in warm milk. The girl was sitting at the table with a deck of cards in front of her. She did not care for the food. Impatiently she pushed the dish away so that the milk slopped over onto the cards, which were spread out untidily in front of her. More than ever she seemed like an overgrown child. Anna Lena felt sorry for this mute creature. Then she noticed it was Schordenius's finest deck of cards the girl had got hold of, the old set of Tarot cards which he kept wrapped in a piece of silk and hardly dared to touch himself because it was so fragile.

'Dear me!' cried Anna Lena. She rushed up to the table and started gathering up the cards. But the girl held on to as many as she could, and said the first words Anna Lena had ever heard her utter: 'Give them to me!'

Her voice was pleasant, but she sounded authoritative rather than pleading, and would not let go of the cards until Anna Lena had found her another deck, which was newer and had prettier pictures. Only then did she manage to smuggle away the old Tarot set and with shaking hands put it back in its drawer.

She had been gone for twelve years. This was a sworn fact. Another fact was that the Linderskjöld father and brothers did not like talking about it. In a well-lit and well-informed world, the inexplicable has a shaming quality. At best, it is forgotten, and life goes on as if it never happened. Possibly this was what her father and brothers hoped to achieve with their silence.

And the girl – why would she not speak? Frightened? Forgetful? Now that she had returned to her frail and chilly body, she was a bitter and alien presence. She prodded Anna Lena's braised veal, and puked like a cat after her father had lovingly made her eat. She had returned to the world of warm stoves, small talk and domestic routine, but it probably left her indifferent or even mildly disgusted. Skord noticed that she actually brought out the repulsive aspects of daily life: smells in particular seemed more obtrusive. He closed his eyes and thought of the forest. The thoughts were vague, a mixture of old and new. The singing under ground. The murmuring. The eternal chatter of thousands of voices in the waters of the streams. Damp star-moss. The smell of sun-dried lichen on stony slopes. And ferns. The fur of a small, quick animal that has been basking in the sun. Not a cat. Not a fox either. It was the scent of marten or weasel. Gleaming coat, glittering black on its back. A stoat!

A stranger, and awkward in spite of being so small, she sat on the settee doing nothing. She was to be magnetised in order for her to return to warm stoves and stale-smelling rooms, and to the memory of what had happened to her one August day more than twelve years ago – and also to the ability to let people know about it. If she so chose.

She was to be made to want to so choose.

This would mean a great deal for the reputation of Kristiern

Schordenius. He asked them to leave and wait in the room next door while he made another attempt to magnetise her. At first her father hesitated. But Skord assured him that so far nobody had been hurt by his manipulations, not even in the most serious cases of enfeeblement.

When he was left alone with her, he first lit his pipe and sat for a long time without addressing her. He even avoided looking at her. Casting a quick glance at the settee, he saw she was observing him. Anna Lena had told him of the weird fact of her playing with the Tarot cards and not wanting to let go of them. He went up to the mantel and took a deck in his hand. He sat down and started shuffling the cards. Now she looked alert. He said nothing, but began laying the cards out on the table in front of the settee. Now he got to hear her voice for the first time: 'Give them to me!'

It was not a childish voice. There was authority in it.

'Well, now, my dear lady,' he said.

He pulled the cards together again. Then he sorted out Sceptres, Swords, Coins and Chalices, putting them in a pile which he deposited in the desk drawer. Xenia stayed on the settee and watched him intently. He had the Major Arcana left in his hand. He shuffled the twenty-two cards carefully and then handed them to her to cut. She came closer to the table, but obviously did not know what to do. He showed her and shuffled again. When she had cut the cards, he laid the honour cards out in three rows with seven cards in each and the Fool alone above the rest.

'Now choose a card,' he said.

Roughly, with both hands, she grabbed as many cards as she could. He reached out and held her right arm. It felt sharp and bony, like a fox's shank.

'One only,' he said.

She let go of the cards, and he laid them out again.

'Take one card. Take the one you like best, Miss Linderskjöld.'

And so she took, unhesitatingly, the Star. She quickly retreated to the settee, sat down with her legs pulled up under her and scrutinised her catch. He was baffled and tried to make his voice as steady and calm as possible when he asked, 'And what about that card did you like especially, Miss Linderskjöld?'

He had hardly expected her to answer, but she said, 'The crowberries.'

There were no berries at all around the naked girlish shape on the card. She let the water pour from her two beakers into the dancing stream. Above her head the large star glowed among the flowers of heaven. A bird sitting on a branch in a small tree was flapping his wings, perhaps longingly. The large earthly flower was in full flame, its petals reaching up towards the heavenly flower bed. The image was orderly, but full of ingenious inventiveness. There were no crowberries, just as there were no crows, foxes, buzzards, ravens, wilderness, disorder, piles of dead branches, tumbling waters or terrifying mountains.

'I like crowberries.'

On hearing her voice for the second and third time, he noticed that it was beautiful. It was not weak or nervous. It sounded determined.

'But surely they don't taste of anything much?' he objected cautiously.

'They taste of water.'

'True,' Skord said quietly without taking his eyes off her, 'Water is good for you. You must remember that. You are not to forget to drink.'

'Is there water inside me?'

'Yes.'

'Is it live?'

He did not know what to say.

'The water inside me, is it like the water underneath the soil?'

What did she know about the water underneath the soil? And how could he ask without frightening her back into silence? Or could it be that she was not afraid when she retreated into her wordless state, like a weasel hiding under a stone?

'Is there water underneath the soil?' he asked softly.

She nodded without looking at him.

'Live running water? Or water in holes and pools?'

'There is live water flowing along, and there are still waters too,' she said. She came to the table again and looked for another card she liked. This time it was the Moon. She looked at the crayfish in the dark tarn so thoughtfully that her tongue, which had come out to moisten the dry, flaking lips, stopped in one corner of her mouth.

'Is the water dangerous?' he asked, but got no answer. The tip of her tongue protruding from the corner of her mouth, pink and a little swollen, looked rather grotesque. Or obscene. He was relieved to see her face change expression as she got hold of a new card. With her right hand she stirred the cards on the table, collecting those she snatched in her left. She took seven cards, and seemed satisfied. She withdrew to the settee with her loot and settled down to look at them one by one.

The Fool made her giggle. She stayed there for a while, holding the card and staring at the torn seat of his pants and the dog hanging on to his backside. The laughter bubbled inside her, but her lips were still closed, and she said nothing about why she found the picture so funny. She looked at one card after the other, very attentively. She laughed heartily at the Hanged Man. Skord saw her small even teeth, which should have been white. Their cleaning had been sorely neglected. She seemed to take as little notice of her clothes and hands. Her nails were bitten to the quick. Her neck was streaked with dirt, and the lace round the neckline of her blouse seemed to become grey very quickly.

After sitting in silence for a long time, his pipe snorting and snoring, while she kept flicking through the cards first once and then once more, laughing, sighing and sometimes giggling, he bent forward and said in a low voice, 'It was most thoughtless of you to do what you did in a strange house.'

She looked up, and they stared into each other's eyes.

'You must remember you cannot stay without water for more than three days and nights at most. On one occasion I myself was without food and water for a considerably longer time, and I regard my survival as a miracle. They could have taken you away from here. How would your soul have found you? I warn you most earnestly not to repeat this reckless behaviour. You won't get much older if you do.'

Her eyes seemed to become blacker. Skord started shuffling the cards left in the Tarot deck. He felt weak, as if he had just recovered from a fever crisis. He had said only a few very straightforward words, and she had listened without dissembling only for a short while. Still he had a feeling that what had passed between them had left them both exhausted and hot, and close to hissing like foxes.

Then suddenly he noticed Anna Lena by the door. He did not know for how long she had been standing there. She held her hands under her apron and, as always, her right eye had a slight squint. It was a long time since he had thought this looked soulful.

But still, she was soulful. Full of care and patience. Full of a tender and watchful love, which had grown stronger during the years of fading visions and dampened tremors. Worst of all, Anna Lena appeared to know what would happen. He did not know, but still he felt galvanised.

The next day old Linderskjöld came alone. He was very upset. Xenia had vanished. When the maids woke in the Norrmalm house of the Gewaltige's widow, the girl's bed was empty. They had started looking for her, first in the house and then outside in the lanes. She was nowhere to be seen, but one of the maids finally came across an old beggar woman who had spent the nights in the gateway to Funcken Lane. She had seen a genteel miss in her nightdress, with a checked blanket over her shoulders. She had been with old Hat, sitting on the coach box next to him with her back to his load. This was in the small hours of the morning. Linderskjöld had difficulties finding the driver because his real name was nothing like 'Hat'. That was what he was called, because he always wore a large three-cornered hat with a cockade when carrying out the duties pertaining to his office. He disposed of the privy bins.

In the end he had found her in a shed outside the South Toll Gate. There sat the old man, bragging away, and there was Xenia, listening, frozen but otherwise intact. She smelled of faecal matter, of course, and the hostess and her maids had to see to her clothes in the kitchen and scrub her in a tin bath.

'Why did she follow this man? Why did she climb up on his stinking wagon?'

Linderskjöld did not sound as if he thought Skord would be able to answer his question.

'I'll take her home with me,' he said. 'I dare not stay in the city. And I cannot find it in my heart to lock her in.'

'Permit me to try just once more,' Skord asked him.

'Will it be of any use? Is her mind not utterly closed?'

'Not entirely,' Skord said. 'Before the next attempt, leave me to talk to her alone, please.'

When they arrived the following morning, she was again indifferent and droopy with lassitude or possibly still half asleep. But she seemed to wake up when they were alone together. She did not curl up on the settee, but stopped instead in the middle of the room and looked about as if trying to find something. He pulled the deck of cards out of the inside pocket of his coat.

'Give them to me,' she said, in a fierce and commanding tone.

'Answer my questions first.'

She sat down on the settee to wait, silent but impatient.

'Why did you run away?'

She did not answer and looked out through the window.

'Why did you leave home that night? Why did you drive off with the old man? You will get hurt if you keep on doing these things.'

She snorted. He could not work out if it meant there were no such risks, or that she knew all about them already.

'Your father will have to lock you up,' he said. 'He should probably have done so before. But he did not have the heart. Where is your heart, Xenia?'

She tittered suddenly. 'I always put it in the large copper pan, that's where. When I tire of dragging it about with me.'

'The cold water must have leached into it, that's what I think.'

She giggled and walked up to him, holding out her not very clean hand. 'Please give me the rest of the cards,' she wheedled. 'I've put my heart under a stone on the bottom of the sea, it's not worth talking about it any more. Give me the cards.'

'I want to magnetise you first.'

'Why?'

'Because your father and your brothers want it. Sit down now and let us try.'

He started without preparation and she descended almost immediately into a state of inertia. After only a few minutes her eyes closed and her breathing sounded like that of someone sleeping. Skord called Linderskjöld.

'I believe we've reached the goal now,' he whispered. 'She's in the third stage. Her senses have stopped functioning. I shall now, most carefully, lead her down into the fourth stage. This will mean she enters the magnetic sphere.'

He bent over her and urged her in a low voice to answer him when he asked her questions. 'Xenia, can you hear me?'

He thought her eyelids trembled a little. Linderskjöld sobbed and took out his handkerchief. His agitation was so great that Skord could hear his breathing choke. 'Good God, dear good Lord in heaven,' he mumbled to himself.

'Can you hear me?'

She did not answer with words, but he thought he sensed a twitching of her face, a faint shiver.

'You can hear me.' He raised his hand over her. 'Answer my question now,' he said.

She changed her position on the settee. Quickly, like a small animal, she rolled over on her side and curled up. At the same time she let go of a noisy and unmistakable fart.

'That's enough of this!' Linderskjöld stood up. 'Stop this. Get up! Come!'

When she did not obey, he went up to her and grabbed her under the arms and lifted her out of the settee. She could stand upright, but had to be supported to the door.

'I must conduct her out of her magnetised state!' Skord cried. 'My dear sir, it is highly inadvisable to interrupt a session.'

'This is undignified,' the old man exclaimed. 'There is no hope in what you can offer. Let me past, sir! I beg of you . . .'

Anna Lena tried to talk to Schordenius when they had left, but he made her leave the room. She kept herself to herself for the rest of the day, and did not even dare ask whether he wanted something to eat. By the evening he left for a bite in a tavern. He drank a great deal and slept heavily after returning home. In the morning she brought him something to drink and told him she had received an envelope from Niklas Linderskjöld.

'Money?'

'Yes. The others have gone back home.'

He grabbed the cup and threw it at the pier glass, shattering the mirror into a big star. Anna Lena cried out from fright and grief. What was he doing? Was he mad?

She could go to hell if she still didn't understand. Couldn't she understand anything?

Well, yes. More than he thought.

Fame had been within his grasp! Esteem! But what did she know about esteem? Self-confidence, the respect and deference of others, society's trust – call it what she may. You walk into a room, those already there might not fall silent but the conversations get a bit fitful, and people turn to look. You are somebody. Could she understand that? No, of course not. All she ever wanted was enough to get by on and bits of additional tat. A chandelier with prisms, and a taffeta dress with a boned bodice. A pier glass! Credit at the butcher's. Right? Enough? But esteem – did she know what that was, what it felt like?

'I do, you know,' Anna Lena said, remembering her own time of glory. 'Once upon a time people looked at me, no trouble – some of them seemed quite stunned.'

'Oh yes, yes,' Skord said. 'The female in Corpus Christi Wynd. That's who you were. It just about became a matter for the attention of the police, as I recall. Had you forgotten that?'

No, she had forgotten nothing.

Well, then. Anyway, the fact was this goddamn stupid little bitch had destroyed his prospects, completely ruined all he had founded his hopes on! Anna Lena countered sensibly, but with some caution, that prospects are only prospects after all, and what was the poor girl supposed to have destroyed, exactly? But she could do nothing to calm his fury. He was raging, beside himself. He did not listen to her. His eyes did not register her standing in front of him, full of watchful patience and hiding her hands under her apron. Spitting with anger, he aimed a powerful glob at the tin spittoon in the corner by the stove, only to hit the hot brass door instead, where it started cooking slowly.

A barmy little miss! Who had been lucky enough to be born into a well-to-do family, and have a father and two brothers brimming with anxiety and good intentions – and faith! 'Can you doubt this child's soul has true nobility?' My arse! She's a madwoman. Should be in Bedlam! If it had not been for that faithful, adoring father and those loving brothers, she would have been chewing her apron strings in the madhouse by now. He never wanted to see the silly goose again. He had had enough of fitting females. Had it not all been within his reach – fame, esteem? She had raised his hopes, indeed, she had embodied that hope. And then she had shattered it. Unwittingly. Without willing it. Or had she done it on purpose? A small flare-up of ill-will maybe, beneath all her lassitude.

He did not ever want to see her again. Never ever in his entire life did he want anything to do with this half-crazed, possibly totally mad female.

But then he would not have to, Anna Lena pointed out. They had left, hadn't they? As she had told him.

'To hell with it!' Skord shouted. 'To hell, that's where they've gone,' he added as she backed towards the door.

Nothing more was said about the whole affair. He sunk into a gloomy, sullen silence behind the shut door.

And there he stayed virtually all the time until the arrival of the letter from Abraham Linderskjöld. He would visit the privy, of course, and sometimes go down the street for tobacco and beer. His mouth smelled bad. His hair grew unchecked and left grease on the collar of his coat. The black curls, growing ever longer and wilder, told Anna Lena of the passing months. Otherwise, it was a curious period of stagnation, of almost timeless brooding. And she went hungry once more.

She no longer had credit at the butcher's and had to sell the chandelier with its prisms. The clients kept on calling at first, but Schordenius was not receiving. She stood outside his door, entreating him as insistently as she dared. But who the hell did she think he was? A charlatan? A trickster who could repeat his fucking performance no matter how he felt inside, or about things around him? Could she not grasp that he had been wounded to the core, that his force was failing him?

Anna Lena told the fortunes of shop girls and tavern maids in the kitchen to the best of her ability during this long winter while they waited for the force Xenia had drained from him to return. Instead, after six long months, there was a letter from Sånga and all she needed was to touch it to sense the force it contained.

All along the river people could tell the name of the place where the girl had disappeared. The Kelpiehole, it was called. Kelp'holl. A black tarn, round and deep, surrounded by a thick forest of firs. She had often walked there with her mother; on no special errand, just out for a promenade, like the upper-class folk they were. The mother wore long skirts which dragged in the grass, and carried a small parasol covered in lace like the flowers of cow parsley. Many eyes watched them but no one warned them about the tarn. That class of person never listens to what ordinary people have to say anyway, and besides it was worth biding to see how it would go. No one was surprised when it happened in the end. The mother came running down to the home farm one afternoon, on her own. She was heard by those who had been about in kitchens and barnyards, and they said she was greetin' then, and skrauchin' like any common mither. And she had lossit tha' silk umbrella.

Linderskjöld had married twice. The first wife was the daughter of a pastor in Härnösand, a respectable and hard-working woman, who had borne him two boys. She died giving birth to the second child. A few years later he married again. He had travelled down south and returned with a bride who was older in years than the first one, but very romantic. The maids told to attend to her found her incomprehensible, and so Linderskjöld had to employ a housekeeper.

It is hard for people from the south to settle down to living below a vast, dark forest along a torrential river. During their first summer the light drives the sleep out of their sore eyes. In the winter the dark and the cold get to them, and they feel dulled to the core and only want to sleep. Many eyes watch as they try to get through the first winter and endure the hopeless dreariness of the slow change of winter into spring.

She wanted so much to find her feet, because she had followed him out of a desire for all that wild, melancholic and grandiose scenery she had heard and read so much about. She read a lot. Reading was her greatest pleasure, even her passion. She was convinced that the landscape around her new home would have an appealing, perhaps terrifying wildness. But left on her own, she was not quite able to distinguish the appealing from the terrifying.

When she met the widower from Sånga, he had told her he usually wore a travelling pistol in his belt during journeys. At least, he would when riding up towards Skule and had planned to go north of the forest. She could not quite fit this image of him and his life by the river with what she saw as his newly married bride. Linderskjöld wore his dressing gown well into the day, changing by mid-morning into a blue coat with brass buttons, and he liked rice pudding and fresh cheese with cinnamon. Linderskjöld loved innocence, simplicity, good manners and rusks with warm milk. He also loved flowers, especially blue ones, and he loved children – clean children – and flowing water. Generally speaking, he valued everything natural. That was why he had arranged for a park to be planted round the house, more or less in the English fashion. On the first morning of her new life in the house by the river, she woke to find Linderskjöld sitting at the side of her bed with a powder-coat over his shoulders and eyes shining like forest forget-me-nots.

'Here I am,' he said, 'a man who loves simplicity and calm, who prizes loveable innocence more highly than well-read profundity and wild melancholy, in short, who prefers a dish of curds to a galantine of partridge.' She listened to him in utter astonishment. She did not understand why he told her this.

At Sånga life was not wild, but above it stood the forest and below flowed the river, with its vast tracts of water and strong currents. It was dangerous. The forest too could be dangerous. When Linderskjöld married again, the boys were already old enough not to need watching. Besides, as children they had always been quiet and clean, and sensible to boot. It was different with the girl born in the new marriage. She was spirited and curious about everything her big brothers engaged in. When she saw them riding, wrestling or shooting with bows and arrows, she wanted to join in. Her brothers thought she was funny, a small, brown-eyed, easily annoyed creature who wanted to do what they did, regardless of physical strength. They often let her have a go. But Linderskjöld asked them to take care, for God's sake. There was something about her, an angry courage and a fiery temper, which made her take silly risks. It was not just that he was afraid she would get hurt. He was concerned about her state of mind, especially her intensity, which seemed to him abnormal – at least in someone of the female sex. When she became a little older she would seek out the farm workers. They too thought she was funny, with her lively face and many questions. But she did learn many things neither her father nor her mother wanted her to know. By the time she was eleven years old, she had already persuaded the estate gamekeeper to take her out hare hunting many times, and fishing in streams and tarns. Perhaps nobody would have found out if she had not gone missing one autumn evening, and people had been called out to look for her. In the end she had come back on her own, wet through and frozen. When her father interrogated her, she had to admit she had been out with the gamekeeper. She had stayed behind to wait for a runaway hare-hound.

It got quite dreadful, even for Xenia's mother. Linderskjöld, who was normally gentleness personified, turned on her and held her directly responsible for the girl, who had been allowed to run so wild that she could be missing for hours before anybody noticed. The gamekeeper was dismissed. Before he left, two farm hands helped the owner of the estate deliver a physical reprimand. Xenia received a vigorous talking-to, which she listened to with bowed head and lips pressed tightly together. Her mother wept. Linderskjöld knew he should have been very strict with the girl, but she was his darling, more so than his sensible and obedient sons had ever been. A few weeks later he gave her a small, white, long-haired dog. His idea was that she would find it easier to stay put if she had the dog to play with. She called him Prinz and took him along on a lead when she went walking with her mother. The maids had scared her with talk of the wild animals in the forest, and warned her these might take the doggie. That is what they called him.

They walked so often along the path up to the small round tarn that Linderskjöld finally obliged his wife and had a seat placed next to it. He would have preferred her to go walking in the small park he had planted, but she seemed not to notice how much he cared for it. One must adapt, he preached to her. If you cannot make ivy and pear trees grow on account of the frosts, then there are always hops and the resilient cherry trees. If the mind gets desolate when darkness falls and cold creeps in, then it is time to take out the embroidery frame or start writing lots of letters. His first wife had set up sixteen-shaft cloths. The heddle-notes for a cloth like that were something worth pondering on, and distracted one from too much thinking.

But throughout these long years, six months always dark and six months almost painfully light, she had not been able to settle. In order for one to do so, the door must be firmly shut on wildness and melancholy. Instead, she seemed to look for such things, to speak about them and even praise them. In the spring, before the gnats and midges had hatched out and started to swarm around everybody with warm blood, she liked to take the path up to the tarn and rest on the seat with her book. Together with Xenia she listened to the harsh and monotonous song of the brambling. When she counted the beating of her pulse at the wrist, she found there were always seven or eight beats between each whistle. Apart from the brambling, there was the sound of the wind high in the tops of the fir trees, and the rustling of the cold water among the stones on the bank. Two ravens living somewhere on the slope above the tarn talked to each other. Their language came so close to being understandable that it frightened her. Everything that concerned the people on the estate, the things they talked and worried about or enjoyed, in fact, the whole life that had been given her to live, was at such times hard to comprehend and without meaning. It seemed to her that the cold water slapping against the stones, and the murmuring in the tops of the fir trees, called forth other voices, burbling, chattering, tittering, on notes at the same time suggestive and incomprehensible.

Late in the summer, when the early frosts had taken all the wee whining things in the air, she would go back and look again at the dark-green reflection of the forest in the water. The birdsong had quietened by then, and the banks were calmer. It was on one such day in August that it happened, on a sunny afternoon when the tarn was quite still.

The girl was walking her dog along the bank. It was warm. She had taken off her hat and jacket and put them on the seat. Underneath it stood her black boots with her stockings stuffed into the tops. Xenia was wearing only a small chemise and a skirt when she disappeared.

Her mother never noticed what happened. She believed she had just looked up from her reading and they had spoken together. Then the girl was gone. The mother thought the girl must have run a little way into the forest. She called out but did not feel worried. She read a bit more and waited. Then she called again. But Xenia did not answer.

That was it. No more.

They searched the forest with dogs and people. They dragged the tarn. But they never found her. Not a trace, not a rag or thread of what she had been wearing. Nothing. The dog disappeared too.

No one who had seen Charlotte Linderskjöld come running down from the Kelp'holl, her face pale grey and her mouth open and screaming, would have been likely ever to go back to the tarn of their own free will. But her husband went there every day. And the workers on the farm of course had to go along and look for the girl. He wouldn't give up even after a week of dragging. Her mother finally realised Xenia was lost for ever. Dead. Gone. Taken. But her father continued to go up there on horseback, and sometimes she went after him. She would sit on the seat and stare out over the waters of the Kelpiehole, even though the autumn evenings grew darker. It was as if she no longer feared anything. As if darkness could hold no more terrors than had that sunny afternoon.

When the winter came she mourned the death of her daughter, but this was something her husband could not do. He carried on searching, and again and again sent people from the farm to watch the tarn in case the girl came back. They did not always do as he told them. Why go if there was no purpose? And it was dangerous. This had always been said, but now there was proof.

His wife had believed he would surely accept it in the end. But this did not happen. During the winter before Christmas, he kept riding into the forest and would sometimes be away for the whole brief period of daylight. This made her conscience torment her even more. After Christmas, during the bleak days of January when light itself seems lacklustre and darkness holds no comfort, she fell ill from grief and guilt. There were those who said it served her right, and she should not have taken the girl where no sensible person would go. She became so feeble she could no longer get out of bed. One morning the servants realised she was seriously ill, and she deteriorated quickly without anyone quite getting to grips with what was wrong with her. At first she had complained of headache and dizziness, but after a while she just moaned like a child. The housekeeper was just as much at a loss as the maids. She touched the sick woman's forehead, and found it cold and covered in sweat. About an hour later, she suffered from cramps and fought for breath. They sent for Linderskjöld, who had not been at home when she was taken ill. When he arrived, she was dead.

He had a very beautiful tombstone made for her, which also bore the girl's name. On Sundays, many went along to the cemetery in Sånga to read the text. It said:

XENIA LINDERSKJÖLD

Loved in Heaven

was called away by inscrutable Providence

Her Mother

My Dear Wife

CHARLOTTE GUSTAFA KRAUSS

followed her Daughter in Death

The Mercy of Providence left Two Sons

with their Grieving Father

CARL CASIMIR LINDERSKJÖLD, ESQUIRE

who raised this Stone in their Memory

The widower did not ever marry again. He shrank, and his light-blue eyes became runny and bloodshot. They said it might be because he was constantly out riding, as if still looking for tracks or explanations. He came back home with soaked clothes and boots caked with mud. He got aches and pains from the cold and the long hours on horseback, and his back became bent. People said that he had the stone cut with Xenia's name to force himself to believe she was dead, and he never spoke about her except in terms of a beloved and much missed dear departed.

One day in spring, almost twelve years later, one of the farm hands was on his way on horseback up into the forest to fell sappy birch logs for burning in the stoves of the estate. It was a cold May morning with hardly any leaves to be seen except on some of the smallest birches on the south-facing slopes. A couple of ice floes were floating on the tarn. The farm hand looked at them as he rode past, and thought that the ice had broken up very late that year. But he also remembered that the Kelpiehole would remain frozen for longer because it was so far in among the dark fir trees. Then he caught sight of a girl sitting next to the tarn. She was crouching down among the stones on the bank with her arms wrapped around herself. Although the morning was so cold she had no clothes on. He of course thought he had seen a ghost, and turned right round. He lost all his vigour and courage, and dared not pass the Kelpiehole in order to continue on his way up to the felling. When he came back down the hill he told the maids of what he had seen, and what he had felt and thought. They gossiped with the housekeeper, and so Linderskjöld got to hear about the apparition his farm hand had seen. In the afternoon he rode very slowly up to the tarn. The girl was still there, crouching among the stones and very cold. She seemed not to understand who he was, and became frightened when he approached her. He had to speak to her the same way he would to entice a wild runaway heifer. She retreated to the edge of the forest and did not want to come out again. Finally he got close enough to throw his coat over her shoulders and take her home. Somehow, it seemed she recognised him.

S kord arrived with the first ship going into Härnösand after the ice had broken up. He got himself a horse and rode inland. When he reached Sånga he had covered fifty miles in fourteen hours and was so stiff he could hardly get down from his horse. He slept in a barn, waiting for the cocks to crow and the smoke to rise from the chimneys.

He had lived through a whole winter of inactivity, and after receiving the Linderskjöld letter he had been forced to wait a long time for a suitable ship. If someone had asked, he would not have been able to explain the urgency which gripped him the moment he arrived in Härnösand. He did not ask himself any questions. When at last it was bright morning, he stepped out into the yard and brushed his coat before riding on to the Linderskjöld estate.

It was announced to Abraham Linderskjöld that a gentleman had come calling. Nowadays, if there was a request to see the owner, it was Abraham the maids went to tell. He sat at the secretaire, entering figures in a ledger with a marbled cover. He heard a cough and turned round to see a gentleman who was not really a proper gentleman. He was a man, as thin as could be, with a polite manner and sharp eyes. He bowed deeply with his left hand pressed against his midriff and one foot put in front of the other. With his right hand he gestured expressively, indicating his wish to serve, not to say his humble desire to oblige, all of which was contradicted by the watchful eyes. Linderskjöld had not seen anyone bow like that since he was a child. After a few moments of confusion he recognised Schordenius. He had bits of straw sticking to his sleeve. Of the famous doctor and magnetist only the lively look in his eyes remained. His clothes were modest – not exactly worn or patched, but it would not take long before the bottom of the sleeves started fraying. The most remarkable thing about him was his age. Linderskjöld remembered him as a man closer to fifty than sixty. Seven months had passed since they last met, yet judging by his appearance it could have been seven or seventeen years ago. He was not bent, but his thin frame had something elderly and dry about it. There were streaks of white in his thin black hair, which reached his shoulders in curls so excessively long that they should have been tied back in a pigtail in the fashion of by-gone days. Linderskjöld wanted to wipe down the green-tinged black broadcloth to free the coat from hairs, which seemed to have a tendency to fall out. How was it possible a person could age so rapidly?

Schordenius had a deck of cards in his hand, bowed again and said he had travelled up from Stockholm in order to hand it over. His behaviour had neither rhyme nor reason. Abraham remembered having written something about the cards. If Xenia was left to handle the seven cards Dr Schordenius had given her, she developed a greater interest in the world around her. He had requested, though without insisting, that the honoured Doctor should send the rest of the deck, should it not inconvenience him too much. It was not possible to purchase decks of cards of a similar kind up here in Härnösand or in any nearby town this far north. And now, here was the Doctor with his cards and his incredible bowing. He offered his services.

'We have agreed that Xenia should not be magnetised,' Abraham said, a blotchy and fierce blush rising on his cheeks. 'It was a joint family decision.'

'And very wise too!' Schordenius exclaimed. 'The case of Miss Linderskjöld is an exceptionally interesting one from the scientific point of view, but it proved unsuitable for magnetising. However, a gentle education following modern scientific principles would be appropriate, and here I am delighted to be able to offer my services.'

'How...?'

'As *gouverneur*. Instructor. Tutor.'

'That would be no life for you, my dear sir!' Linderskjöld said.

He felt all at sea. To say something, he asked the Doctor to join them for their evening meal in about an hour's time. He did not know what else to do or say, and would have preferred to draw the curtains, lie down on the sofa and try to sleep.

Life, for me? Skord thought as he sat on a seat in the apple orchard, waiting for suppertime. Life has been left behind down there. Everything I have thought of as my life for so long, my own life, is left somewhere in the shape of a suitcase and a couple of crates of books. Without a master.

What can be found here then? he thought. Something better?

Something Other, that is true. Here, the wind blows. You can hear birds calling.

'Well, now, what kind of life does one live?' he said, sitting at the supper table and helping himself to dried bean soup, thickened with milk and accompanied by rye bread and brine-cured ham. 'One has very little, indeed, not much at all ... travelling about with a suitcase and a crate full of books.'

Abraham stared at him over his soup spoon, but old Linderskjöld ate with concentration and showed no particular interest in either the guest or his errand. He would have preferred to speak about his beehives.

'I shall value these quiet and rural surroundings in which to complete writing my thesis,' Skord said. 'Miss Linderskjöld's exceptionally interesting casus will enrich the development of my hypothesis. In Stockholm the demands on me are very great. My patients ... they give me no peace. Enough said. I am at your service.'

In fact, what Stockholm used to be like he now remembers only poorly.

To follow the soup, they were served slices of boiled salmon with potatoes in cream sauce. Old Linderskjöld praised this root vegetable, of which he had imported no fewer than twenty-four different varieties. Some of these, for instance the egg-shaped variety now being served, with its shiny bluish peel, surely had just the qualities needed for cultivation in the soil of this river valley, and he would predict it was likely in the foreseeable future to be on the menu in most gentlemen's homes. These days, only the easier, more pleasurable forms of farming caught his interest. A great believer in honey as a nutritional product and health-giving substance, he engaged in beekeeping and was for ever expanding his apiary, for which he himself supervised the construction of frames and hives. He had also run a small mink farm, but had been forced to let it go because of the stench. However, he still took a paternal interest in this line of farming, and saw to it that there was a steady supply of slaughterhouse waste and fish debris going to the crofter who had taken over the cages and breeding stock. He managed the brewing of beer on the farm, and had organised the replanting in better soil of the entire crop of hops. He was also keen to improve the spinning flax, and rode out to speak to crofters and farmers in the valley, emphasising the importance of keeping the flax fields free of weeds and giving flax the most humus-rich soil.

He seemed as restless as he had been said to be just after the disappearance of his daughter, and then continued to be after the death of his wife. But he did not refer to these misfortunes now, and of course lacked any obvious reason for travelling through the forest or along the roads looking for tracks. However, his conversation indicated he was riding about as much as ever. Hundreds of concerns and worries seemed to preoccupy this kindly soul, and yet Skord got the impression that the old man was rather distracted as he spoke of preparing furs and spinning flax.

He mentioned his daughter in kind but unemotional terms, suggesting that her first priorities should be to get her hair under control and learn to sit properly with her knees together. But he had no objection to her receiving an education.

Abraham looked uncertain and tired. He had said only a few words during supper. When they had finished their bread-and-butter pudding, he asked the housekeeper to show Dr Schordenius to one of the guest rooms.

He met Xenia again that very evening. She sat close to the fire, with the doors to the stove open, stretched out like a cat, with her eyes half-closed and her whole being receiving the warmth of the burning logs. When she caught sight of Skord she showed no surprise and asked no questions. But she looked into his eyes in just the same way she had the first time they met. To him it was as if all watchfulness and all pretence had fallen off him, like an old and ill-fitting coat, and he sighed involuntarily and deeply.

The spring evening was chilly and a French window had been left open. Apparently she had not grasped that she should close it to keep in the heat from the fire. This arrangement meant that one side of you grew hot and the other frozen. He pulled up a chair and sat down next to her. Outside a blackbird could be heard warbling, and choruses of other birds chanted around it. He observed that she was listening to them.

Sitting close together in the cool room, he found her rather less strange and awkward than in Stockholm. Her dress was cleaner and her hair neatly combed back from a central parting. She smiled when he gave her the parcel containing the deck of cards, and her hand, closing round it, was less thin than before. He had wrapped the cards in a small silk handkerchief he had bought in the Christmas market on City Square. She seemed pleased with both gifts. She spread the handkerchief in her lap and stroked it with her hands. She did not clutch greedily at the cards, nor did she run off to keep them for herself.

'Do you want me to tell your fortune?' he whispered.

She nodded and let him have the deck. He shuffled it, and made her cut the cards and choose one for herself. Then he started putting cards down in a star-shape on a small table with a lyre pedestal next to her chair. On it was only a cup of milk she had not wanted to drink. A crinkly skin had formed over the top. He laid the cards for the Past, face down in just the way he used to do for the Future. Then he asked her to turn the cards and say what she saw. This was how he came to understand that, for a long time now, Xenia had not been aware of any order among the events and relationships she had encountered in the course of her life. To her, everything seemed distinct but shuffled by chance, exactly like cards in a deck. Since they last met each other, she had attempted to comprehend how other people lived their lives, how life started with being a toddler, then toiling over homework and then went on to other and greater things. If asked, a normal, healthy person could immediately list an orderly sequence of life events. This sequence was in fact the only way in which people were able to interpret their lives.

But for Xenia there was no predetermined internal order governing the images from the past. These were just as likely to present themselves at random as conform to the rules she had learned. He realised that she had laboured to master the rules of life's card game during the winter and now knew, though in a rote-learned and mechanical way, that she had been a child, running around the apple orchard with a puppy called Prinz, at a time much more distant than when she met Dr Schordenius in Corpus Christi Wynd. He also realised it was possible to ask her many things and she would answer – if only one knew the right questions. Perhaps she had never forgotten the period between her disappearance and return on that cold May day now almost a year ago. Perhaps it was just shattered into thousands of fragmented images all mixed into the same great bank as the rest of her winnings in the game.

She found it very difficult to link certain items. She could not understand, except in a learned-by-heart way, that her admired and much loved brother Abram should be the same person as the tired, amiable and overworked Abraham who now called himself her brother. She could say it, just like a child who has learned to rattle off an answer to the What-is-it? part of the Catechism. But she described the other one, Abram, with enthusiasm. He was a hot-tempered boy, who came back home from the Academy and told her that everybody had the same rights, that the woodcutter's children should be allowed to go to school and learn to read, that all female children should be called Miss, and that it was unjust to have honey and butter on your bread when others had herring-brine or nothing at all. *That* Abram had slept at night wearing a Jacobin's cap, and Xenia had loved him and started addressing the woodcutter's children as Sir and Miss when she came across them in the places where wild strawberries grew. The other Abraham was always sitting in his office entering figures into ledgers, and had got a little round tummy which stretched his trousers so much the side fastenings were struggling. She pointed this out to Skord, not as an objection to arranging the images in the order he had been suggesting, but as a reminder of how absurd the whole exercise was. Abram could hardly be Abraham, with the little round tummy.

'People change,' Skord said. 'You too must change.' He looked at the small heart-shaped face with its troubled expression. Yes, she was a child, but slowly growing older. And she could not cope with the changes. People had hurried her too much. Above all, they wanted her to have clean nails and be able to curtsey gracefully, not in the abrupt way she did it at present. The new housekeeper, Miss Erika, was very energetic with starch, iron, nailbrush, curling tongs and laundry soap. She had tried to teach Xenia how to crochet. She had started on edging for sheets, but the lace looked greyish and shapeless, and was lying at her feet with the white ball of yarn. However, Xenia did not mind reading. From her mother's library she had taken books by Madame de Staël and Jean Paul to read during the winter. The books had given her a model for her thoughts about life. One thing came first and then came another – as in a novel. But although it amused her, she did not truly believe it, and found it very hard to apply to her own circumstances.

She was much more responsive to her mother than to the other members of the family, and tried her best to obey the gentle but powerful voice she insisted she could hear from somewhere close to her right ear.

'My poor dear child, your mother is dead,' Miss Erika said. 'She died of grief over your disappearance.' But this made no impression on Xenia.

'She died from having eaten eighty-four bitter almonds,' Xenia told Skord.

'Is that so?'

'Yes, the old kitchen maid knows, the one called Jenna. She saw my mother take a brown glass jar with bitter almonds from the spice cupboard. Then she went upstairs and died.'

'Then how come your mother lives and speaks to you from near your right ear?'

'She does that on other days.' But this 'on other days' meant no more to her than an abracadabra, a trick to make her understanding match that of her companions.

As the spring evening became night, they stayed sitting close together, whispering. A shower of rain passed and threw a scattering of drops on the floor in front of the French window. Soon afterwards they heard feet running up the staircase and the housekeeper entered, most upset by the rain getting in. She had noticed from her room that the salon window stood open. But she had not known that Xenia had still not gone to bed. The flounces and crimped ribbons on her nightcap were trembling.

'Miss must most definitely go to bed at once! It is so late – it's night-time. And just look at the floor! How can Miss let the floor get ruined by rainwater? Such a beautiful old floor! Have you got no heart?'

She spoke to her as one would to a child. But Xenia did not understand that one's heart must go out to floors as well and, yes, to all the things within the dear walls, the park, the estate. And to prevent one's heart from being torn to pieces, one must leave to their own devices all those outside these walls, this park, this river-valley estate. A heart may sigh, but must never be rash. A heart may well be allowed a few tears, but not blood and cries.

When Miss Erika left for a few minutes to get a cloth to wipe the floor, Skord said in a low voice, 'Well, do you have a heart, Miss?'

'Oh, that,' she said, with hardly more than a second's hesitation. 'My heart is in the mountain.'

'In Skule? That's bad. And if one wanted to see what it looks like, where can it be found?'

'There's a cave in the mountain, and a wolf is in the cave, and a kid in the wolf, and a tussock of grass in the kid, and on the tussock of grass a dove is sitting on an egg, and inside that egg lies my heart.'

'I bless your heart,' he said in the same low voice, and hurriedly kissed her hand, which was no longer so thin but looked like a small paw. 'It's a good idea to hide one's heart, to keep it fresh.'

The tombstone Linderskjöld had raised over his daughter and his wife still stood in the churchyard. Even more people than before would now come along to read its inscription, because now it had become a bone of contention. This was because the estate owner refused to have it taken away, even though its text was far from correct. The girl beloved by heaven, called away by inscrutable Providence, had returned and went about among them all, quietly enough but looking a real sight, her skirt hem spattered with mud and her bonnet askew. The stone no longer moved people to tears, but instead elicited mirth and irritation. The Pastor had to speak to Linderskjöld and entreat him in God's name to remove the stone. Or recut the inscription.

'The text says nothing that's untrue,' Xenia's father answered. 'She was called away. We do not know if she is back.'

This baffled the Pastor, and he asked for an explanation.

'I do not believe it is she,' old Linderskjöld said, quietly and pleasantly. 'At first I thought so, but now I don't believe it any more. It is someone else. Still, I must ask you to keep this between ourselves, my dear chap. Or the poor creature will be in trouble.'

And so the stone was left standing with its startling and false inscription, because neither the Parish Council nor the Church Board thought it advisable to counter the wishes of the owner of the largest estate in Sånga, never mind that it seemed a case of sheer madness.

Xenia had seen the stone and read the inscription. Her father and brothers did not know this, but Skord realised soon enough. She did not find her own death at all frightening or even strange. But he felt anger towards those who had let her wander off on her own and find this memorial. He also thought about all the things that could happen to her as she drifted about on her own in her muddy boots, and decided that from now on he would always accompany her. Her family seemed to think she was no longer their dear child. Instead of making them feel deeply moved and compassionate, she elicited a distracted pity. There was no more talk of trying to find a cure in Spaa, Pyrmont or Pisa. She was left to faint and recover as best she could. Even Medevi had been dropped as a place to go. Electricity, galvanism, magnetism – no one mentioned these phenomena. After a few weeks, people hardly treated Dr Schordenius as an honoured guest any longer, but rather, like a displaced relative, someone one had to put up with and hand the dish of potatoes at supper. Sometimes he worried about how long even this courtesy would last.

Xenia often allowed him to hold her hand and they would sit together whispering, their heads close together.

'What's your name?' she asked in a low voice.

'Skord.'

She understood perfectly it would not do to call him that within earshot of anybody else.

'What was your name, over there?' he whispered.

But she did not answer that question.

Some days it seemed to him that he had to fight Miss Erika for her soul. Then she would try to crochet some more on the increasingly grey-looking lace, and did not remember how often they had been alone together. When he stepped into the room through the French windows, she reacted with a startled distress which seemed practised.

'I'm alone here!' she cried and stepped back towards the door.

'That's too bad.'

She had reached for the thick plaited silk cord to ring for assistance. But she did not pull it, and instead answered in a voice she tried to make determined though she was already bewildered, 'No, being alone is no bad thing.'

'Do you find it sweet then?'

'No, not that either.'

'What is it like?' he whispered.

But this she could not tell him. She had let go of the cord and started to move back into the room, but slowly and hesitantly.

'There are four kinds.'

'Tell me about them.'

She shook her head. 'They have no names,' she said. 'But they smell nice.'

'You must tell me what they smell like, and then I'll tell you which they are and what they're called.'

'One smells of smoke. One of rain on birch leaves. And the third smells of grass when it's in flower. It rises like steam. You see, it's the kind of smell that pushes its way up and is so helpful and ready to serve it would be a shame if . . .'

'If . . . ?'

'Oh, I don't know.'

'Earth is sine pudore,' he said. 'The fourth one is full of bird calls, if I've understood you right.'

'How did you know that?'

'I can guess,' Skord answered. 'I shan't ask you any more. But allow me to speculate: you have been exploring elementary levels of existence. Four times over. But, dear lady, if you've been gliding through the air in the shape of a buzzard, if you've crawled into a lamprey or cowered under the mud inside the warty skin of a toad – yes, even if you've endured under the asbestos hood of a salamander and wrenched his skin over your own skinless animula—'

She was standing on tiptoe, jumping up and down with delight, and he had to interrupt himself:

'Don't just listen to my words, please, dear lady. If you've been doing these things – and other ones, inspired by the fourfold solitude – they were still no more than games! Reckless games. I too have played them and now care little for them. These are not real adventures, Miss Xenia! And what's more, they are not without danger. I already warned you once. Games for children, that's what they are. High jinks, driven by tedium and aimed at relieving the fourfold solitude. Now, I do know you have been up to many more things. Hunting for hare with Bear-Ear. You've sat for hours by his side in a forest hut, roasting pieces of heart and liver over the fire, tasting his hooch, listening and giggling.'

'What do you know about Bear-Ear?'

'Your father mentioned his name. I've made it my business to find out more about him.'

'He's left!'

'He was pushed, you know that. He was dismissed, with a good hiding from four brave young Sånga farm hands. He has not set foot here for the last twelve years, and isn't likely to ever again. It cost him dear to play with such a fine young lady, and of course he should've known better.'

'Maybe he did know. And still wanted to play.'

'You tempted him! And what for? When they beat him up he said he never touched you – he would never have dared! Is that true? Did he touch you? Answer!'

He had grabbed hold of her thin arm. As she tried to wrench herself free, her face twisted into an ugly grimace. He let her go in order not to see it.

'He smelled of smoke and sour clothing,' she mumbled. 'He was filthy.'

'Really, did that made you feel disgusted? After all, you went along with old Hat. No qualms about chattering away with him next to the privy bins. These are unreal games, and yet dangerous, very dangerous. How do you think these excursions will end, in the long run? Xenia, the world is full of evil. And vicious lust. Imagine that you were beaten, really thoroughly bashed. Or that you got lost, and nobody came to pick you up and take you home. That you had to beg for everything you needed to stay alive. Why did you drive away with the old man they call Hat?'

'Because of his name.'

'That's a straight answer, I don't think!'

'What right do you have to expect straight answers from me?'

'None. But it is still that way between us.'

'What way?'

'Well, I find it hard to express how matters stand between us. And even harder to say how things will be. But when you and I talk, it is with great candour. I'm not saying we are completely open with each other, but that what we do tell each other is true.'

'You only say so because that's how you would like it to be.'

' No, God knows that's not why. I'm not even sure I'd like it to be that way. I just noticed that this is how it's been from the beginning.'

And then there were days when he simply had no idea where he could expect to find her, in the world of Miss Erika or his own. But she never let go of the cards, even though at times she would ask about them as if she had never seen them before. She put the Magician down in front of her and stared at him.

'Who's that?' she asked.

'He can make people see what is not there,' Skord answered.

'And get them to read with their stomachs?'

She tittered. He looked at her, baffled.

'And who's this?' She held up the Devil.

'I have an idea you might know, Miss,' he said.

Silence, for a while. Only the sound of cards slapping against the tabletop.

'It's wise not to tell everything one knows,' he said after a while. 'I think it very wise of you not to say where you've been. It would damage you.'

She said nothing, and he could not read her face.

'If you've been in a world completely different from this present one, then nobody would believe you. You'd be thought ready for the madhouse. If you've been with someone – for instance, with Bear-Ear! – then you're shamed for ever. Even if quite guilt-free from the beginning! No, better tell nobody.'

'Except yourself. Isn't that the way you'd like it?' she said, smiling. But afterwards she seemed to trust him more, and told him she had been attracted to Bear-Ear because he had been able to tell her so much about the forest. Her mother had seen nothing but the mountain ridges shifting from one shade of blue to the next, layer upon layer receding until it became impossible to tell which was the last ridge and which was the first of the banks of cloud at the horizon. She could distinguish the first pale yellowish green of a birch in bud against the dark pelt of the hillsides, and the aspens shifting to red in the spring. But Xenia had noticed pillars of smoke rising straight up to the sky, and wondered where they came from and who lit fires in the depths of the forest. When she met Bear-Ear at the home farm, it turned out he knew all about the lives led up there. The woodcutters, who stayed up there for many days, slept in forest huts and lit fires to fry their cold porridge and their cured pork. When a pillar of smoke rose from the winter forest, he would know the name of the cutter who lit it, and the name of his horse. He watched her father's forest and knew every clearing. In the summer he could tell her who was working up on the moorland leens and lit the fires to keep the midges and gnats at bay. He knew if the smoke rose from a tar pot or from the cookhouse in a cowherd's cottage, where the maid would be stirring the simmering mese cheese. The forest was criss-crossed by paths, and someone travelled along these almost every day. At night the animals would follow the paths to search for new grazing. Predators would follow them too, when it was quiet and dusk had fallen, and they could pick up the scent of prey. He told her that the paw tracks in the soft ground, which looked like those of large, sharp-clawed dogs, were made by roaming wolves. He spotted bear turds on the paths, and taught her to recognise the pungent smell of fox piss in the grass.

She said it had not been a lie that she had first wanted to speak to old Hat because she liked what they called him. In the beginning, it had been just the same with Bear-Ear. His real name was something different, but nobody remembered any more, and everyone called him Bear-Ear, because a female bear had torn off one of his ears.

Old Hat too had been named after the most strange thing about him. In his case, it was the large three-cornered hat, which no one had thought to take off him, oddly enough. Perhaps because he drove his wagon about late at night and was seen only by drunk members of the nobility wearing the same kind of hat. As for her riding with him on his latrine wagon, it was because he knew all the streets in the city in the same way Bear-Ear knew the forest paths. When she first asked, he had told her about it, and then she had felt like going along to see how big the city really was, and where the city limits were and the many streams which ran through it.

'You met old Hat just a few months ago. But Bear-Ear was someone from long ago. Very long ago. Or wasn't he?'

She said nothing and laid out the cards she had collected.

'Stop it!' he cried. 'You can't keep living with your head full of whirling images! Xenia, it cannot be done! Even if it really is like that in your mind, you must learn to choose! Choose order. And don't present me with these random images of yourself. It hurts me. I worry, always. Xenia, something happened! Something must have happened to you. You really were somewhere else. You must remember. Even if you choose not to tell anyone – which may be wise – you yourself must know. You have to decide to believe it, not necessarily for ever, as if you had once and for all found out the truth of the matter, but believe it for a while. Believe, Xenia, believe you're alive. Ask your father to remove that tombstone. The question of whether to stay alive or die cannot be decided on the basis of fleeting feelings. The answer is final, one way or the other. Only you know what it is in your case.

'You see,' he said and started to lay the cards down so swiftly that they slapped against the tabletop. 'Sceptres and swords, chalices and coins. Good and evil. Beautiful and ugly. Appealing and distasteful. High and low. These are the only alternatives. Four of them. Like the flower petals of clustered broom. You see, Xenia, how they're mixed in with each other. Kings and queens, knights and soldiers. High and low. Nobility and coarse folk. You can see which are which, even though they mix with each other. You know. You can see it. You must see. Or else you cannot live here.

'They march in order, first this, then that. Always in order. Every morning when you wake, that's the order waiting for you. One before two, two before three, three before four . . . this is how things must be, and no other way. You see, always the order, all the way to the end. Which is why everyone can look ahead to the end. This is how it looks. No other way. You're free at night, but only then, Xenia.

'Here's a fine gentleman in a large hat. Who is he, the King of the Moneybags?'

'Old Hat,' she said.

'No. You've got it wrong. Don't look only at the hat, like a child. Smell him. Observe the way he moves. Is he good-looking or not? High or low?'

'He doesn't smell of anything.'

'True, money is shit that doesn't smell, my sweet Xenia. Pretty shit. Good. Tasty. And the king wearing that hat is a great and powerful man. Dance with him if he asks you. Go for a drive in his carriage.'

'And the other one?'

'Was a cheat. Wrong hat. You ought to have known from the smell. You could have heard it from the way he spoke. Bad or good? Ugly or beautiful? Sceptres and Swords. Bad or good? Germans or Danes? Everything has its own order. Sometimes it shifts about, moves a little. But you'll notice that quickly enough. The same faces turn up anyway. Don't forget. One before two,

two before three . . . hat before helmet and hood. And you spot the cheats by listening to the way they speak, walk, the very smell in the air around them. That's how it's done. On we go. On we go. Now, look, this is different! There are many other things to show you, truly. Here are the important cards. Do you recognise them?

'Who is this man in the carriage?'

'My brother.'

'Yes, that's your powerful brother. Look at him, see how proudly he sits in his carriage. In front of him the horses are galloping. He thinks he's driving, but he doesn't hold on to the reins. Well, now, we have to entrust ourselves to him anyway, if we want to come along. He drives straight ahead, always ahead. He is not aiming for the sky. He is travelling into the world and forward in time, and the drive is very fast; fast, fast! He knows how we should live, and we had better do as he says because he's got a plan, and we don't. He believes the world will agree to his plan. It's fast anyway!

'The tower tumbles. The trumpet rings out. Smoke and dust fill the air, but the dust settles, the smoke disperses and the grass shoots are coming up. Here goes a man with a lamp, looking for a truth outside the order of the cards. Let him. He troubles no one. The wheels are thundering, the wheels of the world turn on their axes – their turning makes a booming noise. Who's this? Who's the angel with a star-flower on its forehead?'

'That is my other brother.'

'Xenia, you're such a good little girl! You recognise him! Look carefully, this is the angel called Temperance – he pours the water from one beaker to the other and spills not a drop. He's careful and precise and patient. He's a relative of someone else here – can you spot her?'

'The Star.'

'That's right, the Star. She has taken both her beakers and is pouring the water back into the stream. Both of them know a thing or two. They know one must be careful when things are on loan, and sooner or later return them. You know, there are all these other things too, the stars, the birds, the flowers, the angels – so you needn't despair of the world, please, Xenia! But just now it looks bad, the cards confirm it. The wheels are thundering and booming. The highest and most powerful stay silent. Their faces look like faces fashioned for the dead.

'Well, now, you recognised many of these. Father and mother. The brother in the chariot. The magician who twists what you see. Now then. Watch. There is a number on each of them so you know the order they are in. First this happened. Then that. This was the cause of that. Dear Xenia, of course nobody can know for sure, but you must pretend to know. And believe it. If you don't, you can't carry on living here. The tower collapses. The scythe whines. The water pours from the beakers into the stream. The moon stares down into the pool where the crayfish walks. Oh, it's so scary! But you feel it. You know. And you have only got one deck to play. Just one. You must never pretend there are more. Never. If you do, it's the end. Ever further and further away reach the circles of the cards. But there is a limit. There. That is the limit, Xenia. Beyond it there are no people you know, no house you would want to set your foot in, no water you would ever want to drink. They may well be screaming over there, but you can't hear them. They don't exist. You must not keep someone's company just because he has a big hat. You may follow the Magician and the Emperor and your brother in the chariot. No other men. Watch how the cards fly back into my hand and are shuffled. Now they fall on the table again, the same ones but in a new order. You recognise them, though. Now you know them. All are either ugly or beautiful. Distasteful or appealing. Bad or good. Low or high. For each new day, a new pattern. But always the same cards. You will recognise them always. Here: one comes before two, two before three, three before four ... these can pop up everywhere, but you know their proper order. You have decided. Only one has no number, and runs in and out among the rest, appears, disappears, is high, is low, is different every time. That one, Xenia, is the Fool.'

'I don't want to live,' she said and turned her head away.

'You have to. You've already begun.'

The next day she came to him and asked him to do something he regarded as a great act of trust from somebody so reticent. She wanted him to keep a painted wooden box, and guard it carefully. Under no condition was he to try to open it to find out what was inside. He promised to do as she asked. When they met again, he said there was something he wanted to tell her, and that it concerned her box.

He had woken in the night and noticed light shining through the cracks in the little box. Indeed, he had promised her not to try to open it and look inside, and in one sense at least, he had kept his promise. But he had not been able to stop himself from walking up to the box in the dark to examine how the mysterious light could come to be showing through it. He also thought he heard low noises from inside it, but so faint that, lying in his bed at the other end of the room, he could not work out where they really came from. That was why he had got up and approached the box. He then heard a kind of crackling noise from inside it. He was afraid the wooden box was on fire and hurried up close since – as he had said before – he was so keen to protect the property she had entrusted to him. He had not opened the box – indeed not! He had just put his eye to the keyhole from which came the mysterious, flickering light. A little fire was burning inside the box. When his eye had adapted to the dark and the shadows and the small, unsteady source of light inside the box, he realised he was looking straight into a small room. Its walls were made not of wood but of stones and earth. Truly, it looked as if the small fire was burning on a hearth of stones in an underground room, and the room was not empty. There was a small woman sitting on a chair by the hearth.

'And that woman was you, Xenia,' he whispered. 'At least she looked like you and was dressed like you and wore her hair the way you do, gathered in a ribbon at the nape of your neck. And yet – though it was you, and though I recognised you – everything in there was so tiny, it was as if it had been made for rats or small weasels, and not for people. The small woman, who was you or like you, got up from her chair and walked up and down in the room with the stone walls, and it looked just as if she was pacing while waiting for someone. So I got the notion maybe it was me you were waiting for, and called your name. I called out, 'Xenia! Dear Xenia!' Instantly, the light went out, the inside of the box became dark and all around me was dark too. I groped my way back to the bedside table and lit a candle. The box looked exactly as it had when you handed it to me, and I could not hear a single noise from it either. When I picked it up and shook it gently, there was nothing to suggest there was anything but clothing inside, and when I peeped through the keyhole I did not see anything at all.'

She had been listening but said nothing. He did not quite care for the way she looked. She did not smile but her lips curled a little. Had it not been so preposterous, he might have thought she looked disdainful.

'Where have you been, Xenia?' he asked. 'Won't I ever be allowed to know?'

'What do you think it is all about?' she said. 'Do you really think I was visiting a pretty little world? A cosy, dainty world, below the human one?'

There was no mistaking it, she was looking at him with contempt.

'You're a poet, Schordenius. Not that your poetry is very good. Did you read this story somewhere? Are you sure you called out Xenia, and not some other name?'

She turned her back on him and would speak no further about the matter. But he who felt such a weakling when she was scornful, now became angry and asked by what right she used him and kept secrets from him? He asked her to tell him what was in the box. Without a word she took the key from her pocket and opened the lid. Inside were some ragged clothes and a dog's lead.

Later they came to trust each other still more, with the kind of trust which depends as much on holding hands, as on the affinity of vacillating souls. She then told him these were the clothes she had been wearing when she disappeared and had found next to her on the strand when she returned.

'They're very precious to me,' she said, 'and I'm afraid Miss Erika will throw them out. She's for ever chasing up things she regards as rubbish.'

'But how come the torn old clothes are precious to you? And that lead – surely it's practically rotten?'

'It's a way of making sure I know who I am,' she said.

'You must know that anyway. You can remember images from the past. You can tell of things no one has told you. You've seen Abram go to bed with the Jacobin cap on his head, and you knew your father's hunting bitch was called Tirza.'

'That's what he calls his bitches to this day,' she said. 'And what

434

do we know about memories? Are they really any more distinct than dreams? And what are dreams? Have we already been where they happen? Are they populated by memories of those strange places and people?'

But just as she wanted to preserve the life she had led before her disappearance, so also did she protect her other life, though he did not know whether it was cloaked in secrecy or sinking into oblivion. He understood her protectiveness, although she never spoke about it. She had been forced to go there. He felt certain of that. But where to? Where? Because she protected her past, it was possible that she had lived in it from some kind of choice and volition. Such thoughts made him feel sick and wounded.

Most days they were left on their own, but now and then Abraham joined them and sat down to listen to the education Schordenius had been engaged to give her. Niklas had written from Stockholm and insisted the tutor should be dismissed if his scientific educational principles in the main entailed *far niente* and *Schöngeisterei*. This made Abraham sigh deeply. Each time he received one of these exhortations from Stockholm he always tried to find out what teacher and pupil were up to, but his head tended to be too full of cares about the farm and the timber transports to really take it all in. And if he did manage to push his immediate concerns to one side, he usually fell asleep the moment he sat down in a comfortable chair. When he woke he had the impression they had been talking about gnomes, sylphs, undines and salamanders. He asked if this knowledge was essential for a young lady.

'One should not reduce everything to crude reality, dear sir,' Schordenius said. 'One must take *connaissance* of matters on planes other than the immediately tangible.'

'I see, well, I have never been fanatical about common sense, far from it,' Abraham said and rose. He had just recalled that he had to get a load ready for the mill and the driver was waiting for instructions.

But he was not displeased with the education idea. Xenia had not fainted all summer. She let Miss Erika do her hair. It was, however, becoming increasingly obvious that she was no child, but twenty-five years of age and a spinster. Abraham decided to set time aside for social life in the winter, and to arrange Xenia's coming-out.

By the middle of October the snow had already started falling. At first it came down in single flakes and formed a layer covering the ground lightly, as if the net curtain in Xenia's room had been spread across the whole river valley. Then the layer of snow became thick and fluffy; sounds were dampened and the cold felt less fierce. The daylight grew bleaker. Skord and Xenia slept a lot. They hardly noticed that the house was humming with preparations for the winter. Abraham asked his sister if she did not think it would be wonderful to travel in a sleigh drawn by horses with bells on their collars. She would take her patent leather shoes in her bag. Wear a white dress. Her hair would be curled and tied in bunches at her ears.

He told her about the society that mattered, and how things should be done. Wine would be drunk, and it might be served to accompany roasted hare with *sauté* potatoes and three different kinds of *gelée*. There would be dancing, and conversation with young men who would have estates of their own. The talk would be about commonplace things, like the amount of snow needed for sleighing, and what music was suitable for the piano. Not about salamanders. And everybody would take tea and sweetmeats before putting on galoshes and fur coats, and going home.

'She must have a fur coat,' old Linderskjöld said. 'Or at the very least, a fur collar and a muff. We'll go and look out some skins.'

'You shall have a fur collar made from Chinese mink,' Abraham said. 'Isn't that nice?'

She did not answer, because she had no idea if it was nice.

So they set out. The sleigh was made ready for them with sheepskin-lined blankets. Schordenius said he did not want to join them. He stood on the steps and stared after her, as she was pulled along by the innocent horses. They had soft muzzles and gentle eyes, and their warm bodies steamed in the cold air. She had asked him once why they put up with their bridles and shackles and why they did not kick in the chests of those who placed hames on them. Still, off she went. Sooner or later she would return with a collar made from the furs of Chinese minks. Nausea filled his mouth. Xenia, do you want a flayed skin round your neck? He had better leave.

Yes, he had better leave. She would be alone, bitterly alone, even though Abraham would look after her. She would smell of loneliness like the pungent smell of a wild animal. And so would he. He felt cold and sick. Why did we find each other? Why, in this whole wide world, did we meet only to realise it was a mistake? Oh yes, I did make a mistake. Another face peeped out from behind the small face he loved. The other one was twisted and grinning. There was somebody else standing by you all the time, Xenia, ready to step forward and put your face on, like a mask.

Who are you? All your images, talk and smiles, your inventiveness with words and the games you like playing – everything you have displayed to me is dancing about in my mind. How am I to know who you truly are?

The snow kept falling until the evening. It whirled and flew in the wind. He pottered about collecting the few things that were his. Books. Clothes. He wanted to tell her why he was leaving, but felt at the same time such distaste, such revulsion at the thought of seeing her again, he would rather escape before they returned. But his packing took time, as if he were in a dream, and outside the snow kept falling so densely and suffocatingly that he lost count of the hours. Before he knew it, darkness had fallen. A lamp flared far down among the trees lining the avenue, and then he heard the sound of bells. They had returned. He watched from a window, seeing the coachman pull back the covers and help Xenia from the sleigh. The old man went into the house first. He shook the snow off his hat. Doors slammed. By the time they had all entered the hall and were taking off their outdoor garments, Skord was standing at the top of the staircase watching them. The old man was in a foul mood. Miss Erika put her arm round Xenia's shoulders and led her off to the kitchen. At supper she was not at the table. The old man had told Miss Erika to give her a meal in the kitchen. He was in a very bad temper. It was odd to see him like that. Abraham asked what had happened.

'She cannot be presented,' the old man answered. 'Impossible. There's a malevolent spirit in her. She may seem just a little crazed – but watch out!'

'What has she done?'

Old Linderskjöld described how his daughter had been to see the Chinese minks with their fluffy pelts, gleaming with black, grey and white hairs. She had covered her mouth and nose with a handkerchief as she had been told to, breathing in the scent of lavender water instead of the stench from the droppings of predatory beasts, and of stale meat and fish waste. She had seen the thin-shanked, shy animals, and met their eyes. Her father had told her how costly these skins were once properly prepared, and that she herself would be allowed to select those she found most beautiful. She had bent forward, close to the bars of the cages, and looked most carefully, with the handkerchief still pressed to her nose, but said nothing. Well, that was neither here nor there, since he would anyway prefer to do the selection of skins himself.

Then they left the mink farm, and sat down for a while with the crofter in his cottage. Linderskjöld had much to discuss with this man, such as the breeding program and the practice of culling. It was crucial that the animals were clubbed to death, to keep the skin intact. They spoke lengthily about these things, and also about the deliveries of slaughterhouse and fish waste from the estate. The air inside the small house was hot and stale, because the windows could not be opened and the man's clothes were hanging up to dry in front of the fire. Linderskjöld had not found it odd that Xenia left to go outside. She was not on her own for that long.

Later on he said goodbye and when he got outside she was already sitting in the sleigh. But Linderskjöld went round to the mink-farm enclosure with the crofter once more to ensure the man had understood which skins to pick. When they reached the cages, all of them stood open and empty.

At least she owned up. She told them she had let the animals out.

Skord rose from the table and quickly walked out into the kitchen. He was told Miss Xenia had gone to her room and was getting ready for bed. He hurried up the stairs to her door. Once he had knocked, he entered without waiting for her call. She was sitting in bed with her hair plaited and a mug of milk on the bedside table. The milk had a skin on top. Her small face was pale, almost grey, and he went to her and kissed the top of her head, her cheeks, her hands – everywhere he could, he kissed her.

Xenia loves Skord in the same way the swift loves the air she plunges into. The swift knows she will not touch the ground again, not for as long as she lives. Skord loves Xenia the way the salmon leaps in the waterfall. He leaps higher, much higher than he needs to. Xenia and Skord love each other the way bog rosemary and bear moss intertwine – not for show, not for a purpose nor with intent.

It is night and winter. The horses are shaking their bells. They push their muzzles into delicate hay, still smelling sweetly of summer flowers. They are visiting Sånga. The cats creep about in the hay, watching the foreign animals with fixed, gleaming eyes.

The coachmen are eating soup with fatty dumplings in the kitchen. It is hot there. The maids' faces are glowing and their hair is curling at the back of their necks. Outside, the cold is so harsh that the hunting dogs have been let in. Their hearts are thumping. They hide under the table. It is warm and they get the used soup bones and any biscuit twists that have burned in the bubbling lard. The coachman from Dysnäs is allowed a taste of the wine. They all watch him as he swallows a mouthful and it bursts into flower against his palate, a strange, strong, wild taste.

The chambermaids have been drinking port. They are sitting in Miss Erika's room, where all the coats are kept. They are telling each other's fortunes with cards, and their eyes are black with lust and anxiety. They will go travelling and meet dark-haired men and fall in love and be struck by grief, and then they will travel even further afield, and make love with even darker men. The chambermaids have been given the misshapen cream cakes to eat. Their mouths are full of puff-pastry layers and meringue, and their hearts with anxiety and lust. They got the unopened deck of new cards from the room where the old gentlemen are playing whist.

Then somebody claps his hands, and the violins start playing with a mellow singing tone in the strings. Feet begin tramping, and the candles in the chandeliers flutter in the air currents caused by so many people moving at the same time. They start dancing through the house, and the skirts swish and sweep, the heels hammer on the floorboards and the rose geraniums tremble on the windowsills. The thin curtains billow. They dance into the room where the cards are being slapped down on tabletops, pull the old men from their chairs and dance ring-a-roses round those who refuse to get up. When the large white grandfather clock starts striking, they bow and curtsey to it, and somebody fetches glasses and bottles of wine. They join the round-faced clock in toasts to her incurable propriety – but she shows the wrong time, and so they give her three cheers! Then the little lapdogs start barking so hard their silk bows shiver, and Miss Eleonora Riesenfelt's tame squirrel crawls into Councillor Riesenfelt's pocket and makes a warm nest from the big old snuff-handkerchief the Councillor has secretly brought with him.

Abraham is kissing a young lady behind a door. He kisses her daintily at first, as if tasting a piece of confectionery. Later he kisses her wildly and greedily, and the lady does not swoon and kisses him back, and Abraham thinks, 'Good Lord, I'm engaged now! But that need not be so bad. Besides, she tastes divine.'

There are candied cherries in brandy in a large crystal bowl on the table. A matron sits there with swollen ankles, but she has forgotten the swelling and aching. Her feet are tapping to the rhythm of the dances and the sound of the violins. She is eating candied cherries without bothering with a spoon.

The flowers pinned into curled hair fill the air with scent, and are not going to fade for a long while. They have hidden supplies of water in little tufts of cotton wool wrapped in waxed taffeta. The flowers smell sweetly, and as the women dance, their beautiful breasts, which were so decorously still and white with powder, begin to blush and move.

High above them, right at the top of the staircase, two small figures are standing. Xenia and Skord are watching the dancers. Xenia is making little jumps. She would never dare take to the dance floor, and Skord says he has forgotten how. They have been given port and cream cakes, and Miss Erika has lit candles for them up there. They are surrounded by the whole house, which is glowing with light and warmth and the scent of the rose geraniums and the songs of the violins, sounding more and more loudly. Outside, the stars are burning and the whole firmament is singing with light. Skord says to Xenia that tonight she is not to think about what comes before and what comes after, what is cause and what is effect. Tonight the cards don't count.

'Tonight, my sweet Xenia, we are at one with the whole of creation. Tonight we are all where we should be, and nobody is bad or distasteful, and nobody, but nobody, is low, because tonight we just are, we are . . . The great miracle is that anything at all exists this cold winter night, that something moves under the hay, hearts beat under soft brown fur, stars and wax candles shine and the dance of the strings over a small sounding-box of finest wood creates singing that can be heard far away into the night, and somewhere there is warmth that makes grapes ripen to wine.'

Then Skord takes Xenia's hand, and they go to her room and climb into her bed with the already untidy linen sheets. In the bed Skord loves Xenia the way a salmon leaps in the falls, strongly and wildly, even though there are white strands in his hair. And Xenia loves Skord the way the swift dives through blue air, never in her life needing to touch the ground. They make love to each other the way bog rosemary and bear moss intertwine, without purpose or intent.

Freshly shaved and in a good mood, he might be taken for a young man – but only by her. She thought his appearance testified to great elegance and wisdom, and besides he looked appetising, like fresh cheese somehow – a brown-crusted fresh cheese with cinnamon butter. She couldn't get enough of sniffing behind his ear and in the hollow at the base of his throat. They liked doing all the things they found to do with each other in the middle of the day, when nobody really knew what they were up to. They liked doing what they did in the shimmering blue light coming through the drawn blind, while outside chickens were pecking in the gravel and footsteps came and went.

'You must never keep secrets from me!' he whispered. 'I desire you, I desire all that is you. Your present, your past, your future. I want it all! All of it.'

'There are some things that can't be given away,' she answered. 'Not even in moments of greatest rapture. It simply cannot be done.'

But a moment later it was as if she had given away everything, as if it flowed over to him like the waters of a stream flooding the marsh.

She kept her false curls and corset in the top drawer of the chest of drawers. Sometimes she would take them out and dance about with them. The curls dangled, the corset strings flew. She would put on the patent leather shoes which squeezed her feet and chatter in a high fluting voice. Skord would be made to fasten the corset at the back while she pushed up her practically nonexistent breasts to try to present them like cream cakes on a plate. For a few minutes she seemed to have learned it all, although Miss Erika would never believe it. Xenia would make little tripping steps and her gestures would be as well executed as if she had been coached by a dancing master. She did not even omit the small exclamations, and declarations about loving children and flowers, and other feelings coming straight from her little heart.

'There is a malicious spirit inside you, Xenia,' Skord whispered. 'Don't you feel the slightest pity for them all? Where is your heart?'

'Dropped into the punch bowl,' she answered. 'Cool and nice.'

'Just imagine a fragile creature who has learned the little cries and gestures only to have to lie spread-eagled and be ridden by someone who smells of cigars. What did she know when she was dancing and flirting? And fifteen, twenty years later – who is she? After never getting a whole night's sleep for children crying and sodden nappies and earache and small, panting, febrile breaths?'

'She's a goat,' Xenia said. 'An old goat bleating away as she picks flowers, a sentimental goat with long strings of yellow stuff coming out of her eyes.'

Then she turned herself into a small frog, moist but not cold, and lay down beneath him and made him push into her what she wanted of him, and she squeaked and sighed and panted, and then, a long while later, she started giggling. He had to put his hand over her mouth, because steps could be heard on the gravel, steps made by two pairs of boots. One set of steps was hesitant and dragging, the other one brisk and creaking. They turned right round at the peony bush. Brother Niklas had come home on a visit and was walking in the courtyard, in conversation with Abraham.

Niklas, who had started writing his name Nicholas out of admiration for all the scientific advances made in England, was giving Abraham a talking-to because as a young man he had worn a Jacobin cap in bed. When they passed the gooseberry bushes, Abraham must have stopped and sighed, and maybe pulled some gooseberries off a branch to check whether they were as hard and sour as he suspected.

'So you see,' Nicholas said, 'this is what it has come to. The grinning, bestial face of revolution shows itself everywhere it dares. It is sneering at propriety, art, everything with a spark of sanctity and divine spirit. Now the beast wants freedom for all. So you see, such are the consequences of your hollow enthusiasms!'

Behind the blue blind, the part of Skord inside Xenia became as small and cold as a snail. She heard him growl into the pillow and say the beast was inside Nicholas himself.

'An animal?'

'Yes, a grimacing stone beast. He is afraid of what is lurking deep in his own mind. Because of that, he needs to make the whole world safe against wild animals.'

'How should the world be?' Xenia asked.

'I don't know. I've been a medic. And a chemist. This and that. But never a politician.' He sat up in bed with his thin silvery hair in a tangle round his head, and said very forcefully, 'One thing I've never done: I've never been guilty of telling other people how to live their lives.'

Xenia thought for some time, her face in the shadows among the pillows. Then she said, 'Yes, you have! You've told me.'

'Told *you*! You, yes. Of course.'

And it was true that he had told her how much better off she would be with him, how they should travel to Europe and become famous.

'You're special, you could become somebody different.'

'Become what? The magician's help-mate?'

'That's not what I had in mind.'

'Well, what, then? Am I not meant to sit on the sofa and speak in riddles? And what would happen to me when you left?'

'I don't intend to leave you.'

'No? Had you intended to leave Anna Lena? What is her view of it all?'

'She can earn her living by telling fortunes in cards and coffee dregs. She's got the gift. And before I left her I gave her lots of advice. I've looked after her.'

'With words?'

'Yes.'

'Nothing else?'

'Don't despise words!'

'Still, you're ashamed.'

'Yes, I'm ashamed. And I feel guilty. It causes me pain to think about her.'

'There you are.'

There were times when he felt she had become too sensible.

One late afternoon towards the end of the summer, they were so deeply engrossed in each other that it was as if they were asleep in the warm room, though they still made tiny movements. These caused the coverlet to twitch, made the curtain flutter and disturbed the water in the jug on the bedside table. Skord was expelling air in brief gusts – huh! huh! huh! – and Xenia was also breathing very quickly – huhu! huhu! huhu! – out and in, out and in. They were actually both close to losing consciousness when the door opened and Nicholas stood there looking at them. They had never considered how their lovemaking would appear to an onlooker, but suddenly became aware of their nakedness and entanglement; how the sheets were twisted round their bodies and their hair stuck to their faces, how they were pale and red-faced at the same time, and how lavender water and fresh semen made the room smell like a summer meadow.

Nicholas stretched out his arm and stood there as if sculpted in marble. He ordered Kristiern Schordenius to leave his house and never show his face again, on pain of a police charge. Xenia cried out and said they were deeply attached to each other, and clung to Skord with her arms and legs, the way a frog clings to a stone. But to no avail. Skord hurried off to dress and get away, because he remembered what had happened to Bear-Ear, and there was hardly anything he would have found as disagreeable as a truly serious beating.

It all happened so quickly that he did not really understand what it had been about until he was quite a way into the forest.

That night he slept, or tried to sleep, in a rick-yard where Xenia and he had once hidden to spend most of one day doing what they usually did when no one was watching. He could not leave yet. First he had to get hold of a horse, though he could not think how to approach the Linderskjöld brothers with this request. He had once arrived in Sånga riding a small brown mare, but she was long since dead.

In the middle of the night, he woke from his half-sleep on the floor and listened. He thought he had heard the sound of soft breathing through a muzzle and a pair of dilated nostrils. At first he thought he had dreamed a response to his own thoughts, but after a short while he could clearly hear the thud of hooves on the grass. When he looked out into the night, he spotted Xenia, leading a small greyish-brown mare. It looked very similar to the one he had bought in Härnösand. She also carried a food box under her arm.

'Will you come with me?' he whispered.

'No, I can't.' She handed him the box and said she had packed it with things for him to live on for a while. 'I have to stay here,' she whispered.

'Why here? What do they mean to you?'

'I don't know. But I must stay here. I must be near the river, and I must live below the forest. It is necessary. Nor can I exist without the moorland in my life.'

'You would have me! And I would never leave you.'

'I did not ever think you would. But if you took me with you, you would soon have Nobody in front of you in the saddle, and Nobody next to you in bed, and when you looked up from your plate of soup you would look into the face of Nobody opposite you at the table.'

Her face looked stern in the white light. He could only think of

448

it as cruelty, her coming to find him once more, without intending to come with him. She grieved less than he did over their separation, and to be distant from each other did not seem unnatural to her. Her breast was not lacerated, her heart not broken and her soul had not been cleaved as if with an axe. This was enough reason for him to hate her; he wanted to scream at her and bite the thin hand which put the food box at his feet. But he stood stock-still, unable to utter a sound. Soon she had disappeared into the dark. For a while longer he could hear the dragging of her skirt in the wet grass, and then all was silent. The mare puffed a little, and her brown eyes looked at him with an expression he could not interpret. He did not even know what she was called, and tried Slut. But she just stood there, blinking and hanging her head. Anyway, she was saddled, with a bag of crushed corn tied on one side. He tied his bag on the other side, and mounted. He could not sleep anyway, and since the mare seemed a cautious and thoughtful creature, he might as well start his journey in this dim light.

All the next day he rode up into the forest, avoiding the villages by following the cattle paiths round them. He had a few coins in his pocket, and bought fresh milk to drink and a rye loaf from an old woman in a hill croft. When he got far enough to be able to see Skule Mountain, he rode back into the forest and eventually found a drove road. He thought he might stop by some abandoned grazing leen up there, and settle in the cowherd's cottage or cookhouse for as long as the food would last. Sooner or later it should become clearer to him what a penniless little old man could do to earn his living. He had no particular wish to live on, but then, no particular wish to lie down and die either.

But he did want to go to sleep. The sea was grey, shading into black, and dashing itself furiously against the rocks. The marshes were beginning to turn an autumnal yellow, and the sedge was whipped into waves by the rain. The waters of the streams rushed wild and murky over the falls. The ravens cried. But the mare kept lumbering on submissively, long yellow fringe falling into her eyes. Water poured off her flanks.

He slept in a cowherd's shed, and did not really wake up until forenoon the next day, which turned out to be just as windy and wet. Once or twice he had taken a drink of water from the pail he had pulled up before he went to sleep. Now that slurp of water was finished. His stomach was aching with hunger, and he decided to open the box of food as soon as he had collected fresh water from the well.

He never got that far. He was stepping out to lower the pail when he got a stinging blow across his back. When he got back on his feet a young man was standing there, grinning at him with a willow-switch in his hand. Behind him a tense black horse was tramping up and down, and Slut had been tied next to him.

Nothing was said, but the switch urged him on and left no room for misunderstanding. Skord stumbled ahead along the path, and noticed the young man was carrying the food box. He must be faster on the uptake than he wanted to let on. He sat silently on his horse, his tall back bent and without having stuck his feet into the stirrups, which were just a couple of carelessly fixed loops of rope. The black horse walked on as if it knew where it was going. Skord dared ask what their goal was, and got a couple more blows and an answer sounding possibly like up! up! Or was it hupp! hupp! as if to a horse? Upwards they certainly went. Skord was panting harshly, and found it hard to lift his legs high enough to clear stone-falls and heaps of branches. He pointed out that it would help if he were allowed to ride, but the only answer he got was more blows from the switch. The youth clearly enjoyed seeing how much the little old man could stand, and did not let up until Skord collapsed. This was how he came to arrive at their goal slumped across Slut's back. He was alert enough – and had been, for the whole journey – to realise the entertainment he was providing. He was pushed off the back of the horse and a noose was tied round his neck. The bent-backed young man was probably using the rope as a sign of ownership to impress his companions, he thought.

Once in the hands of robbers, it becomes necessary for the captive to prove convincingly that keeping him alive will be profitable or amusing and – most importantly – will not entail any risk. This has to be established quickly. He could not count properly at first, but it seemed some ten or twelve faces were grinning at him. So I'm still amusing them, he thought. But will it last more than a moment? The young man with the whining willow-switch carried a small knife in his belt, which he now drew from its sheath and began playing with. The knife blade had been ground into an awl-like sharpness, useless for cutting; thinking about what kinds of things it might be used for made Skord feel sick. As if this had not been a clear enough sign, someone at the back of the crowd said, 'Slash the fucking bastard! Carve 'im!'

They wanted him to tremble, and he trembled, from fear as well as to amuse them. As long as he kept them entertained, they would let him live.

In the world of outlaws, the stupid men are often more dangerous than the clever ones. It boded ill that the numbskull who had turned up to take his food box, his sack of clothes and his horse, should have dragged him along to this place, allowing him to see who they were and where they were based. Even if they were all as stupid, they would sooner or later figure out that he should be squashed, stuck or pushed to death. And if there were just one clever one among them, he would already have come to this conclusion.

Skord had been rummaging in his bag only a few hours ago and, finding some down from Xenia's pillow, had sobbed as if cut to the quick at the thought of that warm nest and the dear tangled bedclothes. An ugly robber's crone pulled up his shirt and the down floated to the ground; now everything was truly lost and gone for ever. But maybe the tangled sheets still existed, back there. Surely she would not have let the maids near her bed? Wouldn't she want to keep something to remember him by, even if it was just a wrinkled linen sheet? Oh, dearest beloved ... oh, sweetest darling delight ... He had sobbed a little when the down drifted away, and this they found more amusing than anything so far. Then he heard a voice which made him realise that it was not stupidity which had him hauled up to Skule. A man said, 'So that's what you look like? You're supposed to have a well-oiled gob, but I can't say I've noticed it. Your cock must be good at conversing, or your lady-friend would not have found you so *divertant*.'

He spoke these incredible words as if spitting them from his twisted mouth. One of his ears was missing. Where it should have been was a lump of skin-covered cartilage, not unlike a small birch fungus. Skord realised he had encountered Bear-Ear. He was uglier than Skord had imagined.

As ever, all kinds of flotsam had ended up in Skule forest. If only Skord had been less crestfallen and exhausted, and if his heart had not been cleaved as if by an axe and his life's blood poured out almost to the last drop at the feet of Xenia Linderskjöld, then maybe he would have tried a trick or two to get himself away from the company of these great thinkers and turnips.

The one-eared man made a sign to the young man with the switch to let go of the rope and Skord himself pulled the noose off his neck. He brushed down his coat but did not speak. Quite a bit of bullying followed, but it soon became obvious that Bear-Ear had had him brought to take a look at him and talk to him, and was not going to let anyone ruin his pleasure by beating his guest senseless. But Skord stayed silent. They pushed him about and kicked him for a while longer, and the ugliest hag grabbed him between his legs. When they left him alone, he leaned back against a tree stump, folded his arms and tried to look as if he were dropping off to sleep. Then Bear-Ear stepped up to him and kicked him in the side, hard enough to cause a shooting pain in his ribcage and the loss of all his breath.

'Don't you know who we are?' the ugly one roared.

'Yes, I do,' Skord said. 'You are the most repulsive and terrifying of all living beings, and I'm so scared I am shitting myself just looking at you. Now I have to endure an hour or two of your company before I'm butchered, and so help me, I mustn't hint at how much you bore me because then you'll skin me like an eelpout. You are Bear-Ear, who got yourself beaten up by the farm hands because you'd been playing about with a young lady who was too young and too well-born for you. And you plan to show me the long scars on your back, which will never heal completely, and then try to make me believe you kept the soft little lady here in the forest and pleasured yourself and scared her witless and revenged yourself on her until she grew cross-eyed and foolish. I suppose you regale every poor sap and down-and-out you come across with your heroic deeds. So get on with it, Bear-Ear, I'm all ears – I've still got both mine. You can cut one off if you want a right royal amusement.'

No one spoke when he stopped for breath, and Bear-Ear scratched his neck.

'And you have females here as well, I see,' Skord continued.

'Truly evil-looking and wicked old hags. Would they be called Dordis and Lisapeta, maybe?'

One of the crones cried out and the other put her hands over her eyes and said he must be a troll.

'Shut yer fuckin' gobs,' Bear-Ear said. 'This cunt here just picked up your names while he was lying on the horse. He's the kind who'll act dead if it suits.'

'Your mouth stinks, Bear-Ear. Rotting teeth and a throat as scrofulous and greasy inside as an old pig-swill pail. Don't come too close or I'll swoon again. Why not carve me up now, so I don't have to listen to these female lumps of carrion tell me how great they used to be – at whoring and murdering babies, that is. The one standing on your left strangled her bairn with her suspender, or at least that's what she'll say because round here it matters to be worse than the worst. And the other one, whose face looks like fatty pork and a sow's arse, as like as not she sang this song – or that's what she'll say – in the fishing harbours some twenty years ago:

> There once was this little maid
> who jumped in her bed to get laid.
> She earned her keep with her arse:
> ping pong in her cup went the coins
> smick smack went her bum on the loins.
> This maid had lots in her purse,
> 'cause she earned the coins with her arse.

Dear me, I imagine I'll hear much fine poetry of that sort here. No petty thieves, tramps and runaways in this crowd, I'll be bound. Only dangerous murderers and God-hating criminals – I spotted that the moment I fell off the horse. Lord have mercy on my poor soul! And that robbers' cave of yours, I don't imagine there are just a couple of crocks of dried peas you've stolen from a drunk peasant in it, and a tethered kid – no, no, it's stuffed with incredible wealth, and especially church silver.'

Now both the crones were crying that he was a wizard. But Bear-Ear shut them up.

'He heard the kid bleat, that's all there's to it. No wizardry.'

'And the peas! The peas!' they cried.

'He must have seen the pigeons by the cave,' Bear-Ear said. 'Let him get on with it. It's not uninteresting to listen to someone talking himself to death.'

'One of the people on the run is surely a lapsed pastor,' Skord said, 'One of those who provide the last rites on demand. It would be a poor crowd of outlaws who didn't have a real live fallen priest in their midst – not just a runaway schoolboy or children's tutor. No, I'm going to meet a truly heathen priest, sodden with drink and ready to discourse on both Philosophy and Theology. For screw me if he hasn't discovered the answers up here in Skule forest. All this time he has robbed and raped and carved and done all kinds of devil's work, and led the life of a scoundrel and filthy beast. He's been living as a shadow of himself, as a scarecrow, inflicting damage and pain until – and this is his theological and philosophical stroke of genius, likely to astonish the Lord himself on Judgement Day – until, do you see, the evil has become transformed into the best of the good! What's that if not fucking mysticam and cabbalam? He'll go to heaven from sheer utter evil, turned inside out. He's done those he tormented to death a really great service because, in the extremity of their suffering, they will have seen God. Only those who suffer properly are allowed to face God, you see – and your genius priest has worked it all out, even though his trousers are torn and his chin unshaven.'

At this point Skord reached out his hand towards someone drinking from a birch-bark scoop. The man looked at Bear-Ear, who nodded. The man handed over the scoop and Skord drank, letting the water pour down his throat. Nobody else moved. Bear-Ear had stopped rubbing his neck and instead set about scratching a place in his trousers which seemed to itch even worse.

'Calm down,' Skord said, as if his audience had been restless, 'you must have a priest-murderer with you as well. Not an ordinary clot who happened to thump one of God's own regional governors on the head, but a really vicious and calculating priest-killer, who can look forward to various treats if he gets caught, including the rack and decapitation. He's so infernally wicked that he dragged the priest here and tortured the poor devil for several days before finishing him off. He debated with him, putting his knife to his Adam's apple and waggling it a bit, saying things like, "How can a dead person be resurrected, that's what I've been wondering? Answer! How can someone dead and rotting stand up again and carry on living?" And the priest would have gurgled, of course. So the priest-murderer would have said, "Answer, you fat, ugly cunt. How come someone can live who's been buried underground for a hundred years or more, when his corpse is bare bones, if that?" The priest's eyes would have rolled right up and maybe he uttered tiny noises, like a squeezed vole or a sandpiper. But he wouldn't have found an answer, not even when our priest-murderer took the knife away to cut himself a slice of the dried elk-meat. Because the priest must have thought he was being ridiculed. But surely it was not so. The murderer wanted to know. But never got an answer. So now maybe he will turn to me and say, "What a stupid bastard priest!" and then ask me the same question, and waggle the knife a bit, because he probably has an idea that I have a theological as well as medical education.'

Suddenly it looked as if Skord was about to drop off to sleep from sheer exhaustion. The man closest to him kicked him carefully in the same spot where Bear-Ear's kick had struck.

'I'm sure,' he said, 'I would have been shown the priest-carrion itself, had the ravens not got at it first. Nose cut off, cheeks sunken, innards stinking and the chest full of worms and other crawling things. And had I not spent half my life as a medicus – or a doctor, that is – cutting up dead bodies and examining them in detail, then I would be scared shitless. But honestly, just being with you frightens me badly. It frightens me even more than it bores me, and it does bore me something terrible.'

He had heard people sighing while he talked about religious matters. When he closed his eyes and leaned back against the tree stump, he could hear their chests heaving and the air leaving their lungs. Worst was a young man with pale skin tinged with green, who was lying at Bear-Ear's feet. His breathing sounded like the torn bellows of a street-organ. Skord opened his eyes again and looked at them.

'You know about evil, my friends, more than most. And you know about suffering, especially of the meaningless kind.' He gazed very sternly at them in spite of his half-reclining position, and the woman called Lisapeta whispered hoarsely that it was like hearing an angel of God reading from a book.

'Suffering you know already and will learn even more about

when you get caught and punished for your ill deeds, be it in this life or the next. But it won't be meaningless, but in proportion to what you have done – or, even if not, it will be according to what's been written in a law book or decided at a meeting of the Church Board. Many suffer the way you do now. Little children suffer during their lives like snakes in an ant-heap. But when they freeze and cough themselves to death because their fathers have no fuel to burn in spite of felling timber in the forest each day – which might be, say, because the fathers owed the estate for horse fodder so it cancelled out their pay – then I would still not call their suffering meaningless. You see, the fires will be burning so much more cheerfully somewhere else. Not in hell, if that's what you thought, but sparkling, warming and glowing in the great tiled stoves in the mansion house up the road. And when children starve and suffer from scrofulous glands even in the summer, that too has reason and purpose, because the intention is to let better folk – the kind without ringworm and earache and hollow breastbones – eat till they are satisfied. You can ask any pastor or governor, they'll tell you there's nothing meaningless or unintentional about this kind of miserable suffering – it's as full of meaning as there are maggots in an old cheese. But, my dear friends...'

He pulled himself up into a more upright position, and held up his index finger. Everybody stared at this hand, which lacked its outermost finger. Despite all of them having lost something or other in various places, like ears, the tip of a nose, half a buttock, a chunk of lung and, often, teeth, it still seemed to them a remarkable sign and a symbol of something, that this man had a stump where the little finger on his left hand should have been. There was much quiet sighing, and some wept openly.

'But, my dear friends, if there is much meaningful suffering in this world of ours, there are also other, incurable kinds. Our Lord, Jesus Christ, suffered meaninglessly. He stepped down into hell. Nothing mystical about that. It hurt – hurt like hell. It was more than he could stand, and so he died. He believed God had abandoned him. Surely God is the Meaning and the Cause? But Jesus felt deprived of a cause and a purpose for his pain. And since the beginning of time, great numbers of people have suffered as He did. Little children can hurt like snakes, and a snake when he is stuck fast and skinned will hurt like a child. The snake can see no meaning, and is in hell. You see, my friends? That's where you will end up, and maybe you've already stepped down there and tasted what is on offer. So it should delight your black sinful hearts that there is just and meaningful suffering laid on for you by the authorities in an orderly state. Worse is awaiting you later, much worse.'

At this point he leaned back again and covered his eyes with his arm. He was sitting so still that they were unsure if he was asleep again or if he was weeping. And then he said something that struck them as being so remarkable and full of wisdom that they shivered right to the marrow of their bones. He said, 'The female snake has no teat. Her children turn towards the earth to suckle.'

He stopped speaking then, and all around him their weeping sounded like gently falling rain.

Later on they started moving about again and two of them started to prise open the lock of his food box to find out what travelling fare he brought. Bear-Ear gestured absentmindedly at them and they took the box over to him and began unpacking it. They found a cheese wrapped in a cloth, a large loaf of black bread and a dried leg of mutton glittering with grains of salt. From among some linen clouts at the bottom came a noise like the rattling of stones in a fast-moving current. They pulled out twelve good silver spoons with the engraved initials of Carl Casimir Linderskjöld. Skord leaped up at the sound and almost said, 'Xenia! Xenia! You hapless creature!' because now, with her silly or maybe not so silly wish to help, she had turned him into a silver thief. But Bear-Ear rose and patted Skord's back.

'So, that's what you do!' he said. 'Sit yourself down and let's have something to eat. I did notice you have a finger missing. We have a great deal to discuss, you and I, and had better plan ahead. It won't hurt if you give them the word of God now and then. They're living like wild animals in this forest and sometimes beat each other up from sheer boredom.'

Many wanted to speak to Skord about spiritual matters, and one man asked him to let him hear that verse again and sing the tune, because it was the cleverest song he had heard in his life, and so much to the point. And Skord sang until they could all join in:

'Ping pong in her cup went the coins
smick smack went her bum on the loins.'

We live large parts of our lives as if our will were suspended. We live as we have to, or believe we have to, stalled in necessity, bound by the inevitable. Like cows, we stand staring at the wall in front of us, knowing that behind us we will find nothing but our own dung.

Kristernin Schordenius was living among a band of crippled and tattered outlaws who were hungry most of the time. Sometimes he had to ride the brown mare all the way to Härnösand where the shops and the ships were, and cheat farmers and sailors, even though he was in danger ever since the silver cutlery went missing from the Linderskjöld estate. He realised that – at least for the present – time had run out for the outlaws in Skule forest, and only rarely recalled other times, when silver studs had glittered in their belts and colourful feathers swayed from their hats.

His thoughts often played with the idea of the sea, and the bowing and curtseying ships with white sails like wings, which would arrive once the ice broke up. But when the sea was open, Skule forest also became warmer. Life was easier, fish came to life in the tarns and the field-rose hips ripened in damp corners on the banks. Besides, his great incurable love for Xenia Linderskjöld had caused him such grief that his heart shook in his breast when he tried to make his way among people with smooth and well-nourished faces. He could not abide the smell of clean linen or freshly ironed calico, did not care to see baskets of freshly baked loaves or feel the warmth of stoves. He preferred the toothless and the cross-eyed, and liked best of all the company of a runaway schoolboy who had lost his right foot, and whose name was Johan Fluga.

All that was going on up there in the forest he had done before. Everything that rustled in the bushes he had already seen.

Sometimes he gazed at the back of his hand with its swollen, tortuous veins under the dry, wrinkled skin, and thought of how many times he had seen it. There were few things he was prepared to look at again, because he did not imagine the world had much left for him to experience.

One spring evening he was walking up a path in the twilight towards a cow shed where they sometimes stayed. His friend Johan Fluga was walking with him, but for a long time they had not said a word to each other. In a thicket of fir trees he suddenly caught a glimpse of something very dark brown or grey which he felt sure he had noticed before, not long ago. He asked Johan Fluga if he had seen anything, but he said he had not. Skord thought it was unlikely to be a badger, because badgers lumber and waddle. This thing had been moving swiftly, like a fox. And no more than a quarter of an hour had passed since he last caught sight of the greyish-brown creature, striped in white and with black markings – a foxlike animal, too small to be a wolf.

In the night he heard high-pitched sharp barking outside and thought at once of the animal, but went back to sleep. The next day he glimpsed it many times at the edge of the clearing where they were staying, and decided to try to catch it with the help of the limping and hopping Johan Fluga. They succeeded, thanks to the curious behaviour of the animal. When they pursued it, it seemed as if it did not quite want to escape. It sneaked into an old tumbledown cookhouse, so Johan Fluga slammed the door and called to Skord that he had caught it.

When they cautiously stepped inside and tried to see through the gloom, they made out the animal at the furthest end, close to the old chimney breast. Its fluffy fur seemed to have flattened.

'He's dead,' Fluga said in his high voice. 'We scared'm to death.' But Skord said they had better get out and leave the door open. After a while they saw the dark-brown, fluffy creature slip out of the cookhouse and disappear. Once it had gone, Skord went out into the forest alone, sat down on a stone and waited. It did not take long before he spotted the animal. He stayed very still for so long that his limbs went to sleep, and he must have nodded off briefly. When he came to again, it was sitting only a couple of yards away from him, looking far from terrified. He must have been right in thinking it was not very keen to meet Johan Fluga and wanted to be with Skord on his own. He still could not tell what kind of animal it was, but felt sure he had never seen anything like it, and that it did not belong in Skule or anywhere else in the Kingdom of Sweden. In size it was similar to a small dog or a fox, and it had a tail almost two feet long, drooping and fluffy. Its head was small, blunt in shape, and framed by a bushy beard. Its ears were round and so small they almost disappeared beneath the fur. It had black legs and a broad black band running over its shoulders down towards the front legs. The rest of the fur was pale grey rather than dark brown, but its colour shifted as the animal moved.

Skord was watchful now. The grey-brown animal was moving its paws nervously, but did not get up and leave. When they had been sitting there for a while, it started making noises. At first it sounded like a puppy trying to bark, and later growling and hissing sounds came from its windpipe. It seemed upset and strained by its efforts to say something. Skord stayed still and let the growling peter out. In the end the animal got up and walked down the path, then came back and turned to go the same way. It stopped and stared at Skord, still clearly upset. Then it said hoarsely, with great difficulty and much spitting, 'Follow ... follow ...'

Skord stood up at once and followed it. His heart, so long cold and still, was now twitching in a way that made him feel as if his chest held a shoal of little leaping fish. He was wearing a pair of old skin shoes with high tops, and padded along softly with slightly bent knees. Downwards, downwards they went, surrounded by the scent of the forest. Only after a while did Skord come to consider the way ahead, and how long it would be – perhaps as long as the journey he had made with the food box and the twelve silver spoons. He stopped and spoke carefully and politely to the small, eager animal. 'If you are planning to take me a long way, I had better go and find my horse,' he said. 'I propose we take leave of each other for today, but meet here, at this place by this lyre-shaped fir, early tomorrow morning. I'll find it easier to follow you then, and can also bring something with me to eat.'

The animal withdrew into the forest without uttering a sound, but Skord felt they understood each other.

At sunrise the following morning he went on the brown mare to the place where they had parted, and where a fir tree with two trunks formed the outline of a tall lyre. The animal was already waiting and greeted him with a hoarse but distinct good morning. They seemed to be in a hurry, but still found time to talk a great deal during the day, especially when they were travelling along the road and did not have to avoid obstacles. If they heard the sounds of horses' hooves and rolling carriage wheels, the dark-grey creature slipped into a ditch until the travellers had gone. As the hours passed, the sounds from the animal's throat become more and more human, and it became a real pleasure to talk to him. Skord asked what he was and where he came from. The fluffy creature said there was no word in Skord's language for the kind of animal he was. He actually came from the country on the northern bank of the River Amur, and had travelled with an East India Company consignment to distant Europe. He had been caged with his spouse, and endured great discomfort and distress. The ship had been shaken by storms which battered the cargo of china to pieces and stained the bales of silk with salt water. But they had arrived, even though their fur had grown tangled.

'Are you one of the Chinese minks which Xenia Linderskjöld let out of their cages?' Skort asked.

'I'm no mink,' he said, 'but the rest of what you say fits.'

'I've also heard you called a Japanese fox,' Skord said. 'At least, that's what the wealthy old cows in Härnösand call your children's skins, which they wear wrapped round their necks.'

'I'm most certainly no fox,' said the animal.

'Then may I call you Amur, after the great river, so rich in fish, which saw you play outside your mother's lair?' Skord asked. But to himself he called the animal a dog-mink.

Amur could not say what the reason was for going to where they going, except that it was a dangerous and difficult matter, and Skord should urge his old horse to quicken its pace. They shared the food he had brought, and the dog-mink particularly appreciated the cheese. He caught a frog in the ditch and politely returned the favour. However, he was not offended when Skord refused it. Their journey together was so agreeable that it was almost impossible to take in the warnings of danger and need for haste. Skord's heart was beating strongly and warmly. When they came to the point where the road divided, he had so expected them to take the turning towards the river valley and Sånga that he allowed the horse to tramp on quite a distance before he saw that the dog-mink had stopped at the road junction.

No, they were not on their way to Sånga, and it was only then that Skord became fearful and gripped by the wish to travel fast. As it was, they had to halt occasionally to let the mare rest, drink water and eat grass from the verge. Skord slept once or twice in hay barns, and by the time they arrived in Härnösand, his provisions were long gone. But he was not hungry, only nauseous.

The town lay spread out below them, on one big island and many smaller ones. Its rubbish dumps were hidden under swaying roofs of gulls. Grey sails stained by mould flapped in the faint wind from the straits. Smoke was rising upwards from the clutter of houses and cottages. So many carriages and wagons were grinding their way into town that Skord could not imagine how the two of them would get in among the houses unseen while it was still daylight. He might well dare show himself, but his guide surely had to wait for the dark. Then the dog-mink showed him by walking on that, as luck would have it, there was no need to negotiate the streets between the wooden shacks. Their destination was somewhere on a slope above the firth. He went on ahead, between bushes and stones, until they reached a cottage on a rocky hillside. The nettles were growing thick round the porch and the rubbish pit stank of rotten fish. A cur was barking and showing his yellow teeth, but he was tethered by a rusty chain and could not get at them.

'The barn,' said the dog-mink, once again tongue-tied. During these last few hours when they had been travelling close to human habitation, he had found it increasingly difficult to speak. 'But hurry,' he added hoarsely. The words ended in a sharp bark, almost like the scream of a cat, and then he slid into a tangle of elders and disappeared.

Skord did not like what he saw round the cottage and decided to hide until dark. He found some cover in a clump of sparse fir trees, and later the cur stopped barking. When it had grown almost dark, he saw an old man stepping down from the porch to piss. Afterwards all was quiet. He went to the barn in the dank meadow behind the house. As he slowly opened the warped door, he thought he heard feeble whimpering, but no one came towards him. He groped his way into the barn, and in what remained of light found what looked like a stretched-out body. Touching it, his hand registered a smooth coat with short hairs.

It was a quite large but emaciated dog. He took it in his arms and, sagging under the burden, carried it outside. He recognised her in the light of the night sky. It was Tirza. Her eyes were dull and her nose covered in wounds. He thought she had been trying to dig herself out of her prison.

He went to where the mare was tethered in the wood, and put the bitch down in the moss. She could not walk on her own and licked his hand with a dry rasping tongue. He had to find her water from a stream.

She perked up a little after drinking, but still found it hard to use her legs. He realised she had been beaten. The skin over her back was marked by swollen streaks. He had to lift her and put her in front of him in the saddle, and the whole time he was afraid the cur by the porch would start barking and wake the old man. He must have caught the hunting hound and counted on selling her. Her silver-studded collar had gone. Presumably she had tried to defend herself and get away.

'We must hurry now,' he whispered and they started the ride to Sånga in the dark of night. Just like the first time, he rode for more than fourteen hours and arrived so stiff he could hardly dismount on his own.

Abraham Linderskjöld had so many troubles to contend with that he took no particular notice of the old doctor, whom Nicholas had thrown out, returning with his lost hunting bitch. He noted in passing that the man was now wearing Lapp boots with his morning coat. When Schordenius asked to see Xenia, he was given permission because nothing could harm her any more. The bitch, who was very weak on her legs and shaking with fatigue, padded after him all the way up to the bedroom.

A blue light fell on everything in the room, because the housekeeper had pulled the blind down. Xenia was lying on the bed, as she had been for the last four days and nights. Her skin was pale and yellowish, and her lips parched and slightly drawn back from her teeth, like those of a corpse. They no longer expected her to recover because during the previous few hours her breathing had become so faint and irregular that it was hard to detect. The doctor had left to attend to a difficult childbirth, unable to give Abraham any hope. When old Schordenius bent over her, Abraham felt rather touched, because he knew there had been such a heart-felt bond between the two of them. There were moments when he wished Nicholas had never opened the door to Xenia's room that day, after strolling in the garden tormented by a headache and pondering his patriotic obligations and duties.

When Schordenius rose again, Xenia moved.

'Water!' he said, and the housekeeper handed him the tray with glass and carafe standing on the chest of drawers. He put the glass to Xenia's lips and they moved slightly in response. While everyone crowded round the bed to watch, the water ran down her gullet in her yellow wrinkled neck, found its way down and clearly would not spill onto the sheet again.

Abraham slid off the bed, kneeled by it and burst into tears. Old Schordenius stood next to him, brushing and brushing his old hat as if deeply embarrassed. The bitch was lying on the bedside rug, sleeping with deep, trembling sighs.

'With every world that dies, my dear Xenia, die so many more possible worlds that it brings tears to one's eyes,' Skord said. 'They die without ever really having lived, unnamed and unseen. They have just shimmered for a while around the living and real. They have been glimpsed in the haze and they have dirled when the aspen leaves quivered. Elves' lights, troll smoke – these are the things that never were, but could have been. No, my sweet, there's no point in grieving over that which did happen because much of it turned out to be twisted and ugly. But what could have been – now that's something else! We feel sadness at the loss of what we never saw, only glimpsed. We grieve because the many voices in the murmuring forest streams will be lost to those who can hear only water flowing. Oh, my dear Xenia!'

They stayed quiet together for a while, but then she started giggling because he was at her neck and the skin on her belly and the folds of her knees, and his curly hair was now so thin and light, it was as if he had tickled her with a feather. Then suddenly she sat up and said, 'But the world that is about to start up now will surely have something else around its fringes?'

'Possibly, but we can't see it.'

'Why can't we? Our vision must be good enough! We can look at things out of the corners of our eyes, can't we? If anyone can discover that which is not yet, but could become, then it is us, surely?'

She was right, and yet they saw nothing. They stared out into the gathering darkness, blinking like owls. The wind pulled at the aspens, and they could hear the woodcock tie its ribbon of trilling and ringing calls round the wood.

'Why not us?' she asked.

'I don't know.'

But something dies at every stage of time, he thought to himself.

466

I know that much. Oh, my sweet Xenia, we ought to grieve also for what really is, because that too will always, irrevocably, be lost. Lost and gone for ever. It will sink down and in the end vanish from even the last memory. It will have been scattered. Like tall grass in the wind, it will sink back and leave no trace.

'We're sinking, Xenia,' he said. 'Soil and time are covering us.'

'How old are you?' she asked with her characteristic abruptness, even brusqueness.

'I can't answer that,' he said. 'I didn't grow up among human beings who always measure and calculate time. And when I did learn to count, there were still many around who could not tell to the year how old they were. For them the period illuminated by thoughtful calculations only reached back a short while. They could speak of last year's events and maybe those of the year before. But it didn't occur to them to order their lives in decades.'

'You may have grown up among poor and ill-educated people but one can't hear it from the way you speak,' she said.

'They all sank and became invisible, together with their time,' Skord said. 'And maybe we who live now can throw a light on a longer stretch of the past, but it is still in vain. The dark eats time from behind. The largest part of time, the time that has run out, is always hidden in darkness. My birth is in darkness, like that of almost all creatures who have ever lived.'

There could be no doubt that old Schordenius had saved Xenia's life by some medical intervention which seemed indefinable. Abraham felt he could not send the old man packing, but neither did he dare have him living in the house as in the old days. Nicholas wouldn't have approved. So instead he offered him a crofter's cottage. It was just over three miles from the mansion house. Soon Skord got going a quite profitable little business of his own, because his reputation for medical skills was spreading all over the river valley. He looked proper in his black coat and top hat, which he brushed with his elbow so the nap went in the right direction. But there were quite a few who were scared of him because he was known to be up to all sorts of hocus pocus. Maybe he practised this and that which should not be looked at too closely. Some said he was curing maids' troubles. But he was spoken of more respectfully among gentlefolk than peasants.

Educated people laughed at the notion that he could do magic and might even have been involved in making gold. But he clearly had a gift or ability that they could not quite pin down. Besides, he was a learned man who seemed to know many strange things, be widely read and able to speak several foreign languages. He went about Sånga like a relative, a somewhat unpresentable relative, that's true, but one treated with more consideration than might be expected. Xenia and this man were close friends and confidants, and the younger brother, now on his own, allowed them to continue their friendship.

They troubled Abraham very little and led their own life, their secret intense life together. They always had much to talk about. He often saw them engrossed in conversations which seemed endless. Old Schordenius, whom nobody called doctor any more, was never going to complete any scientific thesis about the use of magnetic forces in medicine, that much was clear to anyone who saw him. It was just as obvious that Xenia Linderskjöld was an old maid, probably a bit crazed or at least quietly eccentric. They were two funny old souls, and no one took particular notice of them as they came walking along, speaking eagerly together. She would be wearing an unfashionable bonnet and a light cape, and carrying a reticule and a no-longer-white lace parasol. They looked like two awkward and elderly children.

'They are playing games,' Nicholas said, making an odd face. He and Abraham were standing at the window, watching them as they wandered off, arms tightly round each other, into the neglected parkland. Their course was a little twisting, because they were both speaking so eagerly that neither kept an eye on the path.

'Yes, they have their secrets,' Abraham said. 'But I don't think they're of any consequence. They are living in a world of shadows and presentiments.'

He did not even consider confiding in Nicholas that he had discussed such things with Skordenius, more or less seriously. The whole exchange would sound so absurd and naive if recounted. 'What value can there be in asking oneself questions concerning heaven and the underworld, when able and forward-looking people are busy building a society?' was how he had put it to Skordenius, who of course could not answer the question. What value indeed in people like Xenia and her talkative friend? Waste of time, both of them. Aged children. Had their premonitions ever brought them anything? He really doubted that. Will and intent were things they had forsworn – and responsibility as well. But he wished Nicholas would stop talking about them. He felt a breath of danger; he wanted them left in peace.

'Roads of iron will be drawn through the whole country,' Nicholas said.

'Roads? Of iron?' they murmured.

He had introduced the custom of setting the table with a stand holding two crystal cruets, a salt cellar and a pepper caster. The cruets contained oil and vinegar. He poured equal portions of the contents of both bottles on all dishes served at the table, apart from soups and desserts. He was serious now, as in everything he said, and had no intention of amusing them in any way with fantastic and imaginary inventions.

'I don't mean the roads will be covered with sheet iron,' he said, 'but there will be iron rails. Carriages will run on the rails. They will be pulled by steam engines. Passengers will be transported in the carriages. And freight, of course. It will become possible to cross the country in all directions on these rails.'

'Well, there you are,' Skordenius said. 'They say man is trying to learn to fly as well. So why not iron rails on the roads?'

'For human beings to try to master the art of flying is clearly no more than a fanciful notion. And if such a skill were acquired, and people started flapping about above the ground using some kind of mechanical process, then nothing would be achieved apart from the writing of a few more volumes of poetry. But roads with iron rails belong to the immediate future, and will incontestably prove themselves of utility to mankind.'

Xenia got palpitations when she listened to this. She could not tell why. Anyway, Skord was able to calm her as soon as they were alone. If all the roads in the country were to be equipped with iron rails, they would have to be curved into an endless number of bends. He asked her to think of all the roads she knew, lined with billowing cow parsley, giving off clouds of dust finer than snuff and so much whiter. How could they possibly install iron rails on this bending, rippling, bumpy network of roads, which, he assured her, spread in a similar manner up hill and down dale throughout Sweden? In which smithy were the rails to be bent and adjusted? Who was to compute the curvature and their deviation from calculable shapes such as ellipses and arcs of circles? No, equipping roads with iron rails was just a dream of Nicholas's, who would fantasise about transporting people for his own purposes in carriages pulled by steam engines, and always knowing who was going where. But surely Xenia could see that no one could possibly put rails along the road network of a country? There would always be a bit of road somewhere, unknown to the Stockholm folk, where an old farmer would be bumping along atop a load of moorland hay or some barrels of newly boiled tar. There would be roads where people were dancing. Was it possible to believe otherwise? Could she imagine a country where they did not dance at the crossroads on Saturday nights?

Nicholas had become a minister of state. He explained that this would probably be his last visit to the place where he was born. Duties and obligations might for all the foreseeable future prevent him from such time-wasting journeys. But he had come this time in order to organise once and for all the lives of his nearest and dearest in the appropriate manner. In the first place, the infamous tombstone must be carted away. No more shilly-shallying. A minister in the government of the Swedish king always had presumptive enemies. Such an enemy might well exploit the absurd and quite irrational situation constituted by the display of this tombstone with its false testimonial. In this matter it was no longer possible to take differing opinions into account, not to speak of sentiments and emotional states connected to the disappearance of their sister. If their father had not wished to recognise her, then that was his business. Dead she was not. The stone must go. The sister of a Swedish minister of state is either dead or alive.

Further, concerning the man calling himself Dr Skordenius. He must be evicted from the cottage that had been made available for his use. The cottage should be demolished. The meadow and the potato patch should used for timber planting.

Further, concerning their sister. It was high time that she

470

received competent treatment for the mental disorder accompanied by amnesia with which she had been afflicted since her long and still unexplained absence. Consequently, a place had been reserved for her at an institution for the mentally debilitated near the Danish-German border, in beautiful Schleswig, a place where the deranged were treated in a loving humanitarian fashion which, however, did not exclude firmness.

Nicholas Linderskjöld's family did not submissively agree to follow his directives. Xenia wept and fainted. Abraham's pipe snorted, and he tried, humming and hawing, to explain his own opinions which differed from his brother's. Nicholas, however, stuck to his decisions and went to bed. The journey had tired him. He had been suffering for several weeks now from headaches, nervous tension and insomnia, and could not bear to listen to any objections.

Xenia wept so terribly that Skord had to sit on the edge of her bed and hold her hands. He assured her he would deal with it all, and she must not worry herself.

'How are you going to do that?' she sobbed.

'Wait and see,' Skord answered and looked wicked. She thought he had a squint in one eye.

Pastor Eurén was announced the next day. He used the removal of the tombstone as an excuse to visit the newly appointed minister, and arrived full of expectations concerning the improvements due for the whole locality. Given this exceptionally important connection with a member of the government, one would now find it hard to paint the future of the river valley in bright enough colours.

Nicholas Linderskjöld was sitting in the dining room with the cruet stand in front of him. His greeting was restrained. The Pastor's exposition did not seem quite to get through to him.

'I turn to you as a person of standing, and an incumbent of a Swedish professional position,' he said suddenly. 'I have been poisoned.' He pointed to the two crystal bottles. Then he rose and, referring to his severe headache, disappeared to his bedroom.

The same afternoon he summoned his brother Abraham and asked him to arrange for an express message to be dispatched to the government in Stockholm. 'These are defence secrets,' he said, 'but you have always been such a discreet and reliable person that I dare confide in you what is afoot. Especially since I myself, owing to acute effects of overwork, at the moment lack my usual strength. In brief: hostile forces are approaching underwater.'

'Underwater?'

Nicholas explained he had by now received several and concurring reports of military activity in the Ullånger Firth.

'Might it not be seals?' Abraham asked.

'Abram, you are a kind and unsuspecting person. Unfortunately, military technology has moved on since the Battle of Bornhöft, my dear boy. The enemy is advancing underwater in vessels powered by steam.'

He handed Abraham a densely written document, several pages long and said to contain all the reports about hostile manoeuvres in the Ullånger Firth, and asked him to send it on to the government in Stockholm, while he tried to get some sleep. Abraham quietly left the room. He put the document into the log chest in the kitchen. Towards the evening the Minister called his brother to him and asked if he had dispatched the papers.

'My dear Niklas,' Abraham said. 'Shouldn't you try to get a little something inside you? Miss Erika has prepared a bowl of bouillon with marrow dumpling.'

'I have felt nauseous all day,' Nicholas said curtly, and shut his bedroom door.

At three o'clock in the morning they heard a shot. The whole household leaped out of bed and rushed up to the first floor. Faced by the closed door to Nicholas's room, everyone except Abraham felt a certain hesitation. Abraham tried to open the door. It was locked and there was no sound from inside the room. Xenia cried, short little cries; she sounded like a bird. Abraham told Miss Erika to give her a hot drink. He himself went down to check the gun rack, and found one old front-loading rifle missing. One of his father's gamekeepers, a chap called Bear-Ear, used to shoot wolves with it once. By now Abraham was feeling very tired, and wished he had somebody sensible to speak to. He waited for a while outside the door, and then sent for a carpenter with tools that could be used to pick the lock. Just as it was ready to swing open freed from the lock-bars, they heard a grinding sound as the key turned and Nicholas's voice saying, 'Abram!'

'Yes?'

'I've shot His Majesty the King through the eye.'

He was shaking as if in a fever, and wept like a child when they got to him. They put him in Abraham's bed and gave him hot milk to drink, just like Xenia. The used rifle was lying in his bedroom. There were shards of broken china and puddles of urine on the floor. He had shot straight into the chamberpot.

In the old mansion house by the river, Abraham Linderskjöld tried for over half a year to create a setting conducive to the recovery of his brother. Nicholas had been granted leave of absence, and eventually also his resignation. However, in the end the house-keeper could cope no longer, and Abraham considered it necessary to find professional help to care for his brother. It was time to claim the place reserved at the asylum in Schleswig, and Professor Jessen explained that the prognosis for Nicholas Linderskjöld was quite good: his illness would soon enter into a much calmer stage. He could then go back and be looked after in his home.

'Jaja, ausgezeichnet,' Abraham said. 'Sehr schön. Das passt sehr gut.'

And so he travelled the long way back home, and while waiting for the return of his brother, took up his work and his pipe-smoking again, and his thoughtful evenings. Staying with him were the two kindly and slightly confused creatures whom Nicholas had wanted to evict. He did not bother to remove the tombstone either. He had a strong conviction that it is often for the best to take no steps at all, leave things as they are, and hope for any not entirely satisfactory situation to sort itself out, one way or the other.

At first, Xenia and her friend were very excitable. But everything inevitably settled down to a daily routine, and soon their thoughts about Nicholas came to have a distracted quality.

'You see, I liked him,' Xenia said. ' I did, you know. Though he was an awfully strong-willed person.'

'Yes, Xenia,' Skord said gravely. 'He was exceptionally strong-willed, and may have had a political gift verging on genius. In civilian matters he may have been practically a Napoleon, and we must be very pleased he fell ill.'

'How can you say something so dreadful?'

'Well, I suppose it is dreadful,' Skord said, 'but I'll say it anyway. I have a feeling he could have turned into reality all the things he saw in his visions. The iron rails. The troop transports underwater. But, luckily, he did go mad and all these things will be forgotten.'

'Maybe we can learn to fly instead,' Xenia said. 'If only – it would be such a pretty world, Skord!'

'Yes, perhaps it would be very pretty,' he said.

They had stayed at the dining table after the others had left. The room was going dark, but they lit no candles. They belonged in the twilight of chilly rooms. They liked being in the damp shade of leaves down by the riverbank. They went walking together drifting, and listening to bird calls. They sat watching the dipper dive in the whirlpools near the fall and emerge again, his soft, tight-fitting coat not looking wet at all. They saw the beaver swimming with the evening sun shining on his head, and observed the otters diving from the rocky shores. When the river became packed with salmon, and Linderskjöld's people were out there pulling in the nets, they sat hunched in the alder bushes near the bank, watching the heavy bodies of the fish flash and shiver in the light. Both could imitate woodpecker and jay, and sometimes Abraham had a feeling they communicated over distances with such sounds as the chattering of the fieldfare and the soft piping of the Siberian jay.

They had many expressions and many names for what they were doing. Drifting around in the countryside they called a balsamic reconstitution of themselves. He had to smile when he heard that, and he would not have been without them, even though over the years they often caused him trouble by getting lost.

They were living on the borderline, and seemed at any moment ready to disappear into the forest. They became very vague when asked about directions and goals, and he thought one day they would resolve everything – if indeed a resolution were needed – by simply getting lost for good.

Contrary to what one might have thought, looking at her dry and yellow little body in old age, it was not at all easy for Xenia Linderskjöld to die. There was a big rumpus at first. It all began in spring when she went out riding kick-sledge with Skord on the softening ice. She had to get off and walk where the top layer of ice had given way, and her boots became wet through. Then she started coughing and had to stay in bed for a long time. She was back on her feet, though, by the time the trees were coming into leaf, and took great pleasure in the familiar miracles getting under way on south-facing slopes under the warm sun of early summer.

That year the summer was hot, with stinging flies and bad air. She started coughing again, and now there were spots of blood on her handkerchief. She ran a temperature and had to take to her bed. Soon it became clear that she was going to die, and all around her people were gripped by a sense of urgency. There was running on the stairs, much haste and debate. Decoctions of barley were prepared and carried up on trays and left to cool. They wanted her to take quinine, and Abraham tried to give her some of his best hock. Egg yolks were whisked into broth, and a greengrocer in Härnösand got a message telling him to find out if any of the ships carried lemons.

When she could no longer eat, and only after a struggle moisten her lips with water, they sent for a pastor, who sloshed wine all over her sheets and read over her from his manual. Abraham was almost driven to the brink of despair by old Skordenius, who sat by her bed all the time, raging wildly against the priest and refusing to accept that he could not prevent her death. Towards the end he started speaking to her in a strange way, which was only partly comprehensible.

'My rest is your rest, and my joy is in your joy,' he said,

reaching out for her hands and gripping them with his own. 'Ich have het of thine brest and swetnes in thine worden.'

And then the furious little man wept so terribly, Abraham had to shake him by his shoulders and tell him there must be peace and quiet by Xenia's bed. But he did not listen and shouted instead in his strange and frightening language, 'Ich wolde rather dayen than ben apart fram thee!'

Abraham was about to throw him out there and then, and tell him he was not to return until he could stay calm in the room of the sick woman and show respect for death. But he did also remind himself that it was not just old Skordenius creating a hullabaloo. For a long time now, they had all been running up and down the stairs, rattling trays and cups, reading and pleading. Horse-drawn carriages had thundered up the drive and the gravel had crunched underfoot as messengers arrived with lemons and quinine, and the priest with Communion wine. Dogs had been barking at the messengers, doors had been slamming, and mortars pounding in the kitchen.

Now Abraham ordered that everybody must be quiet, no matter what. The dogs must be kept silent. Horses were not to be driven up to the house. Only he himself and old Skordenius were allowed in Xenia's room. When all was said and done, he could not find it in his heart to throw the old man out.

Abraham pulled the blue blind down over the window. Xenia's eyelids trembled a little then, and she smiled with thin dry lips.

It had been as if everyone had been trying to stop her, to hold her back. But when Skord saw Abraham pull the blind, he realised that this busy, quiet man knew something that was only slowly taking shape in Skord's own thoughts. She needed nothing more from them. She did not even need her own memories or her own name. She had finished.

She was ready to leave all the things that had nourished her and let her grow. She had no use for them any more. Rather than raging, pleading, demanding and appealing, he perhaps had another task to complete. He did not think it would take long. So he settled quietly near her, feet close together, alert and attentive. In this way he could still accompany her, and he realised that she was aware of this for a few more moments.

476

He was glad she was not afraid. Of course she did not know where she was going and what would happen to her. But it seemed she was trusting, as if this trust was all she took with her, apart from herself. He reflected on how such trust does not always lead to safety. The newly born grope for warmth and nourishment. But not all newborns are received in the way their trustfulness expects. He wondered if for her too these moments held uncertainty, and wished he could go with her just a little further along the way.

When she had gone, her body was left behind.

When his own time came, he too was accompanied. The dog-mink went with Skord to the place where he was to die, walking swiftly like a fox in front of him, in the ambling trot he used when there was a long way ahead and his strength must not be wasted unnecessarily. Now and then he would stop to let the old man rest. These rests were not far apart, and the dog-mink did not even pant as he sat waiting for Skord's strength to flow back from its almost exhausted wellsprings.

When they were resting in the big forest under the fir trees, Skord closed his eyes and listened. Through the heavy fringes of the firs he could hear the forest breathing. This sound, these deep and distant breaths, he ought to know better than anything else. But he suddenly perceived the breathing as alien. The one who was breathing had turned away and left him rejected on the ground.

He thought of how he had found his feet in many different places, more than he could remember, without too much pain and trouble. But his true home was here in the forest, and nowhere else. If the breathing in these tall firs had changed and rejected him, then where did he belong? He had always felt this without thinking about it: the forest was the base of his life.

But what if there was no base?

He listened with his eyes closed. What if you just kept falling? If the forest refused to enclose you when you died? Where then would you be?

He asked the dog-mink if they could carry on walking. They must get out of the forest and get higher up. Higher.

They trundled on, slowly and on an oblique course. The path

ended. Both knew they would have arrived when Skord finally could not get up again. This happened when they had reached the upper edge of the forest. Above them the boulders were exposed, and the sun-dried lichen gave off a strong smell, like burnt roasted nuts. It made Skord smile, because it reminded him of so many things. He thought of Xenia's skin and of hazelnuts which he had collected so long ago that his thought had to dive like a tern over a sea inlet to reach the memory. Yes, there had been hazel shrubs in Skule forest then, and they were probably still there. Someone had taken the nuts into her held-out skirt and cracked them and roasted them in a pan. She had been wearing a kerchief round her head, leaving her round, open forehead free. She had known so much! Had her belief and her knowledge been true, a Gentle Lady would soon put her hand on his forehead, which was grey and cold and damp, cover him with a sheepskin-lined blanket and let him sleep while she spoke on his behalf to Someone who already knew all about him. Knew that he had struck people or used his knife on them a few times, and, like a shadow, a scarecrow likeness of himself, led an ugly life. He could almost smell the wool from the blanket, and honey and clean linen, and he thought a dragonfly flew past his ear, buzzing and sending him to sleep, as eager voices spoke for and against his case.

They had stopped next to a stream, and it tinkled and tumbled from stone to stone, down into its basins and bowls, which were strewn with grains of gold and gravel. Sometimes he was aware it was the running water speaking and murmuring, sometimes not.

The stream ran into a small glen where star moss and ferns grew, and the sparse grass was outlined in light, because the sun was low and everything touched by its beams glowed: the leaves of the birches, the pointed fronds of the ferns with brown spots on their backs, the grass stalks, traversed by the finest veins for carrying juices upwards. For a while he saw everything very distinctly, as if he had the sharp eyesight of a buzzard or a goshawk. He felt he had an obligation to praise all he saw, and that no duty like this had ever been given to him, none so important. He felt like telling the dog-mink about it, but they had already said farewell, politely and with their eyes meeting calmly. The animal had withdrawn and left Skord to what was awaiting him. He had not abandoned him, but kept within sight, sitting on a rock.

Then this sight faded, and so did all vision as grey banks of mist seemed to drift past his eyes. But he realised that the mist was inside his eyes. Long after he closed them, the mist continued to drift past. Then he thought something touched his cheek, something soft and fluttering in the wind, and he whispered a name: 'Qinnamon ... Qinnamon...' And he thought, the time will come when the Earth will scrape off everything human like scabs, like crusts of dirt. Then the wind will flow through manes and leaf canopies, and no one but the raven will listen when the raven caws, and no one but the curlew will listen to the drilling whistles of the curlew. There will be silence, there will be silence, and the water will flow clear right down into the pool.

Now the sun sank below the crest of the mountain and deep shade, heralding the dark, fell across him. A cold streak of real mist was rising from the stream, and suddenly he was fully awake and saw it come creeping along; he heard the voices of the birds quieten and the stream repeat its chatter, the same mumbling noise over and over again. When in his tiredness and pain he managed to turn a little, he saw the dog-mink sitting on top of a boulder with his feet close together. The light had stopped glittering in his fur. He was sitting in the deep shade below the crest of the mountain, and his short pointed nose, arched forehead and small ears, and the hairs on his neck and back, were outlined against a sky which still held some light.

Skord was lying with his head against a tussock of grass, listening to the tinkling of the beck over the stones and the murmuring of water, the constantly running and falling water. It was as if voices were speaking to him. Excited and impossible to catch, they kept speaking across each other. He was very thirsty and felt sick.

He knew he was going to die. Although he was not overwhelmingly and incurably ill, he was beyond all medical help and all hope. He was very cold and nauseous. The nausea came in waves through his whole body, which tried to rid itself of it and shook in vain attempts to vomit up the pain.

Is this how death will come? Will it find its way in through cracks and holes, stealthily cause pain and fear? Is he not a great lord, clattering with spurs and sword in the hall? Is he just a tramp? Well, perhaps he knew this, had known it a long time, since in his days he had seen so much fetid and stained flesh, so many crushed eyeballs and burst bellies, so much uncleanliness and shit and rotting mire. But perhaps one expects that it will be different for oneself, more elevated and noble, not to say heavenly and even a little divine. After all, it is one's own flesh and skin and one's very own eyes, which have seen the splendours and shame of the Earth for so long, for such a very long time.

He looked at his hand. Was there not a bluish-brown spot on the back of his hand, a shadow, a mark like that on an apple that has been bruised and is starting to rot?

'This brown hand, this delicate ear I whisper into . . . are you afraid, Skord? We are of the same kind, you and I. That is what is so wonderful. Skin against skin. We are of the same kind. I kiss you where you kiss me, and together we lie as if in a seashell. No one can separate us, and you can hear the sea murmuring in the shell. Your skin smells of the sea. We are lying together under a cold sky, as close as we can to the fading embers of a fire as the Earth spins among sparks in a huge space. If Christ had been incarnated as a Cucumber, my darling, would you have kissed his feet? A warty gherkin, Skord. Creation is rather strange in some respects. It is not hard to imagine that somewhere, whirling through space, there is an Earth where Cucumbers are worshipped and prayers are said to their Father in the heavenly Pile of Manure. Give me your hand, give me your brown hand before it gets covered in spots. Kiss me as I kiss you, like for like, my darling. We are together in the open air. It is cold but we keep each other warm, skin against skin, and your ear is hot under my lips.'

Indeed, he was resting in the open air, but now he was alone. At least there were no suffocating bed curtains enclosing him, no staring knots in roofboards nor damp stains spreading scornfully. He had only just had time to feel relief at being outside under a great empty sky still holding some light, when a face emerged in front of him. It was not a human face, but the face of a huge clock. He could not make out what it meant. There were circles with inscribed numerals, Arabic and Roman. There were curious signs, which might have been those of the zodiac or belonged to alien heavenly spheres, and they turned round and round. But it was not possible for him to work out where the hands were pointing, and what was the intention behind this complicated and cunningly devised mechanism. He thought the face was inclined over him, then that it was coming closer and closer. It no longer smiled, but roared with silent laughter, and from the wide open mouth came the stench of predator, a smell of raw flesh and filth. He cried out in fear, but moments later felt a cool nose touch the back of his hand, and then a tongue lick a greeting at the corner of his mouth. He woke from his stupor, and saw the dog-mink standing quite close and watching him with a concerned look in his oblique, golden-brown eyes. As soon as he saw Skord recover and breathe calmly again, he padded off to resume his vigil on the boulder.

He was not able to give Skord anything to drink, nor could he really say anything by way of comfort or enlightenment. In fact, when Skord thought more closely about it, he had never heard an animal say anything remarkable that it had not already heard from a human being. They had their dignity and their great courtesy, their courage and their patience in pain and loneliness, but they were not inventive. He giggled, because he thought the voices of beck and birch leaves and the whispering of the ferns were nothing but human speech, inventions, strange riddles and cunning stories to amuse and comfort him.

We comfort each other with notions of clocks and a gentle heaven.

We comfort each other with a great wealth of invention to ward off the nausea of death, and its troubles and sadness. We need not die like foxes, and we have good times, he thought. For a few moments his body grew hot, hot all over as if he had a fever, when he thought of what good times he had had. Especially when talking, and very especially when talking with a girl or a creature or a body called Xenia, and with another, whose name he could no longer remember, but who had been a learned and amusing body and actually the cousin of a bishop, and yet another, a third one whose name he had never used, but called Darling and Sweet Thing.

Now, no one will ever say my name again, he thought. In that very moment he realised he himself had forgotten it, and could not recall it. He had said it quickly once when asked what his name was, and he did not know where it had come from. Now, just as quickly, it had been taken away.

The nausea and the cold gripped him so that it was impossible to speculate about or imagine anything. I wish all this would soon pass, he said to himself. I wish I could sleep. And he did actually sleep for a while, and woke again to thirst and nausea and a shivery chill, which, however, seemed to slowly wane. But he had become so stiff and cold he could no longer turn. Then he understood that he would die in his sleep and would not know when it happened. He could not see the dog-mink any more, and could not turn round, but knew the animal was sitting up there on the boulder, watching his friend without fail, and would come down to him if his fears were such that he cried out loud.

The moments of sleep came and went like small clouds over a blank hot sky, and they brought solace. He was lying in the dark, but did not notice any darkness. The stream no longer spoke with voices. It was just water streaming between stones. It was just water. Soon it no longer had a name.

The dog-mink rose stiffly to stand, and came down from the boulder. He padded along to look at the face. Then he got closer and sniffed the body, but lost interest, turned and left on legs that soon became less stiff. By halfway down the slope where the thick-forest started, he had recovered his agility. Now he was softly moving onwards down the path with his usual sideways trot, his foxlike ambling which saved his strength and helped him get back to his lair in good shape.

Skord's cottage was left empty and everything grew tall around it. Saplings and bushes, rose-bay willow-herb, cranesbill, the dirty-blue and poisonous monkshood and the weed they call elk cabbage – these things shot up and suffocated the fine low-growing herbs. There were no more small pink pads of cat's-foot to be seen. Ragged robin, michaelmas daisy, wild pansy, the low, intensely blue selfheal and the sweet-smelling dame's violet all died back as the tall and strong ones invaded. The meadows round the cottage grew coarser. The first raspberry suckers started poking through the rotten boards of the fallen steps, and soon the birch saplings followed. A stoat began by staying in the stone foundations and then entered the hallway, where split birch logs were still piled up, slowly turning grey with age. Soon the air became pungent with stoat droppings. He lived off woodmice which ran in and out of the cottage through their holes, now undisturbed by people. To the stoat, there was no reason or purpose for the cottage except to provide him with the opportunity to catch mice. It no longer held any trace of human scent. An owl's nest was lodged in the chimney.

One day late in the summer when the wind was singing in the fir trees, Groning, who had been alone for a long time now, came wandering along to the cottage where he had seen Skord many times. He had been thinking he should make himself known and then maybe they would speak together a little. But time had passed without his getting round to it. Now he had the feeling Skord had gone, in the same way as the old crone, his mother, once had. She had left behind her bones and skin and ragged clothes lying on the bench. His brother Granarv too had gone, so long ago nobody would ever find his bones. They were overgrown with white-moss and reindeer moss, shiny cranberry plants and wood sorrel, and formed long straight ridges on the forest floor. Yes, they looked like fallen fir trunks, slowly turning into earth. Not even Groning knew where they were because his memory was a feeble thing, and all around the forest there were ridges formed by fallen fir trunks, so long and straight that they could have been made into ship's masts. But sometimes when he saw them he remembered Granarv, who had had a better memory and a stronger mind than he had himself. And when he saw fir trees that had not fallen, he sometimes remembered how he had felled the biggest fir up in Oringen and it came down on top of him. Yes, he could remember how it had pinned down his leg, and how he had been lying there and all the things that wanted to suck his blood could get at him. If he had not got a message to his brother Granarv, it would have been the end of him.

His mind is not strong. His thoughts tend to drift away with his faint memories. His memory often tricks him so that he thinks he is about to meet someone he knows, but then finds it is just a hunched-up tree stump or a fallen tree stretching out arms and hands and claws. When he thinks of ship's masts he remembers how at times he stood on the highest peak near Oringen and looked down to Härnösand, where the handsome ships could be

483

seen looping and swerving like white birds. But at other times he remembers nothing of all this, and he can no longer see any bowing ships and flapping white wings down there on the shining summer sea. He longs for his brother Granarv who could speak about things like ships and masts and sails, about women and churches and trolls and fresh cheese and sweet milk, and all sorts of things he cannot possibly recall or even long for on his own. Groning wanders around longing for longing. There is a hole inside him, and the hole is a very large one because he is a giant.

Reaching the cottage at the edge of the forest, he again remembers Skord, who helped him twice and saved him when things could have turned out very badly for him. He would like to meet his saviour again, but realises it is too late. Too long a time has passed. How long he is not quite sure. Time murmurs inside his head when he tries to think and remember. The spine of the cottage has broken, and all that remains is a silver-grey pile of lichen-covered timbers on top of the stone foundations. Birches and aspens grow through it, and the wind murmurs in the birches and sighs in the aspens. With large hands Groning picks up what is left of the collapsed wood-tiled roof and lifts it. But nobody is inside. There is no trace of the one whose name he cannot remember.

Glossary

breeks	breeches
byke	wasps' or bees' nest
byre	cowshed
deil kens	the devil knows
deil tak ye ... y'orra bummie	the devil take you ... you worthless stupid fool
dirl	ring when struck; reverberate; tingle; pierce (with emotion or pain)
dowter	daughter
dwalm	stupor; fainting fit; swoon
feus	duties paid in return for keeping and using heritable land
girning	whining; rowing; complaining
greeting	weeping
hidlin	hiding place
leen	grassland on (high) moors or by rivers; often natural pastures
licht	the light part of corn seed (separated out by winnowing)
loch	lake
lokkit	furnished with a lock
lossit	lost
kelpie	water demon, usually in the form of a horse which is said to haunt rivers and fords and may lure the unwary to their deaths
mither	mother
norart, soudert	north- and southwards
norwoodsman	man from the north of the forest
paith	steep track; cleft
piece	snack; packed lunch
reel	a rotating device; also a whirling movement
skrauching	shrill cry; scream; screech
Water–Kelpie	see *kelpie*
wee	small, tiny
wynd	lane, narrow passage

Notes

vulgar (base) gold of commerce – was the aim of the adeptus of alchemy.

p.171 *Bosonius* From Bos, the Latin word for ox; the ox is a symbol of the priesthood and one of the figures of the cherubim (Ezekiel).

p.171 *Athanor* Alchemist's oven.

p.172 *Aurelia* Gold; golden; *Felicula* Little cat, from felix, the Latin for cat.

p.173 *Theophrastus* Bombastus von Hohenheim (1493–1541) or *Paracelsus*, originator of use of 'chymical remedies' for disease; believed that illnesses were cured by similars or opposites.

p.174 *Prognostication* Cabbalistic prediction based on signs and on anagrams of letters and numbers.

p.174 *Agnus balat* The lamb bleats; *Cornix cornicatur* The crow caws.

p.179 *arcanum* Secret of nature; an elixir.

p.180 *Cabbala, Gematria, Notaricon* Jewish texts based on ancient metaphysical thought, especially some passages from the Old Testament, and including a theory of numbers central to interpreting and predicting events; by L. Middle Ages linked to alchemy.

p.180 *Yetzirah; Zohar* Books in the Cabbala.

p.180 *Seen, Koof, Raish, Daleth* Hebrew letters which form the name Skord.

pp.183–4 *aurum, argentum, cuprum, plumbum, stannum, ferrum, mercurium* The seven alchemical metals; *sulphur, mercurium vivum* All substances were believed to be a mixture of these two.

p.184 *Stone of the Philosophers* Also *Materia Prima*; the vital starting point for the complex process of alchemical transformation into the Philosopher's Stone; *Philosopher's Stone* The perfect end point of the alchemical process.

p.184 *Lullian* Raymond Lully, friar and mystic (c.1235–1325); practised alchemy.

p.185 *Hermes* Hermes Trismegistus (Thrice Greatest); Greek name for Egyptian god Thoth; thought to have written many texts of alchemy and magic.

p.185 *somnia a Deo missa* Dreams sent by the Lord.

p.186 *Vulcan, Aquarius, Pyrander* Gods and demi-gods from Roman mythology – but the entire dream is alchemical and describes combinations of substances.

p.188 *Adeptus* The successful alchemist; he who has attained the gift of God.

p.194 *spagyric* alchemical; cf. also *spagyric arts;* term probably coined by *Paracelsus* (see above).

p.197 *Kore* The name of the Greek girl who became Persephone, Queen of the Underworld; having been promised by Zeus that he would rescue her if she did not eat, she bit into a pomegranate and was condemned to stay in Hades with Pluto, King of the Underworld, for half of each year.

p.197 *Ouroboros* The great snake which represents Materia Prima in alchemical imagery.

p.200 *viri obscuri* Practitioners of cabbalistic arts; *viri claris et illustris* Men of the world.

p.209 *Ora, puellula* Pray, little girl; *Oratio Dominica* The Lord's Prayer.

p.209 *Nonulli perierunt i opere nostro* Nothing must ever interfere with our work.

p.210 *White One* An unknown alloy.

p.213 *scordalus* Brawler; trouble-maker; *scordator* Pimp; one who associates with whores.

p.215 *Gestirn* Brain; the mind of the Almighty (German).

p.234 *trajectoria* paths.

p.234 *Address of the Cadaver Cypresses, Speeches of Comfort, Honourable Memorials, Candid Tears of Grief* Seventeenth century ceremonial verse spoken at the graveside.

THE LOST RANKS

p.241 *Hier liegt . . .* Here lies/the noble and well-born man/who returned to Heaven/Ignatius Tugendreich/the illustrious and celebrated doctor/also Adwiser and Chancelore to/His Royal Majesty of Sweden/as no one remembers now except for me/His motto was:/With gaiety and wantonness.

p.241 (and p.243) *Fliesset herbe . . .* You bitter springs, flow with tears/sad waves, like mother-of-pearl!/Whimper, groan, complain and moan/in the night before the dawn./No more whispers from pale lips'; these lines, quoted in German, are drawn from authentic memorial verses.

p.241 *Ignatius* As a child St Ignatius was put by Jesus among his disciples as an example of innocence and virtue; *Tugendreich* Rich in virtue (German).

p.243 *Trux* Brusque; rough (Latin).

p.244 *Fliesset, fliesset herbe . . .* Flow, flow you bitter springs/chase, chase you waves of time.

p.244 *Maledicti saxones* Damned Saxons.

p.244 *Only the Elector's companies remained . . .* The Thirty Years War (1618–1648) was a complicated conflict between Catholic and Protestant states, fought mainly in the German lands; involved through a Protestant alliance, Sweden became a major player for a while;

although allied forces under Swedish command were routed at Nördlingen (1634), Sweden fought on.

p.247 *Bald geht es los . . .* It'll start soon. First thing tomorrow morning. What fun – eh?

p.249 *Keziah* Three of Job's ten children were girls: Jemimah, Keziah, Keren-Happuk.

p.249 *Cassia; cinnamon* Trees (Cinnamomum cassia & zeylanicum) from the Far East.

p.255 *Busenfreunde* Best (bosom) friends; *Hohheiten* Sovereigns; *Durchlauten* Highnesses.

p.257 *Weg! Kaputtgemacht* Gone! All destroyed.

p.261 *die verlorene Haufen* The lost hordes (ranks).

p.265 *Die philosophische . . .* The manufacture of metals after philosophical principles, their characteristics, compositions and transmutations.

p.266 *Disjecta membra* Scattered limbs.

p.273 *Horse of the Burn* In Scottish folklore, as in Swedish, horses figure as water-spirits which are usually malevolent.

p.281 *sang de boeuf* Ox blood.

DRAKENSTIERNA'S TREASURE

p.294 *lycopodium* Dust-like spores from club-moss (L. clavatum) used as absorbent powder.

p.324 *justaucorps* Man's long coat; frock coat.

p.335 *master of ordinance* Officer in charge of artillery and ammunition.

p.337 *He heard sighing . . .* From *Masnavi* by the great Persian poet Rumi (1207–73).

p.341 *punctum saliens* The crucial point.

p.343 *Gehenna* Place of eternal torment (Hebrew).

p.348 *Ita, Sic, Tot, Similis, Idem* So, thus, so many, like, the same (Latin grammar).

p.358 *in contumaciam* In contempt of court; (Paykull had refused to attend the court.)

p.360 *Hoc aurum arte . . .* This gold was made with chemical arts in Stockholm etc.

pp.363–7 *a man lived in Stockholm castle who thought differently . . .* René Descartes (1596–1650); influential French mathematician and philosopher; Queen Christina of Sweden brought him to Stockholm.

p.364 *Method* Descartes set out a unitary theory of the universe in *About the World* (1633) but withdrew it after learning the fate of Galileo; published *Discourse on the Method*

(1637) in which the universe is seen as subject to calculable events.

XENIA

p.371 *l'esprit jusqu'au bout des doigts* Witty to his fingertips.

p.376 *Quodlibetarius* Jack-of-all-trades.

p.376 *phlebotomes* Small sharp knives for venesection (bleeding from veins).

p.376 *Sargasso Sea* Area of western Atlantic Ocean containing sargasso (type of seaweed); area of confusion, stagnation.

p.377 *Gustavia* The capital (named after king Gustav III) of the Swedish Caribbean island colony of St Barthélemy.

p.377 *the Disease* Syphilis.

p.378 *Tartarus* Hell in Greek myth.

p.378 *Aeolian* Of Aeolus, god of the wind (the strings of the Aeolian harp make sounds in the wind).

p.378 *Zephyr* God of the west wind; gentle breeze.

p.378 *ignis fatuus* Flitting light – maybe ignited methane; will-o'-the-wisp.

p.378 *Swedenborg* Emmanuel S. Swedenborg (Swedish, 1688–1772); a scientist and mystic; thought himself appointed to reveal the teachings of Christ.

p.379 *sorcier* Magician.

p.385 *caleçon* Underpants; long johns.

p.388 *Gewaltige* Foreman of the [prison] guard (German).

p.421 *Madame de Staël* (1766–1817); b. Germaine Neckar; married Swedish Ambassador to France; political writer and novelist whose libertarianism (she was an admirer of Jean Jacques Rousseau) lead to years in exile.

p.421 *Jean Paul* Johann Paul F. Richter (1763–1825); German political writer, satirist and novelist with radical democratic and egalitarian views.

p.421 *bitter almonds* intense almond flavour but contains toxic hydrogen cyanide (destroyed in baking).

p.435 *[dolce] far niente* Pleasant idleness.

p.435 *Schöngeisterei* Aestheticism.

p.435 *gnomes, sylphs . . .* Mythical beings which belong to each of the four elements: earth (gnome), air (sylph), water (undine) and fire (salamander).

p.473 *Jaja, ausgezeichnet . . .* Yes, yes, excellent. Very good. That suits us very well.